THE
MONARCH'S
FLIGHT

A Romance Novel

LOUIS VILLALBA

G

GADES BOOKS

PUBLISHER: GADES BOOK

The author's imagination created the story narrated here. Any resemblance to events or persons, living or dead, is coincidental.

Copyright © 2021 Louis Villalba
Email: Louis@LouisVillalba.com
Website: www.LouisVillalba.com
Blog: www.TheClassicWriter.com
Publisher: www.GadesBooks.com
US copyright office reg. on 10/12/2005: PAu3-002-791
ISBN13: 978-0-9996677-3-6
REPRINT: November 27, 2023

To my family

ACKNOWLEDGMENT

My late friend Gary Wang edited earlier versions of this novel. So did Frederick Shaffer, a lecturer at Northwestern University who taught me Creative Writing. I wrote this book's first manuscript in 2003. Sherwin Geiderman read it in 2005, and Francisco Aragon, Director, Letras Latinas, University of Notre Dame, perused it in 2008. Throughout these years, many revisions took place. In 2018, Ann Renee Jacobs proofread a recent one. Hildi Goldstein copyedited the current manuscript. I am indebted to them for their friendship, guidance, and efforts. My family supported me on this journey, putting up with my distracted mind, which stubbornly veered toward my writing endeavors.

Monarchs starve
on Mexican trees,
as sap dries,
leaves wilt,
and creatures rise,
fighting for their lives.

Butterflies with empty stomachs,
rucksacks on their backs,
unafraid of fear,
unafraid of life,
flutter their wings to fly.

Through thorny paths,
sweltering heat,
and bitter cold,
a horizon looms afar,
where milkweeds grow.

There are vigilant guards,
walls, mountains, rivers,
forlorn hometowns,
full of tears,
and an open sky
clamoring for justice.

PREFACE

I n the last two decades of the twentieth century, the U.S. economy grew more dependent on illegal immigrants from Mexico. Over the 2000-mile border with this country, an army of minimum-salary laborers flew north to satiate the American industry's never-ending need. The major ports of entry were San Diego, California; Nogales, Arizona; and El Paso and Laredo, Texas. The 4000 border patrol agents posed a minor obstacle. Every year, 450,000 undocumented aliens crossed the southern frontier of the United States. One-third of that number returned to Mexico on their own. The Migra —as immigrants called the Immigration and Naturalization Service— deported 50,000. The rest settled down in this country.

This novel unfolds in the foreground of this diaspora. I began to write it in 2003. But the events described here could have unraveled during any time when waves of newcomers arrived in this country. Most of the recounted occurrences could have also happened to any of us. These people are no different than we are. Their existence teems with hope and hopelessness, illusions and disillusions, happiness and sadness, successes, and failures. This reprint contains some changes to capture the original intention of my first drafts. I hope my readers will enjoy the book and discover inspiration and beauty in its pages.

1

EL NORTE

A spring morning blossomed in central Mexico. It graced the mountains with fresh air and bird songs. A timid sun lit square miles of fir trees disguised in orange foliage. The color of these leaves pulsed, fluttering their black edges with two lines of white polka dots as if the frills of a flamenco ballerina's dress. Restlessness grew in the surroundings. The leaves were alive. They crawled, flew a short distance, and returned to perch on the same branches. The monarch butterfly was about to travel north as its forebears had done for thousands of years. The time arrived to begin their quest for survival, or the creatures would perish and disappear from the face of the earth.

Down in the valley, people also felt their uneasiness. The soil was warm, and flowery vapors filled the land in Toultuca, a little town in the State of Jalisco. On that day in 1982, Salvador decided to move to El Norte. This was the name Mexicans called the US. His life had become an impossible challenge. He could not support Rosa, his newlywed wife. The economic decline began with the closure of a silver mine. For years, this metal brought prosperity to everyone in his hometown. Canteens, banks, boarding houses, brothels, and cock-fighting rings went down the drain. So did Salvador's upholstery shop. He had not paid his rent for six months. He sat in semidarkness and looked at his store before shutting it down. His palms turned cold and sweaty at the prospect of what he was about to endure. The small place had been his world. He let his eyes linger on his limited inventory: a wooden stool, a small counter, a shelf with rolls of fabric, and a toolbox against the wall. In the past, when his business flourished, armchairs, sofas, and car-seat covers occupied the space. He did an excellent job. People in his hometown respected him. Men lifted their hats, and women bowed their heads to greet him.

Salvador eased the door shut and shuffled away. He thought about explaining his decision to the supplier who had sold him the materials for his failed business. He then wondered how to say goodbye to his caring wife and beloved mother. Rosa was pregnant with their first child. Salvador admired the majestic palm trees as his feet hit the ground and inhaled the white lilies' perfume. The parrots' multicolored plumage flustered him. He listened to their singing and chirping, and a slow shiver ran from head to toe. The place was stunning, and the land dazzling. But their beauty paled before the poverty and harshness of life.

Salvador trod along a nearby park. He had passed by this area every day but paid little or no attention to it. There were green mango trees with lush leaves, tall and dwarf palm trees, white gardenias, yellow and red hibiscus, and pink roses. Some children ran around a gazebo. Their playful voices cheered up the surroundings, but foreboding hammered at him. Salvador feared he would never see his homeland again. He stuck his head under the jet of water of a blue ceramic fountain. But the terrible thoughts did not budge. He looked up and saw the sky with an intense blue. Cotton-like clouds hovered over the peaks of dark mountains that cradled the village between their steep shoulders. This landscape had accompanied him every-where since his birth. Until now, he did not conceive of life outside his native land.

Salvador walked by the cemetery but avoided approaching it. Sad memories assaulted him and held him tight for a while. He gazed at it and observed tall, whitewashed walls and a giant cross at the front gate. This color contrasted with the red sand of the holy ground. Tombstones teemed with fresh flowers from the dead's relatives. On the lintel of its main entrance, an inscription appeared bright in the sun:

"This is what the Lord God says to the bones: I will instill breath into you, and you shall live," (*Ezekiel's 37-5*.)

Salvador did not go inside. His courage failed him. His father's remains rested there, as did those of his brother Florencio who had died the previous year. Salvador did not want to cry because a man should never cry. But tears welled in his eyes. He checked around and reassured himself that no one espied him. Powerful feelings plotted to restrain and jail him in his homeland. Salvador could not afford to surrender to them and mustered the strength to block them. He shut his eyes tight and wiped his tears away with a brush of his right arm. Rosa should not see any trace of his weeping. Salvador marched across the central plaza. Mango trees' shadows soothed him. There was a honeyed odor from the fallen fruit on the grayish sand.

A few small groups of people gathered around little carts. The men wore white dresses and big straw hats, and the women colorful costumes. Two farmers were selling guavas, pomegranates, pitayas, vegetables, milk, and cheese in one corner. In another, an older lady wore a black smock and a red bow tied to a bun and hawked corn products, repeating over and over,

"*Tamales! Tortillas!* "

Next to her, a vendor displayed pork and beef. Close by, a cart with live iguanas and their eggs was in front of a group of customers. A Colonial-style church presided over the square. A big golden cross sparkled under the sun atop a tall and graceful steeple. Salvador wandered inside the nave.

These walls had heard his prayers several times a week since Salvador was an altar boy many years ago. Light seeped through stained-glass windows and lit up the images of the birth of Christ and His triumphal entrance into Jerusalem. Salvador stared at the statues of Our Lady of Guadalupe and Jesus in the center of a high altar. The upholsterer had decided his departure after appealing to God for his divine help. But Salvador still kneeled and asked the Holy Mother and Son to protect him on his trip.

At twelve, Salvador wanted to become a clergyman, so the parish priest enrolled him in the King Christ Minor Seminary in Guadalajara. The prospect of a life dedicated to God enthused the youngster. The cassock made him feel like a young adult on the right path to sainthood. He read the Bible in the evening and spent two hours praying in a chapel daily. His vocation ended four years later when he fell in love with Rosa. He quit the institution, moved in with an aunt in Guadalajara, and attended a trade school for two years.

Salvador continued his daily route, reached the top of a hill, and caught sight of his home. The single-room brick house was amid rugged countryside. He had built it with his hands on a homestead plot a mile from the town. His mother-in-law presented him and his wife with the land as a wedding gift. The place commanded a view of the village. From there, Salvador admired the shoulders and ridges of the surrounding mountains. They loomed so close that he sometimes fantasized about touching them. The house had no running water or electricity. He and Rosa walked to a nearby brook to fill several containers a few times a week. Salvador roofed the cabin with planks of wood. A wooden table and two chairs furnished the room. On the right side was a brick oven with several metal pots, and on the left, a wooden bed with a floral blanket. A crucifix and a picture of Our Lady of Guadalupe hung on the back wall. A small, attached shed served as a portable toilet.

At this moment on his daily hike, Salvador raised his arms, took a deep breath, and let fresh air expand his chest. He thanked God for his blessings. In the past, when life smiled at him, his invocation had been more emotional. He spun around and bellowed as if drunk with joy,

"*Gracias, Papá Dios!*"

As Salvador approached his house, he rehearsed what to tell Rosa. He saw a few chickens jumping and clucking beside a small, fenced area. They were the only livestock left. Before the economic disaster hit home, Salvador and his wife owned a few pigs, a spotted cow, and a horse. Now, the puddle of mud in the pigsty was dry and cracked, the shadow of the mango tree no longer comforted the cow, and the wood pole for the horse stood alone near the front of the house. Only two dark-and-white beagles roamed next to a small orchard with potatoes and maize.

From afar, Salvador noticed the white reflection of the sun on the facade, the open front door, and the red geranium flowers that hung from their pots. Their hues contrasted with his somber mood. Next to the entrance, a little window was open, and through it, he saw Rosa doing her household chores.

"It will be hard to leave her," he said aloud as if gathering strength for what was about to happen.

Salvador enjoyed basking in his wife's beauty, her petite figure, delicate demeanor, skin fragrance, black hair — "dark like a moonless night" — and brown eyes. Her gaze reached every corner of his

heart. Her pregnancy made it harder for him to leave her behind. His wife had spoken kind words when he got home tired from work. She soaked his feet in salty water and scratched his tense shoulders with her long svelte fingers. He liked to watch her slender body with the hands in her apron pockets as her hips swayed with the awareness of his sight on her. A honey tint of love sweetened her intuitive big brown eyes. They drilled into him and read his mind like an open book. Nothing intimidated Rosa. She would rather pet her two dogs, but if needed, she could twist a chicken's neck.

Rosa saw Salvador's tall figure in the distance and wondered why he was coming home early. He seldom arrived before dusk. By then, attendants of local stores and farmers' markets had closed for the day and retired to their dwellings. For a moment, his image flashed through her mind: his handsome face, black hair, thick mustache, tall physique, big muscles, and broad shoulders. He was attractive. But she loved him for his peaceful character and brown eyes brimming with goodness. The dogs ran to greet him, clambering around him as she hurried to meet him. He embraced, lifted, and then inched her down on the ground. She kissed him, felt his lips cold, and looked into his eyes. Uneasiness brimmed in them. For a moment, time seemed frozen, like a picture on a video set on pause. Salvador tried to release the words he had earlier rehearsed, but his thoughts mingled and interfered with one another. After several seconds, they broke from his lips,

"I must leave for El Norte." The sentence ratcheted out as if he were swallowing the syllables one by one.

"'The tree grows better in its homeland.' Remember the proverb," Rosa said.

She voiced her hopes Mexico would change. Farmers exported more goods to the US and other countries in Central and South America. Their country produced oil, and tourists flocked to the beaches. New opportunities and jobs would open.

"No, Rosa, beautiful and beloved Mexico but full of corruption. The rich hold power, and the money will end up in their bank accounts. The poor will stay the same."

Salvador talked about Mexico like a prosecutor. Some local governments were run like the Mafia. Criminals and police agreed to quotas of felonies. Judges and prosecutors decided who should endure the weight of their arbitrary laws. Politicians extorted businessmen. Union leaders pocketed the money of their workers.

The entire organization served as an unshakable foundation that maintained the abuse of power. Low-ranking officials — officers, clerks, and tax collectors — stepped on the backs of citizens. These miscreants carried out their felonies with the authorities' savvy connivance. They knew of the corruption and let the rich accumulate unprecedented wealth. The poor lived in extreme poverty. Like toxic fumes, drug trafficking seeped through layers of criminals, police, judicial systems, and government. Vast fortunes were hidden in Swiss banks. Regulated lawlessness ruled these areas where criminals roamed free. The local police protected politicians and bosses — the caciques — who owned most of the land and shops in the area. Citizens feared the cops as much as the crooks. His ranting over, he caught his breath and added,

"Is my life better than my father's? Was my father's better than my grandfather's? I want a bright future for our child and ourselves."

Salvador expressed his anguish and despair. He could not put food on the table. People had no money to pay for the work he did. His store received materials on credit from Roberto's business. He had been patient with Salvador, but his debts had escalated. Soon, the supplier would ask for the outstanding amount, and he did not have the money to pay.

"Dollars don't grow on trees in El Norte," Rosa countered.

"You are three months pregnant and haven't eaten a piece of red meat in months."

"I am going with you."

"I wish you could. But we can't endanger our baby's life."

Facing each other, husband and wife sat at a table over tacos in the evening. Light still shone through the windows, and the semi-darkness enhanced their somber mood. Salvador cast his eyes down and seemed to look through the table planks. A taco held in his hand lingered before his mouth. His lips and throat were immobile as if thick silence hindered their movements. The smell of tortilla and the pungent odor of frying oil wafted through the place. Rosa felt nauseated. She stared at Salvador with her hands resting on the table. He took bites, one out of the middle of the taco, one out of the right, one out of the left. She observed his struggle to chew and swallow them. Salvador performed the task with almost mechanical motion as if ordering each of his muscles to carry out his instructions.

"Would you like more?" Rosa asked.

Salvador shook his head, his eyes on the table. Rosa picked the leftovers up, wrapped them in a napkin, and put them on a plate in the kitchenette. She turned and looked at him. His pose had not changed. He rose from the chair, toddled toward Rosa, and kissed her. It was a long kiss with no passion, his lips asleep over hers. She fought back tears as her mind raced with fear. Rosa recalled all the men in her hometown that had left their wives and children to work in El Norte. Most sent money to them, fed them, and built decent homes. But their absence shadowed their close relatives' happiness. They missed their presence and spent interminable days waiting for their safe return.

"I am afraid," she said, revealing her forebodings.

Rosa spoke of a young farmer who had died crossing into the US. She expressed sorrow for a fellow countrywoman whose son was buried among the myriad unidentified tombs along the border.

"Don't worry," Salvador said. "God is with us. My cousin Mauricio knows someone who will help me."

Some of her compatriots had fallen in love with American women, married them, and never returned. She knew a few, among them Tomasa's husband. He still wired money to sustain his wife and children every month, even though he had married a Gringa in the US. He mailed pictures of his new spouse and their little boy. The complacent wife justified the bigamy. A lonely man needed a woman's caring hands and affection. Besides, she could not leave her sick mother alone in Mexico. Rosa expressed her apprehension, and Salvador reassured her,

"No, my love, that won't happen to us. I love you. I will send for you and our child as soon as possible."

After their meal, they sat outside. The approaching night greeted them with its chilly breeze as the full moon climbed the peaks. Nature sizzled with the evening dew, parrots' restless cries, and kingbirds' tremulous trills. Salvador rested his thick head of brown hair in her lap and let her trace his lips and mustache with her index finger's soft pad. Rosa loved his soft eyes that shone full of devotion to her. She loved the Aztecan slant of his eyelids and the virile Castilian inclination of his aquiline nose. She loved the dimples in his cheeks that froze his expression into a smile and wished this moment lasted forever or, at least, several days.

The couple went to bed, and the closeness of their bodies served as a constant reminder of the impending separation. Salvador held

Rosa in his arms, kissed her, and their tears fueled their inner fire. Inch by inch, his hands caressed her body's warm contours. His fingers lingered at her belly and palpated the early pressure of a growing womb. Love, passion, and sadness fused husband and wife. Their intimacy ended, and a sense of overwhelming closeness grabbed them as though they had exchanged their bodies. The sleepless night grew dark, and desolation ransacked their minds until the cocks crowed.

Rosa got out of bed and grabbed her husband's backpack. She tucked in a clean shirt, a pair of pants, a set of underwear, a bar of homemade soap, a clasp knife, and a Bible. Rosa prepared breakfast, and Salvador served it. He said grace and ate as the aroma of tamales hovered over them. She looked at him and saw the determination on his face. His teeth bit into the food with a decisive gripping, and his swallowing was methodical and rhythmical. He took a small piece of tamale, and dough spilled onto his finger from the cornhusk wrapper. He licked it with his tongue, but it was a bit stuck in the middle of his mustache. Rosa stood up, dabbed it with her finger, sat at the table again, and ate with a hearty appetite. This moment was not the time to mope. A wife must be strong for her husband.

Salvador picked up the backpack and slipped his arms through the straps. He shrugged his broad shoulders twice to distribute the load on both sides of his torso and stepped out. Rosa was at the door to bid him farewell. She sensed the tread of his feet like the throbs of a nasty headache. Salvador kissed her but did not embrace her, fearing he would be unable to release her from his chest.

"Goodbye, my love," he said. "I'll write to you as soon as I get there."

As Salvador walked out, he thought of looking back at his wife, who stood waving him goodbye. But he knew better than that.

2

NOSTALGIA

The fresh breeze from the mountains eased the suffocating heat when Salvador walked on the streets of Guadalajara. The conversations with his supplier and his landlord had been hard. He reassured them he would pay his debts to the last peso. He visited Mauricio. His cousin knew well the whereabouts of the coyotes — traffickers who helped illegal immigrants to cross the border into the US. He had worked as one. Mauricio and an associate smuggled about forty immigrants daily for over five years. Back then, each migrant paid one hundred fifty dollars. Twenty covered bribes to the Mexican police, and the rest ended up in their pockets. Coyotes were always on the lookout for outlaws who hid and waited to steal their money and rape migrant women. In one assault, his associate was killed, and Mauricio sustained severe injuries. He stayed still, and the bandits assumed him dead. After his recovery, he never went back to the border.

The bus station was a few minutes' walk from his cousin's home. Salvador stepped on a bus, sat beside a window, and closed his eyes. He hoped that sleep would numb the thoughts and feelings that sizzled in his mind. After several hours, the friction noise of the wheels on the asphalt plunged him into a restless lethargy. A three-day, 1400-mile trip awaited him. It would unfold a constant change of scenery, mountain after mountain, coasts with calm surf, golden sands, beautiful blue waters, mountains again, one little town after another, another big city, new streams of passengers on and off the bus, a sandwich, or tamales with a glass of cola here and there. The next day, Salvador caught a wink. When he woke up, a new landscape burst into his view. The dry northern country stretched before him with the scorching sun cooking the earth into thousands of cracks. Occasional prickly pears and scattered dark-brown dry bushes stood under the open blue sky. There was not a single cloud. The night fell, and cold set in. He put his jacket on, tipped his hat forward, and tried to sleep.

His thoughts hearkened back to his farewell to his mother and sister two days ago. Elena and twelve-year-old Margarita lived on the outskirts of his hometown. His father and elder brother Rosendo had died, leaving them in a precarious situation. His father passed away two years earlier after a lengthy illness. Rosendo was murdered a year ago when a killer put a bullet through his head as the victim drove his pickup truck to work. The crime had happened a few weeks after he had joined a workers' union. Political motivation might have caused it since he helped recruit several new members. The authorities never found the assassin.

Mother and daughter depended on Salvador's income and what their small orchard, two sheep, and four chickens yielded for sustenance. The sun's silhouette had lifted over the gray mountains and dissipated the morning dew. He felt its warmth on his back. His long-tilted shadow crawled along a dirt path and slipped ahead of him into the flanking bushes covered with purple blossoms. He saw his mother from afar, beyond the green grass, through the evergreen and pecan trees. Her figure stood out, dressed in black and bent over stalks and tassels of corn. Her silvery hair spilled out from the fringe of her black kerchief. She worked at an unrelenting pace as if escaping from the terrible grief that crowded her mind. Even the fresh flowery fragrance and the birds' morning chirps could not fend off Salvador's foreboding—he was about to kiss his mom for the last time. An old black setter sat next to her. The dog raised his head, wagged his tail, and alerted her to Salvador's arrival. She lifted her eyes, looked at her son, and realized something was amiss. Silence overtook her when Salvador confirmed her fears.

"I must secure a future for my son," he added.

Elena lacked faith in the future. Suffering and poverty had accompanied her since her childhood. She took off her kerchief and wiped the sweat from her forehead with a brush of her arm. The mother then turned away from her son to dry her tears. Salvador hugged her tight against his chest, kissed her forehead, and asked her to bless him. He kneeled before her, closed his eyes, and let the pungent scent of green corn rush into his lungs. Her raised right arm cast a shadow upon his eyes as small stones stuck into his knees. The world turned into a globe of brightness around her head, and the mountain breeze clogged his ears. He blinked. His mother appeared before him like a marble statue in the foreground of massive dark mountains. Her muscular legs stood on the ground with disfigured ankles and large swollen veins writhing under the skin. He thought he would be safe if he could throw himself at her sturdy legs and hold on to them. As a child, Salvador had done it so many times. He raised his eyes and saw his mother's tanned and wrinkled face, the flame of youth still burning in her downcast brown eyes. She stared at him with a stern expression. Her callus-ridden right hand drew the sign of the cross over his head as her soft voice invoked the names of the Father, the Son, and the Holy Ghost. She took a deep sigh and said,

"May God be with you, my son. I'll pray to Our Lady of Guadalupe. Say goodbye to your sister. She is feeding the chickens in the coop."

Elena put her kerchief back on. Her hoe lashed out at a speeding pace as tears ran down her face. She made an impressive effort as if physical tiredness could mitigate the pain of a mother. But nothing drove her fears away that she would never see her child again.

As the bus continued, the constant engine noise and the drone of nearby conversations dulled Salvador's thoughts. Fatigue caught up with him, and a restful nap relieved him. He woke up with the first light of dawn and watched the sun rise above brown mountains. The range emerged in the distance with a dense fog under the peaks. He soon espied the faraway silhouette of Santa Ana ahead of him, his last stop before catching the bus to Tijuana.

The Santa Ana bus station lay next to the highway. Small homes lined both sides of the road. Their residents used their porches as shops and displayed articles for sale: boots, sombreros, belts, religious figurines, fruits, meat, cheese, ice cream, tamales, and other maize-made products. Inside, as if time did not exist, young women and older family members sat and waited for a passerby to buy one piece of merchandise. A small bar boasted gigantic signs of Coca-Cola and Corona beer. Two patrons consumed beverages from big mugs at a darkened wooden counter. The air reeked of dry hay. A few dogs sprawled on the sidewalk, and several chickens fluttered their wings and clucked. The bus driver announced the departure to Nogales on the Mexico-US border.

Salvador had a three-hour wait before catching the Tijuana bus for the last thirteen hours of his trip. The sun passed the zenith, and a sweltering dry heat baked the surroundings. He walked into a nearby plaza and sat on a bench under a tree next to a man eating a Mexican flatbread. Short and dark-skinned, the Indian raised his slanted eyes and glanced at him. The glimpse of welcome did not interrupt his munching. He savored each bite while staring at the floor, swallowed a mouthful of food, lifted his head, and introduced himself as Gaudencio. He informed his companion of his intention to get to El Norte through Tijuana. The fellow migrants shook hands and engaged in conversation. Gaudencio belonged to the Totonaca tribe in Papantla, a town atop a mountain in Veracruz. The village's name in his native tongue meant the city of thrushes — the beautiful, velvety-black birds.

"When the sun sets," Gaudencio said, his eyes sparkling with emotion, "clouds of birds pack the trees. No human-made music can compete with their beautiful melody."

His conversation drifted to his shack and small farm in the mountains. Gaudencio had a wife, two little sons, and a young

13

daughter. Growing maize, vanilla, and coffee provided the means for them to survive. But their prices dropped so much in the past few years that he could no longer sustain his family.

The awaited bus arrived late. A few people got on and sat down in comfortable seats. Most carried shopping bags full of foodstuffs. A man brought along a fighting cock in a cage. The angry bird pecked at the iron bars, crowed, nodded, and stretched its neck in a proud pose. Several peddlers lugged their wares— corn products, home-made sweets, and peanuts. A woman pulled out one of her breasts to feed her baby, and two little children wept across the aisle. An overpowering stench and a suffocating heat beset the passengers, but the open windows did not relieve them.

Salvador and Gaudencio sat down together. The two companions talked about coyotes and rates. The one recommended to Salvador— Nacho—asked for two hundred dollars, and that of his companion, four hundred. Rubbing of tires against rough roads and the constant engine noise enhanced the fatigue of the two travelers. They kept their eyes shut and tried to numb their busy minds until the bus arrived at the central station in Tijuana, their destination in Mexico. The place teemed with expansive shiny halls and wooden counters. At midmorning, long queues of red taxicabs lined up in several rows amid a loud din of passengers' voices, hawkers, and heavy traffic. A big blue sign that read "*Buen Viaje*"—have a good trip— stared at them as soon as they stepped out of the station's front entrance.

The new friends headed for Nacho's haunt, Bar El Rancherito. Inside, two patrons in undershirts drank glasses of tequila and flirted with a youthful woman with an excess of rouge on her lips. A burly bartender boasted a leonine face as he stood behind the counter with a big mustache and a large cross on his hairy chest. The lion man eyed the newcomers with suspicion. Salvador explained the reason for their presence. With a roaring voice, the barman instructed them to sit at a table. Nacho arrived at the bar two hours later. He was tall and corpulent and wore an impeccable gray suit, a black Texan hat, and shining leather boots. The barman raised his eyebrows, tossed his head sideways, and pointed to where the migrants sat. Nacho sized up his prospective clients as he approached them. Salvador conveyed to him his cousin Mauricio's greetings. He hoped the coyote could help him and his friend cross the border. Nacho nodded and said,

"I can help you, but I don't know if I can help your friend." He looked sidelong at Gaudencio and asked, "Do you know how to sing Mexicans at the Cry of War?"

Nacho explained the Mexican police might think the Indian companion came from Guatemala or another Central American country. They could order him to sing the Mexican national anthem. Failure to comply would increase the bribe. The coyote said that American border patrols caught one out of five trespassers. The unlucky one had often ventured into the US on his own. This statistic allowed Nacho to reassure his clients of the operation's success,

"You won't be arrested, but if border patrol agents apprehend you, they'll bring you back to Tijuana. Find me, and I'll ensure you get in the second time."

Nacho pocketed the money and instructed them to meet him early that afternoon at Las Brisas, a tavern on the outskirts of town near the border. The pub served as a frequent haunt for truckers. Two hours later, the two friends set off for their meeting point. The "B" on the illuminated sign had burned out, and instead of Brisas—Spanish for breezes—it read "risas," which meant laughs. The joke seemed to augur an auspicious omen for them. Heavy trucks jammed the parking lot of the noisy establishment, where a record player blared out corridos. Cigarette smoke lingered over a crowd of beer drinkers and card gamblers.

Nacho beckoned Salvador and Gaudencio from a stool at the bar. His clients barely recognized him because he wore jeans and no hat. The coyote covered the precautions that wayfarers needed to heed after arriving on American soil. Shave and wear clean clothes, mingle with people, avoid major roads, and keep a watchful eye on any patrol car. These instructions were to be followed until they were far from the border. Nacho drew a big puff from his cigarette, exhaled, and watched the smoke billow over his head. A group of five women and fifteen men stood off in a corner, planning to cross the border from the New River. Nacho pointed to them, twisted his face with disgust, and said,

"That damned river is a sewer full of dead animals, garbage, feces, and chemicals. It smells like hell. The stench and fumes can choke you. Now, with the rain, it turns into a treacherous trap. You can drown in filthy dirt."

Nacho touted his value as a coyote and ushered Salvador and Gaudencio to the parking lot. The trafficker outlined his plan. Two drivers would slow down their trucks, bring them to a halt, and remain in the queue until reaching the US-Customs booth. The waiting time varied between one and three hours. He taught the migrants to hide under the chassis and let them practice the maneuvers a few times. A partner expected them on the other side of the border.

Dense dark clouds covered the sky, and after a while, a pitchy evening set in. Thick fog and a breeze from the sea chilled the air. The drizzle drenched Salvador and Gaudencio and made them shiver with cold. Streetlamps came on, and the fellow migrants were in the dark on the roadside. Traffic lights shone farther down on the US border, where long queues of vehicles lined up to move across. Salvador would be the first to catch a truck, and his friend would follow at the next suitable opportunity.

A few minutes later, a heavy eighteen-wheeler plowed along the road. A dim light flashed from the spot where Nacho stood and signaled to Salvador that he could run and board the bottom of the chassis. Wheels rolled on like a growling monster. Treads grabbed on the road, the engine palpitated, and the pavement shook. The driver slowed the vehicle down to a snail's crawl. Salvador crossed himself.

"Good luck," Gaudencio whispered to him.

3

ROARING DARKNESS

R oaring darkness wrapped Salvador under the truck. His face rubbed against the undercarriage, his hands clutched a metal piece that crossed the frame, and his body hung outstretched next to the drive shaft. He had his feet set on the rear axle and noticed every jerk of the tires. His spine wavered like a bowstring after firing off an arrow.

The U.S. border was a few hundred yards away. A stench of gas fumes riled up his stomach and turned his fingers cold. Faintness threatened to release his hold on the bottom of the vehicle. It could drop him against the asphalt where the tire treads awaited him. A deep breath did not control his nausea, and sweat droplets cropped on his forehead. After a while, the truck stopped, and the driver addressed an official,

"Bananas."

Official and driver plodded toward the back of the vehicle. Salvador saw the driver's running shoes and blue jeans. The Customs official wore wet black boots whose steps reverberated off the bar where the stowaway's hands were clutched. Salvador held his breath and prayed the official would not look under the truck. A lighted cigarette fell on the sidewalk. The migrant watched his black boot stomp on it and twist it against the concrete, leaving a black swath over the grayish pavement. A powerful tobacco odor rushed toward him, making him feel like the trampled butt. His hopes for a decent life in his homeland had been crushed, the burning fire for a better Mexico extinguished, and the feelings for his country gutted out and scattered. His heart pounded, and his body shivered as driver and official climbed into the back of the truck. He heard them chatting but made out no words.

His mind bristled with anger. Why do I have to go through this agony? Why must we go into another country hidden from everyone like criminals? Damn politicians! They and their relatives live well. They don't care what happens to any of us. Maybe some of them do. Who am I to judge anyone? He then felt jealous of the monarchs that crossed the border with no fictitious limits imposed on them. The driver's tread aroused Salvador from his reverie. He heard him return to his seat and saw the black boots trudge alongside the truck cab.

"Hand this document to the Customs officer. Have a good trip," the official said with a Puerto Rican accent.

The slight engine acceleration resounded in Salvador's ears. The truck crept toward the nearby exit. Outside, the driver pressed the gas pedal for about two hundred yards and turned left onto a worn-down road. Thick darkness enveloped the vehicle. The eighteen-wheeler soon slowed down before reaching the depot. Salvador released his feet from the axle and darted them toward the side rail. He adjusted the position of his hands, let his feet hit the asphalt, and launched himself into a ditch.

A dim light signaled the place where his contact waited for him. He brushed the dirt off his bruised elbows and ran fast to the point of encounter. Next to an unpaved road, a husky man sat in the driver's seat of a minivan hidden among bushes. The lights and engine were off. Salvador went into the back and greeted four migrants, who turned their heads and nodded back at him. An offensive stench of sweat mixed with tobacco and foul breath hovered over everyone in the cargo area. During absolute silence, something horrifying overtook Salvador. A sudden sensation of being in a strange and inhospitable land loomed before him. A cold shiver rushed down his arms and legs, and his limbs shook with violence until he held his hands tight and pressed his feet against each other.

"We are waiting for four wetbacks," the van driver addressed his passengers, using a derogatory term for illegal immigrants.

From his seat, Salvador watched the constant flow of trucks on the long, dark road from U.S. Customs to the depot. The fog had lifted a little. In front of a small office, he saw two white workers saunter toward a large semi. A black clerk inspected the truck tires, squatted to check the chassis, sprang back on his feet, and jotted down the info in a notebook. Far away, voices resounded with a hollow echo. Images passed by his eyes as in a movie. He wondered whether the clerk noticed the remnants of one of his shirtsleeves. The exhaust pipe had burned it and branded it onto the metal. He could not inch his arm out of the intense heat for several seconds. Luckily, his skin was still intact.

Incidents during the ride plagued his mind. The truck had moved so fast that any jerky motion might have caused him to fall to his death. The racket of tire treads deafened him, and bursts of palpitations in his heart seemed to fire in unison with those of the engine. Whenever the truck hit a damaged asphalt patch, a shower of little rocks hit him like B.B. pellets. Coil springs wailed like a wild pig as his body bounced up and down. He perceived the shearing force of gravity threatening to scoop him from the bottom. The wind swept under the smoke puffs from the exhaust pipe. It caused him terrible attacks of coughing. His thoughts drifted toward God. The vehicle drove through sepulchral darkness that reminded him of Christ lying in His tomb. He envisioned Mary Magdalene and Mary of Bethany standing before the removed sealing stone. The grave was empty, and two shining angels spoke to them,

"Why do you seek the living among the dead?"

Salvador had faith that God would help him. He would also rise from this darkness and enjoy a new life.

Meanwhile, Gaudencio had jumped out from the side of the road onto a six-ton yellow eighteen-wheeler. He crouched down alongside the vehicle, his head brushing the bottom edge. He boarded the underside of the chassis and curled himself over the spare tire. The engine throbbed, wheels grabbed the road, and the noise grew deafening. The pavement shook. He held on to a metal ring as the monster crawled toward the port of entry.

Time was at a standstill. The heat in the confined space made him thirsty. He listened to the rumble of neighboring trucks and the hawking noise of the swarm of peddlers. They were selling their wares — tacos, T-shirts, jewels, Chihuahua dogs. Some passed so near that he could see their walking shoes. Hunger spurred him to smell the fragrance of *tacos* over the stink of gas fumes. He wished he were at home eating maize tortillas with his wife and children.

The street noise faded as the vehicle entered Mexican Customs. Laughter and conversations between the trucker and officials flared up. A policeman squatted and peeked under the frame. His eyes flashed wide open and enlarged out of proportion to the nose and mouth as if the image belonged to a funhouse mirror. Gaudencio blinked twice to correct his distorted vision. A gruesome certainty came upon him. He thought the bearer of the deformed eyes was about to detain him, but the officer ignored his presence.

After a long while, the truck moved to American Customs, and voices changed. He did not understand a single word. Black boots and blue-and-white sneakers shuffled next to the vehicle. The inspection of the merchandise took place. His trembling worsened, and fear transformed the waiting period into protracted torture. The eighteen-wheeler then headed for the exit, drove for a while, and rumbled down the road one hundred yards. The truck veered to the left, entered the dark path leading to the depot, and slowed down. Gaudencio maneuvered to release himself. Suddenly, a front wheel hit a pothole, and a big stone hurled upward and struck him in the back of the head. He plopped down, and a tire crushed his skull. Unaware of what had happened, the trucker continued his course over a pool of blood. The front lights of the following vehicle illuminated a man's mangled remains. Screams broke out. A few minutes later, ambulances flooded the area with sirens.

From the minivan at the U.S. border, Salvador heard loud cries. The noise alerted Customs agents, workers at the depot, and truckers that something had gone wrong down the unlit road leading to the facility. An uproar of voices burst out that he did not understand. Two emergency vehicles sounded disquieting sirens. Blue lights spun, and their reflections awakened stretches of dark areas. A yellow truck was at a standstill with its frantic driver waving his arms next to the cab. Both sides of the road teemed with debris, wild plants, dry bushes, and soil, leading to an open field. Six dismounted truckers, three employees at the depot, and four officials scrambled to the accident site.

"Let's go," the van driver said. "Something went wrong. Stay quiet, and we'll leave in a few minutes."

The small van crawled away from the border with the head and tail lamps off. The tires ran over the dry brush with a sizzling noise. After a few minutes, the lights came on, and the van crept onto a road. The sudden beams of illumination from the passing automobiles blinded him. The vehicles drove into the yawning darkness behind him. Tiredness made him watch everything go by like a slow freight train. He had not slept for four days. His eyes ached, and his mind ran amok with visions of a black abyss and geometrical shadows.

A few minutes later, he passed by some used car dealerships adorned with multicolor lights. Bars and nightclubs lit the streets of San Ysidro with red flashing signs. The van arrived at a single home with a short driveway, a small front yard, and a few broken windows. The blinds were closed. Inside, he joined a group of twenty-five men and ten women that other coyotes had brought that evening. Gaudencio was not among them. He asked the driver about him.

"What do I know?" the driver curtly replied. "He didn't make it today."

Salvador lay on the floor in the corner of a room no bigger than a prison cell. His head rested on his knapsack, and his hat on his face. His boots entangled with those of the other five male migrants. Whispered conversations kept him awake. Hard tiles pressed on his spine, and shifting his position worsened the foul stench of humanity that hung over the place. He drifted into sleep. Someone crossed over, stepped on his left leg, and apologized. Salvador removed his hat. He regarded a bush with dark leaves through a small window and two tiny stars above its foliage. There was no wind. Moonlight drew a silver swath on the opposite wall.

Salvador's mind drifted to Rosa. He thought of her long eyelashes, her black hair rustling between his fingertips, and the straight line that parted the right side of her hairdo. He cherished other facial features: the smooth dimple in the middle of her upper lip, her crooked lower front tooth, and the little round black beauty spot on the right side of her mouth. He had sent her a telegram from Tijuana and let her know how much he loved her. Rosa was the pillar that sustained his dreams. Her words of caution resonated in his mind,

"Promise me you will not endanger your life. Our child needs a father, and I need you."

He had promised her, but how could anyone predict what might happen during an illegal entry?

4

5

NEIGHBORING WORLDS

The morning after Salvador arrived in San Ysidro, a poker-faced Nacho told him that the border patrol had detained Gaudencio and released him. He reassured him that his friend would cross the border again in a few days. A few hours later, a van drove the illegal immigrants to a large plaza in the center of town near the central bus station. Relatives and friends waited for some newcomers, and the rest mingled with people on the streets.

Mauricio had provided Salvador with the address in Chula Vista for Mr. Lopez, who would help him find a job. The previous night's experience had left an aftermath of soreness all over Salvador's body. His muscles hurt from fatigue. He sat at the bus terminal in a packed hall where four long lines of travelers were purchasing tickets. Twelve buses waited outside. Signs in English and Spanish gave him the impression of a fraternal coexistence of two neighboring worlds. But everything looked different. This place was clean and organized; even its smell was foreign to him. No one smoked. Salvador disliked this habit but now felt an unexpected nostalgia for the clouds of cigarette fumes and coffee aroma in Mexican public places. Something else struck him — the silence that loomed over him. People were next to one another, reading newspapers or books without even peeking at their neighbors. Everyone was together, yet alone. The observation unnerved him.

Salvador saw an old lady with Mexican features who sat munching on a little sandwich. He approached her and asked if she could help him purchase a ticket for the Chula Vista bus. She took a bite, lowered her head, then raised it, gazed at him straight in the eye, and said,

"You are a newcomer, aren't you? You people will never learn. This place is a terrible country. Listen to me. Go home. Do you see how old I am? I am still cleaning houses to survive."

The elderly woman grimaced in disgust and pointed toward a window. After buying a ticket, Salvador sat beside her and drifted into thoughts. Her presence reminded him of his mom, and childhood memories rushed to him. His mother's lips mumbled in prayer as her folded hands rested on the dining table. Her eyes concentrated on a small stack of corn tortillas, a plate of burritos, and a chunk of meat. The aroma of the cooked food lingered over everyone. A candle flame flickered in the middle of the table. Their enlarged and distorted shadows trembled on the wall as if climbing to the ceiling. His brother Rosendo sat next to him and across from their mother. He liked to kick his younger brother's foot and even reach his sister's leg, who was two chairs away from him. His poker face revealed no grimace or gesture. Their mother had been unaware of the game played underneath the table until the evening Rosendo missed his sister and hit his mom's knee. With her eyes fixed on her naughty son, she waited until her husband finished saying grace. She then stood up, grabbed Rosendo's right ear, and pulled him up and out of the chair. His brother exclaimed,

"Mom, I am sorry."

With his neck stretched out, the mother drove her naughty child as he tiptoed and flitted like a bird into a corner of the room behind his siblings. Salvador and his sister snickered under their palms, covering their mouths. His father stared through them in absolute silence. His mother returned to the table and distributed the tortillas and tamales, each for his parents and double portions for the children. Her face was impervious to the situation. There was never enough meat for husband and wife. His mom cut the chunk into three equal parts with surgical precision and forked them onto her children's plates. She picked up Rosendo's, walked toward him, and said with a stern expression,

"If you kick like a donkey, you can eat like a donkey — standing on your hooves."

Salvador boarded the bus to Chula Vista. When he arrived, a bright sun illuminated a city awash with large white, pink, and yellow ranunculus flowers and slender palm trees. Streets bustled with shoppers, fancy cars, people sitting at outdoor cafes, and stores with colorful beach clothing. The shoreline boasted boardwalks and bike trails. He had never seen the sea and looked forward to the experience. The immense water burst upon his view, rippling and shimmering in the sunlight. It was as blue as the sky in his homeland on a cloudless day. Salvador was in awe as a fresh breeze with a lime-like taste caressed his face. His mind soon drifted to more pressing matters than the stunning surroundings.

His deliberate steps led him to the intended destination. He found Mr. Lopez sitting on a chair reading a newspaper outside a little taco store. He was in his late sixties, wore an undershirt and a Panama sombrero, and smoked a large cigar. After making their acquaintance, the old man offered to find him a farm job for a commission — the first two months' salary minus room and board.

The farm was far from the city. The living quarters were twenty small trailer homes on a narrow strip of land. Each housed seven men or seven women in small partitions. The next day, Salvador woke up two hours before dawn and climbed on the back of a truck. The long ride took him and his fellow workers to an enormous field of red strawberries nestled in green leaves. Drops of dew sparkled in the morning sun. Twenty crews of seven harvesters bent over between lines of bushes, picked ripe fruits, and placed them into large boxes.

After a while, his back hurt, but he forged on, now and then wiping sweat from his forehead, and straightening himself up.

A brief noon break reinvigorated Salvador.

He shared tortillas and tamales with his coworkers amidst a joyful atmosphere of jokes and laughs. They soon resumed their labor, and hours later, the sun rouged the clouds and hid behind the mountains. Worn out, Salvador hopped back into the truck and rode back to his quarters. He ate a hearty dinner, thanked God for granting him work, took a shower, and collapsed in bed.

A few days later, two new immigrants arrived at the farm, and Salvador learned of the death of Gaudencio. The news brought him to tears. He kneeled and prayed for him and his family. His friend had never provided him with an address to notify anyone of the terrible news.

Little by little, he accepted the demise of his Indian friend and adapted to his new environment. His daily reading of Bible passages comforted him. Reminders of his homeland cheered him up: singing birds, large trees, grass, warm sunny weather, mighty black mountains. He thrived on hard work, harvesting strawberries, oranges, lemons, grapes, and avocados six or seven days a week. He wrote in dwindling light at night. His letters spoke of his job, the beautiful scenery in the North, how much he missed his wife, and his hope that God would reunite his family soon. He kissed the envelope and retired to sleep.

In October 1982, Rosa notified him of the birth of their child, Humberto, a handsome boy who took after him. The correspondence also contained a blurry picture of his wife with their baby in her arms. To him, the details of his face were sharp. He could even distinguish his wife's happiness in her expression and would have given anything in the world to be with them.

Salvador never felt alone in the middle of his solitude. In the seminary, his teacher, Father Guillermo Milton, had taught him to rely on God for his companionship. His instructions remained imprinted in his memory,

"Talk to Him about your joys, sorrows, and worries. Be grateful to Him and acknowledge all your blessings. Offer Him your love and kind acts. Atone for your evil actions and weaknesses. Get to know Him and relate to Him. Your closeness to Him will help you with your decisions in life."

His learning process had been a long and frustrating path. For a while, he thought he would experience the nearness when the priest lifted the altar bread and wine to change them into the body and blood of Christ. But he perceived nothing. Salvador complained to Father Guillermo that he could not sense God next to him. The priest consoled him,

"My son, persevere, keep praying, listen to your conscience, and you'll soon notice His presence near you."

For several months, frustration made the youngster consider the goal unreachable. On a spring morning, fifteen-year-old Salvador was fishing on a stream alone. The sun lifted behind the gray mountains, dissipating the dew from the small yellow flowers on acebuche trees. Fresh rippling water bathed his bare feet, and the current's musical gurgle rushed among bedrocks. The sounds infused the surroundings with quiet joy. He caught two trout, felt happy, and talked to God about the school, his hope for a devout religious life, and the prospect of helping his fellow man.

Salvador raised his eyes to heaven and saw a large white cloud with a silver edge. It seemed as if God's splendor outlined its contours and drew a breach in the cumulus with a mouth shape. The gap drifted and hung over the mountain. He then perceived his spirit lift as his ears clogged, his chest swelled with air, and his heart rushed. At that moment, he sensed God's closeness as if a short stretch of space connected him to the divinity. God was ready to listen to him. The youngster related his worries and riffled through his consciousness for God's recommendations. From then on, Salvador counted on God's companionship and paternal guidance whenever he summoned Him. The seminarian drew energy from God, much like an electric tram from an overhead electrical line.

Musings kept Salvador occupied on the farm. On the occasional Sundays off, he walked to a small abbey a few miles away and attended Mass. The place was empty early in the morning. He pleaded with God for the welfare of his family amid the solitude. Salvador spent the rest of the day at home, reading and rereading his wife's letters. Rosa reviewed Humberto's new milestones, events in their little village, and her unconditional love for him. He came across the words 'missing you' several times. But Rosa had omitted her dreams where she had made love to him. Her intense desire made her climax while asleep. Erotic scenes erupted in her mind, ree-nacting their passionate kisses the following day. Rosa did not mention her ecstasy when she inhaled the aftershave cologne he had forgotten on the washstand. The fragrance evoked the warm sensation his stubborn stubble left on her chin and lips. It even brought back the ticklish caresses of his mustache. She had been too shy to express these intimacies.

Besides her letters and the Bible, Salvador loved to read newspapers, western novels, and Reader's Digest magazines.

He now and then watched a soccer game and enjoyed a beer at a nearby bar. His coworkers pressured him to stay longer after the match, but he always declined. All his money went to his family. It was not much since he had a meager income after lodging, meals, taxes, and the high commission for wire transfers. His wife handed cash to her mother-in-law, bought staples, and put aside a few pesos. It took a long year to repay the debts to the landlord and the supplier. This employment did not provide him with enough income, so he looked for another job where he could earn a better living.

On Saturday evenings, most workers visited downtown to spend their money. Salvador sat outside his quarters with Felipe, a fellow migrant. In his fifties, the seasoned coworker bore the prominent wrinkles of hard work on his face. His eyes shone with the serene glint of those who had led their lives in the countryside. The sky brimmed with stars that night, and a full moon coated the landscape with silvery shades. Felipe drew a cigarette, lit it, and the dry odor of tobacco rushed toward his young companion. The night's quietness invited conversation. Felipe talked about his decision to return to his home in a small village south of the border. His initial arrival in California occurred twenty-three years earlier when the Bracero Program was in force. The US government terminated the arrangement in 1964. He had come on his own every year in the busy season and returned to his family in the low season ever since.

"I want to stay in the US," Salvador said.

"The majority of Mexicans feel sad about leaving their country and their people," Felipe said. "Many forget how terrible their lives were in Mexico before arriving in the US. They dream of their hometowns and remember only pleasant things. When they return, the blessings they've left behind in El Norte dawn on them."

"I want my child to have a better future than me."

Salvador pulled out his wallet to show him the picture of his son as his face beamed with happiness and pride.

"Very handsome."

Felipe removed his hat, donned it back, and got ready for another set of measured words,

"Life taught me that home is where you work, eat every day, and are treated like a human being."

"Why didn't you bring your family to the US?"

"I am old. I have no children."

Felipe took a puff on the cigarette, exhaled it, let the smoke billow over his head, and added,

"My wife takes care of a mentally disabled sister. We can't move anywhere."

The senior coworker offered to help Salvador find a good job and referred him to Mr. Tello, a friend in Chicago.

A few days later, Salvador sat on a Greyhound bus and left San Diego early in the morning. After several hours of green foliage and lush orchards, the dry and rugged landscape of the Mojave Desert stretched before him. The blue sky blended with almost bare red mountains. Sparse yuccas and prickly pear cactuses fought for their lives. He sensed a closeness to those plants seething under the sun and battling to survive in a harsh world. Passengers rode quietly. Their silence helped his mind drift on and off to Rosa and his son, and the engine roaring lulled him into sleep. When Salvador opened his eyes, Las Vegas was in the middle of a valley surrounded by reddish, brown, and black mountains. After a long night, he woke up to the blushing shoulders and summits of the Rocky Mountains. He dozed through the long, flat plains of the Midwest and reached the outskirts of Chicago after two days.

Salvador could see the skyline as he approached the city from the south side. A hazy mist blurred the John Hancock skyscraper. The expressway to the town crawled with cars, lanes moving at a snail's pace even though the rush hour had yet to start. A glorious morning sun rested above the horizon of Lake Michigan. Sunlight ricocheted off the calm waters, and cotton-like clouds floated almost motionless. On the bus, he could hear the rumble of tires scraping against asphalt. His tiredness and sleepiness did not stifle his excitement as he approached the city where he hoped to fulfill his dreams.

Salvador stepped off the bus, and the summer's humid heat slapped him in the face amid the pungent odor and savor of bus fumes. Mr. Tello recognized him. The older man's fat belly bounced and almost unbuttoned his shirt as he approached the passenger. His welcoming words augured new encouragement and blessings for Salvador. Chicago, the Windy City, whose proud citizens aired its beauty and preeminence, opened its arms to him. His host drove him to the heart of the Mexican community, La Villita. A new chapter in his life awaited him.

LA VILLITA

To a casual observer, La Villita—the Little Village—was like a small part of Mexico transplanted in Chicago. August 1983 had just begun, and all stores displayed their signs and products in Spanish. The area bustled with Mexicans dressed for south of the border. English and Spanish fused into a language of its own. There were Mexican restaurants, mariachis, tequila, margaritas, sombreros, and leather shops with riding boots. Doctors, quacks, public notaries, and lawyers set up offices there. Buses and cars jammed the area. Life blossomed on 26th Street—Mexico Street—the main thoroughfare. The houses exposed their broken windows and scaling walls a block away, where red and blue graffiti marked the territories of different gangs.

Tello took Salvador to an apartment building. The four-story red-brick structure had a stoop with a few cracked steps of cement and loose tiles that ended in the main door. Yellow dandelions populated the dry brownish grass in the front yard, and untrimmed dwarf pine trees grew next to the façade. A sun-faded yellow curtain stirred behind an iron-grilled basement window. It revealed an older man's haggard face and quickly fell back into place. The open main entrance led to narrow stairs coated with a dirty, dark-brown carpet that reeked of decomposed urine.

Salvador climbed three flights of stairs, knocked on a scratched-up wooden door, and soon observed an eye looking at him through a peephole. Fifteen-year-old Antonio welcomed him with a friendly smile. Short and medium-built, the youngster had dark skin, brown eyes, and a sad facial expression that made him look older. The apartment had two bedrooms for seven tenants who spent the nights or rested for a few hours during the day after long workdays. There were only two official residents. The other five hid in the closets or pretended to be guests when the landlord dropped by. Everyone paid the modest monthly rent of sixty dollars apiece. A fan blew at full force and shook peeled-off flakes from yellow walls on the living room floor. The area opened into a small dark-blue kitchen with an empty old refrigerator, a rusty gas oven, and a little white table with two wooden chairs. Mousetraps were in every corner.

The occupants used the kitchen to make coffee or heat the food from their workplaces' restaurants. Any leftovers kept out of the refrigerator soon crawled with cockroaches. These creatures infested the entire apartment and ran into any furniture or wall crack in the bat of an eye. Four pictures of Playboy-centerfold bunnies hung nailed to the walls of a small and messy bathroom.

"We had six bunnies, but the guys are so stinky that two of them choked to death," Antonio said as a grin made his eyes sparkle with a mischievous expression.

"What do you know about naked bunnies?" Salvador said. "You're still a kid."

The youngster ushered the new tenant into a shared bedroom and handed him the key to the apartment. All valuables were kept out of sight, and the main door shut because drug addicts had often burglarized the building.

Salvador accommodated himself, placed his belongings in a corner, and pinned the pictures of Our Lady of Guadalupe and the Sacred Heart of Jesus to the wall. He kneeled, prayed for a few minutes, and lay on a sleeping bag. Outside, cars honked, and radios blared corrido songs. The heat grew intense. He fell into a profound slumber that soon led to a sweet dream:

Salvador saw himself in his home in Toultuca beside a window where Rosa stood next to him. Her entwined black hair hung down her back, and her soft, flowery perfume of gardenias floated through the room. She wore a light-blue negligee and a necklace with tiny red and yellow plastic flowers he bought on a Guadalajara trip. He gazed at her and watched her eyes shine with love.

Salvador woke up drenched in sweat, but he rejoiced in the scenes. He wished he could have kept the vision for hours. His hometown and mountainous scenery struck a chord with him. So did Rosa's tenderness and love. His mood turned somber. But his thoughts then drifted to Antonio, who faced terrible hardships alone at a young age. The idea caused him remorse and stirred up memories of his mother's words,

"You must look back. Looking back, you'll always find people worse off than you are."

Salvador rubbed his eyes and stretched his legs for a few minutes. He walked out of the room and found Antonio sitting in the kitchen. The youngster was waiting for him to take him to a local restaurant where he could buy the fake documents for a job application. Antonio had gotten them at the same place, "Los Mariachis." The secret agency could issue them in minutes: social security cards, passports, work permits, driver's licenses, and green cards. With Antonio, the counterfeiter had written the youngster's age on the documents as nineteen to avoid child labor laws.

Salvador and Antonio left the apartment in the early afternoon and headed for the restaurant. The sun raged, and the thermometer outside a bank read ninety-one degrees. Mexico Street bustled with shoppers. Children jumped in and out of an open fire hydrant's thick gush of water. The new client sat at a table while his young escort talked with the owner, a shabby man in his late sixties. He was at the counter and greeted the youngster with hesitation. He checked outside the restaurant door, returned, and sized Salvador up momentarily. A bulky bartender kept a watchful eye on the newcomers. The papers cost seventy dollars. The counterfeiter ushered his customer into a small back room, and a few minutes later, the migrant held the fake immigration document and social security card in his hand.

Antonio took Salvador to Le Petit Maison Restaurant in downtown Chicago. The youngster introduced his new roommate to Baldomero, a Mexican waiter supervising the bussers and kitchen personnel. Soft-spoken, he had eyes that shone with an expression as trustworthy as a village priest's. The supervisor had worked his way up from dishwasher to his present position in six challenging years. His income increased so much that it allowed him to bring his family to the US. He uttered a litany of instructions to the new employee. Loyalty and honesty were essential qualities. He accompanied Salvador to meet with the owner, who spelled out some words of advice,

"Tell him that if he works hard, I don't care whether he is illegal. If he does a good job, he'll always have a position in my restaurant."

Baldomero translated the sentences. The boss bragged about many Mexican employees who had toiled for a while. They saved money, went to their hometowns, and got their jobs back a few years later. The owner preferred undocumented aliens for unvoiced reasons: affordable wages, productivity, willingness to work seven days a week, and commitment to complete tasks without complaints.

As a cleaner, Salvador began to work at 9:00 a.m. He ended at midnight on Sundays, Tuesdays, Wednesdays, and Thursdays and at 2:00 a.m. on Fridays and Saturdays. Mondays were his day off. The restaurant floor stank as his feet got stuck on the tiles in the morning. The irritating stench of spilled liquor sickened him, but he offered his daily toil to God and took pride in his job. Salvador scoured the bar, tiles, tables, and restrooms. The ladies' sparkled tidy, but the gents' bristled with messy puddles and scattered toilet paper under the urinals. This task made him aware of humans' humbleness and reminded him of Jesus' words to the Pharisees:

"Do you not know that nothing entering from outside a man can defile him? Because it does not enter his heart, but the thing that proceeds from a man defiles the man: adultery, theft, murder."

Salvador spent part of the day in the kitchen with Antonio. His companionship eased the strenuous hours that only two brief breaks interrupted. The resting minutes let him sit alone and munch on some food. Thinking about his wife and boy always made him smile. He liked to reminisce about the day he and Rosa fell in love.

As a child, Salvador had met her many times. But the spark occurred one morning on a summer vacation from the seminary. Salvador was sixteen and Rosa fourteen. The sun shone with fierce radiance as he sat at The Bus Cemetery with friends. A crushed-down motor coach roof pushed against shattered windowpanes and burnt rubber seats inside a charcoal-black single deck. The vehicle lay tilted sideways. The tires were missing, and the chassis rested on the dusty ground. Grass and shrubs closed in on the wreck, and nests of wasps draped rusty corners.

Several years earlier, a fatal accident occurred. The bus tumbled and spun several times along a curb into the trees flanking the road. Ten passengers and the driver died. Four children from Toultuca sat so close to the gas tank that it ignited their bodies and reduced them to ashes. On either side, the smash-up still advertised Queso Colon with a sun-faded picture of a smiling boy and a girl eating a piece of cheese.

A big wooden cross stood several meters in front of the wreckage. An oak plaque with the victims' names hung on the vertical board. Bouquets of wilted flowers reposed at its foot on the ground. The youngsters gathered at the accident site to remember their dead friends on the anniversary of the tragedy. Like all his friends, Salvador wore a straw hat, a white shirt cinched tight at the waist, loose trousers, and a black scarf around his neck. The boys huddled to talk and wait for the girls, who would arrive dressed in their Sunday best.

Rosa showed up first since the cemetery was close to her home. Salvador watched her shuffle down a narrow path on a hill near mountains with forests climbing almost to the top. The sun ricocheted on her black mantilla that draped her head and upper body. Bent forward, she teetered along the trail, her feet searching for safe spots among scattered rocks. To avoid the dust, she pulled the red and blue embroidered edges of her white dress above her ankle. Dirt had already dulled the sparkle of her polished shoes. Shyness gleamed in her eyes when she raised them to look ahead. Rosa wished she had not arrived so early. No other girl was there. A thorn caught the left side of her veil. She turned to her left, yanked it away, and stepped on a stone. She scrambled to keep her balance, pitched to the left, fast to the right, and fell headlong to the ground. The dry shrub branches crackled like twigs in a fireplace. The thorn pierced her mantilla.

Salvador had followed her steps from the shadow of a mango tree. He saw her glittering brown eyes whenever she lifted them. He wondered how she could have grown into a woman in such a brief period. Salvador had seen her skipping rope a few months ago. At the sight of her fall, he ran so fast that his feet almost did not touch the sparse grass that led to her. A dust cloud hovered behind him. Salvador admired her pink face as bright as a nectarine, intelligent eyes that regarded him from the ground, and flowery perfume. He held her right hand and felt the soft and warm contact of her palm and long fingers. He helped her up and said,

"Take my handkerchief. Wipe the dust off your hands and dab at your right knee. You are bleeding."

"I am fine. Go back to your friends, please. My parents will reprimand me if you don't. Besides, you are almost a priest."

"I am not a priest yet."

"I know, but it doesn't matter. I am not supposed to mingle with boys."

The other girls soon arrived and joined Rosa. After brief greetings, they opened their First Communion white-lacquered Mass books and prayed. The boys engaged in animated conversation a hundred feet away. Girls and boys could only get together once the parish priest presided over the ceremony. His towering dark figure plodded down an inclined slope in the distance, puffing and heaving. His black cassock seemed to weigh him down as he drew closer to the youngsters.

The priest was next to the cross a few minutes later, and the ceremony began. Twelve girls grabbed each other's hands and formed a circle around him. Fourteen boys followed suit several feet behind. The priest prayed an invocation and intoned the Salve Regina. Everyone sang along. The girls turned clockwise around the cross slowly, and the boys counterclockwise. The teams whirled under a cloudless sky as gigantic mountains echoed their cheery voices. Some sang out of tune with the rest of their friends. The girls stepped sideways to the left and the boys to the right, their eyes fixed on the cross before them and the fading names nailed to the wooden post. The effort reddened their faces and made their youthful voices rise and drop out of harmony.

Salvador regarded the sun on Rosa's back. He tried to avert his eyes but could not help noticing her shapely figure. Her rounded hips swung under a narrow waist, and the profile silhouette of her face depicted a perfect nose. The sun then illuminated her face. Her lips were as red as the nearby poppies. Her beautiful white teeth burst upon his view when she opened her mouth to sing. His heart palpitated as he closed his eyes and thought,

"Oh, God, why are You doing this? I can't fall in love."

When the song ended, the priest ordered the circles of youngsters to stop and found Rosa and Salvador aligned in front of the cross. Fate had picked them. The priest strode toward Rosa and touched her right shoulder. He instructed her to release her hands from her teammates' and move forward to face the cross from a few feet away. He then ushered Salvador next to her. A wreath of red and yellow carnations lay atop a rock beside the cross. With Rosa at his side, Salvador did not hear his friends' growing murmur. Nor did he see the priest hurry close to them. The seminarian glanced at Rosa from the corner of his eye, inhaled her fresh perfume, and watched her bosom heave. She blinked. He stole another glance. Her brown eyes glimmered with a soft tint, her long eyelashes flickered, and her face struck a bashful expression. His thoughts still raced,

"Oh, God, why are You making me fall in love with this girl? I am supposed to be a priest, am I not?"

Rosa and Salvador strolled together toward the large rock with the flower wreath. All the youngsters sang:

Wait for us in Heaven,
In the green fields full of flowers,
In the blue skies among the stars,
With peace, glory, and eternal love.

Rosa held one side of the wreath and Salvador the other. They turned around and felt the mountain breeze carry the grass scent to their faces. The pair strolled side by side. She gazed at him, her face blushed, and her eyes shimmered. His thoughts sizzled with images of kissing her, embracing her, and marrying her. A warm sensation rushed down his spine that halted his breathing. They eased the floral tribute down and set it at the foot of the cross. The pair pivoted on their heels and lumbered back to their friends without looking at one another. His epiphany thrilled him. Her emotion flustered her. Years later, she would confess she had fallen for him when they were together before the cross.

A few weeks after Salvador was hired, Baldomero organized another schedule. The timetable allowed him to join four Mexican busboys for lunch or dinner. These men toiled hard and considered themselves fortunate. Some tips that rewarded waiters and waitresses ended up in their pockets. Most had worked in this position for over ten years. Several held cleaning jobs long before their promotion. Salvador talked little at those gatherings but enjoyed their humor and camaraderie.

The days passed with no incidents until Miguel, the youngest busboy, saw an approaching van. It displayed the INS emblem — Department of Naturalization and Immigration. He warned his coworkers,

"*La Migra!*"

Salvador and Antonio lifted a wooden cellar door and rushed into their hideout. Other employees had enough time to run through the back door and disappear. Two male immigration officers walked in, one tall and bulky like a professional wrestler and the other muscular and medium height. They demanded that Mexican-looking employees produce identification and work permits. Two Puerto Rican waiters fumed. The impervious medium-height officer listened to their ravings and threats of legal action.

Unaware of what was happening, Baldomero exited the restroom and bumped into the agents. Salvador and Antonio watched from a window in the basement and witnessed how the officers questioned the supervisor outside the restaurant door. He surrendered a fake green card. The tall officer spoke to him in Spanish and examined the evidence. The name and photo on the document matched those of the questioned immigrant. A counterfeiter had replaced the picture of the actual owner with that of Baldomero at the cost of two thousand dollars. The officer asked him the names of the cardholder's parents. The illegal worker shot out the first two names that crossed his mind, but a call to headquarters gave away the forgery.

A few days later, Salvador learned Baldomero would stay in jail for a month and then be deported. His wife and three children would follow the same fate, including his American-born four-year-old son. Their coworker's plight became the primary topic of conversation at the employee meetings in the restaurant. Everyone was sorry for the children since they only knew the US as their country. Their banishment to a foreign land posed severe problems for their fragile minds. The youngest child would have to turn eighteen before applying for green cards for his parents and siblings. The entire matter saddened Salvador and reminded him of the hardships that life imposed on them all.

Salvador realized that moping around or dwelling on adverse events served no purpose. His tiredness at the end of the workday kept his thoughts at bay. He wrote sweet letters to Rosa in his brief leisure time, expressing his love and hope for a quick reunion. She sent him a picture of their one-year-old son. Salvador again realized the boy's resemblance to him. He hung the photo on the wall above his sleeping bag to brighten his days off. Doing laundry, buying food, and reading whiled away his leisure hours. He pored over Joseph's dreams (Genesis 37:1-44) and the novel *Gone with the Wind* in Spanish. This southern saga fascinated him. He now and then listened to a Mexican radio station that blared out over and over,

"Go to Aragon Ballroom. Los Del Norte and their music. This is WBTT radio, La Voz Latina. If drinking, no driving. If driving, no drinking!"

Antonio and Salvador became friends. Life had forced the youngster to mature at an early age. Like those of a stray dog, his eyes could see through anyone who tried to deceive or mislead him. His smile served the same purpose as an animal's wagging tail that reassured those around him of its good intentions. Antonio had arrived in Chicago eight months earlier than Salvador and knew his whereabouts well. His streetwise slanted eyes emanated an air of mystery and intelligence, wielding them to size anyone up. He scrutinized people, assessed situations for danger, and made quick decisions.

Antonio recounted the story of his life to Salvador. His young coworker was born into a poor family in Chihuahua and had two younger sisters. His father worked in construction until he died in an accident three years ago. His mother suffered from lung disease and barely functioned at home. Any minor efforts made her short-winded. She had never married her children's father, so his loss left her with no income. A few weeks later, the family moved to a hut on the outskirts of Mexico City. Antonio began his life in the streets as the breadwinner, cleaning windshields and selling cassettes.

"The streets were dangerous," Antonio explained. "We children united to defend ourselves from perverts. It was hard to make a few pesos. My mother couldn't buy enough food. I often ended up searching in the garbage of grocery stores. We dug the stuff out of the trash before the rats or street dogs. I begged for money from people who didn't care and later hated myself. They passed by and didn't even look at you."

Antonio lived in a brutal world. The gamins resorted to drugs to escape the cruel reality and mitigate their loneliness with each other's company. Most children stole to survive, and others fell prey to pedophiles or prostitution. Drugged and malnourished, they spent their brief lives lying on sidewalks, inhaling glue, until they died of kidney and lung failure. Many were hunted and killed like animals. At home, Antonio's little brother swelled up from starvation like a balloon, and his mother suffered a constant cough that weakened her. The night's chill froze their bones in their dank and dark shanty as they embraced one another. Nothing stopped their shivering. Hunger and cold joined hands to beat them.

"I was so ashamed of that life that I never answered my mother's questions about where and how I got the money or food. I kept my relatives and their whereabouts unknown to everyone on the streets and didn't reveal my actual name to anyone."

One day, Antonio sat on a bench when a mother and her child passed by. The boy threw half of a hamburger into a garbage can. Antonio picked it up, brushed the dirt off, and returned to the bench to eat it. A federal policeman observed him and beckoned him from a squad car. Antonio shook his head and did not budge. Officer Cardenas got out of the vehicle, approached him, and asked,

"Do you want to make a few pesos?"

"I don't know. What do I have to do? I don't do sex."

"I am not a pedophile. Can't you distinguish a decent man from a pervert? Just get in my car, and we'll talk business."

"No, I don't get into anyone's car. You can talk with me right here."

"I guess you don't want to make a thousand pesos."

"One thousand pesos!"

Antonio and Officer Cardenas got into the car and rode for a few minutes to a nearby park, where their vehicle pulled up.

"What's your name?"

"Kiko," Antonio said, using his street name.

41

"Do you have any family?"

"No."

"Yes, you do. I am sure you want your siblings to eat every day and buy nice things for them." The officer paused briefly and added, "Here's the deal. But if you cross me, you are dead, and your family too. Do you understand?"

"Yes, sir. But I am an orphan. I am not lying to you."

"It is easy. I will hand you a package of marijuana. You sell it. We split the money, half for you and half for me. You tell me who purchased it. Then, I'll retrieve the package and pass it back to you so you can hustle someone else into buying it. You give me half of the money and so on."

The children knew well the street bustle — who was selling what and for how much. It was a lucrative business. The gamins stayed away from these rogues. Drug traffickers manipulated them and then slaughtered them like cockroaches. Antonio sold the package to a well-dressed man with a law-abiding businessman's appearance. He did not question the youngster. Antonio asked for 4,000 pesos for the merchandise, but the buyer agreed to 3,000. He hid from Officer Cardenas, walked into a bus station, bought a ticket, and boarded a bus to El Paso. He crossed the Rio Grande two days later and joined his childless aunt in Chicago. She had promised to find him a decent job. The lady loved him like a son. But her affection set off jealousy in his uncle, who accused his aunt and nephew of inappropriate sexual behavior. Antonio again hit the streets to fend for himself two months after he arrived in Chicago.

Every two weeks, Salvador and Antonio walked to the closest cablegram office. Money wire transfers to their families made their sacrifice in a foreign land worthwhile and lifted their spirits. Seldom were they in the mood for watching a movie at a local theater. Every Sunday morning, Salvador attended the 7:00 a.m. Mass before catching a bus to the restaurant. He spoke to the teenager about the need to be close to God, pray, and attend church. Antonio expressed willingness to do so. Salvador awakened him so he could partake in the religious service, but the youngster murmured,

"Yes, yes," as he turned around and fell asleep again.

Once a week, they attended a local school to learn English as a second language. Antonio was the youngest in a class full of immigrants of all ages from all over the world: Chinese, Pakistanis, Indians, Russians, Polish, and Vietnamese. Their fellow students talked and pretended to understand one another. An old Chinese man in a Cubs baseball cap sat beside Antonio and Salvador.

"Do you know the word '*gorra*' in English?" Antonio whispered to Salvador.

"Cap."

"I wanna ask Chinese man where he bought the cap."

"No wanna, I want to."

Antonio turned toward the Chinese gentleman, pointed to his head, and asked,

"Where you buy cap?"

"Not good, not hear… not hear," the old man repeated.

"Not hear?" Antonio repeated. "I don't understand."

"He meant no hair," Salvador said. "The old man is bald… bald like a billiard ball."

"How do you know?"

"I understand Chinese," Salvador said with an earnest expression. He smiled and whispered in Spanish, "I saw him remove his cap to greet our teacher when he came in. The older man thought you were reprimanding him for wearing it in class. Chinese people are very respectful."

Unlike his young friend, Salvador endured periods of strong sexual urges. When his tiredness let up, his flesh demanded satisfaction in the middle of the night. His face flushed, eyes reddened, nose congested, and loins ached with painful heaviness. He roused, picked up the Bible, and read and prayed until fatigue overcame him. Salvador never thought the instinct would assault him with such might.

The incidents reminded him of his stay in the seminary. There, he had experienced sexual desire but had driven it away with prayers. Some mornings, Salvador woke up to sheets soiled with a spontaneous emission. Otherwise, he could manage his libido and did not endure his roommate's torments. Anibal Lopez Marques tossed and turned in bed all night twice a week. He moaned and gasped. The poking and chafing of sheets continued as if an animal were scurrying through thick brush to escape danger. Now and then, whispers of mumbled words interrupted the nocturnal frenzy,

"Damn sex! Damn women!"

After a while, an enormous sigh ended his agony. Anibal then slept like a baby, his snores roaring through the night. A stale, rancid odor hovered over their room the following day as he pulled out his bed blanket to change his dirty linen. The first time Salvador heard him, he asked whether he had been sick. He answered,

"I am older than you. You'll understand in two years."

Now Salvador knew what his friend suffered.

Sexual appetite was not the only change for Salvador. Chicago represented a significant challenge. The lack of mountains infused an overbearing solitude in him, but the shimmering water of Lake Michigan soothed it. Ripples and cloudscapes dazzled him. He watched tamed waves lick the shore while seagulls cawed and pirouetted overhead. Salvador enjoyed the green leafy vegetation in the spring and adapted well to the summer's heat. In September and October, he watched small groups of monarchs alight on bushes, garbage cans, and even old shoes on a beach. Many were returning to the mountains in his hometown. The creatures aroused his jealousy because of their upcoming proximity to Rosa and his child. It was hard to grow accustomed to gloomy, gray weather for days on end. In the fall, he basked in the multicolor trees flamed with red and pink. The first autumnal snow transformed the landscape into a show of ricocheting lights and glowing white upon a lush carpet. Even dilapidated corners and dumpsters turned into glorious decorations. Salvador had never seen snow before, so he touched it.

"It reminds me of the Biblical passages when manna rained down from Heaven," he wrote to Rosa.

A few days later, the smoke from heavy traffic transformed the pristine layers of flakes into muddy slush. The winter's bitter cold and the slippery sidewalks taxed his nerves to the limit, month after month.

"I wish we didn't have to come to a foreign country to support ourselves and our families," Salvador remarked to Antonio. "I wish we had made it at home."

6

HOWLING WINDS

After a year at La Petite Maison Restaurant, the owner promoted Salvador to busboy in August 1984, but not Antonio. The businessman opined his junior employee was too young to work. Customers might realize it and notify the authorities. The teenager believed management had given him the cold shoulder and found himself a job as a busboy in a restaurant near a train station. Seldom did the schedules of both friends coincide at home except in the early morning hours. By then, exhaustion rendered them speechless.

Salvador enjoyed his new position, which allowed him long breaks with his coworkers. A waitress by the name of Elisa joined their gatherings. He liked her because she listened more than she spoke, and her courteous voice inspired confidence. Twenty-two-year-old Elisa was tall and slender and looked like a flamenco ballerina: a straight posture, a thin neck, and silken brown hair draped over her shoulders. Her locks swung almost in unison with her hips' cadence and smooth tread's rhythm. Her presence elicited instant jealousy in female customers whose husbands and boyfriends gazed at her out of the corners of their eyes. Elisa felt their sight on her and considered them blind to their immediate surroundings. In her view, their companions were prettier than she was.

When Elisa talked, her fleshy lips puckered as if about to kiss a flower. Her dark almond-shaped eyes had a stern expression that cautioned ill-intentioned wooers. Her air served its purpose. It worked much like the monarch butterflies' bright orange, which warned predators of the deadly consequences of feeding on them. In the restaurant, she wore an above-the-knee skirt and a collared blouse highlighting her well-shaped breasts. Elisa put on her jeans, a turtleneck sweater, and tennis shoes when her evening shift ended. She lived alone since her honorable US Army discharge a few months ago. Her household chores absorbed her time except for her attendance at a school of paralegal studies in the morning.

Salvador, Elisa, and two other busboys—Alfonso and Miguel— often left the restaurant together at the end of their workday. Their casual conversation revolved around the weather and their jobs. Salvador sometimes talked about his wife and his child, and his companions discussed minor issues about their families. Elisa mentioned nothing about her parents or siblings. After two blocks, she branched off and walked toward a parking garage to pick up her car as her coworkers pressed on to the CTA train station.

On the night of September 20, 1985, Elisa waited for Salvador and the others. Excited, the busboys punched their clock and chatted about the Mexican team's upcoming 1986 Soccer World Cup participation with the waiters. She became impatient, hurried out, and strolled, unaware that someone had followed her and her coworkers for the past week. The stalker hid in the darkness for a chance to accost her. The night grew pitch black and rainy. Elisa rushed toward the parking garage with her umbrella slanted forward and turned from Michigan Avenue to North Water Street on the bank of the Chicago River.

Howling gusts of wind pushed Elisa to the side as water splashed against small piers. Rain curtains blurred the dull lights of tall buildings reflecting on the river. Imposing high-rises towered over her like giant ghosts. For an instant, the wailing faded, and decisive steps resounded behind her. She glanced over her shoulder. A tall figure in a long black raincoat and a hat seemed to have hurried out of her vision. To sharpen her sight, she blinked twice and frowned, but saw no one. Squalling winds slowed her down. She furled her umbrella and wielded it like a sword. The noise of steps got closer, and she ran. Her military experience had trained her for danger, but here alone, the fear intensified. Elisa tripped on a utility hole, slipped, and fell headlong flat on her face. Before she could clamber to her feet, the assailant threw his corpulent body atop hers and pressed a knife against her throat. Her screams drowned in the wind. The attacker rammed his fingers against her cheeks, crammed a handkerchief into her mouth, and threatened her,

"Shut up, Elisa, or I'll kill you."

She recognized her father's voice.

"You, stupid girl, I gave you your life and can take it away. You're mine!"

He pulled her belt open, yanked her jeans down, and ripped her underwear off. Blood dripped down her neck as his thick hand ravished her intimate parts. Panic paralyzed her. Her eyes welled up with tears, and the warm moisture on his right hand enraged him.

"You are a whore. You should have called your parents!" her father said as he unzipped his pants.

"Let her go!" someone shouted. "What are you doing?"

The command and question came from Salvador.

"Mind your own business!" her assailant shouted. "She is my daughter!"

Salvador kicked him in the back. The attacker let Elisa go, jumped up, and turned the knife at him. The rescuer parried the blade with his right forearm, his blood rushing down to his wrist. A second stab pierced the right side of his chest before his aggressor fled. One hand on his deadly wound, Salvador ignored his pain and helped his coworker stand up with the other. Elisa lifted her jeans and pulled the handkerchief out of her mouth. She then realized the severity of her savior's injuries and screamed in anguish.

An ambulance rushed them to the emergency room at Northwestern Memorial Hospital. An intern sutured the thirteen-stitch cut on Elisa's neck. A female gynecologist examined her to determine whether someone had raped her. There was no semen, only blood from the shearing dilating force of offending fingers. She received antibiotics to prevent infection and was instructed to wait for the police. Salvador lay on a stretcher, pale and almost unconscious. Profuse cold sweat broke out from every pore on his face. His blood pressure kept dropping from the bleeding.

The chest wound followed a clear trajectory in surgery, but the knife had severed the pleura and penetrated the right lung. Blood gushed from the torn organ, and his blood pressure collapsed twice. The surgeon feared for his patient's life, but after the two-hour operation, his assistant wheeled Salvador into the recovery room. Elisa waited outside and received word of the excellent outcome of the procedure from the doctors. Barring any complications, Salvador should be out of the hospital in a week or two. Elisa sighed relief and sobbed, aware that her coworker could have died to save her.

She was a private person who never meddled in someone else's life. But she would have risked her life for him or anyone who faced a similar danger. This scenario played out in her mind several times during her military service. Elisa was always willing to accept the ultimate sacrifice for a fellow soldier.

A few minutes later, police Sergeant Ranieri and Officer Laura Benedetto greeted Elisa. The sergeant excused himself and let his assistant talk with the victim. Elisa described the assailant's attack and intimated her father had abused her as a child. Terrible memories restrained her from elaborating on the details of those crimes. Her declaration discussed her coworker's fight when he passed by and witnessed the attack. The officer informed her that Sergeant Ranieri would interrogate Salvador as soon as his health permitted.

The police issued a warrant for her father's arrest. The address that Elisa had provided turned out to be wrong. Her parents, Francisco and Elena, had not lived in that apartment for at least two years. The sergeant called back to inform her of the results of his inquest. Elisa explained that four years ago, she turned eighteen, joined the Army, and severed all contact with her family. Her parents lacked close friends or relatives in the US. Her father had only an estranged sister in Chile, the country her folks emigrated from when she was four. Ranieri said he would use the social security number to locate her attacker. The process might take several days or weeks. In the meantime, the sergeant granted her police protection.

After this conversation, Elisa shuffled into the Intensive Care Unit, where Salvador lay semiconscious. A nurse walked into his small room every few minutes to watch him and monitor the machines and tubes surrounding him. Shrill, ticking, and plaintive noises fused with the bustle of nurses, doctors, and auxiliary personnel. Salvador opened his eyes. Elisa stood, holding his hand at his bedside. He tried to talk but could not, nodding as a sign of resignation. Before retiring home for the evening, Elisa offered to notify his family in Mexico, but he shook his head.

At the hospital, a rough night set in. A low-grade fever lingered as Salvador's breathing grew shallow and painful. Cold sweat burst forth from every pore in his body. He prayed to God and begged Him to spare his life so he could take care of his family. In a different situation, Salvador would have basked in the company of God and longed to join Him in heaven. The images of the Sacred Heart of Jesus, Our Lady of Guadalupe, saints, and angels crowded his mind.

They transported his imagination to a world of celestial music, floral scents, and glorious scenery. These thoughts made him feel guilty. He believed they implied a lack of concern for his wife and son.

The fear of dying assaulted Salvador early in the morning. Visions flashed through his mind. Toultuca cemetery rose before him with tall, whitewashed walls, the giant cross at the front gate, the grounds covered with red sand, and the patios adorned with fresh flowers. His burial site sat next to those of his father and older brother. Their graves bristled with weeds that grew in the cracks between the marble stones. He then saw Rosa crying for his loss with their child in her lap. Her downcast eyes expressed sorrow as tears ran down her face. Salvador tried to wipe Rosa's tears away, but wrist restraints tied his hands to the bed. The unexpected impediment made him drift into a state of semi-alertness. He dozed off for a few hours, and his breathing became slower and more relaxed.

Antonio arrived at the hospital and paced from corner to corner in the waiting room until the first lights broke. A nurse allowed him in. Salvador watched Antonio approach and smiled at him to reassure his teen friend of his improved well-being. A sharp pain cut his grin short. Antonio looked pale and tired. His eyes were on the verge of tears, and his voice choked when he greeted his injured friend. The youngster cheered Salvador up and offered to lend him money for his family if needed. He grimaced and shook his head. Elisa had already taken care of it.

The waitress endured a restless night despite a police escort at her door. Her fears made her toss and turn in her bed. A nightmare aggravated her anxiety. In the dream, her father stood at her bedside with a dagger ready to strike her. Terrified, she jumped out of bed, switched the lights on, and prepared herself a cup of herbal tea.

In the afternoon, she visited Salvador and rejoiced in finding him sitting up in bed. A nurse had raised the head of the bed and propped him up against a pillow to prevent complications. They looked at each other, and her face lit with a tender expression. A deep caring affection wrapped around her heart. It was a strange sensation, different from any other she had ever experienced. Abashed, he might have detected her thoughts, she flushed in embarrassment. He spoke,

"Pro…mise…me…if…I…die… you'd…let… me… wife… know… how… much… I… love… her… and… my… child."

Elisa did so. The few words rendered him short-winded again. A few minutes later, a nurse wandered in, checked his tubes, intravenous infusion, and monitors. She injected him with narcotic medication, and Salvador fell asleep.

Back at home later in the evening, Elisa tried to sort out the emotion that thrilled her entire being earlier in the morning when she saw Salvador. Her conclusion reassured her. Her reaction was born of her gratefulness for his brave aid and disregard for his life. Unbeknownst to her, a feeling stronger than indebtedness had gripped her.

Four days passed, and Salvador was transferred to a room in a regular ward. She visited him every day and observed his gradual improvement. When Elisa walked in on the fifth day of his hospital stay, he was reading the Bible. She sat down, and an expectant silence ensued. Salvador gazed at her as if knowing what she was about to disclose.

"My father began to abuse me when I was a child. One day when I was five, I forgot to pick up my room. He grabbed a skillet full of oil on a burner and poured it down my head. Fortunately, the oil was not boiling. Another day, I found my teacher's pen in the schoolyard while leaving the building. I took it home but intended to return it the next day. My father didn't believe me. He laid my hands on the burners and kept repeating,

'This is for you to remember, so you'll never become a thief when you grow up.'

My hands swelled up like two gloves full of water."

At the mention of her hands, Salvador observed them. The skin was white like a wax doll, the knuckles smooth, and the fingers slender with long pink-nacre nails. Her subtle turquoise veins sparkled at the rhythm of a fine tremor afflicting her hands. She rested them on his bed and tried to hide the shaking. He considered holding her hands to reassure her of his empathy but desisted. Any movement brought on severe pain. Her expression had no self-pity or anger, only sadness and fear. The emotions made her face as pale as the off-white color of the walls.

"The sexual abuse started the day I turned ten. My mother was not at home. He burst into my bedroom, scooped me up into his arms, and carried me into his room. Fear paralyzed me. He kept saying,

'No one will touch you before I do. You're mine!'

He threatened me over and over,

'If you tell anyone, I'll take you far from here and kill your mother.'

After that, he waited for any opportunity to rape me. It happened even when my mother was at home."

Elisa spared Salvador of all the gruesome details. The violent undressing, the groping and fondling, the lewdness in his eyes, and the repulsive touch with his thick fingers digging into her intimate parts. His deafness to her desperate pleas, his fury at her unwillingness to cooperate with him. Extreme penetrations that ripped her insides apart. Blood that soaked through the sheets into the mattress and rushed down her legs. Her tears and loathing at his goodbye kiss on her forehead, and the failure of repeated scrubbing to dissipate his repugnant stench.

Silence fell upon the room. Salvador thought about his parents and the love they had lavished upon him. They would have sacrificed for him. Even now that his pain flared up off the chart, it paled compared to that of his visitor.

Her face blushed. Elisa was ashamed of her parents and what her coworker might have gleaned from her words. She recalled her panic upon the onset of her menstrual period. Elisa misperceived it as her abuser's foul-smelling filth draining from her entrails. A marked weakness in her legs confined her to bed for at least a week. The mysterious illness returned every month. It eluded any explanation until a doctor became suspicious and extracted the information from her. Hours later, her father stood handcuffed, his eyes full of hatred and vengeance.

Salvador had heard of this abuse by a parent a few years ago. He never understood why such an atrocity occurred. Elisa headed home for the evening. Elisa reminisced about her conversation with him earlier that day in her room. Thoughts unsettled her. Her fear did not let up at night, and frightful dreams disturbed her sleep.

The following day, the circles under her eyes revealed her sleepless night but did not dim her beauty when she sat at Salvador's bedside. Elisa informed him that Sergeant Ranieri would take his statement before he left the hospital. Salvador dreaded deportation. Elisa tried to appease his fear and voiced her intention to hire a lawyer since the law granted a crime victim constitutional rights.

"What kind of rights?" Salvador asked in a resigned tone. "An illegal immigrant has no rights."

Elisa reassured him and let him know about the ongoing investigation. Her father had vanished without a trace and might be stalking her to finish the incomplete job. No one knew her mother's whereabouts. Elisa expressed her fears of being alone and regretted having no one to help her. The police escort would not last. The case of a Hispanic woman attacked by her father would not hold their attention for too long. She stared Salvador in the eye with a beseeching look and asked,

"Would you stay at home with me for a while?"

Moved and concerned, Salvador gazed into her eyes and saw her terror but did not answer.

"My apartment has two bedrooms. I can prepare a room for you," Elisa added, casting her sight down. "It'll be as in the military, men and women under the same roof but different quarters."

Her beautiful warm eyes, like Rosa's, affected his heart. He agreed to stay until the police found her father.

The next day, Sergeant Ranieri entered the hospital room where Salvador and Elisa had been waiting for him. Her comforting presence soothed her coworker's nervousness. She translated for him questions or remarks he needed help understanding. The officer reviewed the fake social security card bearing the name of his interlocutor and sensed his apprehension and distrust of the police. In Salvador's hometown, people never called the authorities. No one counted on the summoned cop to behave with fairness. Peasants often suffered coercion that forced them to relinquish their little money. Critical stored-up staples ended up impounded, endangering the survival of the owners' families.

The sergeant acknowledged he knew of his illegal status and reassured him of the irrelevant nature of this information. Salvador was just a crime victim as far as the police department was concerned. His heroism endangered his life to save a young American citizen, an act that would deserve proper consideration. The judge might report him to the INS. Sergeant Ranieri hoped the magistrate would press no charges against a Good Samaritan. But he could not promise that Salvador would not be subject to deportation. The patient's lack of complete command of the English language rendered him unable to express his misgivings with the required precision. He asked Elisa to translate a statement,

"Please, tell the sergeant I came here to work and seek a better future for my family."

Sergeant Ranieri nodded and completed his inquiry into the incident. He then instructed the victim to wait for news from him. The immigrant should keep him posted of his whereabouts if he needed to leave town for any reason. The sergeant thanked Elisa for her help, shook her coworker's hand, and smiled at him with genuine empathy. But the whole interview unnerved Salvador.

7

PAINFUL MEMORIES

E lisa lived on the North Side of Chicago in a white neighborhood with a diverse population: Irish, Jewish, Polish, and German. The area was well lit and clean. The appearance contrasted with the Little Village streets, which seemed to belong to an undeveloped country. New or almost new cars lined the streets. Tall oak trees rose every few feet on the sidewalks and conferred the place a joyful leafy appearance. The neighborhood kept a dignified silence. Salvador did not expect such an oasis of tranquility in the middle of a vast city. The building façades looked impeccable. Their residents took pride in the proper appearance of their properties. Beautiful lace curtains covered the windows, and American flags overhung some apartments.

At first, the surroundings intimidated Salvador. At the restaurant, he had encountered white Americans, who had roamed by him without casting a look or mumbling hello. Their rudeness did not upset him. Salvador preferred to remain invisible until he legalized his status.

He was in the US to work and make a living for his family. He objected to the term undocumented alien as the government called illegal immigrants. It made him feel as if he came from a different planet.

Elisa's apartment was on the third floor of a three-story building. At the street level, the main door opened into a lobby filled with a refreshing fragrance. The long stairway boasted an elegant vanilla carpet and a varnished dark wood handrail that sloped up to a landing before her apartment. Her cozy place boasted two large windows that overlooked the tops of the oak trees rising from the street below. His room had a closet, a wooden nightstand, and a chair. A crucifix presided over his comfortable bed, and a picture of a prairie with a watermill and horses adorned the opposite wall.

From a window, Salvador observed the surroundings. The area lacked the warm closeness that people enjoyed in the Little Village. If a neighbor walked by another, they ignored each other. Their behavior confirmed his notion that the more money people had, the less they needed to relate to others.

One might entertain the impression that no one knew anyone in this part of town. Yet, as soon as Salvador had moved in, everybody noticed him. He was a stranger among them, someone different who aroused fears. They voiced concern that their neighborhood could fall into the hands of the Hispanics, and their property values would drop. Salvador tried to make eye contact and smiled at them, but they disregarded his overtures. In the evening, he told Elisa about his impromptu surveillance. She remarked,

"Here, the neighbors can bring you a cake the first day you move in. After that, the neighbors ignore you until something bad happens. Everybody then pitches in to help one another."

"Hispanics make friends very quickly," Salvador said. "It isn't often a strong friendship, but at least people talk to one another."

Elisa invoked her neighbors' excellent points, such as decorum and respect for each other. People never threw garbage in front of anyone's yard, cleaned up after their dogs, did not blast music from their cars, or allowed gangs to roam their streets.

Salvador did not mention his present situation to his wife. He did not want to worry her since he expected to return to his usual residence in a few days. But two weeks passed, and news of the detention of Elisa's father never arrived. Salvador continued his close relationship with God, thanking Him for sparing his life and Elisa's and protecting his family. He improved and ventured out a few times. It took a while for his shortness of breath to improve enough to stroll two blocks. He then attended Mass at San Jerome Church. The little red brick building boasted two belfries, a lovely arched portal, and a graceful nave that invited the faithful to peace and quietness. A statue of the Virgin Mary was on one side of the main altar. It reminded him of his devotion to Our Lady of Guadalupe and evoked tender memories of his homeland.

Salvador soon realized that the children and teenagers in the neighborhood knew one another. These youngsters attended the same schools and rode their bikes outside. Their behavior aired the bigotry they had learned at home. What parents dared not to state, their kids spelled it out in no uncertain terms. A Spanish proverb rang in Salvador's head:

"Only children and drunks tell the truth."

The youngsters passed by Salvador and shouted,

"Wetback, go home!"

As he strode by them, they spat onto the ground, rode their bikes fast, and drew up behind him in a menacing way. Salvador showed no sign of fear. He grew up around bulls and cows and realized that these children exhibited similar behavior. If the animals sensed any weakness in someone, they would attack him. In the Little Village, he grew used to ignoring gang members who gathered on street corners. Salvador disregarded the thugs and strolled by them so calmly that they ignored him. He wondered why these fortunate youngsters could harbor hatred toward their fellow man in such a well-to-do area as Elisa's neighborhood. After a while, the whole harassment died down. Salvador sensed their indifference. Even the children paid no attention to him.

In Toultuca, Salvador had never experienced discrimination but realized that people were also racist in Mexico. Poor Indians considered themselves inferior to mestizos — people of Spanish and Indian descent — and these citizens regarded their place in the society beneath the *Gueros*—white Mexicans. *Gueros* held the most critical positions in government and corporations.

Salvador believed bigotry against his fellow compatriots in the US had several roots. Part of it resulted from the immigrants' misperceptions, unfounded expectations, distrust, and lack of understanding of their rights. The language barrier also stood out as a significant obstacle. But the most sizeable contributor was people's lack of acquaintance. The unknown fueled fear. Hate groups touted the gradual Mexican invasion of the US and the usurpation of jobs by foreign workers. Most Americans did not listen to those laughable arguments. But Mexicans' Indian features still fanned embers of racism in many whites. Salvador concluded these people were shortsighted and unable to see beyond a human being's surface. Yet, many called themselves Christians and prayed to God.

Salvador never told Elisa about these experiences with the local youngsters. He wanted to spare her any worries. In the area, there were a few receptive people like Mrs. Newman, an older lady with thin, overdone reddish hair. She walked her little white poodle every morning and bowed her head to greet Salvador. He returned the nod from the window. Mr. Loomis smiled as he hobbled along with the help of a cane. He often stopped to talk to his new Hispanic neighbor about how the weather in Chicago affected his bones. The older gentleman ended up inviting him to a cup of coffee.

Loomis' first-floor apartment brimmed with footprints of the owner's Turkish heritage. His parents had arrived from the old country more than a century ago. The main door opened into a small room that contained a large bookshelf, a rocking chair, a coffee table, a gray-blue rug, and two armchairs. A large tapestry dazzled the wall with the image of the Church of Saint Sophia in Istanbul. Thick brown curtains with red floral designs draped a large window. An aromatic scent permeated the air. Mr. Loomis brought a golden tray with two small white porcelain cups. The Turkish coffee was so thick that it quivered and rose in the container like a mercury column in a thermometer. Salvador sipped it. His tongue turned almost numb.

Mr. Loomis praised Elisa and called her Salvador's wife or girlfriend. His companion corrected him. Their relationship was a friendship between two roommates and coworkers. But the host paid no attention to his young guest's words. His mind was engrossed in the story he was about to relate. Mr. Loomis had met his late wife, Myrna, in Istanbul, where she had succeeded as a belly dancer. He fell in love with her at first sight, married her three months later, and brought her to this country. Mr. Loomis never separated from her until her death. The older neighbor's thoughts then drifted to Elisa as he paid a compliment,

"She looks like a woman that a man can fall head over heels with her from the first day."

Salvador blushed and praised Elisa for allowing him to heal from his injuries at her home. He talked about Rosa, his lovely wife in Mexico, whom he loved very much. Mr. Loomis gazed through his recent acquaintance as if the young visitor were an excuse for his monologue. He had also been married to a worthy woman when he chanced upon Myrna. By then, the marital relationship with his first wife lacked passion and became routine. Salvador mentioned his son Humberto, who lived with his wife, but that remark did not sink in either.

When Elisa came in that evening, Salvador noticed something bothered her. Her eyes did not shine with their usual sparkle, and her jaw was tense. He related his conversation with Mr. Loomis and thought she would get upset. But she did not. Instead, her face relaxed and gained a pinkish tint. She sketched a smile and asked him to disregard the older man's words since "he meddled in the life of everyone." Elisa then sat deep in thought. Her eyes were downcast, and her elbows rested on the table where Salvador chopped lettuce and tomatoes for their dinner. He knew the severe issues his roommate confronted. He indulged her with affable silence as she pondered her situation.

Her mind revisited the news that police had provided her — her parents' last known address and the information their neighbors had volunteered. After her mother's death two years earlier, her father moved away without leaving a forwarding address.

Her mom's loss struck her. Her ambivalent feeling resurfaced. It wiped out her dreams that mother and daughter would someday start a new relationship after the father's demise. Elisa still resented her lack of support and unwillingness to help her. Her lukewarm kisses, distrustful hugs, inexpressive face, and indifference to the abuse. Her cold and robotic-like caresses and her anger against her only daughter because of her husband's detention. Elena considered Elisa a troublemaker, someone who interfered with her life. Her mother's words still inflicted pain on her,

"You're a disgrace. What did your father do for you? He gave you your life and did you a favor. He made you a woman and prepared you for your future husband. You should have stayed quiet and enjoyed it."

Elisa had never overheard her parents arguing or even quibbling. She wondered whether the aloofness of her mother resulted from her father's psychological abuse. Maybe, as a child, she needed to believe so since children without love grow like listless plants in the shade. Sudden sorrow overcame her, making her feel like one of those dying leaves. Her tears welled up, escaped the control of her eyes, and rolled down her cheeks.

A light fixture with four arms cast a dim light upon Salvador. He was in the kitchenette behind a counter that separated him from Elisa as he prepared two chicken sandwiches. She hadn't moved from her seat next to the dining room table. A silence reigned that was only broken by his back-and-forth steps from the toaster to the stove and meat searing on a grill. A sharp odor of onion wafted around.

Elisa lifted her head, looked at Salvador, and addressed him in a strained voice. Her father remained on the loose. He never spent time in jail, even though he got two years' probation and a restraining order that forbade him to return home for five years. By then, Elisa would have turned eighteen and moved out. The judge's instructions did not faze the complacent wife, who often met the husband in her bedroom in the middle of the night. Elisa grabbed a large knife from the kitchen and locked herself in her room. Her father knocked on her door but never tried to force it open. On one occasion, he cried out,

"Eventually, anyone who harms me will pay for it."

The wife did not want to upset her husband and ignored everything he did. Elisa wondered whether her mother had endured similar abuse as a child. The couple attended Mass every Sunday and deceived their neighbors, who thought the world of them. Her father bandied about the name of "Our Lord" in his greetings. Even when he came home drunk, he knew how to fake sobriety.

Elisa's confidence awakened memories of her companion. An incident had contributed to his departure from the seminary. But he had kept it to himself because it aroused his anger and shame.

At ease with Elisa, Salvador revealed his secret for the first time,

"On one occasion, I also suffered sexual abuse. When I was in the seminary, a priest grabbed my genitals in a confessional. He said, 'Your organs belong to God.'"

Salvador related the scene of pedophilia he had endured. His terror in that church in penumbra and silence, the rough touch of the evil priest's hairy hand, his nails sinking into the offending fingers. His steps ran along the lateral aisle, his cassock pulled up above his knees, his eyes on the main door, an exit that never got close enough. The smell of burned wax from the dark altars. The niches where saints and divinities seemed to have abandoned him. His mind's inability to register any image—no one to whom to pray for his deliverance—and the ghostly voice after his flitting steps,

"Come back. I haven't given my absolution to you."

The abusive priest did not give up. That evening, he assigned Salvador's roommate, Anibal Lopez Marques, to the nocturnal Eucharistic Adoration in the chapel. He wanted no one to witness his planned misdeed. Shaking like a leaf, Salvador fell asleep and did not realize the pedophile had invaded his bedroom. A hand taped his mouth as a massive body suffocated his young one. The whispered words were as obnoxious as the assailant's foul smell of sexual excitation, sweat, and alcohol,

"Stay quiet if you want to become a good priest. This is a holy act blessed by God."

Amid tears and prayers to the Almighty, Salvador wrestled the attacker and kicked him out of bed. The priest rushed out of the room before the young seminarian could remove the gag and scream for help.

Salvador's meeting with the rector worsened his disappointment with religious life. Msgr. Lorenzo Ruiz Ordoñez questioned his accusation and wondered whether the seminarian had suffered a nightmare. He blamed it on the youngster's dislike for his teacher, who had given him poor grades. Salvador could not provide any evidence to prove his case. The evil priest received a different assignment in a town far from the seminary.

The sexual abuse incident in the school caused Salvador great distress. Losing spiritual innocence hurled him down a cacophony of prayers, but he could not overcome his feeling of filth. It was hard to accept that the priesthood harbored some criminal minds. The pedophilic attack weakened his vocation, and Cupid killed it when he saw Rosa at The Bus Cemetery and fell in love.

The first month of healing ended, and Salvador got well enough to return to work. Life in Elisa's apartment was quiet and organized. His coworker was an attentive companion who was always ready to help him. She encouraged him to speak English and master the language. They enjoyed breakfast together: rancheros eggs for him and cereal and milk for her. After exchanging a few words between bites, she left for school, and he got ready to commute to work. In the late afternoon, they would meet in the restaurant.

Their workday at the restaurant ended in the evening when they languished with tiredness before they slumped in her car and drove home. Their brief conversations revolved around her school and his family. They avoided any discussion about her father, whose whereabouts were unknown.

Elisa's police protection had ceased two weeks after her assault, so her life routine outside her apartment bristled with fear. At home, she experienced relief from Salvador's companionship. However, he became uneasy with his financial contribution to the household since he paid only for electricity and gas. Elisa reassured him of the fairness of their arrangement.

Several weeks passed, and Salvador heard nothing from the police or government agency. He hoped they would ignore his illegal status. Elisa scheduled an appointment with a lawyer, and she and her roommate headed for the law firm's office. The November morning shone with a cold sun, and the trees flanking the Chicago River were almost naked. A few yellow leaves still hung from their branches, and the rest formed a thin carpet of variegated browns on the ground. The waving surface of the greenish water sloshed against the riverbanks, splashing yellowish foam.

Attorneys Leventhal, Levy, and Williams resided in a high-rise and overlooked the Chicago River as it meandered downtown. The structure boasted a steel skeleton and an entire exterior of glass panels. Like giant mirrors, these walls glinted in the sunlight, outlined kaleidoscopic, multicolor figures, and reflected the images of the boats and cars passing by. They conveyed a continuous motion.

A vast hall with high ceilings served as a reception area where clerks in livery directed all visitors to the different law firms. The fast elevator took Salvador and Elisa on a swift trip to the twenty-first floor. Inner inertia and anxiety turned their ascent into a roller coaster ride.

The elevator opened to a luxurious reception with a mahogany desk, a circular counter, lush black leather sofas and chairs, and carved wooden lamps. Mariela, a paralegal at the firm, wore a gray suit and sat in an armchair, waiting for Elisa and Salvador. Blonde and tall, her slender figure towered over the expected visitors when she greeted them. Her parents had immigrated to the US from Argentina, so she spoke fluent Spanish and English. The friendship between the two women had begun in the military. There, they shared the same assignments and spent extended periods together. Their bonds had tightened even more since Elisa started her internship in the same legal firm. Mariela welcomed her friend's roommate with a smile and praised his bravery. A subtle blush reddened his face.

Mariela ushered them into Attorney Rueda's office and excused herself. Born in Colombia, the lawyer had arrived in the US at the age of eight. He graduated from the University of Chicago and specialized in immigration law. His short stature and baldness did not lessen his clients' trust since his tenor voice and the firmness of his handshake inspired confidence.

The attorney addressed a crucial issue — the likelihood of a Notice to Appear from the INS. This summons initiated the deportation proceedings. He warned Salvador to prepare for this occurrence because of the unpredictability of the agency.

Rueda discussed the client's decision to stay employed in the restaurant and unleashed several questions: his family in Mexico, date of entry in the US, jobs held, income statements with proof of tax withholdings, and fake social security number. The attorney then directed his attention to Elisa. He analyzed the events on the night of her assault and asked if she had engaged in a romance with Salvador earlier.

"No, not before or after," Elisa answered, her fingers interlaced so hard that their tips became bloodless pale. She rested her hands in her lap, straightened herself in the chair, and added, "We are coworkers and roommates."

8

LOVE AND PASSION

E lisa's feelings toward Salvador intensified. His presence uplifted her spirit like a balloon full of hot air. The sun's glow made her feel full of life, the colors intensified, and music filled her with sweet thoughts. She refused to accept these signs and the implication she had fallen in love with a married man. After a while, their cohabitation led to a certain intimacy without embarrassment. They did not interfere with each other and left their chores, such as showers or quiet baths, for the few idle hours each spent alone. Otherwise, they took turns. Salvador considered himself a guest and kept everything neat.

On his Mondays off, Elisa came back from school in the early afternoon and found Salvador reading the Bible. He studied English, wrote to his family, or pored over the weekly letters Rosa mailed him. A subtle change in his feelings occurred. When he read her warm words such as "I love you" or "kisses," her voice either did not resonate in his mind or produced an echo that the distance muffled. This change was also noticeable in one memory. He often reminisced about the day he had made love with Rosa in an open field. The encounter happened one day when the newlyweds replenished their water containers in a nearby brook. Salvador sidled toward Rosa, kissed her, and whispered in her ear,

"There is no one around. Let's do it."

Laughing, she waded into the reeds next to the stream. Salvador rushed after her, crushing grass and jostling tall stalks that rebounded on his body. The peppermint-like scent of torn foliage scurried from their feet like frightened rabbits. He heard the noise of rippling water amid the rocks mixed with her giggles ahead of him. Strips of her white dress flashed through the brush as Rosa hurried away from him. Salvador caught up with her. The lovebirds fell into the grass, and the perfume of lilies enveloped them. He kissed her, lingering on the warm swell of her red lips as her eyes shone with the greenish tint of passion. Salvador caressed her heaving breasts and felt the sleek texture of her inner thighs as she thrashed around. Rosa played hard to get.

In the past, these images excited Salvador and aroused his entire body. But lately, the scenes reassured him of his love for Rosa but no longer awoke the animal part in him. He blamed these changes on tiredness. He still waited for his wife's letters with eagerness. A recent one enclosed a picture of her and their child. Salvador shuffled into the kitchenette and showed it to Elisa. She complimented Rosa on her beauty and Humberto on his handsomeness. She voiced her wish to meet them and wondered whether he had informed his wife of their acquaintance and current situation. Salvador had not notified Rosa. If he did, he would have to tell her about the attack. His wife would be afraid and believe his life was in danger. He preferred to let her know when the police apprehended the fugitive father, and their living arrangement ended. Elisa stopped putting away groceries, frowned with concern, and said,

"I shouldn't have put you through this ordeal."

Salvador expressed his gratitude for her caring attention. His recovery would have been much more challenging if he had stayed with his roommates in the Little Village apartment.

A few weeks after this conversation, Sergeant Ranieri informed Elisa his six-month search ended with the discovery of her father's corpse. He asked her to come by and discuss certain matters that could be handled only in person. She drove to the police headquarters and found the sergeant sitting at his desk. Four days ago, her father hanged himself from a tree in Troy, Michigan, leaving no note. During the weeks before the suicide, investigators traced three incidents of pedophilia in the area and looked for a man whose characteristics fit Mr. Ramirez'. Her father used candies to entice three five-year-old girls with dark hair and light skin like Elisa's. The children identified him from pictures, and his fingerprints matched the ones on record from his booking years ago. He must have realized the police were closing in on him. His body lay in a morgue in Michigan. The official offered Elisa to review the photographs of the suicide scene. She declined and added,

"Please, put him in a closed casket. I'd appreciate it if you could spare me from seeing his corpse. His presence haunted me while he was alive. I don't want it to continue after his death. But he is my father. I'll bury him."

Elisa took advantage of the opportunity and inquired about Salvador's case. The police had notified the INS. Sergeant Ranieri reiterated his opinion. The agency would prefer to track criminal illegal aliens rather than prosecute a hard worker and courageous man like Salvador. But there was no certainty. Elisa returned home, relieved, as if someone had removed an enormous burden from her back. Her exhilaration mixed with uneasiness. She wandered about and prayed for the soul of her progenitor, trying to erase from her heart any hatred she might have held against him.

That evening, as Salvador and Elisa drove back home, she informed him of her father's death, her conversation with the sergeant, and the circumstances of the case. He decided to help her with the burial before moving out. She thanked him and said,

"You can stay. We don't interfere with each other. We're good roommates. Let your wife know. Explain to her. You save me some money and have a comfortable place to stay."

He reaffirmed his decision. Elisa offered him her home if he ever needed a roof over his head.

Three days later, on a warm March 25, 1986, Salvador and Elisa left for Michigan. The morning sun shone over the vast cemetery in Troy. A sepulchral silence reigned. A few black squirrels roamed the fields covered with dry brown grass and a few puddles. In a black suit and a constrictive gray tie, Salvador felt sweat run down his forehead as he and Elisa walked abreast toward the gravesite. She looked unsettled in the dark blue coat that failed to mitigate her shivering from the cold. They stood together, the sun on their back, their shadows stretching over the excavated tomb into sunlit grass. An overpowering smell of wet soil wafted from the dug ground. His thoughts drifted into the evening when the father assaulted the daughter and almost killed Salvador. It seemed unreal and even ironic that he was present at his burial. Elisa fought her strong aversion to the man who had caused her so much suffering. Her lips quivered, mumbling prayers, but her mind resisted her words. Her eyes watched with relief as two gravediggers lowered the casket to the ground.

No priest attended the interment. Salvador opened his Bible, raised his eyes to heaven, and summoned God. Two white clouds coalesced into an hourglass-shaped cloud. Salvador interpreted the vision as a divine answer. God would erase his terrible memories and those of his roommate with time. Months and years would heal them. A cardinal now warbled from the top of a nearby oak tree and ended Salvador's reverie. He gazed at Elisa with a warm stare and noticed a tense grimace on her lips. A blink reawakened the sparkle in her eyes. She glanced at him. Her heart flamed with love for the man who now towered over her. She grabbed his left hand and squeezed it tight as she heard him read from Corinthians,

"So, we fix our eyes not on what is seen, but on what is unseen. For what is seen is temporary, but what is unseen is eternal."

For an instant, he could not think of the meaning of these words. Nor could he think of his pleadings to God for Elisa, forgiveness for their attacker, or hope the evil man repented before his last breath. All he could think of was Elisa's eyes—the rapturous beauty the morning sun drew on them. The brief spell embarrassed him. He completed his prayers and steered his thoughts. Their task was over, and they drove back to Chicago.

In the car, Salvador revisited the moment he had been before the grave and read from the Holy Scriptures. A weird and detached sensation overtook him as if he had impersonated a priest. Salvador had never regretted leaving the seminary, not even during harsh times. He thought no one should hide under a priest's cassock to secure comfort or avoid financial distress. His decision made him happy—his wife, child, and job—and he looked forward to continuing his honest living. Salvador wanted to serve God from a unique perspective and respected most priests' loving labor and sacrifice for their fellow man. Quite a few friends from the seminary led exemplary lives. All professions bore bad apples. He disagreed with how the Church handled these miscreants. The hierarchy should not cover up their evil deeds and reassign these criminals to parishes where they could continue their heinous acts. Salvador had never overcome disappointment with his religious life. But he found peace of mind away from the bureaucratic and rigid structures of the Church.

The steady roar of the car engine and the constant flat scenery propitiated a calming effect on the driver and the passenger. A few hours later, darkness enveloped their vehicle. Soon, the dazzling lights of heavy traffic announced the nearness of Chicago.

Elisa broke the silence,

"Those people buried in the cemetery were like you and me a few years ago. Their earthly love, hate, illusions, and hopes all ended there. No second chance for them."

"No, Elisa, you're a believer. Their goodness remains with us, with the people they helped while alive. And their evil persists too."

"People don't realize that."

"There is nothing else in this life except being good to one another."

"That is right." She took her eyes off the road for a split second, looked at him, and added, "We don't think this way and often act as if we'll live forever."

"My father used to tell me, 'Live as if you will die tomorrow and as if you will never die.'"

Elisa continued her silence. Salvador observed her praying, her lips moving in slow, rhythmic motions.

That night, Salvador did not sleep well. Desultory thoughts surprised him. He saw Rosa in his dreams, but now images of Elisa also cropped up in his nocturnal scenes. His mind concentrated on the terrible events his roommate had confronted when an epiphany scared him.

Elisa and Rosa shared the deep fervor in his heart. He blamed the change on his gratefulness to Elisa for her kindness. Nightmares woke him up. Salvador watched Rosa and Humberto fall down a massive precipice and screamed for help. He sat up in bed and panted awhile. Two hours later, Elisa's bloody dead body flashed through his mind as her father stood, laughing, next to her corpse. Salvador turned the light on. He then evoked God's nearness, talked to Him about his fears, and pleaded for his family and Elisa, who suffered so much.

Elisa's sleep was also restless. She wondered what she had done to deserve such terrible abuse at the hands of her father. She could not understand why God allowed people like her parents to conceive children. Her behavior would be so different if she were a mother. There was so much love burning inside her. Elisa was ready to turn it over to a good husband and their children. She pictured Salvador leaving her, and goose pimples ran down her chest into her belly. The fear of losing him grew with her insomnia hours. But she reasoned that he belonged to his wife and his boy. The argument did not put her mind at ease.

The following day, Salvador prepared his belongings and placed them inside two suitcases in his room. He came out and saw Elisa sitting at the kitchen table. She wore a light green silk robe with a black tulip on either side of her chest and crossed lapels. Her vacant eyes stared at the yellow flowers on the blue tablecloth. Her mind still tried to reason out the upcoming farewell to the man she had fallen in love with. The aroma of coffee drifted throughout the hall and mixed with somber silence.

Salvador dragged himself toward the kitchen. His steps hammered his brain as much as his thoughts. He pulled a chair to sit in front of Elisa. The scratch of its legs against the floor hurt his insides. He wished this moment were over and the last goodbye had already passed. She raised her eyes and sketched a melancholic smile. Their eyes met, and a flash rushed through them. Desires bounced and leaped, caroming in their imagination like pinballs. Perplexity overtook them at the awareness of their thoughts. Their unspoken love for each other burst into the open, exposing their naked hearts. Salvador thought of God, sin, all his conversations with Him, right and wrong, his wife and child, and his promises at the wedding. Nothing worked. His blood rushed through his body with uncontained ardor. Flustered, he tried to dispel the passion that made his legs quiver. He shuffled around the table and poured her some coffee. He asked,

"Cream?"

"No, no, I'll do it."

Elisa scrambled to reach for the cream in the middle of the table, her hand stumbling against his. Her touch aroused him. He pulled her toward him and embraced her. Her breasts' warmth was on his chest, and his image on her loving eyes. His hands cradled her face, and her skin arose aflame. Salvador felt dazed. His lips were drawn to hers like an uprooted tree into a tornado. She shuddered.

Salvador lifted her in his arms and, blind with her kisses and caresses, teetered through the hall into his bedroom.

He bumped off against the walls. She intoxicated him with her breath on his cheek, her lips' syrupy taste in his mouth, and her soft perfume. His thoughts reverberated. I love her so much that I can't control my feelings. Oh God, pardon me, pity me. I lack the will to stop this. His right shoulder brushed against the doorframe of his room. Salvador turned her body forward, squeezed her against his chest, and saw the morning light seeping through the window. He noticed her eyes full of love and passion. Down below, her red lips surrendered to his soft caresses. A deep breath pressed her bosom against his chest as her hands clasped his flesh.

The bedspring squealed. The lovers locked their eyes as he lay on top of her. They perceived their tender fusion, warm savor, the torrid cradle where their bodies slid against each other. A sensual scent hovered over them as his hot palpitations penetrated the volcanic fire of his beloved. And the eruption occurred. Their calm bodies blended like seawater in a river estuary.

Their sexual climax over, Salvador held Elisa close to him. He regarded her. She looked beautiful, like a monarch that had just completed her nuptial dance and spread out her wings. He dozed off. After a while, Elisa stood up and prepared to go to school. He wished her goodbye with a prolonged kiss and continued his nap.

When his brief snooze was over, Salvador sat up in bed. Her fragrance enveloped him in a cloud of sweetness and remorse. Traces of their intimate encounter were no longer present in the room. His clothes, which had earlier lain scattered next to hers on the floor, rested folded on a small wooden chair. He closed his eyes, shook his head, and cried. He wished his mind were as well arranged as his shorts and undershirt. Ashamed, he lay down and pulled the flat sheet over his head as if hiding from God. His spontaneous act reminded him of the biblical passage where Adam and Eve concealed themselves from His view when they fell into sin. Salvador wondered why God allowed him to harbor such an intense love for a woman other than his wife in his soul. His perplexity evoked the triumph of Jesus over inescapable temptations after fasting forty days and forty nights in the wilderness. Salvador buried his face in his knees. He had failed because he was not Jesus. The Devil, a fallen angel, enticed the Son of God, but he, Salvador, was an insignificant human being.

Salvador took a shower and wished the soap would cleanse his body and his sinful remorse. He grabbed his clothes, dressed, and scanned the surroundings again. A mixture of sadness and nostalgia seized his heart. He picked up the suitcases and, on his way out, sat at the table and wrote Elisa a note,

Dear Elisa:

I am sorry about what happened this morning. It occurred because I fell in love with you. But it was wrong. I am married and have abused your friendship. You are good and deserve an honest man, free to love you and make you happy. I am going back to my apartment. I beg you, don't call me. It will only worsen my pain and yours. I will be your friend forever. If I can help you in the future, please get in touch with me.

With love,

Salvador

9

"MANUEL'S LABOR"

S alvador moved into a local motel in Aurora, Illinois, one of the
fast-growing suburbs. Young families escaped from a colossal
city's lack of safety and inconvenience. New small towns sprawled
along its outskirts. Streets and courts flanked by single-family homes
cropped up overnight. Buildings, businesses, schools, and hospitals
rose from the ground.

Salvador found a job in construction, an industry that employed
many undocumented workers. He became a laborer in the 12-hour
workforce. These people often held two full-time positions. His
assignment comprised the most complex tasks. The veteran employ-
yees nicknamed these taxing duties "Manuel's labor" because only
Mexican immigrants handled them.

Several weeks passed, and Salvador rented an apartment with
three coworkers. Alone and far from the city, he could not get over
the loss of Elisa. Her laughter and smile had vanished from his life.
Salvador realized the inappropriateness of his feelings but revisited
the love scenes he had experienced a few weeks earlier. Elisa's image
hung over him like abundant flowers on a magnolia tree: the warmth
in her eyes, the way she lowered her eyelids, her face flushed with
tenderness. He thought about her long, delicate fingers with her red
nails, her warm, caressing hands, and her fleshy lips close to his.

This predicament cannot be happening, he pondered. I love Rosa.
Perhaps I don't care for her enough. Life in a village only allows you

to meet a few women. In the seminary, I tried to consider them sisters with no physical attraction. It turned into an impossible goal. I did not endure as terrible nocturnal ordeals as my roommate. But I fought temptation so hard that, some nights, I ended up exhausted. School activities did not allow me any contact with the opposite sex. My imagination created the desired images. It was another factor in my decision to quit the priesthood.

But how can this deficiency account for falling head over heels for Elisa? I love Rosa. She is good—so is Elisa. She indulged me with caring feelings and tenderness. I didn't realize it was love that I felt for her, not just gratefulness. I wonder how an educated woman like her was smitten with an illegal immigrant from a small town in Mexico, someone without a college degree. What are the reasons for a man to love someone? Are there any? One falls, that's all, no logic to it.

My love for Rosa might have been born because we grew up in the same town. There were others available. My stay in Guadalajara offered opportunities. I met several schoolmates, vain girls with many futile fantasies in their minds. I courted Vanesa. Her constant talk and grandiose ideas unsettled me. She wanted to become a celebrity. On our way to a discotheque, she skipped no shop window without looking at herself in the glass. Vanessa accomplished the obsessive task with a not-so-subtle turn of her head and an awkward pose. It was as if a peacock swaggered next to me. We danced and kissed. Her lips had a thick and dry texture and contrasted with Elisa's moist and warm lips, which tasted like raspberry.

These reminiscences send bolts of heat down my entire body. My heart runs fast, and everything rushes inside me. I am going crazy. Rosa is a virtuous wife and mother who does not deserve my unfaithfulness. She showed her great affection for me many times. Rosa said she loves me more than anyone in this world. Her loving attention never faltered. She inspected my socks for any holes and darned them with care. One must scrutinize every inch of the garment before finding a trace of her mending. When Rosa noticed my Sunday shirt collar worn out, she unstitched it and reattached it inside out. Her job had such perfection that the shirt looked brand new. She spared no effort to make me happy. Her contagious joy spread everywhere in the house like a floral scent. There is no excuse for my sin of infidelity.

My nerves and tiredness play dirty tricks on me. I have even lost track of the reasons I came to *El Norte*. I wanted to open a new horizon for my son, Rosa, and myself in a country full of opportunities. Falling in love derailed my plan. I never even envisioned this slip would happen. Sometimes, it behaves like a blessing and makes me happy. Other times, it turns into a curse, and guilt assaults me. I should repent and atone for my improprieties but can't. Nor can I talk to God because I perceive Him far from me. The humongous gap looms between us that my mind can never bridge. My sin defiles me and makes me unworthy of His companionship. I know my love for Elisa is not lust or desire for her body, but there is some of that, too. The human soul and flesh cannot be torn apart any more than one can scoop oil out of the water with one's hands.

Salvador's thoughts exhausted him. A long nap did not soothe him. He hung a picture of his child on his bedroom wall to affirm his love for Rosa and Humberto. Images of the Sacred Heart of Jesus and Our Lady of Guadalupe waited in his Bible. The book had been closed since his carnal sin. He did not attend Mass or go to church.

His state of mind reminded him of how he had suffered after he had committed his first mortal sin. It happened at eleven. Under his brother's mattress, Salvador came across a picture of Raquel Welch in a swimming suit. The actress' statuesque figure with bare legs and rounded breasts captured his imagination. Lusty thoughts tormented him with their immoral nature. His flesh rebelled. He hid in a haystack out of God's sight, relieving his sexual tension. Salvador remembered poking out of his hideout with stalks blinding his eyes and caking his clothes. They reeked of a spicy odor. He brushed the grass from his eyes and garments but was unclean.

The dirt seemed to have encrusted his body. A terrible itch blazed up in his legs and arms.

Now, Salvador also felt dirty, unworthy of God's paternal friendship, and immersed in guilt and self-deprecation. His filial entitlements had crumbled in his mind. He turned into a Prodigal Son. But his lack of repentance was even worse. But how could he regret making love to Elisa? He loved her with all his heart. Nothing stopped his obsession with her. Salvador reassured himself this situation would pass, and time would ease his lovelorn sickness. But weeks passed, and the relief never arrived.

Antonio, now and then, phoned him. Their conversation revolved around their daily routine. In the last phone call, the youngster talked about the gossip circulating among his former coworkers at the restaurant. These tattletales had commented on the unexpected resignations of Elisa and Salvador. Criticisms of sanctimoniousness fell upon Salvador. After his big talk about his wife and son, he seduced a gorgeous waitress and eloped with her. Antonio tried to correct them but got nowhere.

Antonio noticed Salvador's depressed voice and wondered whether the mood had to do with Elisa,

"If something happened between you and Elisa, please tell Rosa."

"Even if something happened, which is no one's business, what good will that do?"

"People change their minds. If they fall in love with someone else, they divorce and marry the woman they love."

"You have no right to get involved in these things. When the time comes, I'll tell my wife about my injuries and my association with Elisa. It would be up to her to ask me questions."

Salvador's construction job kept his mind occupied. Deep inside, he craved Elisa. The sensation flared up on his days off. He sat in his room, thought about her, and conjured up her image. His entire body lit up like fire. This vividness contrasted with the somberness of his surroundings. Salvador had a mattress with a brown cover on the floor and a chair with a scuffed cushion that sank beneath him with a pitiful noise. He ate at a small square table with wads of folded paper under two legs. His belongings were piled up in a corner.

It was cloudy outside. A persistent drizzle wetted the land. A few small oak trees swung dressed in green foliage and dripped raindrops like sad tears. The temptation of returning to Elisa often afflicted him. He stopped short. His commitment to his wife and his son had grown roots in his mind. Salvador had promised Rosa to fulfill it at his wedding proposal in her home. That day, he wore his Sunday best — a gray suit with an open-collared white shirt and black shoes — and sat on a wooden chair. His eyes locked on a photograph of three silver-gray donkeys with snow-white muzzles that drank from a pristine creek. The background image boasted imposing dark mountains. His left foot jerked up and down. His future mother-in-law sat across from her daughter on the opposite side of the room. In black attire, the old lady perched as still as a piece of charcoal. She smacked her tongue against her mouth's roof behind tight lips, stressing the sternness in her expression.

A long braid with a red ribbon bow rested against Rosa's left breast area of her white blouse. Her brown eyes gazed down at her green skirt and black shoes. Her hands lay interlaced in her lap as her fingernails scratched the dress. Long silence chilled the moment. A window to his right illuminated a picture of Rosa's late father on a black horse. He wielded a whip in his hand. His face sketched a smile while his grave eyes scrutinized his daughter's suitor from head to toe. Salvador contemplated the door before him and restrained the temptation to run away. His cough lashed through the dense stillness. The mother tossed her head to signal an order to her daughter.

Rosa stood up, walked to the middle of the room, and opened a holy gospel with the title written in golden calligraphic letters. The book rested on a small wooden table, and a black page ribbon showed a selected passage — *Mark 10: 6-8*. Rosa read it:

"In the beginning, God made them male and female. For this reason, a man will leave his father and mother and be united with his wife, and the two will become one flesh. So, they are no longer two, but one."

Rosa strolled toward Salvador, handed him the holy book, and smiled. Her eyes twinkled, and her nose tweaked in a charming gesture. The mother instructed him to place his hand on the text and asked,

"Swear with your hand on the Gospels that you would care for Rosa for as long as you live?"

The words choked in his throat, but he nodded his acceptance.

"Don't be nervous. You may kiss my daughter's hand."

Salvador stayed stock-still until the mother moved. She pushed herself up with her hands against the chair, climbed to her feet, and shuffled toward the door. He stood up. He had often caressed Rosa's hands, but her palms were warm and silky that day. Her dainty fingers and nacreous nails quivered. She stared into his eyes. A cloud of flowery scent wrapped him when his lips met her vanilla-flavored skin. He thought he could never stop kissing her hands.

Salvador's thoughts now drifted back to his conversation with Antonio. He wanted to ask whether condemning his son to a fatherless existence would be fair. Nothing could justify staying so far away from his homeland other than the welfare of his family. Salvador held the conviction he must carry out his duties and follow God's commandments. He had submitted to Him to serve His church as a devotee out of the priesthood. But a mortal sin occurred. If he died, he would go to hell. Even this thought did not bring him to repentance. Another memory played a significant role. His parents hammered into him his way of thinking, over and over bombarding him with their favorite maxim,

"Duties before devotion," and his father always added, "Never forget that."

Weaning his mind from Elisa proved impossible. The six-month period with her became as vital to him as the several-month diapause to a monarch. This state lengthened its longevity several times to fly 4,000 miles back to Mexico and start a new life cycle. The epiphany rendered him so remorseful that the doldrums overtook him. He appealed to the thumping of hammers, lifting massive beams, and balancing danger on scaffolds to keep his mind numb. The day's work drained him and subjected him to a dreamless slumber.

10

COLD BED

W hen Elisa found the note from Salvador on the table, sadness overcame her. His room was a cruel reminder of his absence. The bed was still covered with a bedspread printed with blue and white flowers. But the empty built-in closet frowned with naked hangers dangling from an aluminium bar like vampires inside a dark cave. The dark wooden chair next to his bed, where he had set his folded clothes, was empty and lonely. The crucifix still hovered over the room, fixed, immobile, unmoved, as if nothing had happened on Jesus' watch. A faint fragrance of aftershave lingered in the air. A pair of Salvador's black socks peeked out from under the bed. She picked them up, deposited them in the laundry bin, and searched around but found no other item belonging to him.

Tears ran down her cheeks. Their salty taste stirred up vivid memories. Salvador laughed when she told him about the dog in the park. The animal peed on her shoes when she was reading a book. His expression of surprise when he picked out the chocolate ice cream he had earlier tucked into the refrigerator. It had turned into a chocolate shake and dripped from the paper cup. Or the day he wore a new jacket and forgot to cut off a conspicuous price tag, which dangled from the back of his garment. She grabbed a pair of scissors to cut it off as he rushed sideways in a knee-jerk reaction. They laughed until their tummies hurt.

Elisa honored his request not to contact him. She knew of his commitment to his family and believed he would be happy with them. For a while, her decision not to fight for his love was steadfast in the daytime and wavered at night. Her mind composed letters in her restless sleep. The words sounded so logical that she was tempted to wake up and write them down. They gained a different meaning at daybreak as if the sunlight had faded the lines out. After two weeks, she reassured herself she had made the right decision. Her suffering eased off. She finished her paralegal training by the end of the month and moved to the neighboring state of Wisconsin.

Elisa ended up in Milwaukee and concentrated on performing well in Attorney Michael Kaplan's legal offices. Her promptness, efficiency, perfectionism, and initiative made her a great asset to her new employer. Mr. Kaplan boasted a distinguished appearance enhanced by gray sideburns and elegant suits in his early fifties. His single three-story home was in the downtown area, near the lake. His garage flaunted three sports cars: a red Mercedes, a blue Porsche, and a yellow Ferrari. He looked upon the place as his castle. Michael Kaplan dreamed he would someday share it with his future beloved wife. But his quest to find his better half had so far been unsuccessful. He always found an excuse for failure: "She is after my money," "She is not religious enough," or "I don't like her family."

When Elisa worked for him, Mr. Kaplan envisioned she might be his queen. He invited her to lunch under the pretense of work. At the restaurant, her face flushed and blanched on and off. She went to the restroom three times. Elisa refreshed her face and relieved her persistent nausea. She blamed her discomfort on some food poisoning. Her boss realized her difficulties, postponed their meeting, and urged her to go home and rest. That afternoon, Elisa visited a doctor who ordered a few tests and asked her to return in two days. He confirmed her pregnancy. Salvador's child, she said to herself as her face lit up with a big smile. Her sudden happiness turned into sadness. Her beloved was not there to share the pleasant news with her. Nor could she tell him. Loneliness overtook her, but the child meant so much to her that her joy soon returned.

Elisa informed her new boss of her state. Mr. Kaplan accepted the news with some reservations. Her future maternity leave concerned him. It was hard to do without her services so soon after her hiring. Her valuable contribution to his firm convinced him to continue her employment. An unacknowledged personal interest hid under this apparent unbiased judgment. He sometimes believed Elisa might be like other women he had met—fickle, illogical females who never thought straight. But his opinion wavered. He did not understand why she had been so sincere with him and acted as if nothing had happened.

At their next working lunch, Mr. Kaplan took a more personal approach and asked questions about her pregnancy and her baby's father. Elisa expressed her love for her former roommate and explained he did not know of her condition. Avoiding any detail, she added,

"I don't want to harm someone I love."

"At least he should recognize your baby and help you financially," Mr. Kaplan said.

"I expect no one to understand my reasons. I am blessed. God has allowed me to conceive a child out of love."

Elisa's pregnancy evolved through the stages as smoothly as her life in Milwaukee. She lived alone in a rented apartment near her workplace. Home preparations for her baby soon occupied much of her leisure time. She had endured isolation during her lifetime. Now, the constant companionship of someone in her belly mitigated her sadness. The windfall of hormones in her early pregnancy enhanced her beauty. Her skin gained a silky luster, her cheeks brightened, and her figure blossomed.

Four weeks later, Elisa got a clean health bill on her gynecologist visit. The next day, a sheriff handed her a subpoena. It instructed her to appear in court as a witness in the case of Salvador Gómez. Elisa was eager to see him, but some uncertainties created considerable anxiety. She doubted whether she could hide her deep affection from him. Her eyes might betray her and shine with the incredible love she cherished for him. Will he resent what happened between us? Will he blame me for the incident? She pondered as her mind sped up. No, he won't. He loves me.

There must be so much guilt. Love should not evoke those feelings, but it does. He might change his mind and want me by his side. Oh, God, that would be so wonderful. That dream lies beyond my reach. But God should grant me enough strength to fight it. I must help him overcome his legal problem and let him decide about our future. If only he knew I was carrying his child. I can't tell him. Cutting the father from my child's life doesn't seem right. What can I do? I don't want Salvador to feel obligated to be with me or care for us. He might lose his family. His wife wouldn't understand if she learned her husband had a child with another woman. It might make him happy, but he might resent the loss of his family. He wouldn't turn hostile. But I wonder whether it would be healthy for him or my baby. He must decide on his own whether he wants us in his life. I don't know what to do. I am damned if I do and damned if I don't.

She did not get a wink of sleep the night before the hearing. The following day, she rose from bed alert. Her blood rushed from her excitement. She caught an early Metra train to Chicago and let her eyes sway over the unfolding green scenery as if pinning her visions on her feelings. Her heart hollered to run, embrace him, and whisper her love to him. There were inner screams that wanted to tell Salvador about his child growing inside her. She restrained her emotions. Her facial expressions would convey her resolve to help him now or in the future if needed. She wished he would realize her immense happiness if he ever chose to live with her.

11

THE COURTROOM

Summer had just arrived. Salvador waited for the day of his hearing scheduled for the following week. Sweat poured from his forehead, and his muscles twitched all day long. He met with Mr. Rueda. His lawyer reviewed several questions the judge might ask and informed him that Elisa would testify on his behalf. Salvador had not forgotten her. His heart still searched for her like a wayward monarch returning home during the fall migration. Palpitations wore him out. He longed to see her but also feared that moment. His prior commitments dictated to him what to do, and this awareness saddened him.

A few days later, on June 25, 1986, Attorney Rueda and Salvador sat on a bench in front of the platform of a presiding judge. They whispered some essential details to remember in court. Other defendants' relatives and friends awaited their slated times, drifting in and out of the courtroom. When Elisa walked in, a smiling Mr. Rueda signaled to her to sit at the back of the room. Salvador turned his head and looked at her over his shoulder. His eyes lit up, his face reddened, and a shiver ran through his body. She sat in the second row, next to the aisle, behind the bar. Her light-gray dress stressed the color of her hair and contrasted with the redness of her lips and the intense brown hue of her eyes. Amid the courtroom murmur, with his future at stake, Salvador could not think of anything but his desire to run toward and embrace her.

His glimpse had overlooked the curious people behind the railing. Two middle-aged women in black were beside a young gentleman in a dark blue suit and an older adult with his right palm on the silver cobra's head of a carved wooden cane. Five young women in colorful dresses chatted and giggled in a quiet voice. It had been so long since he saw Elisa that, at this moment, nothing mattered but her. His mind sizzled with a thought: if only she sat beside me and held my hand.

In front of Salvador, a court deputy in a blue uniform regarded everyone in the room with suspicious eyes. The official folded his arms in front of him in a combative attitude and gazed at the court reporter. Her beady blue eyes examined her purple fingernails and scratched off the excessive skin in her cuticles.

The prosecuting attorney wore a black suit and a blue tie and sat alone at his table across the aisle. He pored over a black book full of documents. Salvador pondered whether that man held the key to his irremediable sentence. He envisioned himself on the witness stand, all eyes on him like a criminal. The broad platform with the judge's bench loomed before him like a symbol of omnipotence. Salvador was alone, and Elisa was far from him. He glanced at her and blinked, embarrassed, but did not avert his eyes. She smiled at him, her cheeks carved dimples, and her eyes unveiled her warm heart. He sketched a grin, and his entire body tensed up. Her heart raced. She tried to avoid any giveaway sign, but her cheeks blushed.

The officer announced Judge Helen Atkins' entrance into the courtroom. Everyone stood up as the magistrate strode toward her desk. Mr. Rueda asked her permission to approach the bench, and she nodded.

"Your Honor, my client is the illegal immigrant who endangered his life to save an American citizen, a young woman."

"Yes, I looked over the papers you filed. Let's proceed. Is the prosecution ready?"

"Yes, your Honor. My name is Stanley Cooper. I am here to prosecute the case against Mr. Salvador Gómez, who entered this country by San Ysidro, California, in March 1982, disregarding the laws of the United States. Mr. Gómez did not seek legal admission to this country, waiting in line with other law-abiding immigrants in Mexico. Instead, he jumped ahead and trespassed the border of our nation. The migrant secured no job before coming in and snatching one from an American citizen. Like many of his illegal compatriots, he contributes to the unemployment of the American worker.

"His invasion is an assault on our sovereignty. Your Honor, Mr. Salvador Gómez and his fellow illegal immigrants do not arrive in search of a new homeland. They form their communities, decline to mix with the rest of the population, grab as much money as possible, and abandon this land. They seldom achieve or desire knowledge of the English language or our society. Our welfare system sustains their heavy burden, whose cost amounts to billions of dollars. Mexican illegal immigration represents a danger to the United States as a nation. I know of the defendant's feat to save the life of an American citizen—a courageous deed expected from anyone, anywhere in the world, under the same circumstances. His civic duty does not erase his disregard for the law. I am, therefore, requesting his deportation to Mexico."

"Mr. Rueda, it is your turn."

"Thank you, your Honor. Mr. Salvador Gómez represents a new breed of pioneers. He crossed the border and endangered his life to seek a new homeland. He worked without rest day after day to build his dream—a better life among free people. His English is not the best. But even after long working hours, he studied the language and attempted to communicate with every one of us. He is a person of good morals. He has worked, paid his taxes, and obeyed the laws of the land.

"Most Mexican illegal immigrants arrive looking for temporary employment to feed their families in their homeland. Yet, many grow roots among us, seeking a haven of liberty, safety, and justice. Mr. Gómez's commitment to our society has gone beyond the call of duty. One day, unexpected circumstances demanded he should sacrifice everything he had, including his life, to save a fellow citizen in danger. He did not hesitate for a moment, and his heroism almost cost him his life. The United States of America was born of the courage of settlers and immigrants like Salvador Gómez. Therefore, I request you grant him a permanent residence green card."

"Thank you, gentlemen, so much for your grandiloquent speeches," Judge Atkins said, "Now, please address the issues. This case is not the only one I must rule on today."

Attorney Rueda related his client's stay as an undocumented worker, his eagerness to work, and the fulfillment of his duties. Affidavits from employers provided ample evidence of his moral character. These companies would rehire him if he so desired.

"To show that Mr. Gómez is not an ordinary man," Mr. Rueda added, "I am calling to the stand a witness: Ms. Elisa Ramirez."

The courtroom deputy opened the railing gate, and Elisa walked toward the witness stand, focused on the judge. Salvador heard the tread of her high-heeled shoes echo throughout the courtroom. Elisa did not avoid peeking at Salvador's back as she approached where he sat and passed by him so close that she smelled the fragrance of his cologne. His eyes rested on her straight shoulders, swinging rounded hips, and long swaying hair. The ceiling lights ricocheted on her locks. She eased into the armchair and stared into the emptiness beyond the room. He lowered his eyes. Both realized their feelings and the need to concentrate on the task. Judge Atkins swore Elisa in and observed her expression. Under her remoteness and cynicism disguise, the judge brimmed with an intuition that the witness' eyes revealed the truth more than her words or oaths. Mr. Rueda addressed Elisa, who displayed confidence and self-control. After some preliminaries, he directed her attention to the events that had occurred the night of the attack.

"Ms. Ramirez, what was the first thing Mr. Gómez said to you?"

"He asked me how I was as he helped me get back on my feet."

"Did he tell you he was hurt?"

"No, he was worried about me, but I saw he was severely injured as soon as I looked at him."

"Objection, your Honor, the witness is not a doctor," Mr. Cooper said.

"Just describe what you saw," Mr. Rueda said.

"There was blood running down his right arm, which he held against his chest. I stood up and saw blood gushing out from the right side of his chest."

Elisa's answers revealed that Salvador had faced grave danger to his life. It was the turn of Mr. Cooper to query her.

"Ms. Ramirez, how long have you known Mr. Gómez?"

"About a year and a half."

"Were you friends before you were attacked?"

"No. We just worked in the same restaurant."

"Was there any romantic relationship before the incident?"

"No."

"Your Honor, I don't think this line of questioning is appropriate," Mr. Rueda objected.

"Your Honor, I want to establish she wasn't a regular citizen he helped, but someone he had known well and might have had a relationship with."

"You may proceed."

"Ms. Ramirez, were you intimate friends?"

"I already answered that question. No, we were just coworkers."

"Are you now engaged in any romantic relationship with him?"

"No," she answered over Mr. Rueda's objection.

"I withdraw my question. When was the last time you spoke with Mr. Gómez?"

"Three months ago."

"I have no more questions."

Elisa remained seated with her legs uncrossed. An open side of the witness stand let Salvador admire her knees and the onset of her shaped thighs under her skirt. Her eyes roved over everyone in the room and lingered a little longer to regard Salvador. She sketched a smile. He saw her teeth white like pearls and noticed that she had blossomed. Her bosom looked fuller, her skin sensuous, her eyes brighter, even her eyelashes were longer. Her gorgeousness struck him. She had grown more beautiful since he saw her several months ago. An aura around her face disclosed her happiness and made him wonder about the reason for her joy. The observation caused him to feel guilty. He thought he might have been a terrible influence on her. Her interrogatory over, she walked by him and stole a glance. His reiterative thought hammered his mind — if only she sat next to me and held my hand.

Based on Elisa's testimony, Judge Atkins decided and asked Mr. Cooper to approach the bench. Her face showed anger as she leaned and whispered to him,

"What are you trying to do? Are you crazy? You bring this case to court when the U.S. Congress is about to consider legislation to grant amnesty to over two million illegal immigrants!"

"Your Honor, my duty is to defend our country's laws."

"Mr. Cooper, laws are enacted in a democracy to be enforced by people with goodwill and common sense. You may go back to your seat."

Judge Atkins issued her ruling and awarded Salvador a green card. Salvador hugged Attorney Rueda, raised his eyes, turned his head over his shoulder, and scanned the spectator area. Elisa's seat languished empty.

Back at home, Salvador found himself lonely and sad. The joy he should have experienced at receiving the legal status never came to pass. The green card stared at him, but his eyes welled up with tears. He missed talking to Elisa, sharing the marvelous news, and hearing her cheerful voice. This moment would have been exceptional if she had been with him, but she was no longer in his life. He envisioned Rosa, but she was so far away. His wife would have listened to him, rejoiced in his new status, and held his head on her lap. Her calming influence comforted him. Rosa differed from Elisa, but she knew him well and always put things in a proper perspective.

Salvador missed God since he could not reconcile with Him. His sin grew insurmountable. At night, his mind strayed from control and entertained thoughts of getting close to Him again. But he felt adrift and agitated in daylight like a wind-stirred kite free from its restraining string. Repentance was far beyond his reach. Salvador wanted to pray and thank God for the outcome of his court case but to no avail. His wound remained open. He doubted whether it would ever heal because of the strength of his love for Elisa. The ingrained feelings for his wife could not restrain it. Both women's images sometimes fused in his head. His mind now deformed them and transformed their figures and faces into a monstrous gargoyle, rousing restlessness. Religion had steered his thoughts, priorities, mood, and life. Those guidelines capsized and sank.

His eyes rested on a letter from Rosa in a pink envelope on a small coffee table. He had received it that morning. Anger overtook him momentarily, but he could not point whether it was at himself, his family, or the world. Resentment filled him with guilt and pangs of shame. He trod toward the coffee table with resolute steps and grabbed the envelope. Salvador decided against opening it and set it back on the table. It was late, and a restorative sleep was essential to him. A strenuous job awaited him the next day. He tucked himself in the sheets, changed his mind, fetched the letter, and read it,

"*Dear Salvador: It has been four years since you left. You would think I would be used to being without you by now. But I am not.*"

He read his wife's account of her steadfast love. Every sentence spurred his remorse. He loathed his unfaithful thoughts and his fits of love for another woman. Her description of his son's charming little ways did not help him either,

"*Little Humberto has found a wounded sparrow chick in the orchard. He put it in a small cage and fed it with water-soaked bread. He wants to send it to you when it grows up and learns how to fly so you don't get bored so far away from us.*"

By the time he finished the letter, his mood was more down in the dumps. He placed a pillow over his face. It was as if its weight could choke his self-deprecating thoughts. The darkness brought back the image of Elisa, along with warm arousal that extended to his loins.

He tossed and turned all night and woke tired the next day. An interminable day of hard work added to his tiredness and ended with a night of deep sleep. A few days later, he regained his composure and wrote a thank-you note to Elisa,

"Dear Elisa: Thank you for everything you did. The green card is of great help. Please forgive me for expressing my feelings. When I saw you in court, my heart jumped inside my chest. I am trying to live without you, but it is hard. I don't know if I will ever be able to.

Salvador"

He never felt so disoriented, not even when he had left the seminary. He was a youngster and knew he would adjust to a new life. Hope cheered up his expectations, and challenges spurred his desire to excel. The hardest part was dealing with his parents' disappointment. Salvador received their letter and feared what it might say, so he tore the envelope's edge and removed the paper sheet. Much to his relief, his parents backed him up and praised his courage to pursue happiness in another profession or trade of his liking.

His persistent grief over the loss of Elisa loomed in his heart with stubborn defiance. Only the passing weeks dulled his depression and nervousness to a manageable degree. He espied a blurry luminosity at the end of the tunnel, but the deep pain never went away. His distress turned into a persistent discomfort as if the swelling had receded and inflammatory remnants had encrusted his heart's layers.

One night, a sudden, unexpected attack surprised him. Salvador woke up choking from a sound sleep, sat in bed, and pushed his hands against the mattress to expand his chest and inhale. It did not work. He noticed cold sweat down his forehead, palpitations, chest heaviness, and tremors. An unknown force drove him and rushed his insides like a high-speed locomotive. Five minutes later, the spell halted as fast as it had begun. Salvador did not know what to make of it and blamed its occurrence on a late evening meal of black beans and guacamole. He slept well the following nights.

A few days later, Salvador strolled to a launderette, picked up a newspaper, and read about a baseball game. Another episode grabbed him and put him through the paces, gasping and panting for air. He laid the paper on his face, so no one watched his spell. It lasted two minutes, soaking the paper in sweat. He recovered his poise, blamed the condition on his stressful work, and reassured himself of their disappearance after several weeks without these attacks.

His life lacked luster. He forced himself to daydream about his wife, but the trick only lasted a few minutes. The face of Rosa soon adopted Elisa's features, and he often thought about his last minutes with his beloved ex-roommate. The vivid images burst into his mind, and scenes unraveled before him. Elisa had been too modest to pose naked in front of him. She stood facing him, covered by the flat sheet. Her eyes glowed with love as her hands maneuvered underneath the linen to fasten her bra.

"Salvador, darling, are you well?"

"I am fine. I am just sleepy."

"Are you sure?"

"Men become zombies after making love."

"I never made love to anyone. I mean of my choice, someone I love. You aren't upset with me, are you?"

"No, I have to think, Elisa."

"I understand."

She put her dress on, let the sheet drop to her feet like a deflated ghost, and said,

"We have been friends for a long while. We respect one another too much to pressure each other into doing anything."

Salvador nodded. Elisa stepped into her high heels and brushed her hair. It shone in the penumbra. He still heard the echo of her receding footsteps as she sauntered to the door and bid him goodbye,

"I'll see you later." Her voice sounded like the joyous peal of a bell.

12

A CAR VIEW

After the verdict, Elisa dashed out of the courtroom and returned to the Metro Station. She sat on a train car and let her memory drift to all the events that had taken place at Salvador's hearing. Some uneasiness found its way to the surface when her mind assessed some of her answers to the interrogation. She had not lied under oath but stretched the truth a little. Intimacy between Salvador and her occurred in the last throes of their relationship. It was a beautiful, unintended accident. The disclosure of her last-minute lapse would have been unfair to Salvador. The judge might have perceived it the wrong way. Besides, the prosecutor's questions were inaccurate and unfair. What was the point? Her friend had risked his life before any romantic involvement occurred.

Elisa reminisced about the events that occurred on the terrible night of her attack ten months earlier. She witnessed how Salvador removed his shirt soaked in blood that gushed out of his chest and right forearm like liquor from a punctured wineskin. The torrential rain diluted it and formed black puddles on the pavement while gusts of wind howled. A moldy stench wafted from the river. Faintness overcame her, and the ground seemed to tilt underfoot. Elisa held on, grabbed a strip of cloth Salvador had torn from his shirt, and tied a tourniquet above his open flesh. Salvador pressed his left hand against his chest as the shadow of death blanched his face.

Elisa pleaded to God not to let Salvador die as he wobbled, cheering her up.

"Don't worry. I'll be okay," he said as if his mind had mastered the power to restrain him from crossing the boundaries of consciousness.

Her screaming for help barely rose over the stormy evening noise. A few minutes later, a police squad car pulled up. An officer stepped out and rushed to the crime scene, clutching his hat with the left hand amid the blare of a portable radio and urgent calls for an ambulance. Salvador could no longer stand up and lay on the pavement. An emergency vehicle's siren wailed from afar. It took two or three minutes for the spinning lights to bathe them with red sparkles.

After setting Salvador onto a stretcher, the paramedics lifted him into the ambulance, secured an intravenous line, and placed an oxygen mask on his face. Elisa sat next to him, held his hand, and fretted at his face drenched in sweat. He mumbled a few unintelligible words and closed his eyes. Afraid that Salvador might not reach the hospital, she squeezed his clammy, chilly hand to wake him up. He gaped straight ahead, his vacant eyes roving upwards or sideways. Her fear intensified, as did her imploration to God to spare her hero's life.

Still far from Milwaukee, Wisconsin, Elisa regained awareness of the train chugging down the track. Her disappointment surfaced. She resented the prosecutor had not asked her about details of her assault. On the witness stand, she would have done anything for him, even lied. His green card afforded her great satisfaction. She sat back and smiled, but her grin ceased, realizing she could not see him again. A tear escaped her control as she pictured Salvador at the defendant's desk. When she walked by him, his intense eyes had met hers at close range, his mind opening to hers like a readable book. His face shone with a deep love for her, and a tense expression revealed uncertainty about whether to rush to hug her or stay put. Anxiety spread his nostrils and made his chin dimple tremble. She saw his right hand reach for his neck and release his tie. Emotion had tightened it. If she had sat next to him, holding hands, the world would have faded.

Back again to the inevitable reality, the wagon's wheels moved with a rhythmic thumping. The noise deadened the feelings of Elisa, who soon observed the Milwaukee Train Station in the distance. On her way home, the taxi driver's head rested upon the seat behind a partition screen, his right hand on the steering wheel as the taximeter jumped ten cents at a time.

A traffic signal turned red. The car stopped with a squeal of the brakes and a soft jolt. Next to the vehicle was a church with an elegant arched portal and a Jesus' Sacred Heart statue above an imposing door. Elisa pushed her face against the right window, looked up, and admired the base of a bell tower with a clock showing 3:20 PM, its dark circle framed by two pilasters and a pediment. Her eyes did not reach the belfry. Her futile effort reminded her of her inability to understand the full scope of Salvador's commitment to the commandments of the Church. The shaft of this bell tower glittered in the sun and cast a shadow on a white skyscraper behind the old structure.

The contrast made her ponder the bright areas of Salvador's character: his goodness, generosity, integrity, willingness to help others, and trustworthiness. There was no darkness in his perso-nality. He would have been an excellent priest. *The Church and I lost him,* she thought. *But humanity has gained a man of integrity. I can't even fathom his remorse for his slip. I found myself powerless to stop what I desired with all my strength. Even now, I won't repent. Those minutes were the happiest in my life. If I could relieve him of his burden, I would. His transgression unleashed guilt and self-deprecation. We committed a mortal sin. His love for me must have loomed enormous for him to fall into such a temptation.*

The taxi resumed the ride, and Elisa realized she had not read the basilica's name. *I wonder whether the same thing happened to me with Salvador,* she said to herself. *I might have paid too much attention to details and missed how much affection he stored in his* heart, an out-of-control fire that lay in wait. I don't understand how he fell for me, a woman scarred by sexual abuse, someone who grew up in a different culture and background. My religiosity sputters and falters like an old car. I believe in God but attend Mass only a few Sundays and never read the Bible. Maybe I should go to that basilica every week. Why did my attention skip through essential information like its name? Before our intimate encounter, I did not read love in Salvador's eyes or capture a single clue when it was born.

In the next few days, Elisa felt depressed and concentrated on her job and pregnancy. Her heart pounded, and the surplus of blood feeding the fetus made her warm and excited. She visualized the baby's face in some of her dreams, but the following day, she did not remember whether it was a boy or a girl. Prayers and loving thoughts eased none of her sorrows about Salvador's absence. Mariela phoned her to tell her about an envelope she had received from Salvador. It contained a sealed letter and a note requesting she forward it to Elisa.

"Don't send it, Mariela. I must stay away from him. I can't afford to open that letter."

"He probably thanks you for helping him get the green card. It must be a brief note."

"I am sure it says more than that."

Silence hung over the phone like a precipice. Mariela envisioned her friend with her head bent back as her eyes contemplated the bare ceiling, the handset dangling from a hand. She had observed this gesture on her friend before when circumstances had become tough to handle. What Mariela could not now visualize was her deep frowning and teeth clenching that evinced anguish. She heard a deep sigh that signaled her friend's willingness to continue the conversation.

"You can't always run away from him. It would be best if you answered his letters. If you love him, fight for his love."

"It wouldn't work for him. He came to bring his family to this country and build a future for them. I can't become an obstacle."

"He loves you."

"He might be fine with me for a while. But his commitment to his family would impede our happiness."

"I don't think you should decide for him."

"Mariela, it was his choice to leave. I asked him to stay."

Elisa's voice showed the strain the subject caused in her. It gained a high plaintive pitch as if she were on the verge of tears. Mariela knew her friend did not cry, but a storm brewed in her mind that could not break loose. Otherwise, Elisa would not react. Perhaps it was a hopeful sign the time had come for her to confront the issue. Mariela did not budge,

"People may change their minds. Some decisions are made in a rush, too close to an incident, causing a tremendous impact on them."

"That does not mean those decisions are wrong. The earlier you make it, the more you put your heart into it. Later, the mind takes over. The heart is what counts."

"Oh, Elisa, you are so hardheaded. Do you want me to open the envelope?"

"No. Tear it up, please."

Elisa stuck to her plan of avoiding any contact with Salvador. This unread letter became a source of jitters and stressed his absence from her life, worsening the doldrums of missing him. Doubts about her decision to destroy it without learning its content haunted her for a while. Elisa figured out Salvador had mentioned his love for her and expressed frustration and inability to do anything about it. Yet uncertainty plagued her. She might have been wrong, and he could have said something important. This possibility seemed farfetched as another conclusion strengthened — communicating with him would only delay her painful adjustment to their permanent separation. Elisa considered asking Mariela if she had given in to curiosity and opened the envelope. But she knew her friend would never poke into her intimate life without permission.

It took a while for Elisa to feel at ease with her choice. One morning, she woke up with an irresistible appetite for a corn tortilla. Her nose even smelled of the thin round bread Salvador often baked for her in the morning. She threw some clothes on, walked to a nearby grocery store, and bought it. It did not taste the same but, at least, quenched her intense desire. A few days later, guacamole struck her fancy, and soon after that, *pan dulce*—sweet Mexican bread. Elisa knew of these cravings during pregnancy but never expected Mexican cuisine to become the target of her little whims. Salvador had reached deep into her heart and mind. Even her most mundane hankerings were woven into her love for him.

13

CAFÉ SONORA

Milkweeds in the US provided monarch butterflies with food, nurseries, and homes for their newborn offspring. On the underside of leaves lay the miraculous metamorphosis of eggs into larvae, chrysalises, and butterflies. Like their colorful counterparts, many Mexican immigrants brought their wives along, and others sent for them later. The process of Americanization of their children began. Salvador followed suit and filed requests for the permanent residence of his wife and son. He explained the process to Rosa in a letter two weeks after his court date.

"Be patient. My lawyer says it will take several years before they approve it. He will do his best. I plan to visit you as soon as I can."

Rosa sensed his mood between the lines and deduced something had stained their love. Praying, crying, and long stares into emptiness did not relieve the bursts of apprehension that overcame her. A dream flooded her mind:

She watched herself walk naked in the middle of the central plaza. Her hair was in disarray, and tears ran down her cheeks as her hands covered her intimate parts. The market bustled with shoppers who gazed at her like a stray dog. She saw Salvador amidst them. He wore an elegant gray suit and a blue tie, regarded her, and opened his mouth to call her, but no sound came out. She rushed toward him with open arms, but he vanished.

The dream worsened her mood. Even romantic scenes were turning into nightmares. She no longer watched Salvador make love to her, stroll hand in hand in the countryside, or play with Humberto. Nor did she observe happiness in his face or hear words of deep affection for her and their child. Daydreaming ceased. Visions of their anticipated first reunion disappeared from her imagination, and the doldrums set in. Salvador had meant everything to her and absorbed all her thoughts and desires. Her conversations revolved around him: "Salvador said so," "Salvador would have wanted it this way," "Salvador will stand up for me no matter what happens." He was her life.

Rosa feared the worst and asked Salvador to arrange for her and their child to travel to the United States so they could spend a few weeks together. He dismissed her request and promised to bring them to Aurora, Illinois. His plans included saving money to prepare a home for them before the INS granted their visas. He was candid and emphasized this sentence in a letter, but it did not reassure Rosa. She noticed his lack of mention of God and realized the omission had been going on for a while. This observation confirmed the ungodly sentiments that brewed in his mind, and her misgivings worsened when the lines did not acknowledge deep affection for her. His words lacked passion and ended with,

"Kisses to you and Humberto from your husband who loves you."

The farewell did not appease her; the lukewarm words changed her mood and perceptions. She saw flowers grow pale and bird songs turn sad. The mountains closed on her, the sun shed angry heat, and the moonlight spooked living creatures. Her weeping child toddled by, grabbing her skirt, but she ignored him and drifted into darkness, her eyes wet from crying. She let the house fall into disarray, took refuge in bed, and stood up only to feed her son or help him get dressed.

Rosa's mother became alarmed. She had been waiting to hear from her daughter for three days. The elderly lady found her in bed with her face down, all the curtains open, and the sun suffocating the room. Little Humberto was sobbing in a corner. Tears ran down his face, and snot dripped from his nostrils down his lips.

"Rosa, what's happening?" her mom asked.

"I am losing Salvador."

"Your husband loves you. He promised to take care of you as long as he lives."

"His love is dying. I can sense it in his letters."

"Women go through periods of insecurity. For your child's sake, you must think differently."

"I can't. I don't know what to do."

Her mother tried to calm Rosa and reasoned with her, wielding some arguments. Young people placed too much emphasis on love and did not realize a marriage contract entailed much more than that. Every married couple went through awful times and faced difficulties, but these problems ended up tightening the links between the spouses. Her experience confirmed her opinion. Her husband had been a dutiful man but had also engaged in sexual affairs. She concluded with caution,

"Men are men. They are tough to handle. Get your act together and fight if you must. But don't hide your head in the sand like an ostrich."

After their conversation, the grandmother fed her grandson, made coffee, and left.

Rosa suspected another woman in Salvador's life, an idea that caused her severe distress. The more she tried to avoid the thought, the more it stuck in her mind, her foreboding so intense it paralyzed her. Her mother's words lingered in her mind as Rosa packed for her departure to Guadalajara. She wrote a note and explained her decision:

"Mamá, don't panic. I left for Guadalajara with Little Humberto. We are going to El Norte to meet Salvador. Don't tell him anything. I'll call you when I arrive."

Humberto and Rosa arrived in Guadalajara in mid-September 1986. The city bustled with traffic and pedestrians. A fresh breeze from the mountains tempered the sunny morning heat. Rosa ignored her surroundings and barely noticed the cars and the murmur of passersby's conversations. Little Humberto pulled her arm and dragged along her side with his eyes wide open.

El Heraldo, a major newspaper, displayed multiple listings of traffickers who offered their services to transport anyone into the US with no hassles, or so they promised. In various Mexican towns, a well-developed network connected the human cargo to their organizations on the border. A friend referred her to a lady. She warned Rosa about the danger of crossing to the US with a child. A group of reliable coyotes would safely deliver mother and son to their destination. The service cost seven hundred dollars, most of the money saved from Salvador's checks. But she needed to rescue her family.

The next day, Rosa and Humberto boarded the bus to Nogales, Sonora. The vehicle rode full of men. A few women traveled alone or with children older than her son. The boy sat in a window seat and stared at the surroundings, storing moments destined to oblivion in his memory. Rosa kept her alertness, focused on her child and the purpose of her trip, and dozed off only after holding his hand. Humberto now and then cried out of tiredness. She reassured him his father would soon take him to the zoo, where he would watch those lovely animals that his dad mentioned in his letters. On the three-day journey, the bus ran through ever-changing scenery from the south of Mexico to the northern states — sunny, rainy, foggy, bright, dark, green, blue, dry, deserted, bustling, cold, warm. All passed by them as on a movie screen. The vehicle's constant roaring transformed these landscapes into a monotonous, non-descriptive view.

In moments of quietness, her thoughts drifted to her husband. She conjured up her imagined vision of the other woman in his life. She must be a Gringa with rounder hips than mine, Rosa thought, and most likely blond. Men enjoy new sweethearts with a hair color different from their wives'. Rosa envisioned her laughing with her fleshy red lips open to unveil perfect white teeth to Salvador, the jealous spouse becoming upset as she tried to turn these thoughts off. Her mind did not obey, and the brazen images lingered. Little did she know there was more resemblance between Elisa and her than she had ever dreamed: deeply in love with Salvador, the expectant mother of one of his children, an attractive brunette, courageous, dedicated to her man, and ready to sacrifice her life for him.

In the late afternoon, the bus reached Nogales, Mexico. Folks dozed off at their siestas under a cloudless steel-blue sky. The September temperature hit 94 F, cooking the spacious streets where shingle-roofed arcades afforded the only protection to the beleaguered pedestrians. A few rundown Chevrolets and Fords rattled on under the casual look of several business owners who sat at their store doors. Two blocks away, Rosa and her son stepped onto Obregon Street. The place bustled with shoppers looking for pottery, glassware, leather, and jewels. Child beggars roamed the sidewalks in tatters while other youngsters sold toys, watches, or cassettes. Peddlers hawked their merchandise — shirts, hats, colognes, dresses, and homemade food.

Rosa espied the lighted sign of Café Sonora, walked over, opened the door, and shut it behind her to prevent the scorching air from coming in. A noisy, overstrained air conditioner kept a cold room temperature. Two men were at the bar, drinking coffee and smoking. A bartender in his early forties leered at her from the other side of the counter. She asked for her hired coyote, Mr. Negron, and the brute grumbled at her to wait at the table in a corner.

Humberto slept while his mother watched other travelers wander into the café: eight men, two couples with five teenagers, and a pair of newlyweds. The adults lumbered in with tiredness and fatigue in their faces. The refreshed children played and giggled. One hour later, short, heavyset forty-and-odd-old Mr. Negron sauntered into the cafe, a warm and reassuring smile on his face. He addressed the migrants and outlined his plan. That evening, everyone should carry a small bag to the path of entry that would take them through the hilly countryside onto the border. An unpaved rural road would then lead to Nogales, Arizona. The patrol agents' enhanced surveillance could complicate their journey. A new supervisor had tightened security and reinforced the integrity of his officers, who now refused bribes, detained migrants, and returned them to Mexico.

"Nevertheless, I'll make sure you arrive safely at the Tucson Bus Station," he added. "From there, you'll be on your own."

At night, Mr. Negron guided them along a hill near Nogales, Arizona, across well-irrigated orchards with abundant tomatoes, potatoes, and lettuce. The migrants trod alongside the road for about an hour and approached the town on its eastern edge. A vehicle with flashing blue lights rushed toward them. Two agents stepped out and signaled them to return to Mexico.

The migrants stayed at The Desert Inn, slept on straw mattresses, and shared a toilet. Mother and son tossed and turned all night as her mind strayed toward Salvador. Rosa brooded on the anger her husband would feel if he knew she and her child were sleeping in a forgotten town in the middle of nowhere. He would balk at their exposure to God-knows-what dangers and the bed bugs that crawled all over their mattress. The tiny creatures caused terrible rashes and itching. Doubts about her impulsive decision overtook her; her breathing rushed, and her heart raced. Prayers did not relieve her distress, and the child awoke and cried out of irritation and fatigue.

The group tried other nearby itineraries for the next two consecutive nights with disappointing results. On the morning of their fourth day of lodging, Mr. Negron walked into the inn and unveiled another attempt to cross the border. The selected location was close to Rio Santa Cruz, several miles east of Nogales. The group would tread all night. He sounded confident of reaching a road where a team member would wait to transport them to Tucson, Arizona.

The next day, a small truck arrived at the inn. It rumbled in with a sun-faded, dark canvas top and a rusty engine that rumbled and trembled. A young driver in a Mexican hat jumped out of the vehicle as a revolver swung from his belt. He muttered a few words to Mr. Negron and leaped back into the truck. His older partner climbed on the passenger side, carrying another pistol. The coyotes feared gangs of bandits who had assaulted them, so the pair kept a close watch on both flanks of the road.

Rosa sat squeezed among her fellow travelers with her child in her lap. The sun seared the route with temperatures over 95 degrees, making Humberto struggle for air. She moistened his forehead with saliva. The truck tires hurled scuds of dust and sand that hovered motionless over a road where no car or sign of life stirred in never-ending drylands. Hills stretched far off before them and ended in a horizon of tall, dark peaks. The ride lasted about two hours.

The sun hid behind the mountains when they reached the Santa Cruz River. It penciled their silhouette with a red halo. The sky glittered in a burning crimson above the sweltering soil. A soft rippling sound announced the nearness of a stream of shallow water that crawled through the stones on a creek bottom. Several curved-billed thrashers perched in a few willows, hackberries, and sedges that lined the banks. Their songs cheered the place's loneliness. Except for the driver, all the occupants exited the truck and rushed down to refresh their faces.

"Beware of snakes!" Mr. Negron shouted. "They also like water."

From the river, grassland, small cacti, and desert shrubs scattered among rugged rocks and bare soil. The group plodded on in the evening, each migrant carrying a gallon of water except Rosa, who hauled two gallons slung on her back. Her load grew heavier with time and worsened when her son rode on her shoulders. To keep him calm, she talked about mountains, a bus waiting for them, and an upcoming meeting with his father. Her arms numbed, and her feet tripped over rocks on the path. They threw her balance off several times. Motherly instincts kept her son safe on her shoulders even when she almost tumbled down. The child fell asleep after a while. She held him in her arms and let his body slump, his head bouncing up and down.

An eerie cold crept in at nightfall. The frigid breeze from distant mountains seeped through their clothing and blankets. The chilly and brutal darkness on the Sonoran Desert borderlands loomed ahead. Their steps resonated with the crunching of dry grass and the scraping of gravel amid overwhelming silence. Overhead, a star-riddled sky and a full moon illuminated the migrants with ghostly lights on the rugged hills along their way. Silent prayers rose to God as men, women, and children plowed on among cactuses and prickly pears.

"Listen! Did you hear that?" a migrant said.

"What?"

"The hissing."

"Watch out!"

"Oh, Jesus!" someone cried out, jumping aside.

"Shut up!" Mr. Negron whispered. "What is going on?"

"A large snake."

"Do you want the *Migra* to arrest us all?" Mr. Negron said, scowling. "If you howl again, I will eat you up, not the snake."

Rosa staggered under the heavy weight of Humberto in her arms, and after two hours, her legs weakened, and her arms tired out. Mr. Negron urged everyone to hurry. The night never seemed to end, but it did, and light pink colored a few clouds atop the mountains. Behind the range, the sun climbed above the peaks and simmered the frosty air into sultry heat. Her child scurried on next to her, but after a while, he sat on her shoulders. Her clothes got drenched in sweat. The child's heaviness intensified as she shuffled on, exhaustion making her feet wobble. The newlywed young man saw her fight to keep up with the rest of the group and offered to carry her son. But Rosa trusted no one with her son's care, welcoming the overture but excusing herself because Humberto would cry. Mr. Negron announced a ten-minute break and warned everyone in need of a private hideout in the bushes about snakes and scorpions.

Rosa's fatigue eased when she put Humberto down, but the respite soon ended, and the migrants continued their challenging trek. The men killed three big snakes and missed a king specimen that measured at least seven feet. A scorpion bit a child, but the creature did not belong to a venomous species. By noon, the group reached a green valley a few miles north of Patagonia, Arizona. After plodding through cattle ranches and orchards with tomatoes, pimentos, and squash, the migrants arrived at Highway 82. Worn out, Rosa put her child down and sat on the ground, her hands swollen and her feet in pain. A few minutes later, a van picked them up and took them to Tucson.

The uneventful last leg of the trip with mountainous sceneries soothed Rosa and made her fall into a restful slumber. Humberto awakened her when the van rolled into Tucson Greyhound Depot on a quiet Sunday afternoon. She got off the bus, bought their tickets to Chicago, and rushed to a phone booth. Her heart raced as she dialed the number Salvador had provided her in the case of an emergency. The phone rang. Salvador and his roommates jumped to answer the phone since they were unaccustomed to receiving calls on Sundays. Far away from home, everyone dreaded these unwelcome disruptions of their rest. The voice on the other end of the line often brought terrible news about parents, spouses, or children. Salvador lifted the receiver before his roommates.

"Salvador?"

"Rosa, what's going on?"

"Don't be afraid. I am in Tucson, Arizona, on my way to Chicago. Please, say nothing. Humberto is also with me. I couldn't take it anymore. I need you."

Salvador could not believe his ears or utter a single word. He was angry she had exposed herself and their child to the dangers of illegal entry. The emotions overcame Rosa. Only a few reassurances came from her lips between sobs when she wanted to convince him of their child's well-being and her own. Salvador had seen her so long ago. Her face flashed before him, but her features blurred and sharpened on and off as if he were focusing images with binoculars. He experienced a great desire to see, kiss, and embrace his boy for the first time.

Thoughts rioted in his head. How will I react when I see Rosa? Will she sense my love for Elisa? She must have perceived something was wrong with me. How did she reach this conclusion? Women can detect these feelings with their sixth sense. The way I look at her might give them away. Or she might notice my love for Elisa in my voice, the touch of my hands, a negligent gesture, or my subdued mood. I don't even know if I can make love to her. I love her, but it is a different love. I still look forward to seeing her. But I am not ready. I still need to adjust to the loss of Elisa. My duties are my duties. I must do what I must do for my family and continue my uphill battle.

14

THE RICH SUITOR

The day Rosa traveled to Chicago, Elisa reached her sixth month of pregnancy. Her face glowed with beauty, and her belly barely stuck out. She often reminisced about her intimate encounter with Salvador, evoking his warm lips, his caresses on her skin aflame under the silky lingerie, and the heat of his words in her ears,

"Elisa, I love you with all my heart."

Salvador breathed peacefully while asleep. The mirror reflected joy on her face after the consummation of her love for him. His brown suitcases were next to the wall, and revealing chaos surrounded his bed. Their scattered underwear, the pillows on the floor, the bed linen in disarray. His hairy toes peeked out of the light-blue cover stamped with green leaves. She picked the room up and shuffled out in a cloud of excitement. Her mind still resonated with the thump of her apartment door when she left for school. The irritating noise aroused a terrible foreboding. But as soon as she stepped outdoors, nothing in this world tainted her glorious moment.

These memories did not keep her doldrums at bay. She suffered persistent signs of missing Salvador—inner restlessness, subtle tremors in her hands and lips, his continuous presence in her mind, and stubborn resistance to wake up in the morning and face another day. These signs of depression ended up affecting her unborn infant. Elisa did not feel its movements for a while. Concerned, she visited her obstetrician, who let her listen to the newly formed heart and reassured her of her child's health. The doctor warned her the fetus reacted to her state of mind and advised her to control her mood. He also detected a soft heart murmur that required evaluation. Most likely, her pregnancy accounted for the abnormality. It posed no danger to her health. But it awakened her fear of dying during delivery. This tragedy would leave her baby in the state's hands. Elisa sent a signed testament to Mariela and instructed her to contact Salvador if this eventuality were to happen.

That night, Elisa had a dream. Salvador fell in love with a baby boy and was mesmerized, staring at him through the glass in a neonatal unit. The blond mother lay in bed in the hospital and eyed Salvador with a coquettish smile. Elisa reacted with jealousy to his infatuation with the child. His spellbound face flashed before her over and over and caused her considerable anxiety despite the incoherency in the scenes. Elisa pondered the implicit message in the dream. Humberto always filled his dad's life with joy, but devotion to his son never roused her resentment. Salvador had been a faithful partner with a strong religious background that strengthened this conviction. At the restaurant, she witnessed how an attractive blonde handed him an envelope with her phone number and a key to her apartment. He returned it with a courteous smile. A waitress made advances to him, and he always declined the offer. The only blunder in his conduct had occurred because he had fallen in love with Elisa. Her concerns about his wife's learning of her pregnancy had brought about the oneiric images. Rosa would misjudge and berate him for fathering a baby out of wedlock.

A few days later, Elisa's cardiac test was normal, and her gloom tapered off, strengthening her love for Salvador. She would have preferred to marry him before their son's birth, but their situation vetoed this course of action. She stored her disappointment in a soft corner of her heart and wrapped it with good memories. Her conversation with Salvador on the previous Halloween unfolded. Salvador praised marriage as an institution that enhanced a couple's happiness. Smiling, he extolled children in a family even though "the little ones created a chaotic hullabaloo." She bought candies and chocolate for the neighbors' boys and girls. Salvador joined her at her apartment entrance. She loaded a table with sweets and waited for the troupe of trick-or-treaters to knock on their door. The grin never left his face when he watched the children in costumes — Cinderella, Superman, Zorro.

"Why haven't you gotten married?" he asked her.

"I am waiting for the right man."

"How are you going to find him? You turn down the invitations from all the guys."

"Those people are not guys. They are jerks!"

"*Hijole!* I am glad I am not in the market."

They laughed their heads off.

Christmas had also been precious despite her father being on the lam. That evening, La Petite Maison Restaurant bustled with patrons. Elisa and Salvador worked hard until late and attended Midnight Mass. Tiredness coaxed her into sound asleep before the priest proclaimed, "Go in peace to love and serve the Lord." He awakened her, and she shook like a little chick with a thunderclap. The following day, Salvador looked sad, missed his family, and whiled away the hours reading the Bible in his room. Elisa cooked Mexican-style turkey to cheer him up, stuffing the bird with walnuts and plums. Salvador encouraged her from his bedroom,

"That turkey smells like heaven."

An excess of butter caused the oven to catch fire. Salvador heard Elisa's screams, rushed to help her, and found smoke in the kitchen and a pitch-black turkey in the range but no flames. Upset and frustrated, she sat crying with elbows on her knees and her head between her hands. He comforted her and suggested finding a restaurant. They drove around for an hour, found nothing open in their neighborhood, and ended up in a small fast-food restaurant in downtown Chicago. There, they gobbled down hamburgers and fries with cans of coke.

Elisa spent her leisure time getting the room ready for her future offspring. She knew it would be a boy, for a recent dream had featured him toddling with Salvador and her along State Street on their way to the Chicago Theatre. A ring suspended from her long hair also supported this clairvoyance. Instead of spinning, it swung back and forth above her belly. After her epiphany, the baby's name became a priority. Salvador was out of the question. If his father ever recognized him, their identical forenames and surnames would confuse public agencies. Jesus, Joseph, and John appealed to her, but they evoked biblical scenes and called for a life of sainthood, a significant burden on a child. She ended up naming him Carlos after the doctor who had discovered her father's abuse. The name fitted the family roots well and boasted an attractive sound.

Elisa avoided thinking about her private matters whenever she worked at the legal firm, ensuring her pregnancy did not interfere with her duties. Michael Kaplan complimented her for handling Mrs. Louise Lerner's case, an octogenarian who lived alone and faced an order of eviction by the American Patriot Bank. Without her knowledge, her only son had taken a home equity loan in her name. Ms. Lerner had not paid monthly premiums since her son's death five months earlier. Elisa noticed the "L" in the signature on the bank document did not match her client's, and a handwriting expert confirmed the observation. This kind of attention to detail made Elisa an invaluable asset and helped Michael Kaplan win several victories in court in the past few weeks.

To celebrate the latest success, he invited Elisa to lunch at The Fireside—a quiet restaurant where customers avoided loud conversations. Lamps shone with dimmed brightness, and windows boasted delicate blinds that permitted some daylight to seep through them. Soft ambient music rendered the place a romantic atmosphere.

"I am not a spring chicken, but I am not old either," Mr. Kaplan said. "I have given much thought to what I will tell you. It would be wonderful if you and your expected baby became my family."

"I am blessed with your friendship. But it would be best if you did not worry about my child and me. We'll be okay."

"I can offer both of you my love, protection, and home. I am asking you to be my wife."

"I respect you. You are kind and generous. I love you as a friend but not as a husband."

Her words bristled with sadness. Mr. Kaplan argued the necessary conditions for marriage were mutual respect and friendship. That romantic love would grow later in the relationship. Elisa did not budge. Michael Kaplan possessed integrity and honesty, and his good deeds and charitable work lacked any fanfare or intended personal gain. Mr. Kaplan indulged her with respect and kindness. But her love for her unborn child's father abounded, vibrant and intense, and no one could ever replace him in her mind and heart.

15

LUKEWARM KISSES

Rosa settled in her bus seat and looked forward to a joyful reunion with Salvador at the station in Chicago. At night, she slept, daydreamed about her husband, or watched her son's quiet breathing. The new day distracted her with majestic vistas of the U.S. and provided a brief respite from her constant ruminations. After hearing Salvador's voice on the phone, she felt he had never left home. He shouldn't love someone else, she thought. His voice was stifled with strain, as if he had forgotten his family. There is another woman. I sense her presence in his mind. I don't deserve his unfaithfulness, for my fidelity has been absolute. I have never thought or dreamed about another man since I belong to him. The border crossing was dangerous. I risked my child's life and my own. The mere thought raises gooseflesh all over my body. But as my father said,

"If you want something, you must pay a price."

In my hometown, several men never returned from El Norte and broke their families apart. It will never happen to me. I'll keep my loved ones together and fight anyone who tries to split us apart. If he has forgotten me, I will win his heart back. This situation should never have occurred. Oh, God, let me be mistaken, and everything is a figment of my imagination.

Mother and son arrived in Chicago in the early afternoon. Salvador waited as their bus pulled up to the terminal. The door opened, and he observed the travelers exiting the vehicle. Some rushed toward welcoming relatives or friends while others, alone, lifted their gaze toward the busy city streets. Rosa helped her son off the bus. They strolled toward the reception area where Salvador stood. The sight of his son next to his wife dazzled him as he welcomed them with an open smile, the child illuminating his heart like a rainbow would a cloudy sky. He had never experienced such tender feelings of love before.

Salvador observed his wife's radiant face, but she looked somewhat different from her stamped image in his memory. Her beauty prevailed, but the rings under her eyes revealed the previous week's ordeal and something else. She had aged. This insight caused him to feel guilty even though he knew that no one controlled the inevitable passing of time. He drove them home in the old white Chevrolet he had purchased a few days earlier. An awkward silence settled over them. Salvador sensed his wife's curious eyes on him, her face revealing joy and concern simultaneously. His expression was uncertain, but he was happy to see Rosa and little Humberto.

Salvador arranged for a room at a nearby motel. He wanted to spend this significant moment alone with his family. At night, he kissed her, snuggled up to her body, and rested his head beneath her left breast as if hiding his shame. She caressed his hair, closed her eyes, and perceived a subtle trembling in his body. Doubts and remorse besieged him. Would he ever love his wife as much as he had before he arrived in this country? Since his adolescence, he cared so much for the woman next to him. Yet, he did not notice the ecstasy he had expected a year earlier when he envisioned their re-encounter. The events of the past twelve months had changed him. He worshipped Rosa and cherished her presence next to him. But Elisa's absence roused his resentment. Touching Rosa reminded him of Elisa. Looking at his wife's eyes brought on him the blurred hybrid face of both women. He blinked a few times to focus and dispel his vision, but it persisted, fixed on his mind. He kissed her goodnight.

Rosa stared at the ceiling and thought about a maxim her mother had taught her,

"Marriage problems are resolved in bed.'"

She turned around, embraced him, and kissed him on the mouth. Her lips' velvety warmth aroused him as her kiss lingered. It was as if she wanted to transfuse back into him the amount of love that had leaked out of his heart. Softness and tears flooded his eyes. Salvador wondered whether his reaction came from repentance, sadness, happiness, desperation, guilt, missing the other woman, or all the above. Salvador made love with her. When it was over, he curled up and fell into a troubled sleep. If only he could have asked for the help of God or prayed to Him. Salvador could not and had yet to attend Mass or sit in a church to approach Him.

Rosa watched her husband shave in the bathroom with his shirt off the following day. A finger-length thin scar glittered on the right side of his chest under the light of a ceiling lamp. Alarmed, she got out of bed, darted into the bathroom, and shut the door. She stood on her toes, embraced him from behind, and rested her chin on his right shoulder. He showed her the other scar on his right forearm and explained what had happened: Elisa's assault, his intervention to save her, hospitalization, and convalescence at her home.

Salvador's eyes focused on Rosa's face in the mirror as he talked. He saw her features transformed. The subtle closure of the left eyelid had moved to the right side; her parted hair, to the left, and a beauty spot was now on the left upper lip. A grimace of concern carved in dimples on her cheeks, opening her eyes wide in perplexity. Her looks turned into that of a stranger, a change that rattled him. The pad of her index finger traced the line of his silvery scar on his chest. She eased her nail across its intricate surface, and its color warmed into a soft pink. His forearm scar's borders stretched, rugged, with fibrous bands unyielding to the strum of her finger. Silence fell upon the couple. Rosa broke it when she sat on the toilet lid,

"My God! You could have died," she said, her face as white as the shower curtain. "You didn't tell me anything."

"What for? I didn't want to scare you."

"How is Elisa?"

"She is fine. She lives in Wisconsin."

Thoughts bristled in her mind. She heard the toilet of the next-door guests flush and their voices hollow and indistinct as if they belonged to a remote past. So did all the questions that assaulted her calm. She thought the past must talk to the past, and past things were best left at rest or might come back to haunt you. And the present must speak to the present. Elisa was no longer in her husband's life, and his wife came to claim her property. Her presence would also serve as a reminder of his obligation to his family, but his words praising Elisa still resonated in her mind,

"A beautiful woman with a golden heart."

The efforts of Rosa to recover her husband's heart had just begun. She realized a long battle loomed before her but strived to convince herself Salvador had given up this woman. Her thoughts dispelled any hesitation. He still loves me and will fulfill his promise before God at our wedding. Our unbreakable marital bond must stand firm and honor his reassurance to me before he departed for El Norte. He'll follow God's commandments. A religious man like him cannot disregard them. For God's sake, he is almost a priest! Salvador shall comply with his fatherly duties and not let our child — whom he loves so much — grow without his daily presence.

After a few days, Salvador found an apartment close to his place of work. Their fellow tenants were illegal immigrants from various parts of Mexico. It was unkempt. Broken doors, torn windows, dirt, poverty, and desperation bristled in the dwellings. Several families crowded into each of the small, unfurnished apartments. Rooms teemed with sleeping bags and boxes that stored their few belongings. Children were dirty, snot streaming down their nostrils, running and screaming through the lobbies and stairs. A mouse scurried a few feet from them, and two cockroaches climbed a wall, oblivious to the human presence. The next-door neighbors, Emilia and Anselmo, greeted the new tenants. The husband warned the young couple about the dangers to Humberto's health,

"Make sure your child doesn't eat the scales from the walls. They contain lead and can damage your child's brain."

Exposure to this metal led to mental retardation and nerve ailments in toddlers. Some tenants drank and engaged in the physical and sexual abuse of women and children. Disputes among neighbors abounded. Teenage pregnancy raged, and drugs and guns grew rampant at the local schools. Salvador heard these critical things about the neighborhood but did not think it would be so terrible.

Positive behavior also occurred. There were no school buses, but a few parents got together and carpooled around the children, each contributing money to pay for the gas. The teachers worked hard to instruct children who spoke no English, and their Spanish faltered. Education ranked last among the priorities. The faculty members could hardly teach starving students who ate their only decent meal at school. Bilingual education received meager subsidies. Since these kids' parents did not vote, politicians neglected them.

The environment toughened up the Gómezes. But a few months into their lease, tragedy hit their next-door neighbor. Their 12-year-old son Enrique died in a drive-by shooting near the school, the scenes at the funeral home haunting Rosa and Salvador. Sobbing, the deceased's little brother Tony settled in the first row of pews with elbows resting on his lap and his head on both hands. Before the prayer stool, his parents, Emilia and Anselmo, stared into emptiness, their eyes red and tearful from constant weeping. Their teenage daughter, Maria, was next to Emilia, stroking her mother's hair and dabbing at the sweat on her forehead with a handkerchief.

Salvador and Rosa canvassed several safer neighborhoods. Rosa found an evening shift at Supreme Poultry Incorporated in Aurora, Illinois, to afford their new dwelling. A windowless central shop kept a freezing temperature to prevent spoilage and deterioration of meat.

The employees had to wear woolen gloves over a plastic pair and a hat with earflaps to protect their ears from frostbite. Inside, the cold was so intense that they saw their breath.

Sixty-three Mexicans, most undocumented workers, toiled on assembly lines. Over and over, employees unloaded cartfuls of chicken breasts on large tables that held at least five hundred pounds of poultry. Twelve giant conveyor belts carried trays. Rosa stood next to one. Over and over, she bent her body and stretched her arms out to snatch two chicken breasts from an ample counter. Rosa inspected them for damage, wrapped them, and deposited them on an approaching tray. Three coworkers followed the same steps down the line to fill it up with eight pieces. The machine rolled forward, delivering twelve containers per minute. At the end of the chain, a fellow worker cloaked the tray, stashed twelve inside a box, and piled ten boxes atop a skid. A forklift scooped it up and drove away. After a while, Rosa's hands swelled up. Some days, she could barely endure their pain but continued working.

Her Mexican supervisor, a burly man in his early fifties, had been in the United States for fifteen years. He did not consider his subordinates, ogled the female workers, and looked down on the men. He approached Rosa daily and whispered obscene suggestions, but she ignored him. On one occasion, he pinched her behind, and Rosa slammed his hand with a tape dispenser. She did not tell Salvador about the incident since she needed the money. The majordomo—as Mexicans called their supervisor—also mistreated her coworkers. These people supported their families and bore their superior's abuses because of their illegal status and dire necessity. When the subalterns complained of pain, the rogue mocked them,

"You, lazy wetbacks. As soon as you enter the States, you turn into ballerinas. I have pain here. My shoulder hurts. My back aches. You forget that you used to toil in the fields like beasts."

"The supervisor treats us like animals." A woman worker took umbrage. "He deprecates being born Mexican. That is why he hates his guts and ours. But papers don't make him a Gringo!"

"A Gringo, that is what we need as a supervisor," another woman retorted and then voiced an obscenity, "*Hijo de la shingada*! Papers don't give him the right to offend us."

"I'd like to squash him like a cockroach," said a man standing at the end of a line.

Rosa did not get involved in her coworkers' tirades. She believed that if her supervisor did not abuse her physically, she would stay calm and wait out his harassment. With every revolution of the belt, with every tray of chicken, her job wore her body away like sea waves would a coastline. But Rosa persevered because she must do her part and improve her family's future.

Her efforts paid off. The couple found a studio in a residential neighborhood in Aurora, Illinois. Rosa relished a cozy kitchenette and a little family room that provided her household with comforts she had never enjoyed. Husband and wife continued their period of adjustment. Memories of Elisa hovered over them like a ghost who shared their living quarters. Salvador sometimes saw a glimpse of her whenever he turned his head to watch his wife do household chores. Any pleasant scent conjured up Elisa's perfume. Her voice called him out when he dozed off after a heavy meal or rested from a long workday. It jolted and disoriented him, beaming him back to her apartment in Chicago. Salvador regained his composure, but her absence evoked frustration and resentment that lingered for a while. Arguments sometimes broke out between husband and wife. Salvador believed Rosa should have waited for him to secure their home before embarking on a risky trip. She voiced her fears and alluded to the temptations facing a lonely man in a foreign land.

"There are temptations everywhere," he replied. "But I did not go out. I worked twelve hours a day, six to seven days a week."

"Something in your letters made me feel you have fallen for another woman, perhaps Elisa."

"Would you stop guessing? Ask me any questions. I'll answer you."

"I need not do that. You smiled and told me stories when you arrived from work in Toultuca. You looked happy. Please tell me if you want our son and me to return to Mexico. It would be hard, but I would accept it."

"Let's not argue. Marriage has always been challenging. I love you. I want you and my son here with me. We will regain our previous happiness."

A few days after this conversation, Salvador came home from work and saw his son rush toward him, his childish face flushed with joy. The boy reached for a silver medallion of baby Jesus that hung around his neck, handed it to his dad, referred to it as God's image, and explained Rosa had given it to him. The gesture awakened his dad's gratefulness to Divinity since Humberto shone as His most precious gift. This awareness prompted Salvador to forge a renewed relationship with God. He visited St. Nicholas Church in the evening.

The place was far from home. Salvador had passed by it frequently but paid no attention. The church rested large and solemn, boasting a tall bell tower and elegant pointed arched windows. Inside, overhead arches joined in the middle of a high ceiling in the central nave, the design rendering a mystic atmosphere conducive to meditation. He walked toward the front rows. His eyes fell on the crucified Christ that hung above the main altar underneath a stained-glass window. His steps echoed. On the left side, next to the west transept, three old ladies and a middle-aged woman waited for a priest to hear them in confession. Salvador kneeled and stood up twice to leave but reconsidered his decision. He needed to repent of his transgression, and embarrassment gripped him. His secret sin loomed large; his heart raced, and his palms turned cold. He attempted to convince himself of his remorse and pleaded forgiveness to God, but his words sounded hollow.

An hour later, his turn arrived, and Salvador slunk toward the confessional and averted his gaze from the priest. He then glimpsed his face through the lattice of the screen door and espied an old cleric who sat with his eyes closed as in a nap. The penitent kneeled and crossed himself. Salvador's words were brief, to the point, mechanical, as if a robot had articulated them. He had committed adultery, fallen in love with the other woman, and stayed away from her to forget her. A fierce battle went on. The word remorse never escaped his lips, nor did he shed any tears. The priest did not react and mumbled a long utterance about God and His infinite compassion for the sinner. He advised the layperson not to infringe on God's laws, absolved him, and wished him peace.

Restless freedom wrapped Salvador when he walked from the church. There was no exaltation, just relief from the burden lifted off his back. A bitter sensation soured his mouth since the sin seemed to have left an aftertaste. The resistant tang clung to his tongue and soul. He perceived no reconciliation with God but accomplished some accommodation with Him and returned to his Bible, Mass, and prayer. Rosa and Humberto joined him to worship on Sundays. Everything seemed to have returned to the way before his transgression, except he no longer sensed God's nearness. Salvador missed His close contact, the relationship that had helped him in his daily life. He now considered himself a foster child—someone who craved the love of his surrogate father, held fast to his adopted home and feared to be found unworthy and subject to expulsion at any moment.

A few months later, his choking spells restarted with a vengeance. Most attacks occurred at night while he was sound asleep. He rushed to the bathroom until the signs of illness wore off a few minutes later. Rosa did not wake up. A doctor might have found the cause. But the next day, he felt so well that he procrastinated week after week and forgot his ordeal until the next episode.

Rosa had her problem to contend with—her ongoing fight with what she perceived as her husband's deficient love. She understood why Salvador's kisses had become less passionate. They were no longer newlyweds. Besides, conjugal love changed as couples got older. Her uphill battle bristled with signs of his resistance. His goodbye kisses did not linger on her lips, and hugs were infrequent.

In their homeland, Salvador had often lavished her with beautiful bouquets of wildflowers. He gathered them as he trundled on his way home— bright orange or red dahlias, yellow daisies, and blue and purple convolvulus. His unselfish and considerate lovemaking attended to her needs and satisfied her. Now, the sexual act turned impersonal and lacked the tenderness he used to indulge her with. His orgasms languished. In the past, his climax had petered out into a long snuggle and lively chat. Now, it came to a sudden halt; he turned his back toward her and fell into a swift and profound slumber. Rosa did not consider his fatiguing job enough reason for his performance.

Despite these problems, the husband and wife tried to put the past behind them and focused on improving their life. They planned to move to a different suburb as soon as it was affordable. Their dream envisioned their own home—a house with a little yard at the front, a patio at the back, bushes, small trees, a lovely porch to sit and chat, and excellent neighborhood schools. The goal required hard work, and they were ready for it.

16

BARREN LOBBIES

S t. Mary Hospital in Milwaukee commanded a lovely view of the Lake Michigan shoreline. Hemmed in by steel-gray waters, Bradford Beach displayed an expansive strip of off-white sand populated by large white seagulls. A thin layer of snow covered the grass on this chilly December morning. Elisa's water had just broken, and she rode in a Yellow cab to the hospital. The driver talked to her, observed her painful grimaces, and comforted her until the vehicle pulled up in front of the building. She pushed the car door open, held on to the frame to keep her pregnant belly from throwing her balance off, and eased her feet to the ground. Her steps were slow, her back arched backward, and her legs slightly apart beneath her precious load.

A wheelchair rolled her to the delivery floor, where the ward station bustled with clerks and nurses. The clinical personnel kept track of the progress of the deliveries on dozens of monitors. A soft-spoken black nurse ushered her into her assigned area through dimly lit and barren lobbies where a few visitors were at the door of some rooms. Their presence sank Elisa into forlornness, prompting her to place a hand over her belly to relieve her emotional pang. Her baby's kick raised her navel like a nose in a ski mask, and the lump slithered on her stomach and disappeared by the right flank.

In her room, monitors scrolled with delivery graphics and vital sign recordings. A uterine contraction surged on the screen. Elisa closed her eyes, concentrated, and talked to baby Carlos as though he were already in front of her. If only he could help her with the delivery. The clock seemed at a standstill as machine noises echoed in the silent room. A nurse checked the dilatation of Elisa's cervix and asked,

"Are you sure you don't want an epidural?"

"No, thanks, ouch!" she felt the mighty power of heaving muscles, rendering her speechless. "I want to feel my son."

The contractions grew intense, her face reddened with pain, and cold sweat ran down her forehead. Elisa wiped it off with the back of her hand. I wish Salvador were here with me, she thought. He could have held my hand and looked into my eyes with the appeasing power of his. For a moment, claustrophobia overtook her as if the walls were closing in on her. The nurse returned and, after a cursive inspection, announced with a pleasant smile,

"Your child is coming. This baby is ridiculously hairy!"

From that instant, Elisa knew that Carlos would take after his father. A big grin crossed her face because, after all, she would have Salvador with her. The thought comforted her, but another uterine contraction halted her breathing, hit the bottom of her pelvis like a catapult, and grabbed her loins fiercely, bringing her back to reality. A sudden snap resounded, and a swift wave of relief ran throughout her body. Carlos' cry burst out as air rushed into his lung passages and set off for his life on Earth. Elisa looked at her boy and peeked at the calendar on the wall: December 20, 1986, an excellent day to be born, she thought.

The delivery took sixteen hours. Elisa embraced her child, and frisky happiness overflowed inside her with a sensation far more robust than any other experienced by her before. Seven-lb. -five oz., nineteen-inch Carlos thrashed about, his eyes wide open, capturing every detail of his new world. His dark irises shuttered on and off, the whites of his eyes shone with dark blue color, and his mottled red cheeks flushed from his birth struggle. His pinkish skin gleamed with a golden glow.

When the nurse carried the baby to the nursery, a sharp silence fell over Elisa's room. Alone, she set her eyes on the empty black leather chairs at her bedside. No one sat there to share her child's birth. On the vanilla wall across from her hung a picture with two oak tree branches forming an arbor, blue lake water peeking through it. The scenery calmed her lonely moment. There were no loving parents, brothers or sisters, or husbands to celebrate the delightful news. It was just desolation that had loomed over Elisa since the nurse left with the child in her arms.

When the baby had lain in her arms, the mother rejoiced in his companionship. He dazzled her with his presence, lifting her spirit and changing her life's meaning. Elisa stared at her child, his soft, nacreous skin warming her hands and breasts. A fresh, wet-clay-like scent enveloped her as Elisa cuddled him like a porcelain doll about to break into pieces. The child clasped his lips around his mother's nipple and sucked her milk with hungry gulps. He seemed to imbibe her happiness, goodness, and tenderness to enrich his life forever. Awestruck, Elisa saw the first-morning lights seep between the blind slats of her window. She welcomed the gorgeous day that augured a bright future for her son.

Elisa waited for her baby's return, opened the nightstand drawer, and found a small mirror and a Bible. The holy book drifted her into memories of Salvador reading in his room. He concentrated so much on the passages that he never heard her calls. She slunk toward him and tapped his shoulder. Startled, he bobbed in his seat and said, smiling,

"I am sorry. One of these days, I'll buy you a handbell."

Elisa did not even flip the book cover. She had already experienced enough sadness in his absence and needed no other reminder. She picked up the mirror. Her face lit up with pink cheeks as dark circles framed her eyes with tiredness. Her hair was unruly. She smoothed it out, put on lipstick, and saw herself beautiful. The image surprised her. Elisa did not remember the last time her good looks had impressed her. It must have been when she was a child. To her, her newborn baby cleaned the grime accumulated in her soul over the years of abuse. I should stay beautiful for my new man, Carlos, Elisa thought. Will he be a lawyer, a doctor, or an influential politician? I want him to be kind and honest, a man of integrity like his father. Will he love his single mother? He might be ashamed of introducing me to his friends. No, he won't. He must grow independent and proud of his heritage. How will he react when he learns his maternal grandfather's story? Will he understand the reason his father never raised him? Her barrage of ideas led to a restless sleep at night.

Mariela walked into her hospital room the following day with a bouquet of roses. She scrutinized the baby briefly and proclaimed Carlos' resemblance to Salvador, confirming the mother's observation. Mariela again questioned Elisa's decision to keep the father of her son in the dark. But Elisa did not budge.

Her discharge from the hospital occurred the next day. Mr. Kaplan waited at the main door to drive the mother and the child home. Cold and crisp, the morning awoke with a thick layer of soft mist that shielded the lake water as sunlight rebounded from icy pavements. She heard the joyful voices of children at play and listened to their lively romps. Flocks of finches flew around, and a red cardinal perched on a small fence in a deserted soccer field. Life welcomed its brand-new offspring. Elisa rode in the back seat with the baby in her lap while Mr. Kaplan kept his eyes on the road. He offered to hire a nanny for the child to facilitate her return to work as soon as possible. She acknowledged his suggestion in a resigned tone. Silence cloaked them as he steered the vehicle. Now and then, Michael Kaplan stole looks at mother and son through the rearview mirror and wished he could soon be part of their family. The idea thrilled him. Losing his parents long ago, the absence of close relatives, and an earlier quest for money had filled him with loneliness. After a while, his voice broke the stillness,

"You know I still want to marry you. Nothing will make me happier. I love you and your baby."

Elisa nodded at his comment but reminded him she had already addressed that issue a while ago. When they arrived at their destination, he pulled the back door open, helped her get out of the car with the baby in her arms, and handed her a small diaper bag with baby supplies. Elisa thanked Michael Kaplan and shuffled home. She huddled over Carlos and whispered endearments as if nothing existed in the world but herself and her son.

17

NOCHEBUENA

T he year 1986 endured a tragic onset for the country with the
space shuttle disaster in January, but it ended pleasantly. In
November, Ronald Reagan granted amnesty to three million illegal
aliens who had lived in this country since 1981 or earlier. The
bonanza left out five million undocumented immigrants, the
majority from Mexico. Salvador would have been one if he had not
gotten his green card in court. The impact of the amnesty
skyrocketed. Legal immigrants surged in the late eighties and early
nineties, reaching about two million annually. In the late nineties and
first three years of the twenty-first century, almost one million people
got legal status annually. Two-thirds were undocumented US
residents, and one-third were foreign relatives of naturalized American citizens or legal immigrants. About half arrived from Latin
America. A high percentage had not completed their high school
education, so most faced a challenging future as part of the working
poor.

Christmas season began, and immigrants got ready for the
celebration. Far away from relatives, they sank into nostalgia but
leaned on each other to ease it. Latinos gathered on Christmas Eve—
Nochebuena—for a celebration until the next morning. Mariachi
songs, *villancicos*, beer, and turkey enlivened the occasion. The
grownups interrupted their fun and went to midnight Mass or *Misa
del Gallo*—the Mass of the Cock. (In olden times, peasants took their

cocks into the local churches on Christmas day and listened to their repeated crows.) These revelers lolled their Christmas Day away in a drowsy state, resting their voices and stomachs. In the meantime, their Anglo-Saxon counterparts stayed well awake and relished their dietary abuses.

That year, the holiday looked auspicious for the Gómez and their Mexican friends. They planned to celebrate Christmas Eve together and thank God for his blessings. No one took for granted good health, decent jobs, and a roof over their heads. These graces required much effort. In the early evening, Salvador rattled his beat-up Chevrolet onto their hosts' driveway and walked into the multicolor-light-festooned home. Lavish food awaited them in a dining room with a Nativity set and a Christmas tree. After enjoying tapas and entrees, everyone reveled in the finished basement until well into the morning. The party ended with effusive hugs and well wishes for Feliz *Navidad*. The hosts and guests promised to meet again.

Everyone at the party considered the Gómezes a happy family. No one realized the hard times they endured. Rosa contended with Salvador's choking spells since she woke up one night and found him sitting up, pale, short of breath, with cold sweat, and his arms pressing on the mattress. He was about to flee from the bedroom and hide. The next day, she took him to their family physician, Dr. Antonio Ramos, who earned his medical degree from the University of San Luis Potosi in Mexico and graduated with honors. He then completed five years of residency training in surgery at the University of Illinois. His office in Joliet, Illinois, bustled with walk-in patients, insured and uninsured. He diagnosed Salvador's condition,

"You have panic attacks. Stress, fatigue, frustrations, fears, and unhappiness can set them off. Sometimes, we find no reason."

Had Rosa been superstitious, she would have concluded her husband was the target of a curse. The women in her hometown believed in spells and touted the curative powers of some remedies, such as peppermint oil, lobelia, aniseeds, almond oil, or parsley tea.

Other requisites for the healing ceremonies included hair, fingernails, or sweat gathered from the sick and candles. A brief verse followed a recital. Rosa did not believe in curses or spells. In her view, the attacks resulted from the grotesque attempt of the present to talk to the past. Communication broke through the barrier of time. She concluded the severity and frequency of her husband's attacks measured his attachment to the other woman whose ghost still seemed to linger in their home.

Rosa counted on the gradual separation between the present and the past to abort this miscommunication. The first year did not wear down the image of Elisa in Salvador's mind. He sat in an armchair and pretended to read, but his brain brooded over his absent beloved. His thoughts basked in scenarios of what his life would have been if he had stayed with her. He pictured himself holding her hand and escaping far away with her, their faces full of joy. This imaginary elopement infused freedom into him and transported him to the forbidden Garden of Eden. He considered his sin like Eve's. Hers had condemned humanity to pain and mortality, and his own doomed him to sinful yearnings and desire for another woman.

Salvador thought of Elisa's unselfishness. She had given him up. She never tried to win him back or prevent him from abandoning his commitments to his family. These ruminations made him feel guilty, and his mind sped up like an unbridled horse. Salvador wondered why fate made him fall in love with Elisa. He asked himself what would have happened if he had stopped her at the court hearing and shouted how much he loved her. People sometimes confronted painful choices like his temptation to leave his family. While his vigorous love for Elisa grew out of friendship and passion, the one for Rosa was slow, steady, and firm like rolling iron drums. The former relied on equal partnerships, and the latter on his leadership of a marital union whose bonds tied husband and wife. These included their child, holy matrimony, upbringing, homeland, his duty toward God, the family, and the Church. None of these restraints erased his feelings for Elisa, and he wondered whether this eradication would ever happen. The dilemma might get resolved in his mind but never in his heart. These soliloquies always reached the same conclusion: some questions had no answers.

A few times, Salvador could not fight the temptation to contact Elisa. He called Mariela, who returned none of his calls or repeated the same litany,

"Please, don't ask me. Elisa is fine. That is all I can tell you. I can't reveal her address."

Mariela told Elisa about his frantic calls. The news saddened her, but she expected time to heal their wounds and hoped he could find happiness and peace of mind with his family. His last call to Mariela elicited a humiliating backlash,

"Don't call me again! Elisa doesn't want to see you!"

Salvador stopped calling, drove to the law firm headquarters, and found his access denied for various reasons. "He did not have an appointment," "his business was personal," or "Ms. Mariela Sanchez was not available." He waited for her and watched the main building door from the bar across the street. She used another exit. He espied her going out with a coworker, but when he attempted to get near her, she rushed into a taxicab and vanished.

Trivial events or circumstances evoked flashbacks in Salvador. The trigger often resembled situations he had experienced with Elisa during their months of cohabitation. On one occasion, he turned the TV on, and the movie "A Man and a Woman" popped on the screen. The sequence brought back the evening the pair had watched the same scene. He pointed out the remarkable similarities between her face and that of actress Anouk Aimee, and she countered his observation with witty banter and demure laughter,

"Oh, c'mon, Salvador, it must be the chemicals in your burritos, or you need glasses."

On another occasion, he drove along a local street in his car and saw an oncoming vehicle whose driver looked like Elisa. His thoughts drifted back to the rides with her after work. Images burst forth. The scenes relived the explosive love in his last hours in her apartment. He perceived her skin's caressing softness, her lips' velvety texture, and her breasts' rounded contours. These censurable sensations beleaguered him but aroused intense pleasure. He clamped his hands on the steering wheel to stem the torrents of emotion and concentrate on the road. The trick did not help. When these episodes subsided, the grime of sin and guilt besieged him for hours.

The inner struggle of Salvador provoked periods of depression that rendered him incapable of playing with his son in the evening. His slow progress caused Rosa's disappointment, and sharp criticisms of her husband flared up on and off.

"I don't understand why you get into these moods. You have no reason. You have so many blessings. God can punish you for being ungrateful."

Salvador resented her meddling with his relationship with God and avoided confrontations that did not solve any problem. In the seminary, discussions about this issue occurred. Some used biblical arguments to support that God chastised men for their transgressions, citing many instances when His chosen people were penalized for disobedience. Others, like Salvador, believed God disapproved of sinners but punished no one before the Last Judgment. As a young seminarian, he agreed with the Catholic Church's implicit policy of discouraging the reading of the Bible by the laic in general. Many passages in the Old Testament could be misinterpreted, particularly as they pertained to God. Salvador had difficulty accepting the cruel acts the holy book assigned to a perfect and infinite Deity. He wondered how a choleric and vengeful Almighty Father could kill innocent women and children.

Salvador's premonition that he would never see his mother again became a reality in September 1987. Her burial plunged him into great sorrow and brought back images of the moments when he was next to Elisa at the cemetery in Michigan. Amid dark Mexican mountains, the scenes should have been more alien to the place than a seagull flying overhead. But this was not the case. His memories of her often had enough strength to surface anywhere.

A few weeks after losing his mother, Salvador and Rosa took their boy to an amusement park. Humberto sat between his parents, enjoyed the Ferris wheel, and laughed and screamed throughout the spinning. The family went bowling. Since Salvador did not know the game, Rosa taught her boy to roll the ball and hit the pins. The circular rides on a swing made the child assert his independence and shower his parents with affection from above. The bumper cars excited him. He wanted to drive alone, but after a convincing argument, the child let his father join him. One crash after another, the laughter of his dad grew intense, and his mom's cheers enthusiastic.

Father and son exited the vehicle, joined Rosa, and the three roamed in the park. She wore a red dress. Her wide smile and the lustrous beauty of her black hair over her bare shoulders called forth Elisa's images in Salvador's mind. He fought them back and blocked them amid a subtle panting. Rosa knew he was thinking of the other woman because his eyes shone with a greenish hue, and he stared at her with an ardent gaze. She had not seen this expression since their honeymoon. The misdirected reaction encouraged her hope that she would soon be the target of that look. The husband stopped cold, held his child with his right arm, embraced his wife with his left, and kissed her softly. The joyful child turned around to hug their legs.

"Thank you," Salvador said, "for making me and our son happy."

That evening, Humberto was tired and retired to his bedroom earlier than usual. Salvador made love with Rosa and tried to withdraw in time. But his wife held him so tight in the heat of passion that he could not avoid the intense finale.

Rosa's pregnancy changed Salvador into a caring husband who took out the garbage, washed dishes, and mopped floors. He feared any effort she might attempt and was ready to indulge her whims. His ear on her warm belly, he often felt their baby's movements and tried to listen to its heart noises, his imagination burgeoning. He talked over and over about the prospective new son or daughter and the likelihood of its resemblance to Rosa or him. His list of names for the baby filled one sheet of paper. Salvador purchased a cradle, brought a big brown cotton-stuffed bear the next day, and placed it atop the tiny mattress. His demonstrations of affection for Rosa blossomed. He often hugged her, kissed her, and brought her bouquets. Rosa realized these enhanced endearments were spillovers of his love for the unborn child. But she welcomed the surge of amorous displays. It reinforced her conviction that she would soon win his whole heart. And the husband Rosa had loved so much in Toultuca would return to her life.

On July 5, 1988, their daughter Lucia was born. A clerk ushered Salvador into his wife's hospital room, where a nurse had washed the baby, weighed her, measured her, and taken her footprints and handprints. The mother was snuggling with her child when the father shuffled in and noticed the bed dressed in white in the penumbra cast by a soft ceiling lamp. The monitor screen was off. The wife rested her back against the headboard as a small bundle swaddled in pink lay next to her chest. An opening in the blanket let him peek at the child's face.

"We have a daughter," Rosa said, her voice choking.

Salvador leaned forward to kiss their newborn's head and perceived her scalp's warmth and smooth brown hair texture. His teary eyes saw her blurry features. He thought about his daughter's gorgeousness and the immense love for her that exceeded even the affection for his own life. His lips lingered on her head as if he were absorbing her scent and taste. Salvador praised Lucia's beauty, planted a long kiss on the forehead of her mother, and murmured,

"I love you. Thank you for the most wonderful gift."

Salvador blinked several times as Rosa handed him the baby. He picked her up, straightened himself, and lifted the child before him. The newborn opened her eyes wide as if staring at her father. He gazed at her, captured the precious image, and engraved it into his memory forever.

"You'll take after your mother," he said. "You'll be as good and beautiful as she is."

In the middle of extreme fatigue, Rosa noticed her husband's expression. It made blood rush into her haggard face, rejoicing in what she perceived as the return of her husband's complete love for her. But Salvador's feelings for the other woman remained dormant like a dormant monarch egg hidden on the undersurface of a leaf, waiting to spring to life as a butterfly. Salvador strived to mitigate and control it. He believed his wife no longer suspected its existence and hoped God would overlook it. But his relationship with Him never warmed to the level before his intimate episode with Elisa. Salvador did not even perceive His distant presence.

Salvador struggled to change this impasse with God. His last attempt occurred when he caught a team member red-handed. The worker was stealing tiles and other materials from their employer. The subordinate blamed his misdeed on severe financial constraints. He could not pay for therapy or purchase a wheelchair for his paralyzed daughter. Salvador had already organized a collection among his coworkers. The serious infraction aroused Salvador's anguish over the need for an incident report. In his view, the restitution of stolen items and the offender's remorse might not atone for the crime.

On his way home, Salvador stopped by St. Nicholas Church. He kneeled in the last row with pleading eyes and stared at a large abstract form of a crucified Christ. The statue hung suspended from the domed mid-ceiling above the altar. Sunlight seeped through the green and red geometrical images of stained glass and cast multicolor patches over two pillars in the nave front. The Mass just finished because incense lingered over the place. His memory drifted to the seminary. After quitting the priesthood studies, he avoided thinking about his nefarious experiences at that chapel. It awakened gruesome details of his sexual abuse. Several years went by before these intrusive sensations disappeared.

A young priest's steps at the altar ended his reverie. The place was empty except for two old ladies in black who sat a few rows before him. He prayed for one hour and found enough strength to talk to God,

"I am sorry, Father. I haven't spoken to You in such a long time, but this incident worries me. Please help me reach the right decision."

There was no answer. A dreadful, dead silence settled in Salvador's conscience. His sinful love for Elisa still blocked his relationship with God. Disappointed, he stood up, dipped his fingers in holy water, and crossed himself before scrambling down the church stoop.

In contrast to the religious issue, his household made progress. In the summer of 1990, the Gómezes surveyed some suburbs to search for a home. They found a little house in a well-kept neighborhood in Naperville with trees flanking a quiet street and white children on bicycles. The single-story house boasted a small front yard and a backyard with tall trees. But what caught their attention was a white façade with blue-framed windows that reminded them of a children's tale. A sign displayed the phone number of the real estate agent, Ms. Melissa Osborne. The couple made an appointment with her.

It was Sunday morning, and the office was empty. Melissa Osborne greeted them. Tall and thin, she towered over Rosa and almost surpassed Salvador. Her black dress, high-heeled shoes, and a silver brooch on the left side of her chest conveyed a professional appearance. Something about the agent unnerved Rosa. Ms. Osborne spoke with assertiveness. But her smile stretched strained between tight mandibles, changing her expression into a forced grin. The Mexican appearance of the potential tenants unsettled the business-woman. She soon recovered her composure and readjusted her disposition to handle minority customers. They would meet a week from today. Ms. Osborne knew how to steer Latinos to specific locations away from white communities. Otherwise, the neighbors would uproar, fearing a decline in home values.

When Sunday came, Ms. Osborne fell ill and sent an assistant, Margaret Loretto. The inexperienced saleswoman did not realize the unofficial restrictions imposed on some ethnic groups. She drove husband and wife to visit their home of childhood tales. The place was empty. Salvador and Rosa admired the small, cozy rooms and excellent housing conditions. Its beauty impresses them. The couple afforded the down payment and mortgage. The next day, the naïve agent informed her boss of their clients' interest in the home. Ms. Osborne went berserk,

"Naperville! Are you crazy? Do you want us to lose our business in the area?"

"I am sorry. I didn't know since you didn't write it down for me."

"Write? You are out of your mind! Do you want us to be sued?"

Her tirade growled for a while. The following Sunday, Ms. Osborne met with Rosa and Salvador. With their financial statements, the couple walked in, ready to sign a contract. Ms. Osborne apologized for the inconvenience her illness might have caused. She focused on some papers on her desk and cooed a few words about their unavailable selected property. Someone had stolen a march on them. Ms. Osborne then suggested Romeoville, a suburb where agencies were ushering their minority potential buyers and renters. But the couple fumed with disappointment. Salvador and Rosa exchanged glances and declined her offer. He considered voicing his complaint: the problem was their race. But his prudence prevailed. What would he gain by saying so? In life, one should choose one's battles, or one would always fight someone in court, he thought. He let it go.

The negative experience affected the Gómezes, who only looked for another home five months later. They met a Cuban real estate agent, Juan Hernandez. Stout and short, he enjoyed a kind disposition. His melodious accent reassured customers of his honesty,

"I have the place for you, a new suburb, a beautiful area. You'll love it over there!"

Hernandez directed them to a new residential area, Bolingbrook, a housing development where a mixed population of whites, Chinese, blacks, and Latinos found a haven. Salvador and Rosa bought a two-story home. It boasted a small front yard with two young oak trees and a backyard at the edge of a forest preserve. The upper floor contained two bedrooms, and the lower a cozy family room and a spacious living room. In the kitchen, a large French window opened to the backyard, letting in plenty of sunlight. There, Rosa kept the grass impeccable and enjoyed her roses.

Their house bloomed in the winter of 1992, ready to host the Christmas celebration. It was their turn. For most of their guests, the past six years had flown so fast that it felt as though the Bush presidency and Gulf War had never occurred. Bill Clinton, a president-elect with a boyish face, had won at the ballot box a month earlier and waited for his inauguration as the new commander-in-chief.

Salvador festooned the oak trees with strips of multicolor lights and arranged a sizeable wooden Nativity in the front yard. The cold yellowed the grass, and the thorns in naked shrubs replaced the roses. A layer of snow under the trees sparkled in a feeble sun. Rosa still fed squirrels on her patio and rejoiced in the doe's frequent visits and the births of fawns before her eyes. Several pairs of red male and reddish-gray female cardinals perched on branches and warbled before dawn every day. Their songs replaced the crows of the cocks that, years ago, had announced the upcoming of a new day in Toultuca.

Husband and wife worked at their jobs, he in the daytime and she in the evening. Lucia attended preschool and Humberto public school, both siblings speaking English like a native and getting excellent grades. Salvador found comfort in his family. Every morning before heading for the construction site, he kissed and hugged his wife and children, thanking his aloof Almighty Father for all the blessings.

18

STUCK TO A GHOST

A fter the birth of Carlos, life smiled at Elisa. She became a key employee, and Kaplan and Associates Law Firm promoted her to office manager. Her knowledge, commitment, and initiative contributed to the corporation's growth. Her job kept her busy away from home, where her son lavished almost constant happiness on her. But Elisa did not get accustomed to so much joy. The past years of terror and sadness were never far away in her thoughts. Now and then, uneasiness settled over her. She foreboded that terrible times would return because she did not belong to the lucky group of people who navigate life with barely any adversity—those for whom a thriving existence was as carefree as drinking a glass of water. It took a while for her to dispel these gloomy thoughts that stuck in her mind, like chewing gum to a shoe sole.

A sizeable chunk of Elisa's past required definite closure—her parents' departure. The project loomed so large that she postponed it several times. Her beloved's absence, pregnancy, and nursing took all the wind out of her. After two years, Elisa began her inquiries into their last known address. Her mother, Elena, had blossomed in her absence, worn multicolor dresses, and often visited a hairdresser. She died during sleep a few days before Christmas 1983, sinking her husband into melancholy. His drinking sprees ended up in wailings like wolf cries that roused the neighborhood.

Several weeks after her father's suicide, Elisa received from the police two items found in his apartment. Francisco had disposed of his belongings before his death, but an unsettled state of mind made him overlook a black-leather briefcase and a large black-and-white picture of his wedding. The former lay under his bed, and the latter leaning against a wall in the bedroom. Elisa removed the photo from the frame and momentarily glanced at her parents' black-and-white figures. It had hung at home for so long when she was a child that she remembered every detail of the images. Elena sat wearing a white wedding gown, a white crown adorned with tiny pearls, and a rosary that dangled from her left hand. Her face sketched no smile, and her vacant eyes espied at a lost horizon. Dressed in a black suit, Francisco stood beside the bride with a stern expression, a carnation in his left lapel, and a crucifix in his right hand. As he had explained, the cross and rosary meant his firm conviction to form an exemplary Catholic family. Elisa rolled the photo up and stowed it away in a wooden chest at the foot of her bed.

Almost six years passed, and Elisa picked up the briefcase and propped the rusty clasp open, its screech bringing chills down her spine. It contained a red velvet jewelry box, a missal, and her mother's diary. The box gaped with a repulsive stench and disclosed an array of darkened silver rings, necklaces, and a few one-dollar coins. The missal had a black cover and worn pages that had yellowed over the years and crackled at the touch. Elisa realized her finger pads passed over the same passages her mother had stroked years ago, their fingerprints fusing. Her indifference to this thought surprised her. A few paragraphs in the diary caught her attention,

"Santiago, September 12, 1961. Francisco bought the tickets for our trip to Chicago. We are going through terrible times, but I do not get upset. When I married, I decided to always submit to his orders. Is obedience not what our mother Church expects from a wife?"

"Chicago, December 4, 1963. Elisa was born two days ago. I have lost my husband because he looks at the baby and pays no attention to me. Francisco loves her more than he loves me."

Nowhere did she find any mention of her father's abuses, just a litany of jealous words and expressions of relief at the departure of Elisa for the military.

"After so many years, I have Francisco all to myself. He is affectionate. This evening, for the first time since we arrived in this country, he surprised me with an *alfajor*. He knows how much I like this pastry."

The mother addressed no loving words to her only daughter. Elisa consigned the missal and the diary into flames in her fireplace and tossed the jewelry box and the briefcase into a garbage can.

Elena's remains rested at Saint Boniface Cemetery. It was next to the intersection of Lawrence and Clark in Chicago, close to the couple's home. Only her husband and the parish priest had witnessed her burial. Elisa visited it to determine whether the headstone acknowledged her existence or confirmed her estrangement from their lives. Her grave was in the middle of long lines of tombs that stretched across the holy place. On a rainy day, under a large black umbrella, Elisa stood before it and braced for any unexpected emotion. A small square marble headstone was flush with the ground, its edges overgrown with brown grass. The persistent pounding of the rain and the abrasion of dust and soil had worn an inscription away. She read it,

"ELENA RAMIREZ, BELOVED WIFE, January 12, 1939; December 18, 1983."

Elisa shed no tears and experienced no disappointment but tranquility at the final closure of a pending chapter in her life.

Elisa knew well where the origin of her fortitude lay: her seven-year-old son Carlos. He had a handsome face and a gigantic bag full of unexpected questions. At school, his teachers considered him an excellent student, proficient in English and fluent in Spanish. Besides his mother, Rosalba had molded his gregarious personality. She was a 65-year-old childless widow who had been caring for him since he was a baby and loved him like a son. Carlos requited her devotion and called her Tata, an affectionate name for a governess in Spanish.

Carlos listened to Tata's story quite a few times. A wealthy Peruvian doctor had smuggled fourteen-year-old Tata into the US from Peru, uprooting her from her birthplace — the Chanchamayo Valley at the foot of the Peruvian Andes. The tropical forest brimmed with little rivers, waterfalls, lakes of blue waters, green parrots, hyacinth macaws, and multicolor quetzals. In the morning, the sun rose over the peaks covered with perennial snow as Tata enjoyed the melodious songs of the crimson topaz and oropendola. Her forefathers lived on plenty of fish and game.

Rosalba's parents experienced the throes of that bonanza. Soon after the white man had arrived with their promises of a new God and prosperity, hunger and desolation had raged throughout the aboriginal homeland. When she turned six, her parents harvested coffee for a wealthy landowner seven days a week. The master let them stay in their hut and paid them a meager salary. Natives could no longer support their families, and many of their children died of white people's illnesses.

The man who became Rosalba's master arrived at her parents' home on March 27, 1977. The youngster espied him coming on a black stallion, his black boots, white suit, and large white hat resplendent in the sun. His silhouette aroused fears as if a ghost were approaching. Her parents sat dressed in black outside their hut, mourning her eleven-year-old brother Raimundo, who had died a month earlier. When the rider arrived, her father ushered him into the shed.

The transaction was carried out, and both parties shuffled outside. The doctor showed no emotion, but a grimace of sadness twisted her father's mouth. He addressed her,

"Rosalba, this gentleman is Dr. Eduardo Lorente. He needs someone to help his wife and his future children. He is exemplary and will always provide for you, so you never go hungry again or lack shelter. There is no life for you here. If you stay, I am afraid you'll suffer the same fate as your brother Raimundo."

She watched her father hold back tears, his face barely able to hide the horror and pain of the moment. Rosalba did not cry, kneeled, and asked her father to bless her. She never learned the terms of the deal or how much money the master had paid. A few days later, a plane flew her to Chicago. The doctor got her through customs and immigration with no problem. For thirty years, Rosalba lived as a serf in the basement of his mansion, taking care of the house chores, husband and wife, and their two children. She led a secluded life until a Mexican landscaper saw her, fell in love with her, and helped her elope with him. He had died a few months before Elisa hired her.

Tata enjoyed telling tales with moral lessons to Carlos. The stories, intonations in her voice, and her facial expressions influenced the immature mind. His mother's sweetness combined well in Carlos' personality with the integrity and sense of duty his governess inspired in him. Tata's values were born from living in the tribe and the coping skills of Elisa during her terrible childhood. His role models had learned to survive in a cruel world. But they steered away from overprotecting Carlos and stressed his freedom of decision.

Michael Kaplan also contributed to Carlos' upbringing. Uncle Michael — as Carlos called him — took him to some basketball and baseball games. Elisa considered him her boss and best friend. His respect for her, love for her child, and loyalty bespoke his kind heart. But Elisa never grew to love him in any other way because she longed for Salvador. Michael Kaplan seldom persuaded her to accompany him to the theater or opera house. She declined most invitations to discourage any false hopes of romance.

Sadness overtook Carlos when he saw his schoolmates' fathers waiting for them at the door. He thought how wonderful it would be if his dad were among them. The youngster would have run toward him and hugged him. Questions about him popped into his mind. Elisa evaded them until one day she sat down and answered questions. Carlos learned that his father was from Mexico and had saved his mother's life. She urged him to be proud of his dad and love him with all his heart, yet she fell silent to a simple query,

"Mom, why doesn't he call me?"

"He can't. You are too young to understand the reason."

The wittiness of her son called Elisa's attention to the depth of his reasoning. His looks made her feel as if Salvador were close by since his eyes wore the same expression as his father's. His grimaces resembled his dad's when he disliked some food, smiled, or raised his eyebrows in concentration.

Elisa's vivid feelings for Salvador never dulled over time. When the cold weather came, she liked to wear the black socks he had forgotten in his room. The mere thought the garment had touched her beloved's body uplifted her mood. She stretched her legs before the fireplace and basked in the red glow that warmed the precious cloth on her feet. Before retiring to bed, she washed the socks with a soft detergent, hung them to dry on a hanger, and stowed them away in impeccable condition. To her surprise, one night after this routine, she enjoyed a vivid dream:

Salvador looked handsome, his vanilla skin, dark hair, and eyes full of love. He and Elisa walked with their arms around each other's shoulders. She noticed her heart throbbing along with his. The stars shone in the quiet night as the lovers leaned against a wall and kissed, their tongues swerving inside each other's mouths. Their steps resounded on a deserted street that led to a small bridge overlooking a river she could not recognize. Ballast stones paved the two arches under which the water crawled.

"I hear people coming," she said.

"It is okay. Let them come and see how much we love each other."

They hugged in the moonlight as water ripples sprinkled the air with music. Salvador stood against an iron railing and encircled her with his arms. Elisa sensed him as warm and adorable in her entrails as their surroundings. Children giggled, and groups of people passed by, paying no attention to their amorous embrace. She became conscious of their intimacy, but no uneasiness hung over her. Loving him was as natural as eating.

Once her dream was over, the sweetness of the evoked sensations lingered. Elisa sat before a dresser whose mirror reflected the honey-hued eyes of a woman in love. She looked at her profile right and left. The intense emotions had reddened her cheeks and lips, and the years without her man had left untouched her stunning beauty. Her long black hair dropped down her shoulders with a sleek shine. Elisa brushed it, and the caresses of her comb brought gooseflesh to her entire body. She applied lipstick and moistened her lips, the fruity flavor evoking the texture and taste of her beloved's passionate kisses. His tiny bites nipped her mouth inch by inch from corner to corner. Without the nightgown, her radiant skin shaped her curves as her bosom rose with a deep sigh. She blushed momentarily, donned her clothes, and put on her shoes.

Her pink pillows and silky sheets lay in disarray, as did her quilt blanket with red and yellow flowers. The bedding revealed the ardent turning and tossing that had followed her erotic dream. It had been more than eight years since she made love to Salvador. Yet the scent of her apartment the morning after their intimate encounter surfaced from her memory — the crisp warmth of his bedroom immersed in her flowery perfume and his leathery male fragrance. An intense desire overtook her. I can't afford to experience these feelings after so long, she thought. My God, why do I want him so much? Her eyes then caught sight of the white porcelain figurine of Jesus nailed to the dark wooden crucifix. His face hung with the chin almost resting on His chest, and an expression of immense compassion radiated from His half-open eyes. She said to Him,

"I know it is a sin, but I thank You for allowing me to dream of him."

Elisa phoned Mariela and brought up the subject of Salvador after avoiding it for a long time.

"Why don't you forget him?" her friend said. "Go on with your life. It has now been too many years."

"Oh, you don't understand."

"No, I don't. Why didn't you do what most civilized people do? Get married?"

"He is married."

"And so are most people who tie the knot nowadays. They are divorcees."

"Tell me how he is doing."

"He is fine. I saw him when he applied for citizenship a few months ago and came to our office. He, his child, and his wife became citizens. Their little girl was born here."

"You didn't tell me he had a daughter."

"Life continues for everyone, you know. You are the only one who lives stuck to a ghost."

19

INJUSTICE

The Gómezes continued their daily efforts to achieve the American dream, the path growing long and arduous. Rosa was healthy but had delicate physical features. If you grabbed her wrist, your forefinger and thumb overlapped two or three fingerbreadths, and her elbow fit in the palm of your hand.

Six years elapsed, and the repetitive job at Supreme Poultry Incorporated imposed a tax on her body. Her wrists thickened, and the shining, rounded, bony features that had once set off her graceful anatomy became a deformed mass. Congested veins undulated beneath her skin amid swelling that extended to the entire hands. Her fingers ratcheted with hard nodes between their joints that resembled those on rigid boughs. In Mexico, Rosa had enjoyed long, slim fingers with nacreous nails and soft hands with minor skin roughness. Her daily routine comprised household chores, attending to a few farm animals, and caring for a small orchard. These tasks weathered her skin but caused no deformities. When Salvador courted her, he caressed her hands, covered them with kisses, and often remarked,

"Your hands are so pretty and shapely. They are like those of a doll."

She requited his endearments, petting his face and using her fingertips' soft pads to touch the delicate complexion of his eyelids, lips, and earlobes.

With her eyes closed, Rosa still outlined the shape of his facial features but could not perceive the texture. Some nights, she woke up and shook her painful hands, triggering sharp jolts of numbness in her fingertips. Sleep evaded her, and the attempts to achieve it subjected her to constant tossing and turning in search of an elusive, comfortable position. Fatigue overcame her. In the morning, her eyes reflected her nightly battles and bore deep dark circles beneath them. Salvador remarked about these changes, but Rosa blamed them on "just plain aging." She continued working. Rosa helped pay the mortgage and saved a little money for the children. Reporting her condition at work was out of the question. She had seen too many coworkers fired and replaced the next day with young blood.

Two years later, on February 9, 1994, the conveyor belt rolled at the usual speed, but Rosa could not wrap the chicken pieces fast enough. The muscles in her hands then cramped, and her fingers bent inward like a claw. Her scream prompted a worker on the line to press the emergency button and stop the belt. Rosa could not move her hands. Her face turned pale, and tears ran down her cheeks. She held her palms against her belly and huddled over them as if hiding them from pain.

A coworker took her to a nearby clinic, the Advance Occupational Center, where Rosa lay on a couch. Ms. Lambratanos, a corpulent nurse with bleached blonde hair, checked her blood pressure. She asked the patient some questions, her face brimming with the impatience and indifference of someone who complied with her daily routine without giving it any thought.

"My hands are lot of pain," Rosa said.

"What did you say?"

Rosa's fractured English and thick accent exceeded the understanding of her interlocutor. The nurse had already experienced this annoyance with Latinos. A change in a vowel, ae mispronounced as a, and she did not catch a single word of what these people said. From how Rosa pronounced *hands*, Ms. Lambratanos did not distinguish it from *hens*, and *pain* sounded like a *pan*. Any thick intonation blocked her brain. Her organ behaved like directory-assistance machines that did not recognize even the numbers a second-language English speaker carefully enunciated.

Rosa wondered why this misinterpretation occurred. In Spanish-speaking countries, most people from diverse birthplaces communicated with one another with minimal effort. A Chilean had no problem conversing with a Puerto Rican. Latinos could even talk with Americans who spoke Spanish with a heavy lilt. The English language required accurate pronunciation, which did not spare English-speaking peers. Even in the British Parliament, representatives from various areas of their country resorted to writing the questions to understand each other. Most native speakers tried hard and used common sense to comprehend foreign-born individuals. But Ms. Lambratanos did not.

A few minutes later, Dr. Manford swaggered in and smiled at Rosa. Bald and obese, he rumpled his rugged face with a sarcastic smile that stretched a brown-dyed mustache. Dark-framed glasses hid wary brown eyes. He asked the nurse whether she had performed the urine test. This procedure consisted of a detailed drug screening. If the company got lucky, and the test strip detected alcohol or traces of an illicit substance, the responsibility for the accident would fall upon the worker. It would save the employer a considerable sum of money. The finding would also strengthen the relationship between Supreme Poultry Incorporated and the Advance Occupational Center, whose business depends on referrals from the 400-employee factory.

The doctor examined Rosa's hands. Her wrists were swollen and deformed, her fingers bristled with reddish discoloration and congested veins, and her fingertips had thickened and ballooned like sausages. He touched them, and the entire limb jolted away. He addressed the patient in a pidgin Spanish,

"Hacer una rayo X."

The nurse ushered Rosa into a room next door. A few minutes later, three X-rays of the hands and wrists hung on a lighted box for the doctor to read. He concluded that she had nothing serious, labeling the condition as arthritis and adding,

"You and I aren't getting any younger."

Munford ordered a painkiller, an anti-inflammatory medication, a muscle relaxant, and a few physical therapy sessions. He expected her to return to her regular job the next day.

Lambratanos accompanied Rosa into a large treatment room where two men and two women lay on beds separated by plastic curtains. Their legs stuck out beyond the dividers. A male therapist in a white jacket walked from bed to bed, applying cold packs, heating pads, or skin electrodes for electrostimulation. He greeted Rosa with a subtle grin, examined her hands, and assured her he would take excellent care of her. His courteous demeanor made her feel at ease. Rosa read his name embroidered on the chest pocket: John Milos, RPT. His thin figure, pale blue eyes, and blonde hair reminded her of a magician she had watched at a circus in Guadalajara as a child. The reminiscence comforted her. The therapist attended to five patients at the same time. As he spoke, two demanded his attention, one because the electric shocks hurt him and the other because of loose patches. Mr. Milos placed ice packs on Rosa's hands and returned half an hour later. He immersed her hands in a paraffin solution with medication and confirmed that her symptoms had improved.

That night, the pain awakened her whenever Rosa dozed for a minute. Her hands' swelling worsened so much that she feared the inflammation would shut off the blood circulation. Rosa envisioned clots in her veins that bypassed obstacles in her wrists and plodded upward in her arms. The next day, she called her employer and talked to Mr. Pedro Lugo, an Ecuadorian American, in the personnel office. Rosa had missed work for the first time in almost seven years. She spoke to him in Spanish,

"I need to see my family doctor. He knows me well. My hands are bad. I think I am getting blood clots."

The superior instructed her to attend physical therapy at the Advance Occupational Center under Dr. Munford and added,

"You can see your doctor, but we will not pay. Remember to bring a note, or you won't be able to return to work. Let me remind you, there is no guaranteed job."

Lugo knew the law. It provided Rosa with two doctors of her choice whose services were covered by workers' compensation (WC) insurance. But he did not inform his employee of her rights. What the law ordained did not matter. Mr. Lugo followed his boss's rule: the employer and the WC insurance would not pay a penny unless the court forced them. He expected the insurance company to designate a treating physician who would look after employers' interests. Any other doctor would milk the system and grab as much money as possible from them. However, studies proved that their misgivings were unfounded. Besides, most insurers hired well-trained adjustors who monitored medical care. Rogue employers and insurers preferred ignoring the laws and taking their chances in a WC court. There, they found some arbitrators who favored their views.

The last word about WC cases in Illinois rested upon the Industrial Commission. The panel is comprised of members appointed by the governor and approved by the legislature. Some held law degrees, and others had just received a crash course. They balanced the interests of the patients with those of the employers. Legislators feared that some companies would move out of the state if payments for WC cases got out of hand. The appointees named twenty-eight arbitrators with similar credentials to face a gigantic task: seventy thousand annual claims. Most settled, but they still heard twenty-five hundred cases every year. The lawyers and the courts tried to make sense of a system run amok. Many workers waited for several years to resolve their issues.

Despite her insurance company's objection, Rosa visited her family doctor, Antonio Ramos. His examination diagnosed her with bilateral carpal tunnel syndrome: Bridges of thick ligaments compressed the wrist nerves against the bony canals next to the palms. Repetitive movements at work had caused little tears in the ligaments. The body repaired them with thickened fibrous tissue, narrowing the channels until they suffocated the nerves, and pain turned intolerable.

"Can you fix the problem?" Rosa asked.

"I think so. But I will know once I study your case. I will prescribe medication for inflammation, X-rays, blood tests, and a nerve conduction study. You cannot work until further notice."

The next day, Rosa went to St. Joseph Medical Center in Joliet, where Dr. Ramos was a well-respected medical staff member. At this institution, Spanish-speaking patients felt comfortable since bilingual personnel assisted them. In the admitting office, soft-spoken Ana Gutierrez addressed Rosa with the formal 'you' in Spanish — *usted* — as customary in Colombia. People used the casual *tú* — thee — in most Hispanic countries. Rosa explained what her job entailed, the accident, and the symptoms. The clerk filled out several forms and phoned Mr. Lugo, who informed her that the company had not reported the incident. Ms. Gutierrez requested that he notify the insurance company so she could contact an adjustor and get the approval for the prescribed tests.

Adjustor Gwendolyn Robbins worked for Secured Insurance for fifteen years. Tall and thin, she wore a stern face, and her greenish eyes lacked the glimmer of youth. Her slouched gait and bent-forward neck conveyed the need to hide from everyone. No smile had embellished her expression for a long time. A lonely spinster, Ms. Robbins dedicated her life to her job. Years of trying to climb the corporate ladder yielded little or no success, and her dashed aspirations rendered her resentful. Her strictness with medical providers saved her company considerable money. As the month's employee, her boss recognized her efforts frequently. But these accolades have yet to materialize into any promotion. Now, one shone on the horizon.

In the morning, Ms. Robbins riffled through the claims received the day before. The monumental task overwhelmed her. She randomly grabbed half of them and tossed them into a waste basket. The providers would mail them again, she thought. With luck, if they ever did, the filing date might have passed. Ms. Robbin paid the cheap claims and held those worth over a thousand dollars to be reviewed. The company required that she retain payments for these bills for as long as possible. She hoped to come up with an excuse to deny them. Latinos were easy targets because many were illegal aliens, afraid to voice a grievance. These workers never learned their rights or raised any fuss. The insurance company also knew any complaints to the Department of Insurance in Illinois would go unnoticed. These entities were not under the jurisdiction of any state or federal agency, a significant loophole rendering them unregulated.

The answering machines at Secured Insurance loomed before the providers like the Great Wall of China. Their repeated rings triggered greetings from a recorded message that promised Ms. Robbins would return the call. Remorse sometimes surfaced in her mind. If only I were working for a trustworthy insurance company that paid the claims on time, she thought. She might have got such a job, but those companies did not pay as much as Secured Insurance. These moments of weakness and guilt lasted for a few minutes.

This morning, Ms. Robbins listened to the messages and heard Ana Gutierrez request the approval of some tests. A call from a hospital required a prompt response. Those institutions wielded power. She had to exercise diplomacy and denied their petitions unless their doctors—the ones Secured Insurance had chosen—ordered the tests. Ms. Robbins returned the clerk's call and claimed no knowledge about the alleged injured worker. She disapproved of the studies.

"Isn't this a recognized WC injury?" the hospital clerk asked. "You must have an accident report from the employer. Ms. Gómez was seen and treated in a clinic at the request of her company."

Her reasoning hit a hard brick wall since Ms. Robbins repeated her usual excuses. Rosa provided the hospital with her private health insurance plan offered by her employer for no work-related conditions. If the WC insurance denied benefits to the injured employees, their health plan, by law, would have to cover the services. Ms. Gutierrez rang the office, and Ms. Robbins answered the phone since Secured Insurance also underwrote that policy. The adjustor parroted the company's official position. The patient could only use her private health plan once the Industrial Commission had denied any financial responsibility of the WC insurance for the employee's injury. Ms. Robbins realized this decision might take several years. The worker lacked any recourse. Rosa had two guarantors on paper but none in practice.

Two weeks passed, and Rosa's condition worsened, her muddled sleep deteriorating even more. In the daytime, she iced her hands and ingested painkillers. But this treatment only took the edge off her symptoms. She revisited Dr. Ramos. He phoned the adjustor to get approval for the tests. Still, Ms. Robbins informed him that only Ms. Ruth McGee R. N. — the rehabilitation nurse assigned to the case — could approve the prescribed examinations. The nurse would contact him. These professionals facilitated services to the injured workers and helped them return to their jobs. But corrupted by a few evil insurance companies, some blocked physicians' orders and inveigled the patients into the hands of WC doctors.

Three days later, Dr. Ramos received a call from Ms. McGee. Despite her unfriendly tone, Dr. Ramos detailed a full report on Rosa Gómez, stressing her hands' deformities, swelling, and weakness. Ms. McGee insisted on the lack of objective findings that another examiner could corroborate, adding,

"No, no, you can't convince me. I have requested an independent medical evaluation. I won't approve any test until Mrs. Gómez gets it."

"With all due respect, you are not a doctor. I am."

His words were brushed aside. A few days later, Rosa received a letter from the WC insurance instructing her to see Dr. Morris Krasnow, an orthopedic specialist. It enclosed a twelve-dollar check for her transportation. Physicians used the acronym IME for an independent medical evaluator. The word often evoked derisive commentaries among same-specialty colleagues who translated the initials as 'indecent money exchange' or medical prostitution. Some evaluators engaged in discrediting patients and their treating physicians for a handsome sum. These rotten apples told the rogue insurers what they wanted to hear.

The office of Dr. Krasnow was at 22 Wacker Drive in downtown Chicago. The tower-shaped building boasted white marble floors, and the main entrance was made of glass walls. On the left side of the lobby, an exclusive club served fancy meals for lunch or dinner under the watchful eyes of a tuxedo-dressed head waiter. A large crystal door led to a private garden on the right side. There, the tenants sat, read, or meditated. Tropical plants grew in a serpentine pattern, and seasonal flowers in a giant rose design. Video cameras and security guards in black uniforms kept close surveillance.

Rosa and Salvador perceived these surroundings with uneasiness. Inside the elevator, the couple observed a few stern-looking people. The men wore dark suits with well-matched blue or gray ties, and the women high heels and blue outfits. They all held black leather briefcases amid absolute silence, their eyes gazing at nothing. For a while, husband and wife perceived the occupants' eyes on them. But the effect of express elevators soon replaced this impression. It rushed so fast on their way up that their stomachs seemed to drop to their feet. Most tenants were law firms. Dr. Krasnow and Associates rented the entire 25th floor.

The elevator opened, revealing a plush hall in mahogany with a thick orange carpet and original abstract paintings. Four black sofas and eight chairs formed a symmetrical arrangement along an outer glass wall. The giant window overlooked the Chicago River. Rosa and Salvador exited the elevator and shuffled toward the semicircular front desk. Two well-dressed employees handled the traffic of the busy office. One informed the couple that a nurse was waiting for them, calling their attention to an overweight middle-aged woman sitting on a sofa writing some notes. When the nurse realized the receptionist pointed at her, she stood up and tramped to greet the newcomers. Rosa noticed the tall and overpowering figure of the woman—no waist, dark hair, protruding eyes, an unbuttoned jacket, big breasts spilling over a blue blouse, and her black above-knee skirt squeezing massive thighs and a bulging behind. She introduced herself.

"I didn't know that I had a nurse," Rosa said with a surprised expression.

Nurse McGee asked her about her pain and the circumstances that had caused her state of ill-being. She made a few notations, closed her black notebook, and placed it in her lap. Her smile turned into a stiff grin as if something restrained her lips. Nurse McGee preferred Mexican patients. Their cases were simple to handle since they distrusted authority and did not know their rights. The nurse scorned them as gullible in contrast to their Anglo-Saxon counterparts, "the blue-eyed, blonde-haired whiners" who posed troubles for her and gave her a run for her money. Their calls to the members of Congress or complaints to the State Attorney's Office caused much nuisance. She could still trick most of them into falling into her trap.

Rosa and Salvador waited and observed their surroundings. A man bore a cast wrapped around his entire right arm, another a neck brace. A woman dabbed her tearful eyes as a young boy held her hand. The receptionist broke the silence and let the couple know Dr. Krasnow would see Ms. Rosa Gómez and her rehab nurse, Ms. Ruth McGee. The doctor sat at his antique desk framed by ten diplomas that hung on the wall behind him. As the patient and nurse entered, he stood up. Rosa gazed at his bald head, wrinkled scalp, penetrating brown eyes, and sparse eyelashes and eyebrows. The white lab coat had his embroidered name. He smiled at Ms. McGee and shifted his vision to Rosa.

Krasnow asked Rosa the location of her pain, examined her hands, and ordered X-rays. The session lasted less than ten minutes. A technician ushered Rosa into an X-ray room and took some films. An assistant informed the patient that the doctor would decide in a few days, cautioning her that the independent medical examiner provided only an opinion. Praising the experience of Dr. Munford, the rehab nurse urged Rosa to visit the Advance Occupational Center instead of her family physician. Rosa did not budge and insisted that she had chosen Dr. Ramos as her doctor. The nurse replied in her usual angry voice, her eyeballs protruding even more from their orbits,

"We need to wait for the report of the IME before we approve Dr. Ramos' orders. We won't pay for unnecessary procedures."

On their way home, the disappointed couple silently rode under a tepid winter sun. The Eisenhower Expressway bustled with cars. The cold froze the fumes out of the exhaust pipes, casting small clouds attached to them like poodles' tails. Amid the roaring traffic noise, Rosa bore terrible forebodings that caused her apprehension. She voiced them,

"If I cannot work again, will you still love me?"

"Of course, Rosa. You are my wife."

"Perhaps you love me because I am the mother of your children."

"I've loved you since I was a youngster."

Rosa enjoyed his genuine love. She recalled when he kissed her hand, and his eyes lit up talking about their hometown and the ceremony at The Bus Cemetery. Reminiscences of their wedding night always brought a smile to his face. Dressed-up bride and groom got in bed and shed their wedding clothes under the sheet in a pitch-dark bedroom.

Rosa realized the passing of time had favored her husband's marital love and dulled the memories of his forbidden relationship. She no longer sensed the other woman hovering over them like a ghost in a haunted house. But his growing demonstrations of affection had plateaued in the past year. Rosa knew this amount of love was the best she could get and accepted it as a reasonable compromise with life. Salvador's feelings for Elisa lingered in the background. But his yearnings no longer amount to an obsession or illness clinging to his bleeding heart with teeth and claws.

Two weeks passed, and Dr. Krasnow's opinion never arrived. Dr. Ramos phoned the adjustor. Ms. Robbins instructed him to request it from the rehabilitation nurse. He called Ms. McGee, who referred him back to the adjustor. The nurse and the adjustor ducked their responsibility, switching it from person to person the same way a ping-pong ball gets tossed around from player to player. This strategy wore out providers and patients. Ms. Robbins finally informed Dr. Ramos that she would not send him the four-page report. Only the patient's lawyer could get hold of it.

Of Cuban ancestry, Luis Mejias was a junior partner in the Williams, Cerullo, Zimmerman, and Mejias law firm. His astute approach to business for the past twenty years had brought him quick recognition. A network of referral sources sent him clients for the modest fee of two hundred dollars a case. His business flourished. Tall and handsome, he boasted combed brown hair, dark eyes with a cheerful look, and a smile that lit up his face. An impeccable complexion, a thin physique with big biceps, a chest framed by elegant double-breasted suits. Flashy ties and pocket squares, and expensive white shirts with golden cufflinks. He drove a red Mercedes convertible.

One of Rosa's coworkers handed her his phone number, commending Mr. Mejias for his professional honesty. The attorney accepted her case despite his awareness that there was little money in it. Latino workers made meager salaries and received low monetary compensation for injuries. But if the case lingered, the unpaid wages would accumulate over the years. This money, plus the final settlement award, turned into a significant amount. Twenty percent of it ended up in his pocket. If he agreed with his client's employer, he might walk away with a decent check for a minor effort.

Mejias heard of Dr. Krasnow's notoriety. The legal and medical communities considered him a hired gun, an insurance hack. When the lawyer called Ms. Robbins to get the IME report, she became furious that Rosa had retained a legal counselor but hid her anger. The doctor's four-page narrative began with a disclaimer that no contractual relationship existed between him and the worker. Dr. Krasnow had no malpractice risk if he made an error. The attorney explained the report to Rosa. Its wording and length defied her comprehension. After seeing her for a few minutes, she did not understand how the doctor had written four pages. His conclusion sounded familiar — arthritis unrelated to any work activities. The attached instructions urged the worker to return to her regular job with no limitations.

Ramos read the report and called Nurse McGee. She returned his call three days later. The nurse stated that she no longer handled her case since the IME had determined that Rosa did not suffer from a job-related condition. Dr. Ramos then called Atty. Mejias. The lawyer assured him he would continue seeking the approval of the tests and treatment. A week later, Rosa received a certified letter from her employer that read:

"We notified you through your attorney that you could perform your regular duties. Since you did not return to work, we terminated you on July 10, 1994."

Rosa's pain worsened. Her right hand shrivels and turns cold and blue. A mere touch felt as if someone applied a torch to her skin. She avoided contact with it and used her left for simple daily chores. This hand hurt and lacked strength, but the discomfort was tolerable. When Humberto celebrated his twelfth birthday, the occasion loomed large because of financial constraints. Previously, she had hung a *piñata*, decorations, and party favors. The task now bristled before her since she needed to use both hands. Rosa climbed on the chair and struggled to tie one balloon after another. Each step caused her eyes to tear, but completing the arduous task made her smile. She basked in her child's joy when he entered the embellished room. Rosa paid for her efforts. Her pain became so excruciating that she shut herself in her bathroom, iced her hands, and cried.

Time crawled when one was in distress. Rosa stopped working three years ago. She still awaited a fair ruling from an arbitrator to allow treatment of her condition. Dr. Ramos suggested that Rosa go to the University of Illinois in Chicago and receive treatment for a modest amount. But things were tight at home. She could not afford to travel to the city since Salvador's income barely covered the home mortgage and family needs.

Rosa had not got a single dollar since her injury. The Labor Department denied her unemployment compensation because she officially left her job. No Public Aid or disability benefits were available to her since she owned a home, could allegedly hold a position, and her husband worked. Frequent calls to Atty. Mejias led nowhere. His answers disappointed her — negotiations with the insurance continued, his office requested an emergency inquiry, and the arbitrator had yet to grant the session.

Salvador felt responsible for Rosa's physical deterioration and mental anguish. Life had not been easy in *El Norte*, for money did not grow on trees, as Rosa had remarked years ago. They had worked hard, enjoyed good times, and endured hardships.

The moment of truth approached, and Rosa's hearing was scheduled for February 20, 1997. She and her attorney, Atty. Mejias, would face Atty. Harold Speer, the counsel for the defendants — the employer and the WC insurance company. This lawyer had worked in this capacity for twenty-five years and saved sizable amounts of money for his clients. Scarred by severe acne, his face glared with an intense gaze that bespoke his strong concentration on the matter. He dressed well with no frills and wore a red tie to mellow his rough countenance. His prominent belly heaved with every breath, and his voice sounded loud and intimidating.

Some attorneys for the defendant flinched when Atty. Speer's name came up in a conversation. He dug into the most unlikely aspect of the cases of WC to discredit their clients. He obtained videos of unsuspecting plaintiffs. The scenes featured the injured worker during activities such as getting into a car, shopping at a supermarket, or performing any other daily chore. Atty. Speer displayed extraordinary expertise in the careful selection and editing of films. He spliced sequences together so the recording would incriminate the plaintiff. It looked as if the worker attempted to defraud the employer in cahoots with the physician. Mr. Speer dismantled the cases and had them dismissed.

The attorney for the defendants tried the same deception with Rosa but could not put together any case against her. Atty. Luis Mejias knew Atty. Harold Speer well. The colleagues sometimes ended their workday chatting over glasses of whiskey. The informal gatherings occurred at a bar near the State of Illinois Building, the home of the Industrial Commission. A few days before Rosa Gómez's hearing, both lawyers met at that building in one of the glass elevators on their way to an arbitration session. The cage overlooked an enormous hall that resembled a covered stadium.

"Harold, today's case, Mr. Sheldon Frey, is simple," Atty. Mejias said. "He fell from a ladder and suffered multiple fractures. Let's avoid this court battle."

"How much are you asking?"

"Ninety-five thousand dollars."

"Luis, you are asking too much."

"For a negligible amount, I can throw in the pot other pending cases."

"Forget it. Sheldon Frey is a big faker. Besides, I have a good arbitrator."

"Just give me twelve grand for Rosa Gómez, ten for Pedro Sanchez, and nine for Ceferino Cuevas. Their salaries are minimum wage."

"Rosa Gómez is not even an accepted case."

"Her settlement is low—four thousand per year off the job."

"Luis, I can do better than that."

"These cases are only worth spending a short time on. My clients will be happy with little money."

"You are out of your mind."

"You are passing up a generous offer. I'll see you in court in a few minutes."

In his mind, Atty. Mejias added the amount of these settlements: $99,200 for his clients and $ 24,800 for himself—an excellent yield since he did not need to spend time in court or prepare the cases.

The arbitrator did not buy Atty. Speer's defense. The brilliant argument of Atty. Mejias had brought out the past working history of Mr. Sheldon Frey and showed the severity of the injuries. The arbitrator awarded the worker 98,000 dollars. No salaries were due. Sheldon Frey had received checks every month, and the WC insurance had also paid medical and hospital bills. The verdict was excellent. Seventy thousand tax-free dollars went to the worker.

The attorneys left the State of Illinois building together. Atty. Mejias' face shone with the money sign and that of Atty. Speer with a solemn expression that could not hide his disappointment. A gin and tonic made him forget today's losses. The lawyers discussed everything except work: football, baseball, politics, and women. After an hour, Luis Mejias said goodbye. The chums would again battle against each other at Mrs. Rosa Gómez' hearing the following week.

Her case was assigned to Arbitrator James Townsend. He had been in labor relations for several years before his appointment to the Industrial Commission, dealing with employers and employees. In inner circles, fellow judges knew of his controversial private opinion about the Latino worker. He believed their frequent lack of health insurance prompted them to blame their jobs for all their ailments. Statistics did not confirm his notion. But nothing dissuaded him— not even sound reasons. To him, only definite evidence should warrant a favorable decision in their cases, not just reasonable proof, as he accepted from other plaintiffs.

James Townsend had a lanky figure and knitted eyes that revealed distress. He dressed well, posed as a successful man, and resented the role that life had assigned him. His small glasses emphasized his long nose, and his lips looked so thin that one could barely distinguish their edges from the rest of his face. He seldom talked but listened to all the details provided by attorneys, his watchful eyes set on the petitioner.

The day of Rosa Gómez's hearing broke cold, cloudy, and windy. Local radio stations predicted snow before noon. Downtown streets in Chicago bustled with pedestrians, who hurried amid overwhelming traffic. The noise and stuffiness of the air hovered overhead as high-rises imprisoned them. People gathered on one side of the traffic light and waited for the walking sign. Their anxious faces were expectant, and as soon as the yellow lamp flashed, the crowd swarmed across the street, dodging cars that still lagged. Everyone reached the sidewalk and dispersed. Rosa and her attorney saw an empty path leading to the door of the State of Illinois Building. They took off their coats in the foyer. It was hot inside this modern structure. Even the employees got sick from the deficient ventilation and airflow.

Rosa looked at the vast interior and experienced a hollow sensation. In the elevator, she felt uncomfortable next to her attorney. He had a blank look and kept silent. His thoughts brooded over Mr. Townsend's reputation. He wished he had a different arbitrator. Rosa feared the outcome of her court hearing. Something in Atty. Mejias' demeanor made her uneasy. She held a faint ray of hope that matters might be resolved and end up well. And the arbitrator would grant her the money that the employer owed her. This country was not Mexico but the United States of America. Rosa reassured herself as she sat in a small waiting area and reviewed the instructions her lawyer had spelled out earlier that morning,

"Dress in a black dress. Do not wear high heels, makeup, or nail polish. One does not want to look too well or happy. People cannot see beyond a person's appearance. Do not smile or make any overt gesture of pain. The judge may think you are faking. If the other attorney asks you a question, always look him in the eye. Keep your attention and only answer a question if you understand it. Check with me if you need clarification on the answer. Your replies must be short and to the point. Do not give more information than is needed."

Rosa had waited for her day in court for a long time. Now that her hearing was about to start, she would have given anything to be somewhere else. Thirty minutes passed, and her attorney returned and asked her to join him. She envisioned a courtroom like one of those that she had seen in the movies: a large room, a big bench on a platform for the presiding judge, a witness stand, a court reporter's desk, a large jury box, counsels' seats, and an audience with several rows of chairs. Instead, she tiptoed into a small room.

In the middle, across a long conference table, she observed Arbitrator Townsend, dressed in an impeccable gray suit and a blue tie. On the left side, Atty. Speer brooded next to the arbitrator and held several large files, his poker face so little as even sketching a smile to greet her. He watched Rosa, assessing her state of mind as one fighter might look at his opponent when he entered the ring. Next to him, a lady court reporter prepared a tape recorder and a stenograph. The arbitrator welcomed Rosa,

"Good morning, please, sit down."

For a second, the quiet beauty of this genuine woman moved him. But he soon reversed his transient softness, turned around, and asked the court reporter to swear in the witness.

"I do," Rosa said, raising her right hand.

"Mr. Mejias, please proceed," the arbitrator said.

"Ms. Gómez, when did your injury occur?"

"February 9, 1994."

"What happened that day?"

Rosa answered the questions over Atty. Speer objections.

"Mr. Speer, why don't you stipulate a continuous objection? You disagree with everything," the arbitrator balked.

"With all due respect..." the defendant's attorney tried to explain.

"Please wait for your turn. I'll let you know when you can cross-examine your witness."

Atty. Mejias made his case, asking pertinent questions — the strains of his client's job, progressive deformities, and the final outbreak of the symptoms. The attorney criticized the WC insurance for denying proper treatment. He had deposed Dr. Ramos a month ago. The evidence showed the defendant's blunt disregard for his client's health. His reproof resounded in the room,

"Their denial has caused a permanent disability."

Mejias continued his argument and voiced condemnation of Dr. Krasnow,

"The employer used the biased opinion of someone who only saw the patient for a few minutes. We should not consider his report. It is a disgrace that the court called these examiners independent. These consultants are anything but independent."

Mejias concluded with a statement,

"I believe that Rosa Gómez needs a proper workup and treatment. We should try to help the worker." He turned to Rosa and asked her, "Please show Arbitrator Townsend your hands?"

Rosa outstretched them. The right looks much worse than the left. It bore a pale whiteness and a sickening shine. Engorged veins enhanced the dead-like aspect. Thin bluish fingers were bent into a claw, and prominent knots deformed the knuckles. Tendons stood out in the back of the hand like rake teeth as her fingers ratcheted down with severe pain. Mr. Townsend observed her thick, matte nails displayed a yellow-bluish discoloration interrupted by several horizontal white creases. He grimaced and said,

"It is your turn, Mr. Speer."

"Ms. Gómez, where are you from?"

"Mexico."

"I know, Mexico, but where is it in Mexico?"

"Toultuca."

"A little town. Did you grow up on a farm?"

"No, sir."

"What did you do in Toultuca before you came to the States?"

"I object to the appropriateness of the question," Atty. Mejias said.

"You already interrogated your witness. You'll have another chance to redirect your questions later. Let this hearing proceed. I'll determine what is and is not appropriate," Arbitrator Townsend countered.

"You may answer," Atty. Speer said.

"I went to a school when I am a child, and I get married, and I take care of my house," Rosa said in broken English, worsened by the moment's stress.

"Well, did you have chickens?"

"Yes, I have few."

"I didn't ask how many you have. Just answer yes or no."

Rosa's face flushed at the rudeness of the man standing before her. She was strong, but her pain and suffering had weakened her. Now, tears threatened to escape from her eyes.

"Did you have cows?"

"Yes."

"Did you milk them?"

"Yes."

"Did you have pigs?"

"Yes."

"Did you pick fruits from the trees?"

"Yes."

"Did you clean your house every day?"

"Yes."

"Did you plant anything?"

"Yes, I got a small *huerta*… I mean, orchard."

Speer's eyes glowered at Rosa, making her cringe in fear. He swayed in his chair and addressed the arbitrator,

"Your Honor, this woman had a hard life in Mexico. She cared for the house, attended to her coop and domestic animals, planted, and harvested. Those tasks are tougher than just placing chicken pieces inside a box. She intends to make my client responsible for something she did to herself in Mexico. Dr. Krasnow's evaluation is based only upon reasonable medical certainty. His training at a major American university, diplomas, and expertise surpass Dr. Ramos's. He was precise and stated with no doubt that Ms. Rosa Gómez has arthritis that preceded her employment by my client. If she has any causation from physical tasks, I have proven, beyond any doubt, that it was her activities in Mexico. Her simple job at my client's company did not cause it. I have no more questions. Thank you, Ms. Gómez."

"Mr. Mejias, it is your turn," the arbitrator said.

"Ms. Gómez," he stopped for a second, sighed, and said, "How many chickens, cows, and pigs did you have in Mexico?"

"Five chickens, one cow, and two pigs."

"How big was your orchard?"

"Little, like my *yarda*. How do you say it in English?"

"Backyard," he said.

"Yes, my backyard."

"Did you have time for leisure?"

"Yes. I sewed my clothes and my family. I cannot do it anymore."

"So, you cooked, cleaned, fed your animals, now and then picked fruits and vegetables, and sewed some clothes." Atty. Mejias paused and added, "But you weren't doing the same thing over and over for eight hours a day, six days a week, for eight years, were you?"

"No," she said over the loud objections voiced by Atty. Speer.

"No more questions," Atty. Mejias says.

Townsend asked Rosa to step out and wait outside for a few minutes. As soon as she left, he let the counsels know his conclusion:

"Mr. Mejias, you have failed to prove within reason that the petitioner's job at Supreme Poultry Incorporated caused her condition. This woman has problems in her hands, but she had them before she entered this country. I will give her the benefit of the doubt for the potential contribution of her job to her illness. I grant her a six-month salary, and the company must refund the expenses she has incurred in the care and treatment of her hands."

"I think that is fair," Atty. Speer says. "My client will not appeal the decision."

"Your Honor," Atty. Mejias protested. "How can I prove anything if the insurance company has denied the tests and approved no treatment? Their adjustors even blocked the use of her private health insurance, alleging that the law states she must wait for your decision. This position is a blunt misinterpretation of the law. I request that you ask the WC insurance to pay for the proper evaluation and treatment of her condition."

"Mr. Mejias, I made my decision. But if you don't like it, you may appeal it."

20

A TRIP TO THE ROOTS

C Arlos turned ten on December 20, 1996. Like most friends, he wore cropped hair, blue jeans, and running shoes. A mixture of Chilean and Mexican traits adorned his handsome face with exotic features. His leadership qualities propelled him to number one in his class.

Advanced for his age, Carlos often wondered why his mother never talked about her parents and avoided the subject. When he was younger, she had changed the conversation to fun times — baseball games, riding horses, or fishing. But this time, Carlos sat at the round dining table, doing his homework. His eyes focused on a thick notebook and now and then shifted to a thick textbook. In front of him, an idled TV rested on a piece of furniture with a few shelves full of magazines. His mother's gaze fell upon him from behind the kitchen counter. She was preparing spaghetti and meatballs for dinner, a loving smile gracing her face whenever her eyes looked at him. He loved to feel her nearby. Onion fragrance wrapped him in a hearth and home ambiance when he turned his head and asked Elisa,

"Why don't you ever talk about your parents?"

In the past, she deflected this question. But this time, her face turned pale, her knife chopped parsley at a speeding pace, and her plates clattered with a crashing noise. Carlos insisted. He spun the chair and faced her, the scratching sound piercing the silence. Elisa made a gesture of disgust and admonished him. He explained the reason for his inquiry. Some friends spent weekends with their grandparents and told him about their elders' gifts, excursions to fun places, and exceptional food prepared for them. Carlos asked whether she had preserved any keepsakes from her parents.

Elisa opened a wooden chest she kept under lock and key and pulled out the rolled photograph. It had yellowed. She spread it out for him, and the youngster scrutinized his grandparents' wedding picture, attires, stern faces, and religious adornments. Their deaths and passing time conferred on their ancestors an air of eternal stillness. It was as if immortality had come to a complete halt and stood paralyzed like a raccoon dazzled by headlights at night. Carlos noticed his grandmother's striking resemblance to his mother but missed the grimace and forced tightness of the lady's lips that revealed a hidden ghastly truth. Nor did he detect it in his grandfather's expression. But if he had focused on his left eye and disregarded his right, he would have seen the evilness the elder had harbored in his soul.

Elisa wanted to satisfy her son's curiosity about his genealogy and arranged a vacation to Valparaiso, Chile, during his spring break. She took advantage that Tata had to stay in Peru for a few months. On this trip, Carlos came in touch with his grandparents' background. The never-ending Pacific Ocean stretched before their eyes. She envisioned the immense body of water as enormous as the void Salvador's absence had created in her intimate life. The years passed over her with relentless speed, and Carlos represented her only fulfilled dream. This trip was as much a search for her roots as an attempt to understand herself.

The mother's maiden name, Zularreaga, gave away the family's Basque roots. An octogenarian former neighbor confirmed that Elisa's mother came to Chile from Spain as a baby. Her parents worked hard, kept to themselves, attended church, and doted on their only child. Their daughter's marriage and her emigration to the U.S. sank them into a secluded world whose chains were broken by their deaths soon after she departed for Chicago. They left no surviving relatives in Chile.

Her father was born in Valparaiso, but his family traced his origin to a small town near Caceres, Spain. Her aunt Frasquita had perished long before Elisa's parents died and left three cousins. One, Iliana, still lived in this coastal town. Married to a doctor, this relative boasted a distinguished air and two lovely children. Her home sat atop the mountains with a breathtaking view of the city and the harbor. Seagulls and pelicans perched on the tiled roof for a while, swooped down the slopes, and continued their fishing trips along the seafront. Iliana had a certain resemblance to Elisa. She enjoyed beautiful dark eyes and the remnants of a gorgeous figure that her repeated motherhood had distorted with a discrete protruding belly. Her gracious and sophisticated manners lacked any fastidiousness. Their mutual grandmother had suffered from temper tantrums and died young of tuberculosis before the cousins were born.

"I am sure there are many things in our relatives' lives we'd rather avoid discussing," Iliana said with a complicit look as if perceiving the looming memories and menacing ghosts lurking around them.

On this trip, Carlos realized his mother's touch lit up everything she did for him. Acting as both parents, she compensated for the paternal absence. He thought about her tenderness, reassuring smile, calm beauty, doting on him, and the large tortillas on Sunday mornings. Carlos longed for her company on his occasional sick days. Elisa sat beside him, cooked chicken soup, squeezed orange juice, set her soft hand on his forehead to check his temperature, and handed him prescription medications around the clock. When he was a child, Elisa had found time to sit on the floor with him and play with his toy trucks and electric trains. As he grew up, their games changed, and mother and son practiced football with padded knees and elbows. His mother was unable to grip the ball with her delicate fingers, but she ended up throwing it with both hands like a basketball.

Back at home, Elisa's efforts to make up for the absence of his father did not diminish the urge of her son to meet him. Carlos hoped Elisa would soon relent, reveal his identity, and let him understand the other half of his makeup. He knew that a sizable part of his face took after his father's. So did his outgoing nature and his serenity. To her chagrin, his conversations about this matter became frequent,

"Why don't we meet him? You mean to say my father is so stupid he doesn't know where we are?"

"Stop it! I will not allow you to refer to him with such disrespect. This discussion is over. You are not mature enough to understand."

The confrontation unnerved Elisa so much that, after a few days, she left early for Saint Anthony's Church. The building towered over the bifurcation of a broad street, boasting a high spire that stretched up to the sky like two hands in prayer. Small arch buttresses and a vertical nave rendered it a slender and modern gothic appearance. Amid solemn silence, two golden altarpieces stood inside: the image of Our Lady of Help of Christians with Child Jesus in her arms and the sculpture of St. Anthony. Elisa kneeled on a prayer bench and lifted her eyes to the Virgin Mary's blessed face. Her prayer from mother to mother spoke about the behavior of their children, Jesus staying behind at the temple to preach, and Carlos' insistent request to meet his father despite her disapproval. She watched Father Pierce walk into the confessional. Elisa bowed to Our Lady, made the sign of the cross, and went straight to confession. She opened her heart to the priest,

"Father, it is about my son Carlos. He has asked straightforward questions about his father."

"My daughter, you know that you must face this issue. First, ask forgiveness from God for your sin. Have you done that?"

"I can't. You realize God knows I'd be lying. I wish I were married to him, but I am not. I loved him. I still do. How can I repent for having my son? That is all I've got. He is my gift from God."

"I am not the one to judge you. It is a matter between you and God. I'd leave that issue to both of you. I am only His humble minister."

"What should I do?"

"Nothing without consulting with his father. But are you ready to do that?"

21

THE CALAMITY LAW

T he outcome of the hearing caused the Gómezes great disappointment, but it did not shake their belief and love for this country. Imperfections were to be expected in a society built by imperfect people. Losing his wife's income did not discourage Salvador, who worked hard for the same company at their new construction site — the Orison Building — six days a week. He made a decent living, but the job provided no health plan. The workers bought their private policies. But premiums skyrocketed beyond their means. The employer valued them and ratcheted up their salaries as inflation and cost of living crept up.

Salvador had a sense of duty and a gift for teamwork. His crew members finished their assignments on time. Little by little, his reputation as a capable leader grew among management and coworkers of all nationalities. Not everyone recognized his efforts and abilities. The company promoted several employees with less seniority and merits than Salvador to supervisory positions. His complaints fell on deaf ears. Management always concocted an excuse. He realized these native coworkers spoke better English than he did. But his job skills surpassed theirs, as did his dedication and efficiency. Salvador complained to his union, but the officials ignored him.

Salvador did not feel bitter, but the injustice brought back the discussion he had shared with Elisa. That day, she sat at a small table in the kitchen over breakfast. Her appearance bore witness to her premature rising. Not a single speck of makeup, her eyelids heavy with lack of sleep, and subtle blue rings around her eyes. Her hair tousled from tossing and turning, the fringe of her long green gown brushing the floor. Even then, she looked beautiful. Her sleepy eyes shone with a charming expression over smiling carmine lips. Elisa remarked that a new male coworker with the same job description earned twice as much as she did. Salvador asked why she had not filed a complaint against the law firm, and she answered,

"My internship will soon be over. In life, you choose your battle wisely, or you will be unhappy all the time. There is a lot of truth in the Spanish curse, 'Let God chasten you with a good lawsuit.'"

In the spring of 1998, a promotion loomed on the horizon. However, the elusive supervisory job did not materialize. Instead, Mr. Dean Fleming, an outsider, was appointed to the position. The subordinates named him "El Rubio" — the Blond — because of his golden yellow hair and impenetrable light-blue eyes.

The new boss was lanky and strutted around, flinging his arms like a cat trying to claw a mouse. His friendship with the influential Alderman O'Connor got him the job.

El Rubio endured an unhappy mood. A year earlier, his wife of twelve years abandoned him and took their children with her. Workers blamed his marital discord on his inability to function in bed. Some swung their pelvises in an obscene gesture to illustrate their point. Latinos believed the wife had run away with a guy from Latin America since they sensed El Rubio's hatred for them. Their Polish counterparts disagreed and opined her paramour shared their nationality. Every early morning, El Rubio lurked around the construction site like a fox preying on chickens. Workers hid from him for fear that whoever caught his eye would get the worst job. Rumor had it the supervisor devised these devil-inspired tasks during nightmares.

El Rubio hated the praises that administrative members and most coworkers bestowed on Salvador. His subaltern excelled as a skilled and versed team leader who possessed what it took to become an outstanding manager. Behind his back, the supervisor laughed at him and called him a 'Mexican wetback.' Salvador avoided encountering his boss and stayed away from him, as did the rest of the crew. One day, El Rubio beckoned him over, pointed to the east side of the building, and said,

"Mr. Gómez, install the ceilings in that area."

Salvador nodded his head.

"You have four weeks to complete the job."

The assigned area was near the place where fellow workers were spraying paint. Salvador smelled an intense odor. He thought some paint fumes wafted toward the upper part of the area and concentrated under the ceiling because of deficient ventilation. The painters wore respirators. Salvador asked El Rubio for a suit of protective gear. He denied it because the company only provided enough for the painters, adding that no one could inhale any chemicals at that distance.

"If there were any vapor," the supervisor said, "it would not reach your site since it weighed more than air, and gravity would settle it down."

Salvador suffered pervasive tiredness, dizziness, and headaches, dragging at work all day long. Three weeks passed, and one morning, Salvador could not breathe well. Dizziness and headache prompted him to read the label on one can of paint. It contained big, frightening names—cristobalite, titanium dioxide, aluminum silicate, calcium carbonate, hydrocarbon, petroleum distillate, and alkyd resin. He read the warning label:

"*Its vapor is harmful. It may affect the brain or the nervous system, causing dizziness, headaches, or nausea. It irritates the eyes, skin, nose, and throat.*"

A law of Nature declared a second calamity always followed the first, and sick dogs caught all the fleas. As if Salvador did not have enough problems with Rosa's disability and financial difficulties, his health also faltered. In the following weeks, his fatigue grew intense, muscle pain flared up, and respiratory problems worsened. It peaked on June 22, 1998, and he woke up short-winded. His chest failed to expand as if something kept the ribs anchored to the lungs. Repeated spells of coughing turned his eyes red and distorted his face. Rosa accompanied her husband to see Doctor Ramos. When the physician asked him how he felt, Salvador's response bristled with humor,

"Screwed and badly paid."

But after the evaluation, the doctor's conclusion was anything but funny,

"You have severe bronchitis and physical exhaustion."

Ramos discussed how stress contributed to his condition — Rosa's disability, lack of second income, insufficient money for expenses, and work problems. He paused for a second and added,

"Your exposure to chemicals is difficult to prove. What I read coincides with your supervisor's contention. These chemicals weigh more than the air and can't accumulate in the area where you work. A complaint will aggravate your stress only."

"Some of my coworkers believe the supervisor might have added something to the paint."

"There are times we must leave things for God to handle on Judgment Day," Dr. Ramos said, shaking his head.

The word God ushered the patient into thoughts. The doctor had not mentioned all the stresses, particularly his dormant longings for Elisa and his estrangement from God. Salvador needed the energy from His presence to replenish the loss from his sickness. Despite the treatment with medications, the respiratory problems persisted, and overwhelming fatigue and muscle pain ensued. He returned to work, but only lasted a few hours because his difficulties breathing became unbearable.

"Go to see your doctor, and don't return until you are well," El Rubio said. "We don't want you in this condition. You may hurt yourself at work."

Salvador hoped to muster enough strength to go back to his job. But his improvement never materialized. Even carrying a gallon of milk from the car to the refrigerator caused him shortness of breath. His frustration grew when his savings dwindled. Salvador had no choice but to ask for help from Antonio, who worked as the manager at Las Palmas Restaurant in La Villita.

Salvador visited his friend on a scorching day when a sweltering sun shone at its zenith. The people swarmed 26th Street in the Mexican neighborhood near downtown Chicago. But Salvador was oblivious to their presence. His somber mood distorted his perception since the sun seemed to be casting only shadows. He walked like a ghost, unaware of noises around him, his mind deep in thought. Every few blocks, he stopped to catch his breath and peered into a shop window. Borrowing money insulted his manhood, but he had to succumb to reality. His family needed to eat and pay his mortgage, or the bank would repossess their home. Antonio sat between the two tall artificial palms that over-towered the restaurant entrance. He watched Salvador lumber along the sidewalk, his heavy breathing and dripping sweat alarming Antonio. He rushed out to meet him and usher him in as he asked him,

"What is the matter with you? Sit down. You don't look good."

"I am in serious trouble. I am losing everything: my health, my wife's, my savings, my home."

"Calm down. I'll help you. I am your friend. We are like brothers."

"Yes, but I feel terrible. I have never asked for money."

"How much do you need?"

"Fifteen hundred dollars to pay the mortgage and buy food."

"I can help you for a short while. I have a few thousand dollars saved. But we need to find a long-term solution."

"I don't know what to do. If I get a little better, I'll work. That is all I ask God, a little health to support my family."

"Speaking of God, I know someone who knows much about tough situations like yours. He could help us. Father Rodriguez, my parish priest."

Father Francisco Rodriguez served in the local church for over twenty years. His parishioners loved him and admired his tireless dedication to the poor and needy. A native of Spain, he had left his country right after his ordination. His thin, average-height figure and sprightly gestures gave away his restless personality and his eyes his goodness and kindness. At 67, his hair was dark, giving him a younger look. If one scrutinized him, his face showed a faint grimace of pain. Some thought his lower back condition caused it, but others knew the reason. The sneer was already there when he arrived at the parish twenty years ago. Its presence began the fateful night of July 18, 1936, in Ronda, Malaga, his hometown in Spain. He was six when the Falangists — fascists — took to the streets on a murderous spree. Father Rodriguez could still hear them screaming,

"Turn the lights off!"

Those criminals called every man out of the buildings and lined them up. In their underwear, his father and ten more people were herded away while Francisco watched the scene, horrified. Her mother reprimanded him,

"Stay out of the window, go to bed. Your father will be fine. He is an exemplary man and has done nothing."

A few days later, he saw his mother crying and overheard what happened that night. The fascists stripped the detainees naked, forced them to drink a full glass of castor oil, and shaved their heads. Early the following day, the rogues shot them to death in front of a wall at the local cemetery.

The post-war hunger almost killed Francisco. The child swelled up like a balloon. He was a studious boy who entered the seminary to further his learning since his mother could not pay for higher education. Soon, he discovered that it was an excellent choice. Helping his fellow man appealed to him more than anything else. His priesthood allowed him to pursue this inclination. Nowhere could he find a better place to practice his vocation than the Little Village.

The Nativity Church was in Zapata Plaza, the heart of the Hispanic neighborhood. The building had a spire barely rising above the neighboring houses and a weather-beaten, whitewashed façade. Two cement steps led to a massive wooden portal with small rectangular doors embedded at the bottom. They were kept open during the day. Salvador lifted his eyes to a large cross presiding over the main altar. A broad white sash draped the horizontal crossbar and hung halfway down on either side of the upright beam. It had the following inscription in Spanish:

"I am the way to salvation. Those who believe in me will live forever."

The images of Our Lady of Guadalupe and Saint John of the Casas — the patron saint of Mexico — flanked the cross. On the aisle hung two murals with the parables of the Seeder and the Prodigal Son. It depicted Mexican farmers and landscapes. Beneath them, small pictures portrayed each of the Stations of the Cross. Inside the nave were rows of scuffed wooden pews.

The place comforted Salvador since it conveyed modesty. It contrasted with the seminary chapel that had reminded him of a giant bonbon wrapped in gold paper. The architectural jewel boasted a rounded shape, oval windows and doors, sumptuous paintings in golden frames, gold-painted Baroque altarpieces of carved wood, and mahogany pews. The image of Our Lady wore a long black cloak with golden embroidery. The teaching faculty justified this opulence because it was "God's home." Salvador never got used to it and did not accept a luxury incongruous with the neighboring huts.

In the central nave, a small door opened into Father Rodriguez's abode. Doña Concha, an older woman who worked as his assistant, welcomed Salvador and Antonio. She had worked for Father Rodriguez since her childless widowhood ten years earlier. From then on, Doña Concha found a surrogate son in him. Her dedication was so unconditional that she worked every day and lived in a small studio next to his room.

"Father will be back in a few minutes," she said. "He went to visit the sick in the parish."

The two friends sat on a wooden bench in a small office with a small desk, a chair, and a tiny crucifix on the wall. A black-and-white picture of Father Rodriguez' parents, yellowed by the passage of time, dangled on the wall. Next to it was a colored photograph of his small hometown in Spain. It showed little white houses in the middle of a valley surrounded by green mountains. Silence hovered over both friends, who spoke only a few words in an inaudible voice as if afraid to disturb the peaceful stillness. A few minutes passed, and they heard the priest's decisive steps as he approached his office. His figure was stately, and his face beamed with a contagious zest for life.

Father Rodriguez had learned to hide pervasive tiredness. It worsened with his long workdays that ended in the wee hours of the morning. Then he lay on his bed, worn out, praying the rosary until the smooth rolling of pearls on his fingertips lulled him into sleep. Otherwise, he tossed and turned in bed all night, thinking about the poor and the sick. Doña Concha always cautioned him about so much work and his painful back that made him limp. But he answered,

"Oh, I am just limping. It is not like I am dying. You know I have a job to do."

Father Rodriguez walked into the room and greeted Antonio and Salvador,

"Here you are! Doña Concha told me you have come to see me urgently," he spoke tenderly. He smiled at Salvador and cast a wondering look, "I don't know you. You must be new in this parish."

"Father, he is my friend Salvador Gómez." Antonio said.

The newcomer stood up and reached for his hand to kiss it. But the priest grabbed his hand and shook it.

"Save your kisses for the ladies," he said, his eyes full of warmth and goodness. His parishioners knew that gaze could evoke kindness in the rudest human being. Now, it recognized a man of integrity before him.

"I don't want to bother you. I am not from your parish, but Antonio insisted I come to ask for your help."

"It is okay, my son, you know what we say in Spain, "Reach out to others regardless of who they are." He added, "Each parish has assigned geographical boundaries, but lending a hand to our fellow man knows no borders."

Salvador explained his situation. Father Rodriguez exhaled a deep sigh of relief and said,

"Thank God we are not dealing with a spiritual sickness, which is the worst condition that can afflict a person. It can pound away at your mind day after day until your very soul gives way. But your matter is only a question of finances. We have the right person who can help you, Doña Concha. She has handled these problems for many years and knows the ins and outs of the system." He lowered his head, opened a small drawer, and said, "But you need money fast. I have a small emergency fund just for that."

His parishioners suspected this fund accumulated from his unspent monthly stipends. He bought nothing for himself, wearing even the same boots for years. When anyone remarked about his ten-year-old footwear, he always responded,

"They work fine. Why should I buy another pair?"

Spellbound by the priest's charisma, Salvador did not reach for the proffered money. Bewilderment loomed over him for a long pause that Antonio seized to address Father Rodriguez,

"Thank you for your offer. But that has already been provided."

Doña Concha took over the meeting and explained Salvador's rights,

"Your employer does not pay sick days, and unemployment compensation is out of the question because you cannot work.

You qualify for social security disability. But those benefits become payable when you are disabled for at least six months. You can sell your home and earn some money. But your equity is too little since you haven't lived there long enough. I mean the value exceeding the quantity you paid for it. Very little cash will remain after your property taxes and overdue mortgage. You should apply for public aid immediately to get some money in the next few weeks. I'll find government-subsidized housing for your family. There are some apartments available.

"Our public schools are decent. Living in this area is not easy, but one gets used to it. Most neighbors stick together to help one another.

You can count on the parish as another home. Father Rodriguez multiplies himself fourfold to help everyone in need. There are problems as in most inner parts of the American cities — crime, drugs, gangs. One should steer children away from them. Nearby Cook County Hospital can help you regain your health at no cost. Once you and your wife get public aid, the State will cover your medical expenses."

The office of the Department of Public Aid bustled with people waiting in line. A sense of despair loomed over the reception area. In the hall, a few people chatted and laughed as if at a social club. For many, public help was a way of life passed down from single mothers to their children since fathers disappeared from their environment. Most were blacks, with plenty of Hispanics and a few whites. Next to the main door, a gaunt young woman was crying. She wore a black dress with faded patches and a frayed collar, and her entire face crumpled into fine wrinkles and sunken cheeks. A security guard asked her out of the entrance as she protested,

"No, I didn't receive my food stamps this month, please!"

"Yes, you did, lady!"

Shame seized Salvador and Rosa because they had never foreseen requesting help from the Government. The mere thought unsettled them. He covered his tearful face with his hands. Salvador had reacted the same way when Doña Concha brought up the subject. But she reassured him,

"You have paid your taxes. It is right that some money comes back to you since you and your family need it. Think of it as a loan. Once you get well, you'll pay it back. Nothing is shameful in it unless you make it a way of life."

The turn of Salvador and Rosa arrived. Mr. Robert Deangelo, a middle-aged gentleman with black-rimmed glasses, approached them.

"Salvador and Rosa Gómez?"

"Yes, sir."

"Please, come to my office."

The couple stood before two wooden chairs, their heads bowed and their bodies hunched as if hiding.

"Please, sit down," Mr. Deangelo said with a poker face without raising his eyes to regard them. "Are you legal residents?" he asked as he scrutinized the forms that Salvador had handed him.

"Yes, sir, we are," Salvador answered feebly.

"What did you say?"

"I said, yes, we are, sir," he replied, mustering strength despite his shortness of breath.

"Are you able to work?"

"No, sir."

"Is your wife working?"

"No, sir, I cannot work," Rosa answered.

"Well, you need a note from your doctor. Here are the forms. Ask him to fill them out and return them to me."

"I handed you those forms. Doctor Ramos already took care of them," Salvador said.

"Oh, yes, you're right," Mr. Deangelo said. "I see that you have worked for several years."

"Yes, sir," Salvador said.

"Well, it entitles you to some benefits. But you are not citizens. It may take a little longer."

"How much longer?" Rosa asked. "We both are sick, and we have children to support."

"We'll do our best. That is all I can tell you."

Deangelo projected a bureaucrat's indifferent attitude of disenchantment with the governmental system and his life. In his view, he had attended to enough Hispanics in the United States who had grabbed Public Aid and stopped working. The official favored the notion that these immigrants cost the Government an arm and a leg. He would not make it easy for them if he could help it.

"I'll call you as soon as we approve your application," he added.

Time passed slowly. It always did when people lacked the means to survive, or sickness plagued their lives. Both conditions applied to the Gómezes. Salvador and Rosa waited day after day for the phone call that could afford them some respite. Four weeks went by, and he informed Doña Concha, who voiced her concerns about the unacceptable delay.

"The agency takes prompt care of its applicants," she said. "But sometimes we need to prod a bureaucrat a little."

Their case's seriousness and proper and timely documentation demanded a quick resolution. When Salvador mentioned Mr. Deangelo, Doña Concha realized their case faced difficulties,

"I wish one of the Indian or Hispanic ladies would have handled your application. Those women can get the approval fast. I'll let Father Rodriguez know what is going on."

A week later, Father Rodriguez joined Salvador at the offices of the Department of Public Aid. The priest introduced himself and requested to see Mr. Deangelo regarding Salvador Gómez' urgent matter. A young receptionist informed the bureaucrat about the ecclesiastical visitor and hurried him along,

"You'd better see him right away, or he'll give you a run for your money. The priest knows Mr. Murphy, who belongs to Work of God, *Opus Dei*."

"*Opus Dei?* What is that?"

"I don't know. I heard it in my parish. These people follow a strict Catholic doctrine. I am sure Mr. Murphy will pay attention to what a priest says."

Father Rodriguez and Salvador walked into Mr. Deangelo's office. On the wall behind his desk was a picture of the Governor shaking his hand. An American flag was in the right corner of the wall, and a state banner in the left. The official did not get up and signaled them to sit down. Salvador spoke first.

"I have been waiting for your call daily, sitting beside my phone. I expected the Government to lend my family a hand now that we need it. It hurts my pride. But I intend to escape this mess as soon as possible." He paused and added, "Mr. Deangelo, this is Father

Rodriguez. He came to help me. He knows about this process more than I do."

"It is nice to meet you, Father. I hope you understand I don't have to talk to you. This matter is between the applicant and the State. Only a lawyer may accompany the individual."

"Well, think of me as a lawyer from the highest court," Father Rodriguez said, gazing at him straight in the eye as if scrutinizing his deepest feelings. "The one where we'll all be judged."

"Mr. and Mrs. Gómez's papers are in process," Mr. Deangelo said.

"You have an outstanding job. You can help the dispossessed. God will reward you." Father Rodriguez wielded a disarming, warm expression that did not affect the bureaucrat's demeanor, his poker face unwavering.

"I beg your pardon, but papers being in process is not an answer," Salvador interjected. "What is it that is pending?"

"Mr. Deangelo, we will not allow you to put off this matter. My parishioner expects concrete answers today."

"I can't provide them today. I'll call you in a few days."

"No, we won't leave until we get a response. You're not the one who watches your children go hungry—" Salvador said as Father Rodriguez broke in,

"Mr. Deangelo. Please call your supervisor, Mr. William Murphy."

"I already told you. I'll call Mr. Gómez in a few days."

"I insist that you call Mr. Murphy."

As Mr. Deangelo hurried out of the room, the priest whispered to Salvador,

"If someone doesn't heed a kind God's appeals, one must seek other connections with the Almighty." He then added with a wink, "*Opus Dei.*"

A few minutes later, Mr. Deangelo returned with an answer,

"Because of the urgency of the matter, your Public Aid is now approved. Please wait outside for a few minutes. I'll have everything ready for you."

"Thank you," Salvador said.

"Are you married, Mr. Deangelo?" Father Rodriguez asked him, smiling as they were leaving the room.

"No."

"Then, as we say in Spain, may God reward your good deeds with a wonderful wife."

"And you."

"What a jerk!" Father Rodriguez mumbled between his teeth.

22

LAWLESS CITY

A month later, Rosa regarded her backyard for the last time. Twenty or thirty sparrows fluttered around and ate breadcrumbs she had scattered for them. A tiny chipmunk and two gray squirrels shared the feast. She and Lucia fed them every day. Several pairs of cardinals perched in two nearby bushes as if gathered to wish her farewell. She closed her eyes, and tears ran down her cheeks. Under the pretext that nothing was left behind, her last walk into the children's rooms ended before a small crucifix. It hung on the wall over the void Lucia's bed had left. She stood in front of it, prayed for a minute, and retrieved it.

The girl could not understand her mother's tears and why her family had vacated her home. She jumped and skipped as if about to start a pleasure trip. In contrast, Humberto bristled with frustration and anger. He already missed his schoolmates and friends. Not even his father's words comforted him. He had heard them so many times during the past several weeks,

"This is only a temporary move. As soon as I get well, we'll be back."

Now that the time had arrived, words meant nothing. Salvador kept his composure despite Rosa's difficulties accepting the vanished years of work and daydreaming.

"Not all," he countered, "We still have our children and each other. Let's count our blessings rather than grieve over our losses."

Antonio hoisted the few pieces of furniture they owned and loaded them into a rental truck. He then waited to drive the Gómezes to their new residence. A somber mood overtook everyone except Lucia, who looked forward to seeing her new home,

"Tito Antonio, how long before we get there?"

But after watching her parents' faces and the muteness of her brother, the girl turned quiet and fell asleep. Antonio tried to distract his passengers but gave up, letting silence rule over them until they reached their destination.

A twenty-story building loomed imposing before them. Faded yellow, it frowned with broken windows covered with cardboard. The intact ones languished with curtains darkened by the passage of time and lack of washing. A few neighbors, curious about the newcomers, peered out from behind them. The outer façade raged with graffiti, overlooking a small plaza where little children played on two rusty slides and weather-beaten swings. Their happy romping resonated throughout the place while older children played a basketball game. Rosa contemplated their new home, and discouragement overwhelmed her. She forced a smile and hid her emotions from her family. Salvador got out of the van and proclaimed,

"Well, it is not too bad. You even have a playground."

At the building entrance, the door lock gaped at them with a sizable rugged-bordered hole that revealed the successful attempt to break into the premises. Mailboxes hung in shambles in the lobby. Some had been forced open. Walls bristled with patches of dirt and ink-pen writings and drawings, some obscene. A large inscription read,

"Lawless City. Enter at your own risk."

Three neighbors chatted in Spanish while Antonio assessed how to move the furniture to the Gómezes' eleventh-floor apartment. An older woman walked out of an apartment on the first floor to greet the newcomers. Her white dress boasted colorful flowers, and her face the features of a Mexican Indian. She introduced herself with a tender voice,

"Welcome. I am Lola. Don't mind the way things look around here. Washing graffiti is an exercise in futility. We erase most of them, and in a few days, they are back. Please ask me if you have any questions. I have lived in this place since my husband died twelve years ago. I hope you come down to have a cup of coffee with me later. I want to give you some advice if you don't mind. It'll be helpful."

Only two of the three elevators worked, and someone had uprooted the emergency phones from the wall. Rosa reached the seventh floor, entered her apartment, and the world sank beneath her feet. A short, dark lobby evinced wall paint peeling off. It led to a faded-yellow family room with a sizable window that opened onto the plaza. The area led to two bedrooms whose harsh blue depressed her even more. A bathroom raged with a rusty, leaky shower and a tub fraught with dark spots, the enamel flaking off. Next to the restroom was a kitchenette with no windows, a cracked countertop, and a sink with a leaky faucet stain. An old gas stove reeked of slimy food around the burners.

The furniture fitted well. Humberto lay on the bed, gazing at the unkempt ceiling. He missed his backyard, reminisced about his former school, and foreboded what to expect at his new one. Standing at the window, Lucia looked forward to joining the children in the playground. Rosa cleaned as much as possible, and Salvador and their children pitched in. After a while, the couple visited their neighbor.

Lola kept her apartment clean and cozy. She prepared Mexican coffee for Salvador and Rosa, and as she served it, words breezed out of her mouth,

"Thank you for your visit. I am from Guadalajara. I haven't been there in many years. It is such a beautiful place. My granddaughter lives with me." Her desultory chat tried to summarize years of suffering in a few sentences. "As soon as I saw you, I said to myself, these are good people and dared to greet you. I never do that."

Then, matter-of-factly, Lola went into several instructions,

"Get two sturdy locks for your door but leave the keys in their holes when you are at home. Fire is even more dangerous than thieves. You don't want to search for your keys at that urgent time. Always look through the peephole before you open the door to anyone. Chains don't work. Thugs can break into your home. In this building, drug addicts keep robbing us. They want money or anything of value that can support their habit.

I know that well because my daughter is on drugs and stole from me. I have no idea where she is.

"Never open the door to anyone you don't know. No exceptions. Use the elevators with caution. Women and girls have been raped there. It has not happened in a while, but you should not ride it alone. Knock at my door so I make sure it is safe for you or your girl.

"Be courteous and always answer your neighbor's greeting but avoid looking the person in the eye. Some may think it is a provocation. Gangs won't bother you if you don't bother them. They sell their stuff, so if you walk by, don't even glance at them. Threaten no thugs with the police. Officers avoid coming here anyway. They are afraid of them. Warn your kid to stay away from the gangs. Every year, they recruit younger and younger boys and girls. Random shooting happens almost every day. Teach your children to duck and lie down flat on the ground until the danger is over."

She paused for a moment, sipped the coffee, and went on,

"You can buy this coffee at Mexico Lindo grocery store. It is a block away. It tastes good, doesn't it?"

Salvador and Rosa nodded, perplexed. Lola continued,

"Anyway, in this building, there are good and bad people. You cannot distinguish them by their appearance. Sometimes, those with mean faces and strange outfits turn out to be pleasant ones. They disguise themselves to fool those who may hurt them. The women here are divorcees or single mothers. Their ex-husbands and boyfriends come and go. They get drunk and beat the heck out of them. Never get involved. It is hard to listen to screams, but if you want to stay alive, do nothing. We must look the other way and pretend that nothing goes on."

Lola poured more coffee into her cup and said,

"I hope I am not scaring you. I want you to stay safe."

"We lived in a rough neighborhood several years ago," Salvador said. "I am aware of what happens, but I thank you for reminding us."

"Some neighbors are weird or dangerous," Lola said. "In the apartment above mine lives a real lowlife. He is always dirty, unshaven, and stinks of tobacco, marijuana, and God knows what. Strange people go up and down stairs all the time, knocking on his door to buy drugs. But there is nothing that we can do. If I report him, I'll be found dead in a corner. We have a crazy older man on the fifth floor, Mr. Juvencio. His family neglects him. Neighbors often find him wandering around the building stark naked. His body is thinner than Mahatma Gandhi's and wrinkled like a prune. He smiles when someone gets frightened. Loco, old son of a gun! Worst of all is the young guy who had a severe motorcycle accident, Juan Polenco. He lives on the twelfth floor. His brain damage turned him into a sexual beast, a scary one. His back is hunched over, and his eyes come out of their orbits. When Juan escapes from his apartment, he stares at everyone who walks by, his eyes full of lust. His mother swears that, before the accident, he was the most kindhearted man who ever set foot on earth. More than once, the police dumped him in the crazy house since he tried to abuse little girls and boys. I don't understand why they don't lock him up and throw the key away."

The first night arrived, and Salvador and Rosa conversed in bed,

"It is horrible to be poor in the US, "she said.

"Yes, but we confronted a similar situation earlier and made it. It is bad to be poor anywhere."

"I know, but here you lose everything. You lose your freedom. You fear because you don't know where or when wild beasts will hurt you. Those thugs are animals. In Mexico, many people lack food and barely survive amid injustice and hunger. But at least, in most places, you can walk around without fear. You are free."

"One cooks cauliflowers everywhere," Salvador said, a common saying meaning that stinky things happened in the entire world.

"No, it is different here. In Mexico, the poor still smile, laugh, and sing. It is different poverty, the one that Jesus talked about in the Gospel, 'Blessed are the poor because they will inherit the kingdom of Heaven.'"

"It is the same. In the US, the poor get used to living in inner-city neighborhoods. They were born here. They have no clue about any other way of life."

"But it is a grim life, full of unhappiness, a continuous struggle."

"We must ensure our children get an education so this never happens to them."

"No, Salvador, it also happens to knowledgeable people. Lola isn't illiterate. Calamity can hit anyone as it has affected us."

"Those are the exceptions. Anyway, the same misery occurs in poor neighborhoods in Mexico."

"I know, but Mexico is Mexico, and the US is the US, a country with a lot of money founded by common citizens. Are they now forgotten? Here, gangs, drugs, and crime threaten us."

"We'll adapt," Salvador said. "We did it before. It cannot be as bad as Lola said. Unless you want to go back to Mexico while I get well and go back to work."

"No, I cannot leave you sick."

"I won't be alone. I'll stay with Antonio."

"No, that is not an option."

An interminable day exhausted Rosa and Salvador, their voices fading like a dimmable lamp when one turned the switch down. Their bodies fell asleep, but restlessness stirred their minds. They tossed and turned; their thoughts still revved up by stress. A peaceful respite quieted them in the wee small hours of the morning.

The desperate financial situation affected Salvador and evoked memories of the promise he had made to Rosa on their engagement day. Amid an intense silence, the young couple kneeled alone in the church with the image of Our Lady of Guadalupe before them. Salvador believed the Holy Mother witnessed their love and endorsed their vows.

"Not matter what, I swear to God, I'll always take care of you," he whispered.

"Do not make promises, "Rosa said, her teary eyes gazing at him affectionately as her hand caressed his. "Just love me for as long as you can. I will love you forever,"

Rosa's old and straightforward statement still carried the same weight. Her injured and worn-out hands did not derail her mission. She cared for him and their children and did her duties to keep her family happy. Her words still loomed over the stain his sin left in their life together.

Rosa and Salvador liked their new place of worship, the Church of the Nativity. The ten o'clock Sunday Mass inspired joy in the families and made them reflect on their blessings. Parishioners wore their best dresses and fleckless black shoes. Young girls sported white veils, and women's black mantillas created a sense of happiness and solemnity.

On their first Sunday, Salvador found the strength to go to Communion. Rosa was surprised to see him in line behind her and their children, his eyes riveted to the floor, face pale, and arms folded on his chest. The children sang "Ave Maria," and incense scent wafted around as if wrapping everyone in sanctity. Salvador was oblivious to this shared grace. His mind was immersed in thoughts. Bent over in piety, the faithful returned to their seats with their faces illuminated. He wished he were them, no conflict in their souls, no remnant of the blemish of a capital transgression, no guilt in their expression. The red tiles of the waxed floor reflected his shadow. The cast image reached his son's black shoes, and the pant cuffs over his heels, making the father feel unworthy of stepping on virtuous footprints. Salvador heard the shuffle of feet approaching Father Rodriguez. The priest mumbled prayers as he imparted consecrated wafers. Salvador turned back to abandon the queue. In a long white lace veil, an old Mexican lady stood behind him with a smile. Her resemblance to his mother struck him and stopped him in his tracks. He inhaled a deep breath and pressed ahead. His wife and his daughter were walking back to their seats, and his son just received Communion. Salvador faced Father Rodriguez, who regarded him with a gentle expression, settled the holy bread on his tongue, and mumbled,

"The body of Christ."

Salvador perceived the bread's lightweight and bland flavor as he tried to swallow it. It got stuck on the roof of his mouth, and scrupulousness urged him to let it melt untouched. The lingering sensation evoked images of God adjusting to his imperfections. A gush of saliva carried it down his throat, and sudden relief overtook him. What happened the next few days proved this consolation to be transient. Salvador tried to feel His nearness, but the presence of God remained elusive.

At one of the church gatherings, Rosa met the newlywed spouse of Miguel, a waiter and Salvador's former coworker. The young woman belonged to a different parish several blocks away and attended a service with a friend. She boasted an ample bosom that contrasted with her tiny eyes under barely any brows, her large lips fluttering without her giving any thought to the consequences. The gossiper asked Rosa whether she was Salvador's second wife. Watching the bewildered reaction of her interlocutor, the impertinent woman added,

"Wasn't your husband married to a waitress? I think her name was Elisa, a gorgeous woman. A little weird. She hardly talked. But men dreamed after her and doted on her."

Rosa scowled at her, excused herself, and hurried away. Back home, she discussed the incident with Salvador, who labeled it as an evil act unfit for any further consideration.

"There are hateful people, busybodies who make up stories," he said. "They don't care whether they hurt anyone. Elisa is a decent woman."

The way her husband pronounced her name, his mouth full of the five letters, revealed the passion and loving memories he kept hidden. In the past, it would have roused the wife's jealousy. But Rosa controlled her emotions and tried to ignore it because she had decided to pardon any indiscretion Salvador might have committed when he lived alone. She continued dusting the furniture and straightening the pictures of her children and Our Lady of Guadalupe.

23

WHEELS OF HEALING

In the heart of Chicago, Cook County Hospital faced a gigantic task. It provided care to an enormous population of indigents, undocumented immigrants, and the uninsured working poor. The hospital opened in 1857 and earned a high reputation for excellent patient care nationwide. An ancient façade with marble columns rendered the place solemnity and a sense of responsibility. Annual statistics were staggering: 700 beds, 24,000 admissions, 150,000 emergency visits, and 500,000 outpatient visits.

It took two weeks for Salvador and Rosa to settle in and seek help. On July 16, the day of Our Lady of Carmelo's festivity, the day broke cloudy, and rain rapped their windowpanes. The few trees down in the plaza were heavy with water dripping from their leaves. Puddles flooded the street except for the narrow sidewalks. Utility holes gulped the whirling water with the same avidity that life was swallowing their ill-fated existence. The couple heard their gurgling sounds as they prepared to leave their building for the bus stop on one corner of the plaza. Salvador unfurled a black umbrella, and Rosa huddled next to him as they floundered on, gloominess hovering over them like the dark clouds overcasting the sky. They sat on the bus silently during the brief ride and soon saw the main hospital building with its tall marble columns. Salvador recalled Doña Concha's words,

"Thank God we have a hospital serving the needy. The poor and uninsured also need care. There, they get free medical services and prescriptions. They have to wait for their turn because there are many patients, but doctors take excellent care of them."

A bustle stirred around the facility. Patients and visitors walked in and out, police officers stood by, and nurses and other medical personnel hurried toward other buildings on the hospital campus. Cars entering or coming out of parking lots and boundary streets crowded with heavy traffic. On the east side was the red brick building of Press St Luke Medical Center and its organized setting. Looking around in awe, Salvador and Rosa lumbered through vast halls, somber and long like tunnels under a mountain, their tall ceilings and dark benches revealing their aging. He stopped every few steps to catch his breath. Coughing attacks seized him and brought tears to his eyes, turning his face purple. Rosa patted him on his back and waited until he composed himself. Both continued their way to the emergency room.

The couple found a long queue of patients who had waited in the reception room for five hours. Most were blacks who sat as if they had spent their entire lives there. A few paced about without uttering a word, their faces in anguish. Many dressed poorly or wore tawdry outfits, while others looked healthy and strutted around with the inner-city Black American's self-confident swagger. Several whites munched on their chewing gum and regarded their surroundings as if they were in a foreign land. Hispanics gathered in two groups, whispering among themselves. A young, blond nurse with thick glasses called patients in.

After a few hours, Rosa and Salvador's turn arrived. Luck was on their side since Dr. Joseph Talbot was on duty that day. Tall and in his mid-thirties, he boasted a round face framed with small round glasses and the gentleman-like distinction of someone born into a wealthy family. Dr. Talbot exuded philanthropic compassion and dedication to the dispossessed. As the new patients shuffled into his office, he stood up to greet them with a smile and a handshake. Rosa told her story. The doctor examined her right hand and shook his head in dismay. Her pale skin bristled with swelling veins, lusterless corpse-like nails, and fingers bent into a claw. She ratcheted them up and down with great difficulty and pain, the discomfort extending to her shoulder. He couldn't believe his eyes. How could a healthcare system neglect its workers to this extreme? He thought. How could some doctors lend themselves to these abuses? Dirty money. Weak and swollen, her left hand looked better than the right. The situation frustrated him because of his fellow physicians' betrayal. He rebounded and said in a hopeful tone,

"Your nerves are compressed in your wrists. I'll ask a neurologist to see you."

Talbot then approached Salvador, whose frequent cough had often interrupted Rosa's interview. His chest fluttered, and his belly swelled with every breath. His bluish discoloration and rattling chest sounds revealed his pulmonary ailment. He referred him to a lung specialist.

Neurologist Dr. Alan Bouffard walked in to see Rosa. He wore a white coat over his lanky figure and long blond hair. A smile warmed his compassionate blue eyes. His brief examination yielded a conclusion,

"I'll do my best to help you, but I can't promise anything. I hope your condition is reversible."

"Reversible? What do you mean?"

"That it might still respond to treatment. I'll see you in my office tomorrow."

In an adjacent room, Dr. Sen Banerji examined Salvador. The physician wore an impeccable gray suit that enhanced his white strands in a full head of thick black hair. Circled by deep dark rings, his dark eyes penetrated patients like an X-ray machine. His hands rubbed a stethoscope to ease the coldness. The doctor slid it from area to area on the patient's chest, each sound evoking pondering expressions and diagnoses,

"You may have chronic inflammation of your lungs or a persistent asthmatic condition. Acute exposure to irritants may have thickened your lungs."

"I don't understand, Doctor."

"The fumes might have thickened the membrane that separates the air you breathe from your blood. Normally, it is very thin and allows oxygen to seep into blood vessels, which distribute it to the entire body. I hope it is asthma—a partial obstruction of the airflow into your chest."

"Do you think you can help me?"

"I don't want to give you false hopes. The prognosis depends on your condition."

Banerji could have been blunt. While asthma would heal well, a dense respiratory membrane would kill him in a few years. The doctor kept this painful thought to himself and avoided unnecessary worry in Salvador. He prescribed blood tests, scheduled a pulmonary study in his office, and bid him goodbye with a subtle curtsy.

Doctors who infused confidence in their patients could improve them before they ever touched them. Hopefulness changed our body and prepared it for healing. That evening at dinnertime, Rosa and Salvador enjoyed some relief. Rosa's fingers improved, the bluishness turning pinkish as her hope kindled the blood circulation. Salvador's coughing attacks shortened and slackened, and the pounding of his heart lessened into a rhythmic throbbing. Tonight, their relief helped them sleep. The next day broke with their optimistic expectation that the scheduled tests would further ease their lives.

Rosa and Salvador stepped onto a hospital elevator where an older black woman requested their passes as she sat before the floor panel. Passengers filled the cab. When it arrived on the third floor, the operator alerted Rosa. She kissed Salvador goodbye, got off, and found herself in front of the neurology office. It flanked a short stretch of a vast hall that led to the inpatient wards. A crackling noise startled her when pieces of ice dropped inside a large ice maker that stood against a wall. Rosa nudged the office glass door ajar and shoved her head into a sizable room with three partitions. The secretary, a thin blonde with thick glasses, offered her a seat next to her desk. Rosa huddled down on a small wooden bench. It was an austere setting — a desk, an old typewriter, a bulletin board nailed to the wall, two hangers, and an end table with a coffee maker. Even the bench where she now brooded looked old and rickety. Junior residents and medical students strolled past her, sharing stories of the patients they had just seen. They filed into a partition where an instructor imparted teaching. No one paid attention to Rosa, her eyes on her painful right hand that her lap shielded. A few minutes later, Dr. Bouffard came in.

The doctor ushered her into a dark examining room at an adjacent office. She lay down on a couch. The doctor applied electrodes to her right palm and thumb. An electrical shock on her wrist jerked her thumb. He repositioned the electrodes and stimulated each nerve controlling her hand muscles. The discharges worsened her pain to such intensity that it burrowed deep into her bones. Its sharpness surprised her. Until now, she had never experienced such torture. The burning feeling rushed from the hand to the shoulder. It reminded her of that of condemned men who had their eyes impaled with red hot daggers. Dr. Bouffard finished the study of that hand, sticking needles into its muscles. Her left hand perceived the sharpness of pokes, but it did not distort it into a terrible torment like the right. Rosa did not flinch.

"I am sorry," he said. "But I have excellent news: your nerves still work. They are slow but are there."

"Will I recuperate my hands?"

"I think so. But you need surgery on both wrists. The left will improve, and the right might also get better. Let me give you a referral to neurosurgery."

Salvador had gotten off the elevator on the fifth floor and arrived early for his appointment with Doctor Banerji. Several fluorescent lights flickered above vanilla walls in a sizeable reception area. In a corner was a desk for the departmental secretary, her delicate scent wafting through the room. A few papers rested on the counter, and a half-typed sheet on a typewriter. He heard the tread of her high heels approaching. The woman wore an elegant blue dress, and her face, statuesque figure, and sleek brown hair reminded him of Elisa's. His heart jumped.

"Are you okay?" she asked.

He nodded.

Salvador thought of his ex-companion. It had been so long since he saw her. She might have found happiness with someone. He hoped so. Time often resolved most issues, and life continued its unstoppable destiny. Feelings for her still lay dormant in an area of his memory. Once one had loved a woman so much, some remnant of that emotion lived inside the person forever. He still blamed his decision on his promise to God before the altar on his wedding day and his child. But an unresolved question remained whether the resolution was an excuse for his lack of courage.

"My husband, I mean, Dr. Banerji, will take care of you in a few minutes," she said, smiling at him as he blushed, embarrassed.

This question hung in the air when Mrs. Banerji called him into her husband's office.

The doctor ushered him into the pulmonary lab next door and conducted the scheduled test. As he examined the graphics, his face brightened up.

"It looks good, Mr. Gómez. Let me perform the last test. Bear with me, please."

Salvador inhaled a medication, the diagnosis bringing a smile to Dr. Banerji's face, and his reassuring words,

"Irritant-induced asthma. Your exposure to the chemicals in the paint changed your bronchi's reactivity." He observed bewilderment in the patient's expression and added,

"Your lungs have become more sensitive to substances we breathe in our environment. Their airways tighten, narrow, and don't allow the air to flow into your lungs."

"Is this something curable?"

"Yes, but I don't want you to make any physical effort. Please take your medications and come to respiratory therapy three times a week. Don't expect miracles. It will be a slow process."

His face lit up, and his eyes closed in a silent prayer. Salvador realized God had pity on him and cared for him. He was sick but was still alive, able to walk and breathe. His family members had a roof over their heads and their daily necessities covered. He hoped his suffering would atone for his transgression and revive his relationship with God.

At Cook County Hospital, forty-five hundred employees attended to hundreds of thousands of patients with an inevitable delay. At the outpatient surgical suite, bright lights, white walls, and marble floors unnerved Rosa. She prayed for a favorable outcome as a nurse cleansed the surgical field. Under his attentive eyes, neurosurgeon Luis Torres numbed her skin and made an incision in her right wrist. The swollen nerve popped out as if screaming from a long compression. He stitched the wound and left a thin line that stretched down her wrist into her palm.

"It looks nice," he said as he smiled at her, winking his left eye with the immediate familiarity of those who shared the same homeland. "No one will ever notice your scar."

"Will it get well?"

"We have to wait, *hermanita*," he said, using a loving diminutive for little sister.

Two weeks later, Dr. Torres performed surgery on her left hand and scheduled Rosa for intensive rehabilitation.

The healing wheels spun forward. To Salvador and Rosa, the sky shone bluer and brighter than ever. Hope removed a black veil from their eyes and plugs from their ears. Even sparrows' chirping sounded happier in the few bushes in their neighborhood. Salvador often sighed, expanding his lungs, and warming his face with blood. Rosa experienced happy tears that ran down her cheeks, wiping them away with her left hand as she smiled.

A few weeks later, on September 8, 1998, Rosa took Lucia to Ashland Grammar School. The ten-year-old girl looked more like a little woman. Her eyes, sleek black hair, and delicate features resembled her mother's, while her vitality and personable demeanor mirrored her father's. She grew excited and kept asking questions. As they approached the school grounds, they heard the noisy bustle of children playing. The building appeared well preserved except for a few gang signs, whose repeated erasure had left a faint trace of their symbols. Enclosed by a fence, the three-story structure boasted many large windows. Its formidable size captured Lucia's imagination, for her former school had been much smaller. An enormous door led to a spacious schoolyard swarming with little children of all races. The area sweltered in the sun except in the fence lee, where the youngest children found shelter.

The same day, Humberto, now sixteen, began the school year at Washington High School, near the Villita. He found it spacious, with excellent playing fields and a comprehensive library that bespoke a well-endowed institution. The schoolmates' appearance surprised him—a mixture of blacks and Hispanics with punk hairstyles, eccentric outfits, and prominent tattoos. The girls used excessive make-up, their lips red like a clown's nose, and their faces white with powder. Most wore short skirts that flaunted muscular legs and thighs like football players. Several normal-looking youngsters gathered in separate groups. In the school hall, a prominent notice read:

"Guns and knives are prohibited on the school grounds. We will dismiss anyone who disobeys this ordinance."

It was challenging to adjust to an unfamiliar environment. Drugs were available. Humberto found that out when he walked into a restroom. A tall boy with an earring hanging from the right ear beckoned him,

"I got great stuff, cheap, marijuana, ecstasy, crystal meth. I can get what you need for a good trip: crack cocaine, LSD—"

"I am not interested.".

"C'mon man, grow up."

Humberto sashayed away without replying. It was no use. He knew of the dangers in the inner-city high schools and just got a taste of it.

The school bullies soon realized Humberto's assertiveness. He did not yield to persuasion or attempts to force him into acting against his will. But they tested him. Three mean-looking teenagers preyed on him in the hall. The rascals waylaid him, glaring at him. Rosendo, the tallest one, addressed him,

"Don't you have any manners? You are new here and didn't introduce yourself."

"My name is Humberto. I know who you are. Now let me through. I don't have time to play games."

Humberto pressed on through them, showing no fear. He knew these bullies behaved like animals that refrained from attacking fearless humans. From then on, they ignored him. Humberto joined a group of students interested in learning and pursuing further education in college. Their conversations ranged from social issues, political topics, science, and college plans. Acting like normal teenagers, they talked about sports, laughed, and joked, the girls chatting about the boys and the boys about the girls. Their low socioeconomic status intimidated no one. They willed to sacrifice for their dreams and counted on financial help and grants to achieve them.

24

BACK TO THE PAST

T welve-year-old Carlos Ramirez grew taller and muscular. His eyes had an expression of intelligence far beyond that of the average boy his age. Two women, Elisa and Tata, continued to dedicate all their efforts to molding his personality. Carlos adored his mother and loved his nanny, who had just turned seventy and planned to retire in her home country a year from now. The older woman taught him to think carefully, make a few mistakes, and learn from them.

His mother stressed his duty to excel in school and respect his fellow man. Carlos also learned from her that knowledge and integrity edified people more than money. She emphasized self-discipline, integrity, and fairness, often repeating the dictum,

"Do unto others as you would have them do unto you."

Religion burgeoned out in the youngster's life. Elisa got upset with Catholicism since Father Mathews had begrudged baptizing her son on account of his out-of-wedlock birth. The older priest upbraided Elisa for engaging in sex before giving any thought to the consequences. A few years later, Father Pierce replaced him and welcomed Elisa, Carlos, and Tata. The three went to Mass every Sunday. They stayed in church the whole morning, his mother and his governess attending Bible school as he learned religious education. Carlos nurtured a curious mind that concocted challenging questions. He asked Tata,

"There is no proof that God exists. Why do you and my mother insist on religion so much?"

"I am not a learned woman, But I know some things need not be proven. Can you touch the air with your hands? No. If you don't breathe it, or the wind doesn't blow it, you would not know it exists. The concept of God is the same. You cannot touch Him, but God is there, around us, always with us."

Elisa's answer to the same question was more pragmatic,

"An intelligent youngster must understand practical things. Believing in God is a wonderful investment. Knowing He will reward you in Heaven for your good deeds on earth can be a powerful incentive to behave. If, after all, God did not exist, you would still have done your best, anyway. What do you have to lose?"

"Well, Mother, I would lose the truth. I would have based my life on false premises."

"The truth lies in goodness, caring for others, loving your fellow man. It distinguishes us from the Animal Kingdom."

These arguments never convinced him but stuck in his mind like post-it notes. Carlos liked to get Michael Kaplan's opinion. The youngster joined him at soccer games or the law office, where Carlos filed papers for a small stipend on Saturday morning. Born into Judaism, the agnostic attorney's views confused the youngster who looked up to him.

"Carlos. You must follow the teachings of your mother and your Church."

"Don't treat me like a little child. I am trying to have a serious conversation."

"Let's talk, man to man. Some people consider God a marvelous invention. Human beings must understand life and death and everything that happens around them. A primitive tribe in New Guinea erected a plane's wreck as their idol since they saw it fall from the sky. As man learns more about Nature, God becomes less and less important."

"Do you believe in God?"

"I do, but the faithful have used Him to harm people. Their behavior made me skeptical and disenchanted with the whole concept. I stay away from religion. I prefer the fairness of laws, and I do as many kind acts for my fellow man as I can through my profession."

In junior high school, Carlos became popular with the girls, who walked by him giggling. He had eyes only for Sarah, a twelve-year-old schoolmate who boasted ebony hair, aquamarine eyes, and porcelain-like skin. Her pink lips and svelte body had blossomed with early changes of womanhood. Her vivacious intelligence tallied well with her unpretentious demeanor and graceful behavior. Despite her magnetic personality, Sarah considered herself one among many, just another face in the crowd. She excelled in poetry, drawing, and piano, enjoying jazz and classical music.

Carlos had known Sarah since kindergarten and worked with her on many school projects. They played, studied, and grew up together. For a long time, her parents, Elaine and Samuel Goldman, a wealthy real estate attorney, paid no attention to her friendship with a Christian boy who behaved and excelled in school. Their only offspring meant everything to them. They were in their forties when they adopted their baby girl. Sarah just learned this information, bringing her even closer to fatherless Carlos.

The curious pair discussed this common nexus and decided to find their natural parents. The youngsters did not miss them. Their mothers indulged them with enormous love, and Sarah's father doted on her. The girl asked questions, and her mom and dad recounted what they knew about her story:

Samuel and Elaine could not have any children, so they contacted a center for adoption in Evanston — the Cradle. It was an institution where movie stars and wealthy couples sought babies, most Northwestern University students' offspring. The Goldmans requested a Jewish child and found their request blessed with a beautiful newborn daughter of Sephardic ancestry. Their joy soared to the happiest point in their lives, the child enjoying their total dedication and devotion.

Their story did not quench Sarah's curiosity. The Cradle kept progenitors' identities secret unless the birth mother and father agreed to the disclosure. Samuel and Elaine paid six thousand dollars to put the process wheel in motion. Sarah soon learned her natural mother's name, Deborah Lerner. The single and childless writer lived in San Francisco and dedicated her time and efforts to her profession.

Samuel and Elaine feared losing their daughter but let her meet Deborah so they could put this issue behind them. Sarah's maturity and filial love reassured them. Ushered by a stewardess, the youngster wandered off the plane and espied a middle-aged woman who held a placard with her name. Deborah wore a white skirt with red roses, a light-blue shirt, and windblown-like ebony hair as if she had never overgrown the hippy years. She shook her daughter's hand and patted her on her shoulder, voicing the happiness of meeting her with an emotionless face.

Deborah lived with two Siamese cats in a small apartment brimming with books and Hindu memorabilia. The birth mother's limpid blue eyes resembled those of the daughter but lacked the warmth of Elaine's. Sarah had never experienced as much love for her adoptive mom as she now felt. Deborah accommodated her in a room with a small couch, a yellow bed cover, and a large red cushion in each corner. On the walls hung many newspaper cutouts that Deborah had authored. The white cats with black faces soon asserted their domain and nestled on two cushions, their blue eyes focusing on the intruder. Under the couch lay two large suitcases with old shoes and skirts. The place reeked of stale cheese and shook like jelly with every tram nearby in the street.

For two days, Deborah talked about her young age and inexperience during her pregnancy. She majored in English at Northwestern University in Evanston. The studies absorbed her time and energy. Deborah loved her daughter but could not take care of her and wished the best for her. She had never set eyes on Sarah before because the institution took her baby girl away at birth.

From an erratic and detached conversation, Sarah gathered that her natural parents had conceived her after a Halloween party. Her maternal grandparents were abroad on a trip around the world, and her mother hid her pregnancy. Deborah was an only child whose mother had abused her physically. She dreaded her elder's reaction. When the Lerners returned from their lengthy journey, their daughter had already delivered and disposed of Sarah. They died several years ago. Sarah's father, Abraham Mederano, was a college mate who studied accounting. The single sexual encounter that engendered the unwanted pregnancy happened the first time Deborah ever attended a celebration in college. They might have drunk more than their share.

Sarah felt sad for her lonely host, who led a secluded life immersed in papers after her first and last attempt to connect with her fellow man. Writing was her only weak link with society. Before leaving, the youngster expressed appreciation to her birth mother because, despite impediments, she never aborted her. Sarah budged to hug her, but Deborah flinched. They promised to keep in contact.

Abraham Mederano was a Sephardic Jew who traced his roots to Cordoba, Spain. His family came to the US from the Balkans in 1905. He lived in Winnetka, Illinois, a wealthy suburb on the north side of Chicago. Samuel Goldman took Sarah to meet him on a Sunday. They drove through gorgeous roads under branches of ancient oak trees that snaked along the blue water of Lake Michigan. Mr. Mederano's two-story mansion lined a vast stretch of a long boulevard.

Abraham introduced his wife Anna and three daughters, 9-year-old Abigail, 7-year-old Daniella, and 5-year-old Miriam, to his guests. The three children boasted fiery blond hair and blue eyes. Mr. Goldman excused himself and left Sarah alone with them until his return in the evening. Abraham could not stop smiling as Anna welcomed his newly found daughter with a hug. His vivid Mediterranean brown eyes and thick dark hair contrasted with his family's Northern European complexion. The children enjoyed their new sister and hung around her, showing her their rooms and inviting her to play.

Abraham inspired a sense of pride in Sarah about her ancestry. She learned of her forefathers' suffering. Abraham illustrated it with books. The Catholic Kings decreed the Jews' banishment from Seville, Cordoba, and Cadiz in 1483 and carried it out in 1485. Their final expulsion from Spain occurred in August 1492. The numbers were staggering for a country with eight million people: 50,000 converted to Christianity to avoid exile; 20,000 died en route, and 175,000 emigrated. By law, they could not take gold, silver, coins, arms, or horses. Bills of exchange became their only alternative, but the state often confiscated them. Most had no choice but to abandon their properties or sell their belongings cheaply — a house for a dress, a vineyard for a donkey. Historian Salomon Ibn Verga described the exodus with words that affected the youngster:

"And so everywhere they encountered afflictions, extensive and somber darkness, horrendous tribulations, rapacity, sadness, starvation, and plague. Some left by sea, looking in the waves for a path, but there, the Hand of God disfavored them, confounding and exterminating them because many of the banished were sold as slaves in every corner of the earth, and quite a few fell into the sea, ultimately sinking like lead."

Mederano did not learn of his fatherhood before Deborah signed their baby away. His name never appeared on Sarah's birth certificate. He did not discuss what he would have done if he had known. Back then, the clueless father welcomed the news that a devoted, well-to-do Jewish family had adopted his offspring. Now that Abraham had just met Samuel, the host realized how much love and effort Sarah's parents had dedicated to molding her into a mature, responsible young woman. His natural daughter could not have fallen into better hands. Mr. Mederano hugged Samuel and kissed Sarah on the cheek. He invited the Goldmans to their home for Hanukah and thanked God for blessing him with new friends.

Carlos' endeavors to locate his father improved when Sarah told him about her search. He devised a stratagem. Elisa turned livid when she pulled out a drawer of his nightstand and saw an open envelope from the Clerk of Circuit Court of Cook County. It was addressed to Mr. Carlos Ramirez. Her son had removed it from the mailbox before she arrived home. The letter asked for the case number and the date of Francisco Ramirez's transcripts so their office could send Carlos the requested information. He was searching for his father's social security number to track him down.

Elisa confronted Carlos. He revealed that he had overheard a conversation with Mariela and learned that his maternal grandfather had assaulted his mother and almost killed his father. Elisa turned livid and said,

"There will be a time when I must break the silence. But I must be the one who decides. To you, Salvador is an unknown father that you are curious about, but to me, he is the only man I have ever loved."

$$25$$

BULLYING

T he first quarter of the 1998-99 school year proved excellent. Lucia got straight "As" in reading, mathematics, and science, and Humberto in algebra, biology, and chemistry. After the Christmas recess, he returned to his desk in the back of the classroom. An overweight youngster shuffled over and sat next to him. The new classmate had the innocent expression of a teenager whose adolescent body had outgrown his childhood mindset. He made no eye contact and concentrated on his work, uttering no word. Now and then, he perceived someone looking at him. If a girl did it, his pinkish cheeks blushed crimson red. When the class ended, Humberto turned toward him and introduced himself. The newcomer's name was Roberto. His weak handshake revealed insecurity and a lack of assertiveness. Humberto and Roberto conversed at lunchtime and shared their common ties — they were strangers in a new high school. As often happens with lonely people, a friendship sprouted as if they had known each other for years.

Roberto had just moved from a small town in central Illinois after his father's death. His dad brought him into this country illegally. His mother toiled all day. He helped her take care of his younger brother and sister. In the morning, Roberto combed their hair, got them dressed, fed them breakfast, and took them to school. From there, he proceeded on to Washington High. When his classes were over, he tended to his brother and sister and worked in the kitchen at a local restaurant until midnight.

Roberto's personality made him a prime target of the school bullies and their leader, Rosendo. The youngster was a recalcitrant troublemaker. Tall and burly, he flaunted a picture of a devil tattooed on his right arm. His eyes seethed with a smug, mischievous expression. He disliked everyone, including himself, and enjoyed intimidating his classmates. Many times, the school officials complained to his guardian, his elderly grandmother. He had suffered a terrible childhood because his cocaine-addicted single mother often beat him. He ran and hid under his bed, but she dragged him out by one leg and lashed against him with any object she found. A few years ago, she abandoned him and walked out to roam the streets. Her departure spelled a welcome relief. Since then, his grandmother raised him, but he never obeyed her.

The band of scoundrels took advantage of any opportunity to call Roberto names—fatty boy, stupid dude, weirdo. They waylaid him while one got on all fours and crawled behind him. Rosendo then toppled him over. The fall knocked the victim out for a few seconds. He picked up his book and tottered away, limping in pain. One day, the bullies snatched his schoolbag and tossed it around, passing it to one another. Another day, one restrained Roberto while another dug into his pocket and plucked out the money his mother had given him to buy food for the family. These rotten apples made it challenging for the youngster to continue attending school, but he had to.

Humberto knew of the different pranks first-year students endured at an institution. The roguery included drinking parties, beatings, or ceremonies where everyone urinated on the newcomer. It had grown meaner over the years. He and Roberto sat in the locker room, ready for a physical education class, when the bullies jumped on top of them. Humberto kicked two where it hurt the most, punched several guys, and thrashed around, beating anyone who dared get close to him. The assailants desisted. But they subdued Roberto, stripped him of his clothes, and threw him against a table.

While he lay naked, Rosendo faked an attempt to rape Roberto. The panicky youngster cried out. Humberto grabbed a baseball bat that was on the floor nearby.

"Stay away from him!" he yelled.

When the bullies saw him run toward them, they regrouped, jeered at their prey, and strolled away. Roberto picked up his scattered clothes, his eyes welling with tears and his face flushing with shame. He got dressed and thanked his friend, who mulled over the incident.

"Those guys are like a pack of wolves," Humberto said. "If you show any weakness, they pounce on you."

Most students at the school coped with bullying and submitted no formal complaints. The victims feared retaliation from the abusers and avoided discussing the problems with their families. Teachers and counselors viewed harassment as a sign of weakness of the assaulted student. The administration offered no recourse since some educators deemed it a typical age-related phenomenon. Others feared the bullies and shirked any disciplinary action against them. Teachers often left their cars in a solitary parking lot and ventured around the school facilities without protection. Incidents of student attacks or threats to them had occurred several times a year.

Faculty members reported their ordeals, but the consensus was the school did not want to deal with the issue. The outcome of their complaints often yielded the opposite results of what they had expected. A colleague, Mr. Perkins, had suffered an adverse experience that had influenced their attitude. During one of his literature classes the previous year, he reprimanded a black student who chatted and disturbed his classmates. The teacher expelled him from the classroom. As the teenager was leaving, he punched Mr. Perkins, who fell to the floor, unconscious. After he had reported the student, the black principal, Michael Brown, called Mr. Perkins into his office and scolded him. The student had unfairly accused him of repeated acts of racial discrimination, but his boss did not waver.

Roberto and Humberto notified the school of the attack. Mr. Brown listened to their complaints and promised to provide safe grounds to the students. He addressed Humberto,

"The school will investigate the complaint. But I don't condone your threat with a baseball bat.

"I am sorry, sir, Rosendo intended to rape Roberto. I couldn't sit idly and witness it. Could you?"

"Young man, we are in my office. I don't appreciate you asking me questions. I'll investigate the incident."

The police captain came to the school. According to the statements of the victim and his friend, penetration had never occurred. They were unable to prove rape or attempted rape. The police considered bullying a school affair, a matter of low priority. Their workload bristled with 'real crimes' that demanded more time than the officers managed to spare. The principal called Rosendo's grandmother. He intended to dismiss her grandson unless the youngster showed a dramatic change in his conduct. That evening, the older woman urged Rosendo to behave one too many times. He became exasperated, threatened her, tied her up, and gagged her. The following day, a neighbor strolled by her apartment and heard her moans. He knocked on the door but got no answer. Firefighters broke into the flat and found the frightened victim on the floor, but she filed no complaint.

A month had passed since the incident. The bullies kept a low profile and the routine precautions Humberto had implemented lapsed. His mind shifted to academic issues as the anticipation of lurking danger dissipated. One evening, his work on a project captured his attention in the public library. He focused so much on this task that he did not realize the sun had already hidden. The bus stop that took him home was two blocks away. He lumbered over a shallow layer of snow that muffled his steps and noticed the chilly breeze of March on his face. The street was dark. There was no moon, and a burned-out lamp hung on a tall post. Lights across the opposite sidewalk cast his tilted shadow upon his path and building facades.

Two cars drove by. Humberto saw no pedestrians. A sudden screeching noise of breaking tires tore through the evening silence. He turned his head, and a baseball bat bashed his right brow. He plunged to the ground, unconscious. Four youths kicked his torso and belly several times. The *gangbangers* stopped their beating when a passerby screamed out for help from a block away. One drew a pistol and shot twice at the witness. He missed. The assailants pinned a note to the victim's jacket, climbed into a dark Chevrolet, and sped away. Letters cut out from a newspaper spelled out a warning,

"MIND YOUR OWN BUSINESS."

Humberto arrived unconscious at the intensive care unit at Cook County Hospital, where a library card showed his identity. The police notified his parents, Salvador and Rosa Gómez. The father drove through the streets, paying no attention to other cars or traffic lights. Neon signs lit his face with variegated colors, sometimes the left and sometimes the right, as if an Indian curse had gripped him. A few raindrops splattered onto the windshield. Rosa huddled next to him, praying. Now and then, some words reached her husband's ear,

"Holy Mary, mother of God."

His mind sizzling with thoughts, Salvador wondered why God had allowed such a terrible event to afflict Humberto. He might put up with any calamity but pleaded with Him to spare his child's life. A pitch-dark parking lot loomed ahead. The couple scrambled out of the vehicle, rushed through the rows of cars, and reached the building.

A police officer was in front of the main hospital door. Groups of people walked in and out. Rosa prayed as Salvador's mind bristled with foreboding. The crowded elevator door opened. An older woman with a cane got out. The elevator ratcheted onto the next floor and let out a young man with a snake tattoo on his right hand and a baseball cap. Salvador sensed Rosa's nearness, listened to her mumbled paternoster, and grabbed her hand. Her skin warmth did not relieve his painful musing. An overwhelming responsibility weighed upon him. He blamed himself for bringing his family to this country. An eternity ticked away before the couple reached the fifth-floor hall next to the intensive care unit.

Humberto was unconscious. In the waiting room, Rosa could not contain her crying. Salvador paced back and forth, the years in the United States flashing before his mind. Did I make the right decision? He asked himself. These times are dangerous everywhere, but there is so much violence where we live. His situation reminded him of a biblical passage. He remembered it word for word,

"After all these things, God tested Abraham and said to him, 'Abraham!'

And he said, 'Here I am.'

'Take your son, your only son Isaac, whom you love, and go to the land of Moriah, and offer him there as a burnt offering on one of the mountains of which I shall tell you.'" (*Genesis 22: 1-19*)

But Salvador was not Abraham. God had already tested him with Elisa, and he failed. The Almighty bore plenty of evidence of the consequences of his prodigal son's misdeed. He loved God with all his heart and soul. He needed no trial and asked God to vouchsafe him only one favor,

"Almighty Father, please don't let my son die."

Humberto woke up a few hours later, but confusion and restlessness overtook him. Dr. Hines, the neurosurgeon on call, informed the parents,

"Multiple injuries have caused his brain to swell. Several ribs are broken, and the spleen is bruised. Humberto will live, but I don't know how much he will recover. The next twenty-four hours should tell us more. You may go in, but don't overtire him."

The ICU bustled with nurses and doctors as young and old patients were close to death. The machine humming and beeping pierced the medical personnel's din of conversation. Nurses scrambled frenetically from room to room, checking on the sick and the equipment. As Rosa and Salvador shambled into the unit, they observed an unconscious man in his fifties with eyelids taped shut.

An older man stared at them, his eyes almost popping out of their orbits. A woman's serene facial features reflected the peaceful acceptance of death.

When Salvador and Rosa saw their son, they barely recognized him. A large hematoma shut his right eye, his limbs flailed around, and his lips uttered unintelligible sounds. Humberto lay in deep slumber but sometimes opened his eyes. He gaped, rambled, moaned, and groped for the intravenous lines until leather restraints held his hands.

A nurse asked the parents to step out into the waiting room. Four women sat crying as three men gazed at them with sad expressions. The night loomed long and dreary. Salvador paced the place again. A clock on the wall kept track of time, the tick-tock submerging anxious relatives into a hypnotic trance. The new day never seemed to break. After a while, the loud voices of workers changing shifts roused along with repeated thumps and bell ringing of elevator doors.

The stealthy hours of darkness had brought fears of death to many visitors and patients that dissipated with the first lights. The new dawn revived their hopes. Rosa and Salvador stayed immobile in their chairs, their eyes red and teary, and their faces faded to an ashen color. She rolled the dark pearls of a rosary, each Ave Maria, each paternoster lifting her pleas to the divinities.

Salvador stared straight ahead, fighting thoughts about Elisa. The place stirred his mind to hearken back to the days when she comforted him in the ICU as he faced death. Unable to stop it, her amorous eyes flashed before him, full of love and concern, and so did her soft hand as it rested on his. Her warmth branded his skin like a brand on an animal's fur. He gazed to the right, the left, at the wall clock marking 7:10 AM, at the large abstract painting with red, blue, and white patches. Nothing dispelled the image or sensations until a young nurse's vigorous tread roused him. She let him know that he and Rosa could visit their son.

Humberto sat up in bed in the telemetry unit. His face was swollen, but the sparkle in his eyes revealed happiness at his parents' presence. He embraced them. Over the next forty-eight hours, he tried to remember any detail that might identify his assailants and help the police. He recalled none, and neither did the witness.

The police discovered that Rosendo had joined the Latin Kings, but his interrogation led nowhere. The grandmother learned of the brutal attack on his schoolmate and confronted her grandson. He denied any involvement. But she perceived guilt in his facial expression. The lady changed her mind and filed a complaint against him for the assault he had perpetrated on her. Despite his pleas, her decision stood. She needed to prevent another serious crime. The police handcuffed Rosendo in the school. The impassive thug swaggered out of the class, smirking at the officers, and winking at his friends.

Three days later, Humberto left the hospital with lengthy rehabilitation and an uncertain future before him. Salvador reacted with anger to his son's brutal beating. How dare anyone attempt against an innocent human being's life? My son's. He is one of the people I love most in this world. His rage lasted until he realized wrath did not resolve problems. He discussed it with Father Rodriguez, who advised him,

"Vengeance poisons the soul. The gangbangers are our kids gone astray. What did Jesus say? 'The hireling flees because he is a hireling and does not care about the sheep. I am a good shepherd. And I know My sheep and am known by My own. And other sheep I have which are not of this fold; them also I must bring.'"

Father Rodriguez believed the primary cause of the problem lay in the family's disintegration. Previously, husband, wife, and children shared their house with grandparents, uncles, and aunts. If a parent died, the extended family compensated for the departed. The children looked up to their relatives as protectors and role models. But now, the youngsters had grown up alone. Many lived with single mothers, or if there was a father, he either toiled at two jobs or too many hours to dedicate time to his children. Both parents worked, so the children fended for themselves. Parents lavished their offspring with abundant gifts to offset their lack of care. Youngsters joined gangs to seek attention, love, a sense of belonging, protection, deceitful self-respect, or a false sense of control of their destiny.

"Then, there are the material aspects—the easy money, drugs, girls, even the gang dress and colors," the priest added. "All these items attract these kids."

"But, Father, have you looked around?" Salvador asked. "It must be a consequence of our neighborhood's severe poverty."

"I don't think so. Poor people don't live like rats. They don't kill or live in fear of what others may do to them. But they bond together and help one another. This plague is a family's illness, but some don't realize that. Parents move their gangbanger children to a different location without uprooting the problem, spreading the infection. Besides, the good neighbors who make it in life—those who can be an example for our children—leave the area, deserting their friends."

"It is dangerous over here, Father. Parents must protect their children. For a while, my wife wanted to take Lucia and Humberto to Mexico. But my son refused, and so did my daughter. But I understand my wife's concerns. While I can put my life in danger for something, I cannot force my family to do so."

At midmorning, Sunday Mass, Father Rodriguez's sermon dealt with the danger the children were facing daily. He talked about the way some became gang members and threatened the community.

"If we are to prevent the gangs' dangers, no one will do it for us but ourselves," he said. "Only if we are good Christians will we finish with this plague. We all know single mothers and undocumented immigrants who are working two jobs to sustain their kids. Children roam the streets alone. What do you think the future holds for them if we don't lend them a hand? It is not a question of money; it is a question of love and caring for your fellow man. Where can a teenager whose parents are on drugs find a kind word or proper advice?"

A few days later, Salvador addressed this issue with Father Rodriguez,

"I am not a hero, but I want to do my best for this community. My family and I believe we have a duty toward our neighbors. You can count on us."

"We all can help," the priest agreed. "We must put our hearts and minds into it. Politicians create laws, police officers enforce them, and judges apply them. They try to solve a moral problem that has led to a crime crisis. As we say in Spain, 'It is like washing a scabby man's head' — you clean it today, and it is back to square one tomorrow."

"We need their help, don't we?"

"But the initiative must come from us. Our family is sick. We cannot jail almost a million gang members. They complete their training while incarcerated, anyway. There isn't any rehabilitation in prisons. When they leave jail, the gang's way of life has seized them. They commit to delinquency more than ever."

Father Rodriguez appointed Salvador to lead the parents' council. Two weeks later, he presided over a meeting. The neighborhood bristled with dreadful news. Assaults on businesses turned into an ordinary event, and owners rejoiced in their spared lives after looking down at a gun barrel.

Ten members of the church committee, five men and five women listened to the accounts of an older man. A young woman with three children — nine, ten, and eleven — lived in an apartment next to his. Addicted to cocaine, the mother engaged her children in selling drugs to support her habit. Men paraded in and out of her home, securing sex and drugs. Without proper intervention, the children's future looked bleak. Social Services investigated her. She was married, and the officials proved no wrongdoing. Salvador volunteered to discuss the issue with her, and Rosa accompanied him. He rang the bell, and the woman held the door ajar without releasing the chain lock. She hid behind it, but not before the visitor glanced at her disheveled appearance — a long, loose nightgown, tousled black hair, and dark eyes with smeared mascara. She growled,

"I don't talk to Jehovah's Witnesses! I already heard everything I have to."

"We are not Jehovah's Witnesses," Salvador said. "We are neighbors and belong to the parish. We want to offer our help."

"Maybe we can talk to you for a minute," Rosa said.

"I need no help. Scram!"

"But your children —" Salvador said.

"You want me to get my gun?" she snarled, interrupting him. "Go away!"

She slammed the door. Salvador and Rosa went home, crestfallen. It would be more complicated than they thought. Their minds wavered from the notion that their neighbors could grow into an extended family. After a short while, they thought it was worth pursuing. A few days later, the time came for everyone to report the status of their assignments. When Salvador entered the meeting room, he observed the members' faces. An eerie atmosphere hovered around.

"I guess you didn't hear the terrible news," Father Rodriguez said. "The young woman and the three children you visited the other day are dead. A few days ago, the husband walked in on his wife having sex with another man. He killed her, her companion, the three kids, and turned the gun against himself."

The neighborhood was fraught with vandalism, attempted murders, arson, and thefts. People grew more frightened every day. When a youngster entered the barrio wearing the wrong color shirt or with a misplaced cap, the gang considered him a member of a rival outfit. They beat him. Graffiti proliferated with impressive speed. Assaults on businesses grew more frequent. The gang's turf was up for grabs, and the area turned into an occupied offensive zone. Residents were up in arms. Organized block by block, meetings took place at the local high school where a mother stood up and said,

"We have let our children organize an enemy army on our streets!".

"I feel better when my son is in jail," another said. "When he is out, I am always afraid that someday he'll be found dead."

Crime besieged the poor neighborhood. A drive-by shooting ended the life of a two-year-old boy. Little Peter boasted big eyes, a sweet smile, and a loving disposition. His mom had just recited a bedtime prayer with him, tucked him in bed, and kissed him good night. He was asleep when the stray bullet penetrated a window in his bedroom. His mother found him dead. The summer of 1999 was about to end as mourners cried over a child's body. Tears might well flood their streets but could not drown the violence.

26

CHILDHOOD LOVE

T hirteen-year-old Carlos adjusted well to Tata's retirement in
Peru. He continued his friendship with Sarah, but Samuel
Goldman looked at their relationship with uneasiness. He spoke to
his wife, Elaine, "Carlos is an excellent boy but is not Jewish. Nor is
his family well-to-do. His mother works as a paralegal."

"Why are you concerned about them? They are children. Leave
them alone. Besides, his uncle Michael Kaplan is Jewish and rich."

"He isn't his uncle. It is time we talk with our daughter."

Sarah's Bat Mitzvah took place on *Shabbat*, December 14, 2000. The
morning woke up glorious. The shining sun ricocheted on thick,
pristine snow on the grass and tree branches. A cold breeze greeted
children and parents as they strolled toward the synagogue. Carlos
wore a black skullcap and sat with Elisa in the back of the sanctuary
next to the middle aisle. Abraham Mederano and his family settled
in the third row. Deborah did not come. The young guests' growing
buzz announced the onset of the event.

Carlos heard the murmur, turned his head, and saw Sarah in a
blue velvet dress that enhanced the aquamarine splendor in her eyes.
Sunlight seeped through the star-of-David-stained windows,
illuminating the specks in the air that hovered over her like colorful
confetti. Even the bronze plaques with the names of the congre-
gation's deceased members threw golden reflections over the left

aisle. It was as if an ancestral jubilee were joining the fanfare. Carlos' and Sarah's eyes locked. She blushed as he mouthed,

"You look awesome."

She smiled.

In prayer shawls, her parents and grandparents paraded behind Sarah. Their admiring eyes were fixed on her. They sat in the first row of seats. Rabbi Mosheim shuffled toward the *bimah* where the Torah lay. His tiny eyes sparkled as if the older man were a boy about to receive a lovely gift. He caressed the scroll with his prayer shawl and kissed the holy garment where it had touched the sacred book. Samuel Goldman strode toward the central reading dais, touched his glasses, cleared his throat, and chanted the fifth *aliyah* prayer in his tenor voice. Grandfather Goldman held on to his silvery cane, limped to the stand, and followed suit. The sixth *Aliyah* resounded in his tremulous voice, dazzling the audience with its ancient allure. The holy calligraphy spoke the words of God, the faith that transcended centuries, continents, persecutions, banishment, pogroms, and holocausts.

It was Sarah's turn to read from the Torah. Amid an expectant silence, her steps echoed until she walked onto the *bimah*. The doors of the ark with gold foliage ornaments were in the background. A marbled column stood on either side, and a blue cupula perched atop them like a crown. The *Ner Tamid*, the eternal light, shone high above this altar. It highlighted Sarah with a halo and cast her shadow down the aisle as if she were rushing to meet Carlos. Her eyes roved from her parents to her friend, searching for his comforting gaze. He smiled.

Sarah pointed at the scroll with a silver yad and guided the *Bracha* reading in Hebrew. She concluded with a blessing,

"Blessed are Thou, O Lord our God, King of the Universe, who has chosen us from all peoples and has given us Thy Torah."

Giggling, several children hurried out of their seats and showered her with nuts, raisins, and candies, wishing her a sweet and joyful life. She stepped off the podium, glowing with self-possession and maturity as if transformed into a woman within a few minutes. Her parents and grandparents stared at her with their faces flushed with love. She sat next to them and listened to the rabbi,

"Welcome, Sarah, into the world of Judaism and the commandments that God handed to Moses. Now, you are an adult and have new rights and duties."

The Goldmans celebrated the party at home. Elisa could not attend, but Carlos did. Food, music, laughter, and gifts abounded. Happiness hovered about the place. Guests sang and danced, and Sarah played the piano, everyone admiring her performance. Carlos and Sarah sat across from each other at a large dinner table. Mr. Goldman observed the youngsters conversing, smiling, and laughing. His apprehension grew by the minute. As dinner ended, Sarah left the table and gathered with a few girlfriends in one corner of the family room. Mr. Goldman seized the opportunity and drew Carlos aside.

"May I talk to you for a minute?" he said.

Goldman ushered the boy into a nearby room with a bookcase spanned from ceiling to floor. He asked him to sit down.

"Carlos, you are an exemplary young man," he said. "I know of your virtues and hard work. Sarah speaks highly of you. For Elaine and me, nothing is more important than our daughter. We are devoted Jews. Today, you have attended the Bat Mitzvah, where Sarah turned into a mature Jewish woman. Do you understand what that means?"

"Yes, sir, Sarah and I often talk about religion. We respect each other's beliefs, and I felt so happy at the ceremony."

"I appreciate that. But you are not Jewish, are you?"

"No, sir, I am not."

"You like my daughter and consider yourself her best friend. Friends would sacrifice anything for the other's sake. You wish the best for her. It breaks my heart what I will ask of you, but I have no choice. Please, leave her alone before you both grow older, and your friendship becomes a serious relationship."

"Mr. Goldman, we are just kids. We have been friends for many years. We play and help each other at school and sometimes at home. That is all."

"Yes, but will you do it?"

Carlos nodded his assent.

That evening after the party, Mr. Goldman spoke to his daughter.

"My daughter, your mother, and I want your happiness. You are no longer a child. She mentioned you had your first period a few weeks ago."

"Mom!" Sarah blushed and complained,

"It is all right, my darling," Elaine said. "Your father must know everything that happens at home, and you are the most precious jewel in our lives. You are everything to us."

"Today, at your Bat Mitzvah, you read a beautiful passage from the Torah and listened to Rabbi Mosheim as he welcomed you into adulthood," Mr. Goldman said. "You are no longer a child. The new state calls for additional responsibilities."

"Your father and I think it is time for you to select the right male friends, Jewish friends."

"Are you asking me to stop seeing Carlos?"

"Is he Jewish?" her father asked.

"No."

"My daughter, you have answered your question." Mr. Goldman kissed her forehead and added, "I talked to him this afternoon. He acknowledged my position. He is a bright youngster."

Sarah had always been a merry child. One could have heard her laugh over and over. Her friends partook of her cheerfulness and enjoyed her zest. But sadness now overcame her. Crestfallen and pensive, she dragged around school with a blank stare. Her friends noticed it, but no one knew the reason for her unhappiness. Carlos espied Sarah shuffle down the hall. His heart raced as she approached him with traces of tears on her cheeks. He put his arm on her shoulder and said,

"It is hard, but we must obey your father. "He paused for a second, looking at her downcast eyes, and added, "I can't see you, but I am your friend."

"I know you are."

Carlos had never seen Sarah so upset. She turned around and rushed away, wiping her face with her arm. His world sank beneath his feet as he, immobile like a salt statue, gazed after her. Recently, he was still a child in primary school and could comprehend his feelings. Everything had changed. Carlos wished he were eight or nine when his mother and Tata safeguarded his joy. For the first time, he savored the bitter pill of growing up, standing alone, and watching his childhood happiness fade away.

27

GOSSIPS

On October 10, 1999, a little more than a year after Salvador's treatment had begun, he woke up invigorated. The world smiled at him. He sang a *Ranchera* in the shower to tell Rose the pleasant news. She also enjoyed some welcome relief. Weakness and severe pain afflicted her right hand but no longer flared up to unbearable intensities. Her left still bore moderate pain. At least her husband achieved a full recovery that brought back their happiness.

Rosa prepared breakfast. Salvador tasted the coffee and relished its aroma as the scent of fried eggs and tortillas aroused his appetite. Humberto observed his father and found him in beautiful spirits. Lucia kissed her dad on the cheek, took a seat next to him, and asked him to buy her a doll as he had often done before his illness. Rosa saw him out and wished him good luck.

The union building rose on the other side of the Eisenhower Expressway. Its solid brick wall faced the thoroughfare like a bulwark. Someone had tried to soften this harsh appearance and painted faux windows and balconies. The casual observer who espied it while racing along the lanes would get the false impression the structure matched well with the surroundings. But during heavy traffic, when the cars crawled, the faded pinkish color of the giant mural turned into a conspicuous eyesore.

Inside, offices boasted no luxuries to avoid the impression of lavishing membership fees on the hierarchy. Salvador sat to wait for

Nick Maltese, the union representative. In the reception room, he met Manuel, a former coworker at the Orison Building. He greeted him and engaged in a conversation. The stonemason updated Salvador on the developments at the construction site in his absence. Shifting political winds had ended the career of the alderman who had helped El Rubio, the supervisor. Mr. Miller's CEO position became shaky, and he retired. His assistant Ronald Madigan replaced him. Dean Fleming lost his job and family since his wife won custody of their children.

"I wonder whether it is true," the tattletale added. "A guy at work swore he saw him begging on the corner of North and Ashland. He wore a tattered jacket and a long blond beard that disguised him. But his deep blue eyes gave him away. Otherwise, he would not have recognized him."

Salvador listened to his ex-friend's gossip, but he did not comment. Dean Fleming, a bum, he thought. Life can change our destiny so fast. I know all about that, don't I? His musing halted when a secretary informed him that Mr. Maltese would receive him. Salvador wondered why the rep rolled out the red carpet for him. Many stories about this official circulated among workers, most of them indifferent. In his late fifties, his obesity disclosed an excessive appetite for excellent food, his only deadly sin on display for anyone to see. He did not beat about the bush and got right down to business matters,

"I am glad to see you back. You have come at the right time. Mr. Madigan called me, looking for a few talented men two days ago. He must assemble a group of well-trained Hispanic workers for a spin-off company. The City of Chicago must grant contracts to businesses owned by minorities. A lot of money is at stake."

Ronald Madigan, a fair businessman, sat behind an elegant mahogany desk. His youthful face reflected a genuine gladness at welcoming Salvador.

"The news of your illness saddened me. I always considered you a valuable and loyal employee with enough qualifications for a promotion," he said. "I would like to appoint you as the chief supervisor of a new company, Hispamer Construction. Several Hispanic businesspeople financed the initiative, as well as our parent company, through the Puerto Rico Bank. We have presented the projects to the lawyers of the City of Chicago. They agreed that the new firm fulfills the requirements for a minority-owned corporation. We will compete for the contract and win the bid. I need competent workers and want you to oversee their selection."

The intersection of Ashland and North at midmorning bustled with cars coming from or going downtown. Some pedestrians ventured outside on that chilly morning in April, most of them on their way to a small shopping mall. The lunch hour was so busy that twenty vehicles waited on both sides of the pedestrian crossing when the traffic light turned red. There, an unkempt, bearded man in worn-out clothes strolled by the cars. A stale odor of smoke and dirt followed him, much like a dog at the heels of his owner. A sign hung from his chest that read, "Vietnam veteran unemployed and home-less, please help me." Salvador approached him and asked him about Dean Fleming, the regular homeless person who worked that corner. The derelict looked at him as if he had fallen from another planet, for no one ever spoke to him.

"Man, don't ask me anyone's name. We, the homeless, have no place or name. We don't even exist. Is he your brother?"

"Yes, we are all brothers."

"Do you have two dollars for a burger?"

"This is all I got, my friend."

He handed him a five-dollar bill. The traffic light changed, and with the money already burning a hole in his pocket, the poor man crossed the street and looked back over his shoulder, hollering,

"Go to the Rotten Yard, next to Saint John's Cathedral. That's the place where the police let us camp out."

The Rotten Yard languished surrounded by high-rises and closed in by an iron fence. Inside, hundreds of homeless people huddled next to one another, each with all their earthly possessions — a stolen supermarket cart full of boxes and ragged clothes. Empty wine bottles, beer cans, and cigarette butts lay scattered everywhere. Salvador felt as if in an ancient leprous colony. Salvador could not understand the reason God let this horrendous squalor happen near the opulence of a cathedral and downtown Chicago. God had sent His son. He cured ten lepers in a village, but only one, a Samaritan, returned to praise Him. Maybe this underworld existed to give another chance to people, to rouse them to help their fellow man. But not even there did Salvador feel His presence.

The homeless stared at Salvador as one might an unexpected apparition, a ghost walking in a garbage dump. Salvador shouted,

"I am looking for Dean Fleming. Does anyone know where he is?"

No one answered. Salvador wandered, scrutinizing everyone's eyes. He thought of men being alike in death and birth and how misery diluted humans into the same amorphous social magma. It annoyed him to search through all that wretchedness amid luxury skyscrapers.

"I thought I had seen poverty," he said to himself.

Salvador espied El Rubio in a cardboard box. His lusterless blue eyes gazed at him, emotionless. A newspaper-wrapped bottle of vodka sat next to him, and a dirty blanket with burn holes covered him.

"It is me, Salvador. I came to talk to you."

"I know who you are. Go away. What are you doing here in the middle of all this garbage? Wasn't it enough that I poisoned you?"

"It is about a project."

"Leave me alone, will you? Can't you see I am dead? This world belongs to the forgotten, and you to the world of the living."

"You are sick," Salvador said.

"I'll be okay. I drank too much. It numbs everything."

"Mr. Fleming, I am taking you to a hospital," he said as a big shiver shook the sick man's body and made his teeth chatter.

"Leave me alone!"

"I am sure you want to see your children again.".

"What did you hear about my kids?"

"The children are okay. They miss you."

"You, liar! Anyway, my ex-wife, the bitch, takes care of them. I have no children anymore. I've got nothing."

"You are their father. A father is a father; no one can replace you. Come on, let's go. Let me give you a hand."

El Rubio could barely stand up, his legs giving way. His face had waxy paleness, lips blue discoloration, and eyes intense redness as a constant tremor agitated his body. The quivering extended to his Good Samaritan as if a bridge had joined them. El Rubio's ragged clothes reeked of alcohol and tobacco. The odor irritated Salvador's throat. He held his breath and put his arm around the hobo's waist, plodding along the yard under the indifferent look of everyone. No one lifted a hand to help. Many did not even glance at them, imprisoned in their thoughts. With a mighty effort, Salvador dragged his ex-supervisor out of the yard.

During the first few days in the intensive care unit at Cook County Hospital, El Rubio suffered frequent attacks of hallucinations. Rats, cockroaches, snakes, and scorpions crawled over the walls and ceiling as he kept shouting,

"These bugs are killing me! Get them out of my bed!"

A nurse sedated him with injections, but as soon as the effects wore off, the horrendous visions and screams returned. His face sweated, his heart palpitated, and his breathing resembled a runner's at the end of a marathon. In between these episodes, he mumbled. On the fourth day, his condition stabilized, and he was transferred to the detoxification unit.

This unit stretched through an entire floor in the psychiatric building. It was next to the inmate unit for the sick prisoners at Cook County Jail. At the entrance, two policemen were guarding access. Before Salvador walked in to visit El Rubio, he observed some convicts. Most were blacks or Hispanics, their envious eyes regarding anyone who strolled by their door. Freedom was only a few steps away and so far from them.

Salvador entered the hall, where several patients paced from one end to the other to control their nervousness. Their behavior called attention to their bewildered expression, blank stares, irresolute graceless gait, and bodies' and limbs' awkward motions. They seemed to have just come off an alien spaceship. A few nurses and auxiliary personnel chatted at the ward station. Salvador walked a short distance and saw El Rubio. He sat at his bedside, a curtain separating his room from the rest of the ward.

"You look better," Salvador said.

"Yes, I feel okay. But I still don't understand why you care about what happens to me."

"I am hiring workers for a new construction company. I want you to work for me."

"You don't need me. There are many well-qualified people."

"Only a few have your experience. Besides, there is nothing wrong if I try to give you a hand, is there?"

"You're Mexican, and I am white. I discriminated against you, laughed at you, and belittled you whenever I could. Why should you help white trash like me? If our situations were reversed, do you think I would have given a damn about you?"

"I don't see any Mexicans or Gringos here. We are two fellow workers."

"Let me give you some advice. Please stay away from me. I almost killed you once because I hated everyone's guts, including mine. How can you be sure I won't do it again?"

"You won't. Life has taught you a hard lesson. When I learned you had lost your family, I felt terrible. I said, 'I had to do for this man as other people did for me when I was in need.' If you can't accept my proposal for yourself, at least do it for your children. They need a father."

"You're crazy, Salvador. Let me think about it."

El Rubio had a hard time accepting aid from a Mexican. In Alabama, society had taught him to despise them as a child. Authorities assigned back seats on buses and segregated restrooms to blacks and Mexicans. Those ideas were rooted in his character. El Rubio remembered his father's words:

"Freeing the niggers was a big mistake. They don't work and will destroy this country. Mexicans are the same, niggers disguised with sombreros."

Dean Fleming also held the opinion that people in Illinois rejected minorities. Those folks shared the same belief but showed more tolerance for Hispanics and blacks. He also thought most people harbored no hostility toward them, just an ambivalent attitude. But El Rubio had hit rock bottom, a circumstance that prompted him to reassess this issue in a different light. He wallowed in the dregs of society where everyone looked alike as if they were grains of coffee grounds. But something more important than external appearance lived inside these human beings: their hearts and souls. These people deserved a second chance to get ahead.

After his epiphany, Dean Fleming accepted Salvador's help and joined Hispamer Construction. The company began building a library as part of the City's multimillion-dollar contract. The hammering noises, beeping of forklifts, roaring sounds of trucks, and workers' loud voices arose everywhere. The work progressed at a staggering pace. Salvador and Dean toiled together in an office. The chief supervisor glanced at his new assistant and observed his joyful smile, his blue eyes glowing like candles. At lunchtime, they rested and conversed,

"How did the meeting with your ex-wife go?"

"I couldn't see her. I have a restraining order," Dean said. "It is my fault. I drank too much and abused her. 'You are stupid. You don't know how to do anything. The house is a pigsty. You are a bad mother.' I pounded her over and over. She cried but always pardoned me, hoping that I'd change. I promised it many times. But my behavior worsened. One day, my verbal attacks ended in my losing control, and I hit her. It was the final straw. She left me and took the children with her. A few days later, a sheriff served me divorce papers."

"People can change, Dean. It may not be too late.

"My wife was an attentive wife and a devoted mother. She loved me, but I turned her life into hell. When I met her, I fell in love with her beautiful eyes. We were happy. I loved her smile and how she talked, laughed, and walked."

Salvador listened to El Rubio's story and watched the eyes of his coworker on the verge of tears. We are human, he thought. We make mistakes and become self-destructive. His mind hearkened many years back to Elisa. His feelings for her had grown powerful and fresh, a relationship born of friendship and passion. The unexpected romance almost destroyed his family. He acknowledged some remnant of love for the other woman because his mind had resolved the dilemma, but not his heart.

Father Rodriguez approached Helen, Dean's ex-wife, to arrange a meeting of her ex-husband with their children at the Church of the Nativity. She hesitated, concerned about her children's exposure to a drunken father. The little ones had suffered enough when they were living with El Rubio. Six-year-old Diane and five-year-old Johnny now attended school and enjoyed a quiet life. They missed their dad, but the mother had explained to them,

"Dad is not living here anymore. He is sick. Once he gets better, you'll be able to visit him."

It took two months for Father Rodriguez to convince her,

"He is now sober and attends Alcoholics Anonymous meetings."

"I am sorry, Father. I must check with my lawyer."

"We won't go anywhere with lawyers, Ms. Fleming. Do what you think is best for your children. When they grow up, they'll hold you responsible for the lack of contact with their father. I understand you put up with a lot of abuse. Dean has told me all about it. He is trying hard. I'll assume responsibility for the safety of the children."

On Saturday morning, the church was almost empty. Two older ladies dressed in black sat in front near the altar, their hands caressing rosaries. An altar boy lighted candles, his steps resonating in the nave.

A young woman eased into the building, holding her two children. Tall and svelte, the newcomer wore black garments and a worried expression in her turquoise blue eyes that contrasted with her porcelain-like complexion. Her facial features were dainty, and long black hair dropped to her shoulders. The little girl shared her father's sky-blue eyes and blonde hair. She dressed in red lace-edged attire. The boy took after his mother — rosy face and brown hair — and had put on a dark blue suit with a tiny blue tie. Diane giggled and looked in all directions, searching for her father. But Johnny searched aghast as if he had never stepped into a church. His memory tried to reassemble his dad's face, which, in the passing of months, had blurred.

Mother and children were in the last row. A few minutes later, Father Rodriguez exited the sacristy and strolled toward them. His face was radiant in anticipation of the joyful reunion. Ms. Fleming stood up to greet him and introduced the children. The priest kissed them and offered them his hands,

"Let's see your dad. He is waiting," he said, then shifted his eyes to their mother and added, "I'll bring them back in a few minutes."

"Father, wish him well. My husband — I mean, my ex-husband."

Revd. Rodriguez wrapped her in a warm gaze and nodded. Dean could barely wait anymore. Salvador had his arm over his friend's shoulders when they heard the steps of Father Rodriguez and the children's voices. As soon as they entered the room, Diane rushed toward her father, who held her in his arms, crying. Johnny froze and tried to match the man's image before him with the one his mind had concocted. Dean embraced him, lifted him, and covered him with kisses.

A few months later, the spring of 2000 bloomed in full swing. Salvador found a red-brick, single-family home with spacious windows and a front porch with flowerpots full of white lilies. On the first floor, an expansive family room and spacious kitchen stretched a few steps above a well-lit half basement. A short stair flight led to the third level with three bedrooms. Bushes and little trees grew along both yards, abutting into a small garden behind the house. Salvador could not wait to tell Rosa. Their new address was in a safe neighborhood, with no gang activity, and not too far from the Church of the Nativity. Life smiled at the Gómezes again.

28

THE LETTER

The ripping noise of Salvador's impatient opening of the letter from Elisa made his hands tremble. The paper seemed to give off the scent that enwrapped his former roommate during all their gleeful months together. The brief note read,

"April 17, 2003

Dear Salvador:

I need your help on an urgent matter. I must meet you in Milwaukee at your convenience. Please let me know when we could get together. Forgive me if this is an imposition since you made the promise so long ago.

Sincerely,

Elisa"

Elisa's decision to contact her beloved came after long and arduous considerations. Her decision derived from Samuel Goldman's opposition to the relationship of sixteen-year-old Carlos with his daughter. The youngsters continued their childhood friendship. Sarah became so depressed that Elaine intervened. Mr. Goldman capitulated and allowed the relationship to continue for a long while until he surprised the two lovebirds holding hands at a nearby park. That evening, the father and the boyfriend discussed the situation.

"I am sorry," Mr. Goldman said. "I can't turn a blind eye and bless your courtship of Sarah."

"I told you I will embrace the Jewish faith. We worship the same God."

Goldman did not relent. His disapproval of the youngsters' liaison did not stem from religious beliefs or race but the unknown paternity of Carlos. The lack of information unnerved him and called into question the ancestral baggage the youngster would bring in. He believed that one wedded a family, not a person.

Elisa visited the synagogue and talked with Rabbi Martin Lehman, who remarked,

"It is hard for Jews to accept an interfaith marriage. In those couples, the Christian fathers endured a hard time approving their offspring's education in Judaism."

"In your case, it is even more complicated," the rabbi added. "There is no patriarch in your family, a father who oversees your son's upbringing."

When Elisa discussed this issue with Michael Kaplan and Mariela, both advised her to contact Salvador. They did not decry her silence over the years or berate her with, "I told you so." On the day Elisa wrote the note, she was working on official papers in the living room. Her eyes gazed at a giant porcelain elephant at the center of a coffee table. Little light triangles dappled the figurine's face after oblique sunrays seeped through the blind slats. Her mind wandered from the summary of a legal case to her son's predicament.

She had pondered nothing else since Carlos brought his problem to her attention. Elisa stood up, shuffled to the kitchen, and poured herself a strong black coffee. With the drinking cup in hand, she stepped on a red rug with golden embroidery and halted before reaching her seat. Her body and her thoughts stalled, paralyzed as in a trance.

Elisa regarded an old photo of her son on the wall. Seven-year-old Carlos sat at a school desk with an open book before him. He wore a gray suit and a blue tie, and his eyes looked straight ahead with intelligence and determination. She lost her grip on the mug. The cup plummeted against the area rug with a muffled thump, careening and spilling the coffee over the thick fabric. She ignored the mess, sat down, grabbed a piece of paper, and wrote the note to her beloved.

Before Salvador received the letter, the Gómezes' life had run smoothly for the previous three years. Their finances blossomed, and their American dream turned into a reality. Twenty-year-old Humberto was in college at the University of Illinois in Champaign, and fourteen-year-old Lucia attended Moreland Junior High. Rosa passed her driver's license test. She bought a red Camaro and found a part-time job as a saleslady at Marshall Field in downtown Chicago.

Three years earlier, Rosa visited her hometown. Lucia joined her, and Humberto stayed with his father. The same vast mountains and the dark blue sky overlooked the unchanged, beautiful valley. On their way to fir forests, the monarchs still perched on the shrubs around the house. Nothing else was like it used to be. Her elderly mother tottered to attend to her house chores but no longer took care of the orchard. A stroll through Toultuca shattered Rosa's memory of the place. The central plaza languished empty. Vendors and shoppers had disappeared since a small supermarket opened in the neighborhood. Whitewash flakes dropped from the church tower, and the old golden cross rotted away, tarnished with rust.

The young people and her school friends emigrated. Only her friend Magdalena stayed in town. She aged and wore tattered flip-flops that bared her clean but unkempt toenails. Her face wrinkled, and her hair rioted disheveled. She had raised six children. The three youngest—two boys and a girl—lived with her. The older three daughters worked as housekeepers in Guadalajara, and her husband still toiled in the agave fields. The irremediable passage of time bristled before Rosa. She had undergone a significant transformation, and so had Salvador.

With her mother and Lucia nearby, Rosa reassessed her relationship with Salvador. She missed him and felt lonely even in the middle of the Toultuca countryside. Her husband loved her. Her awareness of his devotion to her intensified as she gaped at the mountainous landscape. After arriving home exhausted from work, he often washed the dishes and tableware, placed them back in the cabinets, and helped her with the home chores. Salvador sometimes brought her flowers or drove to a Latin Supermarket to get *pan dulce* for her. Some Saturday evenings, he took her to a Latin place to enjoy wine, listen to the piano, and dance. Occasionally, in those evenings, Rosa got into romantic moods, prompting her to appreciate her husband's attractiveness and increase her urge to make love to him.

But the passion had cooled in their marital life. Salvador loved her very much, as she loved him, but their sexual life became part of their routine, predictable, and unsatisfactory to human instinct. It became a scheduled activity like his weekly visits to the supermarket. One could argue that, over time, this change occurred in many marriages. However, there were other reasons:

In her case, unrealistic expectations surged as the main culprit. Her imagination often returned to her hometown, where she viewed her union with her husband as perfect. As for him, Rosa thought he had never completely recovered from whatever happened to him during the time Salvador lived alone. She bore no fault on this issue. Rosa pardoned him many years ago, even though he never confirmed his infidelity or asked for her forgiveness. Now, far away, she realized it would take an extra effort to improve the situation. Rosa decided to implement changes that would transform her spouse into a happier lover.

Back in Chicago, Rosa put into practice her resolution. She consulted a psychologist, Dr. Ann Barbour.

"Mrs. Gómez, you have not done your part. Salvador might have been unfaithful to you, but he stuck with you and kept his commitment. He is an exemplary father and a dutiful husband."

"I pardoned him and forgot his infidelity."

"Not completely."

"I don't sense his full love as it should be. The other woman not only enjoyed his body, but she also kept part of his soul."

"Relationships are never perfect. Mrs. Gómez, you did not keep your resolution: 'The present talks to the present and the past to the past.' Nor did you put it into practice. Let me put it this way: the statute of limitations has expired. Please comply with your decision."

Rosa went on a shopping spree, bought sexy lingerie at Victoria's Secret, got her hair done at a fancy salon, and wore a sexy cologne. Rosa forced herself to revive her newlywed feelings and give herself to him. The couple enjoyed a boost in their marital life. Then, it declined to lukewarm progress. A definite gain remained, but daily matters took over and diluted the energy needed to keep the full bonanza.

Salvador's lack of nearness to God disturbed him until two years ago. That day, he reproduced the conditions of his initial close contact with Him. The chilly morning woke up with a tepid sun that barely lifted on the horizon beyond the mass of skyscrapers. He regarded a gray sky with a few long oval clouds that tinted it bright purplish pink. His car tires screeched in the morning's silence. Salvador drove, prayed a Rosary to Our Lady of Guadalupe, and invoked her name, asking her to help him find the divinity again,

"Talk to Him, Mother of God, plead on my behalf."

The divinity was generous with Salvador, bestowing upon him and his family wealthy living standards. His wife and children got everything their hearts desired, and he enjoyed plenty of earthly possessions. A Hail Mary lingered on his lips when the prodigal son parked his car on the grass between green bushes.

The day shone with bright light. Salvador heard the stream rippling and cardinals and robins singing. A few wild ducks took off the water, quacked, and flew in a V formation. Out of the car, the wetland scent hovered over him. He unpacked his fishing rod and gear from the trunk of his black BMW sedan and shut it with a soft noise. Salvador plodded along a footpath, the sun on his face, his trailing shadow crawling over flanking heathers as his feet treaded on the trampled grass. A cold breeze whispered in the nearby oak trees. He thought of God and summoned Our Lady's aid. Here on the riverbank, the suppliant held the rod like an aspersorium, ready to sprinkle holy water, cast the line into the stream bottom, and talk to God,

"I've got everything but miss You."

Salvador heard the water gurgle among pebbles and rocks. He perceived a distant God. He sensed the faraway presence of the divinity out of his consciousness' earshot. The reason for God's aloofness loomed large before him — his lack of straightforwardness. The remnant of love for Elisa lay dormant in his mind. He tried to erase it. But memories resisted with the same angry force he whipped the fishing line back into the water. No one could fool God because nothing escaped His detection.

From then on, Salvador lived content with the distant presence of God when he prayed. Perhaps one day, the Almighty would allow him to sense Him close and converse with him as in the past. Maybe He would behave like his old neighbor when seven-year-old Salvador found a red jasper ring in a park. The boy fell in love with it and hid it for a year. He then returned it to his neighbor. But the older man returned it to Salvador as a gift for his First Communion. Perhaps God would someday let him treasure the memories of his time with Elisa and still be reconciled to Him.

29

UNFORGOTTEN

A ll the changes in his life did not prepare Salvador for Elisa's letter. His initial joy gave way to a state of upheaval, his mind going into a tailspin. Images of his onetime lover rekindled intense feelings. His temples throbbed. The panic attacks had disappeared six years ago, but they now recurred with a vengeance, sweat and palpitations overcoming him.

Salvador parked near the Planetarium and took a long walk to Navy Pier. It was sunny and a little windy, and the waves lapped up against the stone wall and rippled back to the immense body of water. A few boats lined up on the pier as still as the seagulls that blanketed the jetty at the Chicago River outlet. He drifted into thoughts. What could be the reason for this letter after so many years? It must be something crucial for her. Is she dying? Oh, God, I hope she is okay. She means so much to me. Even from far away, with no communication, I sensed her company. I took for granted that she was always somewhere in Milwaukee, her life following an uneventful course with no significant setbacks. Every time I traveled to Milwaukee on business, I searched for her. I hoped to bump into her as she strolled through a street, entered a store, or left a shopping center. Elisa liked to hang around domestic merchandise stores to admire little trinkets and purchase comfortable pillows. I often roamed through several stores with my eyes focused on any woman with some resemblance to her. I was always disappointed because I never came across her.

Mariela promised me she would notify me if a life-threatening illness or calamity happened to Elisa. I have not contacted the legal firm in two years, not since I made my testament and Rosa's. The paralegal still works there and is probably the one who provided my address to her friend. Has Elisa run into hard times? She would not have written unless something of extraordinary importance occurred. I know Elisa never got married since she accepts no invitation from anyone. Loneliness is painful for a young woman. At least I know she did not forget me. Nor did I consign her to oblivion. The walk calmed Salvador and let him put the note aside for a few hours before he talked to Rosa.

His wife stood on a stool, arranging her clothes and shoes on the upper shelves of a walk-in closet. A Gucci black-leather bag hung from her hand, and the mention of Elisa's name shook the double golden chain of its shoulder straps. Her feet were stuck to the wood plank as if electrocuted by a high voltage current. Her face became pale, and her eyes glared at him with dismay and fear. Salvador helped her down, noticing her fingers were cold and moist. He stared at her and waited for a verbal reaction.

All the years of bearing the weight of his sin flashed through his mind. In the past, Salvador had put himself in Rosa's shoes, but now more than ever, he felt the enormous impact of his misdeed on his wife. For the first time, he understood she had avoided his confession since it would have crushed her. Rosa said nothing as terrible forebodings blocked her mind. In total silence, she turned her back to him and stepped on the stool to continue her task.

"You may come with me," Salvador said.

"No, you must go alone. This time isn't appropriate for me to meet anyone. It is up to your conscience and God to judge your past relationship with this woman. I realize you owe her a favor since she helped you get the green card."

Salvador looked forward to meeting Elisa but realized he needed to be cautious. Although flimsy, his renewed relationship with God encouraged him to seek advice from Father Rodriguez. Salvador and his family attended Mass and other meetings at his old parish at least once a week.

The priest turned the lights on in the empty church and sat in the confessional. The penitent explained his relationship with Elisa, the fateful events that led to his stay at her apartment, and their inadvertent and insidious falling in love. Their mutual affection culminated with an unexpected single intimate encounter. It resulted in his perceived aloofness of God that hurled him into a pitched battle to forget Elisa and reconcile with Him. It had been many years since he had daydreamed of her or conjured her image. But occasionally, joyful memories of their time together still popped up when least expected. Yet, after so many years of restraining his will, Elisa's letter shook his soul's foundation.

"Memories are not a sin. You've repented, haven't you?"

"No, I haven't. I can't be dishonest with God."

Salvador had tried to deplore and atone for his transgression but could get nowhere. His sin of love always woke up and resisted his attempt with invincible might.

"The Almighty God is a father who knows what brews in their sons' hearts," the priest said.

"I sometimes wonder whether God cares about us and watches what we do like an indifferent bystander."

"That happens to most believers and some saints. Mother Theresa of Calcutta struggled through periods where she doubted even the existence of God."

Now that his parishioner was about to meet with Elisa again, Father Rodriguez advised him. He should resist the attraction. Good and evil coexisted in the human makeup. Imperfections and weaknesses were as much a part of us as virtues and strengths. We had the duty to walk the path of sanctity. Our efforts to improve had to be fair and devoid of hypocrisy or lies to ourselves. Humility was at the center of our Christian life. He added,

"Sometimes we fall, and when this happens, we must repent, pick up the pieces, and keep going."

30

THE SECRET

The next day, Salvador drove to Milwaukee. Alone in the car, he attempted to concentrate on the road. His mind flitted from the last time he had met Elisa to his immediate concerns. All these years of taming his reactions to memories did not withstand the upheaval her letter had caused. The confession did not help him. He was back to square one because nothing placated his state of mind. As he drove, the sunrise tainted the flanking foliage with a fiery appearance that matched his burning sensation of anticipation. Capriciously shaped white clouds dotted the steel-blue morning sky as he observed the contrasts and noted the similarities between those hues and his mood.

The point of rendezvous with Elisa was Café Provencal, a little place on Stevenson Plaza. Round forged-iron tables and blue cushion-padded chairs rested on a sidewalk. The area overlooked a central garden with florid gardenia bushes, tulips of various colors, and red roses. She sat, waiting for Salvador. Her heart pounded, and her face bore witness to her sleepless nights and trepidations at the upcoming meeting. Paleness lit her pink cheeks and darkened her under-eye circles. Elisa knew that Salvador would understand the situation and receive her revelation without anger. But she wondered how he would react to the unexpected news.

She soon saw him waiting for a walk signal near the coffee shop. He wore an elegant gray suit set off by a blue-and-white tie, his hair sported a mixture of black and gray, and his bearing struck a note of self-confidence. This effect was more pronounced than in his earlier years when she met him. Time had graced him with an air of distinction. From afar, he locked his eyes on hers, observed her demeanor, and tried to guess the reason for her letter. She uncrossed her legs, tight blue jeans stressing their svelteness and contrasting with the red blouse with black fringe that stirred on her shapely bosom. Her long black hair gleamed as it fluttered over her shoulders.

The intersection bustled with shoppers. Pedestrians hurried and interrupted the view from her table on and off. A big old clock that hung in the corner chimed twelve. The cars stopped, and Salvador was motionless for a moment. A cloud shadow slid over him as emotion riveted his feet to the ground, his eyes still on hers. Crossing the street hastily, a youngster brushed against him, bringing him out of the trance. Salvador strode forward and noticed Elisa's beauty grow intense as he approached. They experienced a powerful urge to rush toward one another and fuse in an embrace. The self-restraint made their bodies shudder. It was as if their last and only romantic encounter occurred yesterday.

They kissed each other's cheeks. The neighboring tables were empty. The children's voices from the garden playground across the street added a note of freshness and excitement to the sunny afternoon. Silence enveloped them as he sat at the table across from her. Their loving gaze turned into a wondering expression as if reading each other's minds. Elisa and Salvador shared the same private thought that the passing years had changed their appearances. But the intense love that lived on in their hearts loomed before them like a giant obelisk—immobile, tireless, impervious to the ticktocks of time. Happiness shone in their eyes as her hands rested on her lap and his right foot swung back and forth.

Elisa apologized for contacting him after so long. She did not want to intrude on his life and cause a disruption in his relationship with his wife. He shook his head and shrugged his shoulders. His smile intensified as he took a deep sigh and filled with words the seventeen-year gap of separation. He looked into her eyes. She did not blink. His hands rested on the table, and so did hers as if bracing for what might transpire in their conversation. His professional life had been successful. The construction company recently promoted him to the chief of human resources. His health was excellent. Rosa was a wonderful wife who worked to make everyone happy at home. Years ago, she toiled so hard at a factory that her right hand became deformed. Their children were their biggest treasure and rendered their lives joyful. Salvador reached across the table, grabbed Elisa's hand, and said,

"There is no excuse. I had no right to do what I did. But the impulse I felt was stronger than any principle or God's rule."

"Don't say that. Don't be so hard on yourself. I was a grownup. I let it happen because I fell in love with you."

"I realized I had failed you, my wife, and God."

"You didn't fail me. You helped me enough. Life can never be perfect."

A waiter stood before them to receive their orders. Engrossed in themselves, the customers ignored his presence. He coughed to get the pair's attention. Elisa ordered his favorite drink, café-latte, with plenty of milk, and Salvador smiled at her act of thoughtfulness. She described herself as a friendly person who prided herself on a joyful, comfortable home and challenging job. Her unmarried and unengaged status had allowed her to dedicate more time to her job. She never dated and refused serious matrimonial offers, providing no reason for her single life. The conversation then veered toward the central issue of their meeting. Elisa changed her language to English to signal the seriousness of the revelation she was about to unveil,

"I hope you don't take what I have to tell you badly."

"We are friends. Nothing can break this bond."

"We ended up being more than friends, didn't we?"

"Yes, we did."

"And I became pregnant and gave birth to your son."

"A son!" he repeated, astonished.

Salvador held tight onto the table's edge, his eyes shining and overflowing with tenderness. He could not believe his ears as a thoughtful grin stretched his face. Elisa explained her silence – her consideration for his children and wife. His thoughts raced. He loved Rosa, yet a big reason he had stayed with her instead of going with his former partner was his child. But he didn't know Elisa was also going to give him a son. That news might have shaken the foundation of his decision. It could have changed everything.

"His name is Carlos, and he is my life," Elisa said. "He looks forward to meeting his father. I can't postpone it any longer. He almost found you on his own."

When Elisa talked about her son, her eyes lit up with immense love. He provided meaning for everything she did and her happiness. Being a mother and a father to him had entailed an arduous job full of rewards and pleasant moments. She praised Carlos as a bright, sensitive, and caring youngster. His school achievements would make any parent proud. Elisa taught him to love his father, disclosing her boyfriend's Mexican origin and married status. She revealed their romance and events that led to Carlos' procreation, stepsiblings, the reason that Salvador had not yet contacted him, and her letter to his father.

"Your wife may feel disappointed with you," she added.

"Rosa is a sympathetic woman. When I explain the situation, she'll understand."

"I hope so. Carlos' rights are now more important than hurting her feelings."

"I know. I love Rosa, and she loves me. She is an intuitive woman and has known for a long time I fell in love with you. My love for you was… is different."

"You don't have to justify anything," Elisa interrupted him. "One cannot explain love. One only senses it."

Lengthy silence ensued as the news took hold of his mind. His thoughts drifted to his new son and the woman in front of him whom he loved so much. Her voice now sounded more ardent than ever before,

"Carlos takes after you. He has your gentle eyes and goodness. Even his gestures remind me of you."

Her words gladdened him, but his happiness soon turned into disappointment for all the years he had lost — birthdays, Christmases, schools, first words. He missed his soccer games, days of sickness, celebrations, and the day-after-day growing up of a young life.

His guilt soared. What could he have done? When he left Elisa, Salvador never considered she might have become pregnant. He should have investigated this issue since they used no protection. His climax skyrocketed to the acme, rendering him unable to withdraw in time. Life was never perfect. He could not possess everything and should appreciate any gift that fate held in store for him. It was never too late to love a son and enjoy sharing one's life with him.

"God blessed my love for you with a son. I've never been able to stop loving you, Elisa. I've tried very hard."

Elisa squeezed his hand. It acted like a detonator that revved up his insides. Salvador felt the warmth of her skin and watched her eyes sparkle. These perceptions transported him to another world. It was a magic dimension with no traditional principles. Neither his vows nor the rules of society nor the laws of God governed this domain where his love for the woman before him erupted with passion.

The passersby's curious eyes, the cars moving along, the aroma of coffee, and the murmuring chat of customers who sat outdoors, all gained a new meaning. Even the nearby flowery scent inebriated his senses. It felt as if Salvador embarked on a time machine and contemplated all those years left behind. His decision inflicted pain and suffering on two women. He subjected Rosa to his depressed moods and panic attacks while Elisa languished, yearning for his kisses in the middle of her forlornness.

"Our son waits for us at home," Elisa said, interrupting his thoughts. "He has been expecting you for so long. He must discuss something important with you. I'll let him explain it."

Carlos was not at home. Unsure of his father's reaction, Elisa did not forewarn her son of his visit. A note on the table indicated he went to a friend's home and would return in three hours. The sun flooded the small living room with a balcony that afforded the view of a park teeming with dogwoods, honeysuckles, and prairie roses. A delightful fragrance wafted around. An open French window let it seep in and mix with Elisa's subtle cologne. It transformed into the heavenly aroma he had reminisced about many times before. Two lipstick plants with several blossoms hung from the ceiling on either side of the balcony. A large picture of Chicago featured the skyline framed by the calm waters of Lake Michigan.

Salvador and Elisa sat next to each other on a light blue sofa, huddling over a photo album on the dark oak coffee table. Their nearness made their faces flush and their hearts pound. A narrow gap separated the one-time lovers, but gravity pulled them close together, and each noticed the touch of the other's hip. Warmth waves rushed through them and stunned them. They welcomed the intimacy vibrations like an endearing jewel. Their shoulders brushed against each other as she bent over to open the album.

The photograph of Carlos stared at them. Salvador could see his eyes reflected in the picture, the shape of his face, and the same jovial expression. Elisa gazed at Salvador, expecting his reaction, her smile lighting her face. He looked at her. His eyes roved over her lips, soft like red petal cushions. A small opening revealed the dainty teeth as the tip of her tongue barely peeked through them in an inadvertent gesture of excitement. It was a sublime attraction for him, a temptation beyond measure.

Salvador recognized the same mighty attraction he could not resist seventeen years ago. He excused himself, stood up, went to the window,

"I love the view from here," he said. "The park, the flowers, the children, people's bustle. I knew you would be successful."

"Salvador, stop it! I know why you stood up. I felt the same thing."

He laughed as she walked to the kitchen and brewed some coffee. She came back with two mugs and some cookies. They went through the entire collection of pictures gathered in twenty albums from their son's birth to the present. Salvador's absence everywhere in the presentation made him feel like a failed head of a family. Feelings of frustration and inadequacy overtook him. He then realized that selfishness provoked those sentiments. The account of mother and son's life did not have anything to do with him, but it was a testimony to the terrific work Elisa had accomplished. He was proud of her.

They kept no track of time. When the outside world popped up before them, their son's arrival hour approached. A few minutes later, Salvador observed Carlos when his child walked into the apartment. He was tall and handsome and had an aura of self-confidence and happiness. His brown eyes examined the father as if catching the meaning of the stranger's unexpected presence. His honey hue of tenderness in his eyes spoke of a sensitive and loving person. His demeanor revealed self-esteem and self-reliance. After a moment of perplexity, Carlos realized who the visitor was. The youngster had seen these man's eyes in his mirror many times.

"He is Salvador, your father," Elisa said.

Carlos stretched his arm out to shake his father's hand and greeted him with a neutral expression. Salvador held his son's hand, drew him closer, and embraced him. Carlos froze. He did not expect this demonstration of affection. The youngster often dreamed of this day. He saw himself running toward his father to let him know how much he loved him, his dad hugging him and smiling. Now that the moment came, it turned out to be so different.

"I am sorry, my son. I've lost so many years of your life."

"I'd lost hope I'd ever meet you."

"From now on, I'll make it up to you."

"I thought you didn't even try to find us."

"No, Carlos," Elisa interjected. "He didn't know. This moment is no time for reproaches. I've brought you together so you can enjoy each other."

Elisa's voice sharpened with emotional strain. She reminded her son of his promise to disregard the past, express no regrets, and forge an excellent relationship with his father. Her happiness blossomed at the scene of her men together, their remarkable resemblance, and their restrained joy. They needed a little push to ignite the chemical reaction of effusive affection.

"Go down to the bistro, have coffee, and talk," she said. "You have so many things to catch up on."

Dimmed candelabras illuminated the high black tables, the magenta stools, and an oak countertop. A powerful aroma of coffee wafted through the shop. The waitresses' blue uniforms infused the environment with a cozy atmosphere, and the "I-love-Paris" melody sweetened it. Cheerfulness seemed to ooze from Elisa's apartment down into this establishment.

Salvador sat over a cup of coffee. Carlos pulled open a can of cola and sat at the table across from him. The youngster talked about school, his friends, his upbringing, and Tata's role. He elaborated on his intention to study law and follow Uncle Michael's footsteps. His mention of Mr. Kaplan as the youngster's role model provoked a hidden jealous reaction in Salvador, but he reined it in. The new dad prided himself on his son's demeanor, maturity, and accomplishments at school. Carlos expressed his love for his girlfriend, Sarah. The situation with the Goldmans created an impasse in their relationship. He acknowledged his youth but did not want to lose such a precious young woman and added,

"One never knows if one will ever find genuine love again."

His words sent Salvador's thoughts back in time to The Bus Cemetery and his sudden crush on Rosa. He was sixteen, the same age as his son. It was genuine love. But several years later, he fell head over heels for Elisa. Another type of love blossomed, fitting his mature age and life in a different country. That created a dilemma Salvador never fully resolved.

He now added Carlos to the equation of his predicament. Paternal devotion flooded a dad's heart when he met his child. This affection erupted with phenomenal strength, regardless of the timing. It could occur with the son in the mother's arms at birth or while sitting before the father many years later.

Carlos ended the pause in their conversation. He looked forward to meeting his new siblings and his dad's wife but voiced some concerns about how they would receive him.

"Rosa is an excellent person like your mother," Salvador said. "It will be hard for her to accept that I have a son with another woman. I hope she can forgive me. I am sure she won't have any bad feelings for you. At first, your brother and your sister will be shocked, but after a while, they'll welcome you."

As they sipped their drinks, father and son pondered. Carlos thought about how wonderful it would have been if he had enjoyed his company over the years. He often needed him. Salvador regretted their ordeal of living separate lives. He realized the tremendous work that Elisa did raising their son. She indulged Carlos with her share of hugs and kisses and those that belonged to him, the dad. Father and son could have recounted each other countless details of their existence apart. Life set their courses like two trains with different destinations. Their comfortable silence meant as much as their earlier sincere talk. An instant trust was born, an atmosphere of love that would burgeon their relationship.

31

BROKEN PROMISE

On his way back to Chicago, Salvador basked in immense happiness. A new son and his meeting with Elisa caused him feelings of unreality, memories of today's events plunging him into thought. His son showed gratefulness over the appointment to satisfy Mr. Goldman's request. It will take place five weeks from this date. Salvador recalled his last words to Elisa,

"I love you. I don't know if I can live without you again."

"Weigh everything, please. Don't rush any decision. You have a family."

His mind drifted toward Rosa amidst the noisy rubbing of the tires and the blurred images of cars whizzing by. He pondered her dedication to him and his different love for her. It was passionless but profound and calm, like Lake Michigan on a windless day, its water level steady over the years. There was rough surf, but no gales, and the feelings inside swam like schools of fish. Sanctified by the sacrament of marriage, his relationship with her withstood the test of time. Until now, his commitment to her and their children had prevailed over anything else.

Salvador then reflected on Elisa, the woman whose love for him transcended time and distance. She remained faithful to memories of their relationship, jilting marriage proposals and attempts to woo her. Salvador reminisced about her beauty. It evoked the radiance of her flesh that sent a rush of warmth down his belly and loins. Elisa also unveiled a treasure for him: the birth of Carlos, his son. After today's events, Salvador wondered whether he could live without her again. And yet, it was hard to conceive of life away from Rosa. His predicament resembled that of a little sparrow trapped in a baseball batting net, unable to find a hole big enough to escape.

The highest intensity of his affection switched back and forth between Rosa and Elisa. It depended on which one was the focus of his attention. At his mature age, his mind lacked an immature person's blinding passion. He understood the reason a man could love two women at the same time. Men created regulations and laws and developed them over the years. Monogamy was a recent development. The Bible provided an excellent account of this evolution. He also accepted why a consensus existed regarding the matrimony of one man and one woman. He approved, supported, and defended it.

But books and laws did not encompass all plausible scenarios in human relationships. Real life was another issue. People make mistakes. In Salvador's case, it was one of love. No lust or other lowly desires filled his heart, but the highest emotion of all. The sinner did not condone his transgression. He was not proud or ashamed of it. As penance, Salvador endured his conscience's assault over the years. Unable to repent, he clung to his sin like a castaway to a piece of debris from a wrecked ship. These musings resolved nothing in his mind and raised doubts about what to do next. These two women were ripping him apart. He would divide himself into two halves if he could.

Salvador felt ecstatic about the day's events and proud to have controlled the enormous desire to make love to Elisa. He realized that would have been a severe mistake affecting God, Elisa, Rosa, and all his children. His relationship with Him was distant and feeble but enough to content himself.

When Salvador arrived from Wisconsin and entered his house, Rosa noticed something significant had occurred. His face was pale. She did not ask him anything and waited for him to start a conversation. He waited until his wife was alone and then sat in front of her and said,

"Elisa revealed a secret she has kept from me since I last saw her seventeen years ago — my son Carlos."

Rosa stared at the magazine in her hands, fought back the tears, and rushed into their bedroom. Facedown, she lay on the bed and sobbed. Salvador remained silent in the family room, his fingers intertwined as he gazed at nowhere. A thousand thoughts crossed Rosa's mind. Her husband making love to another woman bristled as the most painful one. How could he do such a thing? She wondered. Years earlier, before she arrived in this country, Rosa feared Salvador had fallen in love with someone else. The high suspicion of infidelity turned almost into conviction over the years. But now, uncertainty stabbed her heart.

Rosa composed herself, emerged from her bedroom, and tottered back into the living room. The TV was on, making unintelligible noises and flashing images into oblivion. Salvador huddled in the armchair, his back sinking into the cushion as if he wanted to hide. He gazed at her. Her eyes were moist, her face pale, her hair disheveled, and her light blue skirt and flower-stamped pinkish blouse rumpled. Mascara ran down her face. Dangling from a gold necklace, the medallion of Our Lady of Guadalupe had carved a square red spot at the root of her cleavage. Her bosom heaved over a lacy fringe. Rosa had applied makeup before Salvador came home, and her fruity cologne still wafted from her. She looked him straight in the eye and asked,

"Why did she reveal it now?"

Salvador rumbled about what had happened: His accidental falling in love with Elisa, the insidious beginning, the incredibility of what had occurred to him, his fight against it, and his objections to God for allowing it to happen. A grimace of pain ripped his wife's expression as she stood frozen before him with her clasped hands pressing on her belly. Rosa frowned at him as if ready to raise an accusatory finger. He sat straight as his voice grew assertive,

"Rosa, I want you to understand. That slip doesn't mean I don't love you. I love you."

"You don't love me enough."

A vibrant-colored commercial popped on the screen and broke the moment's somberness. Salvador outstretched his arm to reach for the remote on the coffee table, toppling over a purple glass vase with red roses. The container shattered into tiny pieces, and the flowers clumped in disarray. The commotion did not faze the couple. It was as if the mess was a mere reflection of the present state of their marriage. Salvador grabbed the device and turned the television off. Rosa wiped her eyes with her finger, smoothed her skirt and blouse, and passed her hands over her hair. She strode to the brown armchair in front of her husband, plopped into it, and said,

"Elisa knew you were a married man, didn't she?"

"Please, don't judge her. She is an honorable woman."

"Who am I to judge her? As Jesus said, 'For, in the same way you judge others, you will be judged.' God will do it."

"I didn't mean to hurt you. Forgive me."

"How could you fall in love with someone else?"

"I don't know. I fought it with all my strength. Sometimes, it felt like a curse."

"It was a curse. You committed adultery."

"I often asked God why He tormented me by letting me fall in love with someone else while I still loved you. I got no answer. Some things in life have no answers."

"Did she love you?"

"Yes, she still does."

A cloud of dense silence engulfed them. Rosa fell into a deep trance. A gilded wooden grandfather clock that stood in the corner chimed ten times. Each clang raised gooseflesh in husband and wife as they held their breath and braced for the next question. Rosa mustered all her strength and asked it,

"Do you love her?"

"Yes, I do."

"How could you do this to me? I have always loved you more than my life."

"I love you with all my heart. I never stopped loving you. But I also fell in love with her. My son was born out of wedlock, but not without the blessing of love. I am not ashamed of him."

"We are not discussing Carlos. I welcome him to this house as your son. We are talking about Elisa."

When Salvador spoke of Elisa, he gained a warm expression. His gaze aimed downward at nowhere, and Rosa again watched his eyes shine with a greenish tint as his face lit with a longing smile. He praised her motherly qualities, unselfish love for him, and her putting his welfare before hers. Elisa never attempted to win him over and believed his happiness was with Rosa and their family.

"Is that what she still thinks?"

"She left it up to me to decide."

"What do you want to do?"

"I don't know. I am tired. Let me get my things from our bedroom and take them to the guest room. I don't want to be unfaithful to you or Elisa."

"Salvador, you married me before God. You promised to love me until death. We have been together for many years."

"I need to be alone and rest."

"We have two children, for God's sake. I am your wife!"

Salvador shuffled into the main bedroom and grabbed several suits from the walk-in closet. Another trip took care of his ties and shirts. He closed the door to the guest room, put on his pajamas, and lay on the bed facing the ceiling. Out of the corner of his eye, above the bed headboard, he gazed at the crucifix. Jesus seemed to stare at him. Salvador stood up, took the image down, and stowed it away in a nightstand drawer.

He returned to bed and let his eyes rest on a painting of Bosque Colomos in Guadalajara. It hung on the wall before him. The scene brought back honeymoon memories of their visit to this park. With peals of laughter, Rosa ran after the ducks and white herons around the pond. Her lips' taste reminded him of baked cookies. The newlyweds spent their night of love and passion in a nearby bed-and-breakfast. He had loved his wife; he still did. But his feelings for Elisa always hovered in the background for seventeen years.

Salvador lay alone in a strange bed, his nerves shaken, his chest tight, and his feet cold. He thought of Rosa, who sobbed alone next door. Her mind must have been bristling with the smothering weight of his unfaithfulness with another woman. This woman's blood fused with his vital fluids to bear a child— her children's new brother. A sinful stain smeared his wife from head to toe. It was unfair. Rosa was honest, committed no transgression, and did not deserve this torment. He perpetrated the infraction. Salvador pondered God, his sexual offense, and the breaking of His commandments. His conscience repeated his father's warning,

"Salvador, my son, our family is all we have in this life. We live for it. The rest is just pieces of hay the wind carries away."

But now Salvador had two women who bore him children. Love and the laws of the Almighty and society buttressed the first one, Rosa. But blessed with the same affection, the other resisted the passing of time with steadfast persistence even in his absence. In front of him loomed his loneliness, terrible predicament, and uncertain future. When you leave a crucial task unfinished, it comes back to haunt you. All along, Salvador understood this maxim and convinced himself he had resolved the dilemma to the best of his ability, but he had not. It had been pending since he fell in love with Elisa. He stayed with Rosa and fulfilled his obligations, but his heart never abandoned Elisa. His pondering overwhelmed, fatigued, and surrendered him to restless sleep.

Salvador's acknowledgment of his love for Elisa made Rosa feel as ghastly and deformed as her shriveled right hand. Conviction and certainty were two different things. She carried her grief and tried to overcome it but accomplished nothing. Her husband's behavior changed. He nodded or said a few words at dinner and breakfast but joined no conversations, his mind somewhere else. The TV filled the silent void at their table. Not even his daughter, the apple of his eye, broke his spell. Her father wandered around, munched, or fell asleep but never smiled.

Salvador commuted to his office every day. On one occasion, he brought flowers to Rosa, who interpreted his gesture as a sign of guilt. Salvador never mentioned or discussed anything. Rosa knew when he had been on the phone with Elisa because of his eyes' reflective and restless glare. It was as if he had overdosed on emotion. The prayers of Rosa for a miracle allayed no marital woes. Her mind tormented her with reminders of his love for another woman. It hurt her to consider that Elisa and Salvador might care for each other more than Rosa and her husband ever did. Her face revealed the fatigue and despair her inner battles stirred up. She wondered how long they could endure this situation.

32

WIFE AND LOVER

On a Sunday morning, Elisa boarded the Metra train to Chicago. She had often made this trip to visit friends or show Carlos the local attractions, Navy Pier, the skyline, and the museums. The Show of the Stars at the Planetarium mesmerized him. Now, her mind raged with worries. A few days ago, Rosa called her. She wanted to meet in private without Salvador's knowledge, articulating no reason for her request,

"A matter too sensitive to be discussed on the phone."

Elisa detected no animosity in her voice. Her words brimmed with concern, but her tone was courteous and friendly. Her feeling toward her friend's wife had always been one of understanding and respect. Salvador belonged to Rosa. She realized they were spouses. But this fact did not mitigate her anguish at the mere idea of their intimate encounters, and it took her a while to come to terms with Salvador's marital duties.

During two brief periods, Elisa experienced an emotion foreign to her. The first time occurred a few weeks after Carlos was born. She noticed instant jealousy for all couples in love since any reminder of her loss affected her. Elisa missed romance when she watched pairs of youngsters woo one another: their gaze into each other's eyes, blush of passion, quiet tenderness, and intrigue in their laughter and smiles. All spoke of an invisible link that tied two human beings together, a magnetic force that paced their minds and bodies in unison. Even elderly couples who walked hand in hand were targets of her uncontrollable resentfulness.

The second time happened when Mariela informed her friend of Lucia's existence. Elisa rejoiced in Salvador's new family member but felt terrible jealousy. Until then, she had never considered bearing a girl to her beloved. Notwithstanding her late mother's behavior, a daughter livened up a mother's life as a best friend and a pillar of happiness. Elisa envisioned conversing with her, keeping her company, and going shopping. They could do arts and crafts, share women's ideas, help with home chores, and guard her old years. The idea fascinated her. In the privacy of her bedroom, she placed a pillow under her nightgown and admired her profile in the mirror. She fancied her daughter. The little girl boasted a doll's white complexion, puckered lips, tiny toes like necklace pearls, curly brown hair, and large dark eyes.

Elisa thought so much about her daughter that the image invaded her waking hours. She even fantasized about her child, who sat next to her to get her hair combed before the bedroom mirror. Elisa felt her by her side in the kitchen or at the dinner table across from her for two months. One day, a sudden penchant for two items in a shop window caught her fancy — a floral dress with long sleeves and a blue tulle skirt with a ribbon-covered stretch waist. A courteous saleslady asked her about her daughter's age. Embarrassed, Elisa rushed out of the store, hurried home, and cried. The incident dissipated her obsession with the little girl.

As Rosa waited for her husband's lover, she wondered how to identify her. She had never seen a photo of Elisa. She remembered only an envisioned image that stuck to her mind the day she and her son left Toultuca to cross the border. Back then, a few lights trembled in the darkness far down the town. Amid that gloom, she pictured Salvador staring at his lover with a passionate expression. The other woman laughed and stuck her tongue out at him, her eyes full of intrigue. The wagging organ waved long and fleshy. It released a sweet poison that intoxicated her husband with an irresistible desire.

The other woman vanished into plumes of flame that lingered over her and her child like an evil spirit. The brazen images blazed up as if branded in her eyes.

Rosa now hoped this vision would not turn into a harsh reality. The rivals had picked "The Little Mermaid" as the point of encounter, a small restaurant close to where Elisa used to work. The place kept a half-lighted ambiance to reduce the patrons' stress. Customers flocked to the quiet dining room during lunch break. A wall clock chimed eleven, and a lemon-like odor of recent cleaning greeted the early comers. Some were already at the bar; otherwise, the place was empty.

Elisa could distinguish no one or anything in the penumbra of the restaurant. Her mind teemed with the questions that Rosa might ask her. She expected her beloved's wife to want her out of the way. Maybe she held a terrible secret to discourage her from pursuing him. Rosa would attempt to dispel any hope the other woman might entertain for a favorable decision. Women often bribed their husbands' lovers, but Elisa would accept nothing. Salvador was non-negotiable. Her right hand reached for her face, and her cold and clammy fingers ran over her forehead.

In the semi-darkness, Elisa looked down, probed for the steps with her right high-heeled shoe, and then did the same with the left. Her cautious tread navigated a wet floor. Her adjusted vision then focused on Rosa. As agreed, her friend's wife wore a black skirt and a blue blouse with a sizable onyx brooch pinned to her chest.

Elisa needed no cue. She had seen her picture frequently and would have instantly picked her out of a lineup. Rosa sat in a corner over a cup of coffee. A large painting of the Eiffel Tower next to the Seine River hung in the background. Photographs did no justice to Rosa. Her eyes were more prominent and expressive than Elisa had gathered from Salvador's photos. Her cheeks were flattened like a fashion model's, her jaw clenched, her elbows against the chair arms, and her right hand in a white glove. There was nothing provincial about her. Her attractiveness stood out as two men at the counter kept their searching eyes upon Rosa. The dish-and-glass clatter in the kitchen broke the silence.

Now that Elisa approached her, Rosa wished she had never made the call. Her mind, which had sizzled with thoughts, turned blank. The firm handshake with which she intended to receive the other woman did not pan out. Rosa's nervous smile turned into a grimace, and her attempt to stand up and greet Elisa failed. She barely lifted herself from the chair when a subtle tremor overtook her left hand.

Over the years, Rosa had heard about the beauty of her husband's friend from several gossipers. Long eyelashes rimmed her eyes, her raven-black hair reached her shoulders, and her fleshy red lips opened ajar, ready to bid hello to her. A well-tailored gray suit enhanced her shapely body. Elisa took a seat, and Rosa proffered her left hand. The wife noticed the other woman's slender fingers, soft texture, and long red nails. Neither sensed ill feelings toward the other, just apprehension.

"Thank you for coming," Rosa said. "I thought we should meet. We have children from the same father."

"That is frequent these days, isn't it?"

"Yes. On my way here, I planned to tell you to leave my husband alone. I then put myself in your shoes. I don't know what to say to you. But he looks disoriented."

"Give him some time. It is not every day you find out you have a son with another woman."

"I don't know what goes on in his head. Well, I do. He wonders whether to leave me and go with you and his newly found son."

"Has he told you that?"

"No, he doesn't have to. I know."

A young brunette waitress with a black skirt and a white apron poured some decaffeinated coffee into Rosa's cup and added warm cream. Elisa ordered a cappuccino with some sugar. The aroma of the drinks set a friendly tone. The young server reminded Rosa of her husband's initial encounter with Elisa, her insight seething with uneasiness. The emotion surfaced in a grimace that Elisa noted,

"What can I help you with?"

"I don't know if you can. I realize you love Salvador."

"I do with all my heart."

"Not more than me. I have loved Salvador since I was a child. Even now that he has broken my heart, I still love him."

"Then, he should be okay with either of us. If he decides so, it doesn't have to be an acrimonious divorce."

"It will be tough. The children are grown, but it will be hard for them and me too."

"Salvador must decide. I don't want to give him up unless he wants to stay with you. Let's put it this way. You enjoyed him for over twenty years. It may be my turn.

These words had an impact on Rosa. She understood why her husband could have fallen in love with the other woman. Elisa dazzled anyone with her striking beauty and gentle eyes that could penetrate any soul. Other attributes flared out: her air of distinction, ability to empathize with the person in front of her, and capacity to listen to others. Rosa believed she was her husband's best half, and fate had erred and misled him when he met the woman before her. But now she was not sure.

"Ms. Ramirez."

"Call me Elisa, please. Regardless of his decision, I'd like us to be friends."

"I don't think that will be possible. You went to bed with my husband. We can be civil to one another."

"Salvador and I love each other."

"I hope you understand my situation. You are a sophisticated woman, a learned person with a career and a life of your own. Until recently, I was just a housewife. My family is everything. It is all I can show for my lifework."

"Rosa, you wouldn't be here if you were simplistic and unrefined."

The two women ate their lunch in silence. Elisa had a chicken sandwich, and Caesar salad, and Rosa had a tuna sandwich and chicken soup, their thoughts consuming their minds much more than their mouths the food. There was no need for words. Their eyes spoke and understood the dull flickers, half-blinks, and blank stares. Anxiety shone on each of their surreptitious looks at one another. Life played with them, put them through their paces. Whatever the outcome, both would endure the blow. The winner, if there were a winner under these circumstances, would sense the other's pain. Otherwise, how could they call themselves children of God?

A few weeks later, Salvador prepared a small suitcase for his trip to Wisconsin. He packed inside a light brown suit, a white shirt, a yellow and red striped tie, brown shoes, a pair of brown socks, underwear, and a small bag of toiletries. Rosa noticed his disquiet state of mind. He stuffed every item in his disorganized luggage. In the past, she had helped him with the suitcase whenever he attended a meeting out of town. But this time, her husband did not ask Rosa to organize it for him.

His mood changed and turned subdued and reflective a week ago. It happened right after Salvador informed his elder son of a younger stepbrother's existence. Humberto had lived enough to understand the reasons — a man living away, the birth of love for another woman other than his wife, and the imperfections of every human being. His maturity deemed the matter a private concern between husband and wife. It hurt him, though. He had always looked up to his father as a perfect dad, incapable of making mistakes. His father and mother loomed like a bulwark built with a single flesh. All his doubts, fears, and disappointments dissipated against this wall. He pondered the situation, asked himself questions, and concluded that a son should not judge his father.

Lucia posed no difficulties. She liked the picture of her new brother and looked forward to meeting him. He was handsome and worthy of her boastings to all her friends. The girl knew of her family's stress and perceived the strain in her parents' voices. The situation chilled the once cheerful home and hearth she had taken for granted. Her dad's reticence caused part of her impression.

Salvador's thoughts brooded over the conversation with his friend Antonio a few days ago. He had found him reviewing some papers in the small office in the back of the restaurant. The dining rooms were empty, and the aroma of maize and flour tortillas announced the upcoming lunch hour. His friend admonished him,

"Get your act together! I told you years ago to resolve this issue."

"I've worked hard all these years to build a happy family."

"So, you have a new child and two women. You don't know what to do. It would help if you kept your sanity. Think with your brain, not with your pants."

"C'mon Antonio, I came here to talk to you and get your advice. You don't have to chew me out."

The friend did not understand his interlocutor's predicament since Antonio had always seen Salvador content and calm. Life was never perfect and entailed difficulties. The impromptu counselor also realized that Rosa loved her husband and strived to make him happy with all her heart. She had succeeded most of the time.

Antonio remembered the day Salvador lost his job promotion and became a nervous wreck. Rosa asked Antonio to come over for dinner. She served guacamole, grouper a *la veracruzana*, and *chimichanga* — tortillas with shredded chicken, cheese, and rice. A chocolate cream pie added a note of sophistication to her cuisine. She played a *ranchera* music record. Antonio took to the floor with nine-year-old Lucia, and the mother convinced the father to dance with her. Margarita glasses in their hands, husband and wife turned and spun until they dropped, dizzy, to the ground. As their bellies ached from laughter, she said,

"Life is like a dance at home — family, friends… we laugh, cry, fall, and stand up. We'll be okay. There is no reason to get depressed."

Antonio cautioned his friend about the future with Elisa since she might have grown into a different person after the lovers had parted their separate ways so long ago. Salvador could be in love with a ghost and did not know Carlos. The newly found father might end up living in an unfamiliar home with strange people, unable to find his comfort zone. Antonio warned him,

"You would take a big risk."

"That may be my problem. I took no risks."

"Elisa is gorgeous. She can stimulate any man's hormones."

"It is not sex. Elisa is a fine woman and a good mother. I love her."

"Don't be naïve. I don't have to tell you. That excitement mellows down and goes away with time."

"Not necessarily. It changes. Everything does."

"You must consider the terrible stress of divorce."

"I don't fear divorce. I am afraid of the decision, of what it means."

On his way home, Salvador thought about his answers to Antonio's questions. One required further clarification — his attraction toward Elisa had little or nothing to do with sex. For a moment, he wondered whether he was fooling himself. A sudden resurgence of desire for Elisa occurred sixteen years ago.

Back then, he blamed his ordeal on his anxiety and extra fatigue from excessive work. Memories of Elisa's luscious lips, voluptuous breasts, and sleek inner thighs kept him aflame. His longing assaulted him over and over and interrupted his work, meals, and sleep. Pervasive arousals brought on terrible heaviness in his loins that making love to Rosa did not relieve. Nothing helped. Words such as 'woman' or 'love' evoked the sensual image of Elisa. Salvador felt like a male monarch flapping his wings in a spasmodic rhythm as he desperately searched for a female.

At work, Salvador overheard a young man open up to his friends and reveal his struggle with intense lust. Going to bed with a prostitute resolved his problem. He mentioned the name of the bar where he had met her — El Gato Dormido Tavern in Joliet.

When Salvador shuffled in, he found a gloomy place with candles and several bright beer signs half-lighting the bar. Bolero music added intimacy to a small dance floor. Four couples sat at tables, and two women stood alone at the counter. One, Matilda, was a buxom young brunette with a know-it-all smile and light-green eyes as bright as a cat's. Salvador loitered next to her over a glass of Merlot. After a brief talk about the rainy weather and terrible mistakes the mayor of Joliet had made, she asked him,

"Would you like to fuck? For you, it is only fifty bucks."

Salvador paid for her drink. Her well-lighted nearby studio contained a king-size bed against the main wall, a little round table with two wooden chairs, and a loveseat in front of a small TV set. A kitchenette hid behind a partition. He only saw the end of a narrow table with a large cognac glass full of red beads. Matilda wasted no time, and after kicking her shoes off, she flashed her naked body. Her breasts bounced as light reverberated on their pale, splendorous skin.

Salvador observed her perfunctory eyes, the room's coldness, the big bed with crumpled sheets, and the private scent. This odor was not the fragrance that had enveloped Elisa's apartment. The memory adjusted his feelings like the first chords helped a guitarist tune his instrument. Everything in the studio of this woman became foreign to him. He felt as if he had awakened and found himself in an unfamiliar place. No erection, no desire. This woman roused his sadness as a veil of shame fell upon him. He could even perceive God watching him and showing contempt for him. It was loathsome lust rather than honorable love that caused his behavior. The incident ended his lecherous spree.

Back home, Salvador prepared a trip to Wisconsin the next day. In the morning, he bid goodbye to his wife. Salvador eased his lips against hers and planted a smack on her forehead, squeezing her in a long hug. Rosa noticed his trembling and thought his reserved behavior showed he had already decided to go with the other woman but kissed him lovingly.

He stopped to say goodbye to Lucia on his way out. The teenager was reviewing some brochures to prepare for the celebration of her *Quinceañera*. The coming-of-age ceremony would take place in a few weeks. Father Rodriguez would conduct the service, and a party would follow at Rosebud Banquets. As Salvador left, several items caught his eye: a list of guests and long dress patterns for Lucia and her court of honor. A lovely photograph of his daughter bedecked pink invitations. She wore an elegant white dress, a sparkling tiara, and her first high-heeled shoes. The Barbie that would serve as her last doll rested on a table.

"Don't forget to invite my new brother to my *Quinceañera*," she ran after him. "Here, please, take the invitation with you."

33

AT A STANDSTILL

"Elisa, may I speak with Salvador?" Rosa asked on the phone. "He is not with me. I haven't seen him since we dined with the parents of my son's girlfriend four days ago."

Rosa was at a loss. Since she concluded that her husband chose Elisa, her fears of confirming his decision prevented her from contacting him. Her first attempt to reach him on his cell phone occurred this morning. There was no answer. He never arrived home after checking out of the Holiday Inn, where he had lodged. A clerk at the reception desk corroborated his stay. The guest occupied a room for one night on Friday, May 29. He booked and paid for it with a credit card two weeks earlier. The evening of his arrival, Salvador apologized for forgetting his wallet and departed early in the morning before dawn three days ago. The receptionist recalled a brief conversation with him,

"After he handed me the key, he smiled and said, 'What an enjoyable morning. Some people say that one should be grateful to God every morning of a new day."

"I joked with him and asked whether he was a priest in disguise. He replied, laughing, 'No, just a good sinner.'"

Rosa's words plunged Elisa into bewilderment. She thought something must have happened to Salvador. He was calm and happy the evening of the dinner, his eyes sparkling with love for her and their son. She introduced him to Mr. Goldman. Both men walked into a large office, whose main wall boasted a bookshelf that extended from the ceiling to the floor and across the entire wall. It teemed with large books with covers of dark colors. They sat in two large mahogany armchairs that faced a white marble fireplace. Glass doors adorned with a white ivy pattern hid the dark flue. The door and windows were closed, yet they could hear the joyful noise of their relatives in the family room. Even traces of the aroma of a stew cooking in the kitchen reached them.

The wealthy lawyer knew of the construction executive. The fateful story that brought a young illegal migrant and his lovely coworker together eighteen years ago. The reason father and son were separated for so long. Mr. Goldman wondered whether the father behaved irresponsibly. His law studies taught him to examine everyone and every circumstance with absolute objectivity with no interference from emotions.

Salvador was intuitive and sensed his counterpart's doubts. He read them between the lines of their casual conversation about the Milwaukee Bucks and the Chicago Bulls, which accompanied them on their way to their seats. A floor lamp was behind the seats where Mr. Goldman and Salvador sat. The light blinded the guest when he looked at his host. Salvador excused himself, stood up, and positioned the chair facing his interlocutor, a subtle scratching sound interrupting their thoughts. He saw the fidgeting shadow of his host come to a halt over the hearth and vanilla wall and then heard his voice,

"Mr. Gómez, let me apologize for any inconvenience I might have caused you with my decision to meet you."

Salvador expressed his utmost happiness about meeting his son and reiterated his gratefulness for the blessed events that brought father and son together. His words and humble demeanor impressed Sarah's dad. Their discussion about Jewish concerns and duties revealed his outstanding knowledge of the Torah. Mr. Goldman learned of his guest's seminarian studies, and his face lit up with a smile. A conversation ensued that ended with an embrace of mutual understanding.

At dinner, Salvador smiled, laughed, mingled with all attendees, and rejoiced in the radiant happiness of Carlos and Sarah. His son remembered his father's words to Sarah,

"Love at your age is pure. No hidden interest, no corrupting influences, no doubts."

Salvador lifted a glass of red wine and said,

"Please, join me in toasting Carlos and Sarah. I propose we all drink to a long friendship based on love and respect for each other's ancestry."

Salvador sounded sincere and convincing and acted as if he had been a part of his son's life all along. No clues emerged to his desertion of everything in his life, nor any sign of threat to his life. He spent most of the evening with his arm around his son's shoulders. Elisa observed some periods of absentmindedness in her beloved. For a few seconds, he regarded everyone at the gathering as if looking through them from the clouds overhead. She had never seen this reaction before but thought nothing of it and blamed it on the moment's excitement. He kept the thread of any conversation. When she hinted something about his state of mind, Salvador answered her with a splendid smile,

"Yes, I already saw a shrink."

He did not elaborate on the reason for his psychological consultation. Elisa knew it pertained to his decision. He seemed cheerful, smiled, and joshed,

"It is hopeless, Elisa. I am too far gone."

He did not express any frustration about his visit to Dr. Lawrence Whitaker's office, where he had sat alone on a black chair in a room brimming with diplomas. A dark mahogany desk was between the patient and the doctor. Salvador felt a great disappointment at the psychologist's words,

"Only your sound judgment can resolve your predicament."

The doctor apologized for not providing him with the expected answer. No one could save him from fretting over the deliberation and final resolution of a dormant matter in his mind for too long.

"You are the only one who can decide," the doctor concluded. "The sooner, the better."

Whitaker issued a dire warning—the situation in Salvador's mind could behave like an abscess under pressure. Pus might bore through the skin and come out. So could a severe stress break through his mind and surface in some unforeseen form when least expected.

Elisa now recalled her private conversation with Salvador at the party,

"I love you with all my heart, but my stress is overwhelming."

"I am not pressuring you. I want you to be happy with your wife if you decide."

Salvador bid goodbye at Elisa's apartment door and lingered outside, smiling, and enjoying every moment with his beloved. His amorous words overflowed with passion and warmth like his farewell kiss. He shuddered as if seized by a sudden chill, a reaction that made her ask him in. He declined. Elisa watched him leave with confident steps and noticed that he never turned around to gaze at her.

Salvador had not gone to work or requested scheduled days off. A letter with instructions never surfaced. Antonio and Dean, el Rubio, never heard from him. His hotel room revealed no clues since a maid had cleaned it and new guests occupied it.

The police found his dead flip phone in the hotel parking lot. The black lid had come off as if thrown away with violence or run over by a car. They recharged the battery, but the retrieved voicemails disclosed no meaningful messages. Inquiries in the neighborhood and his photograph in the newspapers yielded no information.

Authorities began a comprehensive search for the car. So far, no one reported any sightings. Nor did anyone mention a recent accident involving a vehicle with its license plate or one with the same color, model, and year. All hospitals in the surrounding areas received alerts.

A week passed, and nothing transpired. Father Rodriguez officiated a special Mass for him at the Church of the Nativity, where Elisa and Carlos met Humberto and Lucia for the first time. The mourning half-siblings took comfort in one another's courage to endure the tragedy. Lucia never left Carlos' side. It was as if she wanted to experience her departed father's unknown part that still lived within her stepbrother. Their mothers bared their hearts and souls and conversed out of their offspring's earshot.

"I wish he had been with you, Elisa. I know you would have taken excellent care of him. He was, I mean, he is an honorable man. I wanted him to be happy."

"Let's not despair. We'll find him."

The police posted a ransom for information, leading to finding the missing person. Rosa, Elisa, Dean, and Antonio put up the money. The police found no evidence of foul play or robbery. The car did not turn up yet, and investigators considered other leads. Salvador might be a victim of carjacking or kidnapping, but no one requested any payment. The agents entertained the possibility he had voluntarily disappeared, questioning his relatives and Elisa. In the police's experience, sudden vanishings occurred in families harboring some terrible secret. This problem no longer existed in his case. Another woman in a man's life could pose a threat to his mental stability. The finding had no significance since Salvador did not run away with her. Voluntary desertion seemed unlikely since he had been a loving father, a responsible husband, and a reliable worker.

The uncertainty about Salvador's fate caused great distress to his family and friends. Rosa brooded over the day he left for Milwaukee. She feared he was abandoning her. But he did not take a large suitcase or grab his old electronic agenda with his contacts. The latter still lay atop his nightstand. In the upper drawer, she found his wallet, an act of inattention Salvador had often committed. One would have expected him to be more careful since he was leaving town. It contained his credit cards, ATM card, driver's license, photos of his children, a yellow laundry receipt for his shirts, and a card with his office alarm code. Rosa could not find his silver money clip. She had warned Salvador against carrying the gadget. He exposed wads of bills out in public but often protested,

"Oh, don't worry. I always separate the cash I am going to pay beforehand."

Most of the time, Salvador did not. Rosa now concluded he planned to return to her, his wife. Life turned into waiting for news and fearing it. Time was at a standstill as Rosa felt the terrible vacuum of her husband's absence. She missed him and viewed their marriage in a positive light. This realization brought back scenes of happiness with Salvador.

One occurred the day ten-year-old Lucia celebrated her First Communion. After the religious ceremony, a brunch took place at Las Palmas Restaurant. The venue boasted a large dining room with a forged-iron arcade and a gorgeous veranda that reproduced a Mexican patio. In white, the little girl looked like a doll in a wedding gown. Rosa wore a red dress whose color emphasized the dark hair resting on her shoulders. Salvador hired a five-person mariachi band with giant Mexican sombreros and silver-embroidered garments. Adorned with roses, each of the ten set tables accommodated eight guests whose excitement increased the joyful atmosphere. Three waiters and two waitresses rushed in and out, serving coffee, pastries, *quesadillas*, and tortillas. The aroma of food mixed with music.

In the middle of the banquet, Salvador walked toward the stage where the band tuned their instruments. The accords of *"Las mañanitas"* began. He sang with his eyes riveted on Lucia. The girl sat next to her mother, who faced him.

"El día en que naciste, nacieron todas las flores."

His tenor voice resounded in the room. He strutted toward them in an elegant blue suit as the band followed suit. Salvador posed with his arms open and palms up, a soft grin on his face. The candelabra light ricocheted on the dark hair of his daughter and wife. It trembled in their eyes and illuminated their smiles. He thought about their striking resemblance, about how much he loved Lucia — and his wife, who had borne him his precious gift. Their table got closer as the song wound down,

"Ya viene amaneciendo, ya la luz del día nos dio."

Guests stopped eating, held a pastry or a fork in their hand, and pinned down to their seats. The restaurant personnel and Antonio stood still. Everyone stared at the scene as if a movie screen suddenly stopped. Salvador's face blushed with emotion. He inched around the table toward his little girl and his wife. His heart rushed. He placed his hands on their shoulders as his mind sped up, spurred by his feelings for them. Once the song finished, he bent over, filled them with kisses, and ended with a big hug to Humberto. Like a magician, he grabbed a tray of rose petals hidden under his chair and showered them with delicate blossoms.

Two more weeks went by without information about Salvador. Elisa mourned his loss. As she had often done when his absence became too painful, she opened a little jewel box that she kept under lock and key. Inside was his letter of apology for their first intimate encounter. It lay carefully folded next to a passport-size picture of him. She pulled the note, spread it out, and placed it on her nightstand. The words appeared neat and bright, as if years had not passed. She inched her hand over the paper and caressed it. Before, the dry sensation on her fingers turned into a warm river of feeling that flooded her entire body. Now, it only brought sadness and tears. She read it,

"I am sorry about what happened this morning. It occurred because I fell in love with you."

From the box, Salvador's picture gazed at her, reminding her of the day she took it. It was sunny, and she and her roommate visited his attorney's office to review the case. The young couple strolled around to find a small restaurant where they could have lunch. He looked so worried she devised a way to lift his mood.

"The judge sometimes can grant the green card on the spot," she said. "You must be ready."

"Oh, Elisa, you're much more of a dreamer than I am. What are you trying to tell me?"

"Take some passport pictures and keep them handy."

"Is it for good luck?"

"If you want to look at it that way, fine. Let's go to a booth where you can get four photos for five dollars."

He kept three photos and handed her one to include in his file, but she misplaced it under a book cover. The picture had lain dormant there for several years. One day, when she looked up something, it fell on the floor.

The image of her beloved Salvador brought tears to her eyes. She now admired it again: his gentle and clean looks, a man incapable of harboring ill feelings; his mustache framed his face like a signature on a vital document; the increased separation of his upper front teeth that unveiled his natural smile. Her fingers eased over his mouth. For a moment, his upper lip's softness and tiny protrusion in its middle came back to life. She plucked the photo out, kissed it, put it back, closed the box, and put it away. Thoughts about her love for him lingered for a while.

Elisa still had a faint expectation of finding him alive. Every night, Salvador's loved ones resented going to bed empty-handed with their prayers unanswered. Their hope grew more and more implausible with each passing day. His loss weighed upon them like a tractor furrowing the earth and marked their life with a great sense of loss.

34

PLACID LAKE

Salvador awakened in a strange room a day after checking out at the Holiday Inn in Milwaukee. The information booklet on his nightstand showed he was a guest at the Lakeview Motel in Lake Geneva, Wisconsin. The place was sixty miles west of the road that should have taken him back to Chicago. Salvador needed to learn who he was and how he got there. Dizziness and headaches plagued him. Salvador felt as if someone had beaten him up and thrown him into the room. But no evidence of a struggle could be seen in his lodging.

He stood up, looked outside, and saw the water of a placid lake. A few joggers ran along a promenade next to the coastline. A two-story redbrick building with a central gallery led to a pier that bustled with people about to board two riverboats. Red and yellow tulips, purple dense-blazing stars, and yellow cinquefoils bloomed everywhere. Tall oak trees displayed their lush leaves. Two carriages with white horses waited next to a curb. He opened the window, and chilly air rushed in. It did not clear his head. The area was unfamiliar to him.

Salvador felt nonchalant. The lack of memory of his past lavished him with listless peace. A riverboat pulled out of the dock, and the expansive blue waters rippled and gleamed before his eyes. A wake of white foam rode on the wave crests, rushed to the sides, and disappeared yards away in the calm lake water. Seagulls fluttered over the boat and swooped down to catch their food. The birds cawed, the passengers bustled around the deck, and music drifted toward him. The sun hovered above in a blue sky among white clouds. The golden star witnessed the splendorous spectacle of man and Nature.

But this uneasy calm was an artificial state. Salvador needed to find out his identity. He sat down, examined his hands, and noticed the remnants of calluses on his palms. His thick finger joints showed he had worked hard. Salvador recognized his face in a mirror but did not associate it with a name. A little scar at the corner of his right eyebrow shed no light either.

A picture of a red barn with an extensive field of yellow wheat ears hung on the wall behind the bed. He named the objects in the painting and the room in Spanish and English. The effort did not straighten out his mind, worsened his headache, and blurred his vision. He recited first names, starting with Antonio, Andrew, and Angel and ending with Zacarias, Zaqueo, and Zedekiah, but did not retrieve his name. A call to the reception might yield the one he had registered with. Salvador decided against it because it could arouse suspicion. He feared he might have fled after committing a crime and needed time to think. His underwear revealed no incriminating stains. He took a shower and got dressed. A metallic object protruded inside his pants pocket. His hand plucked out a silver money clip full of bills and a crumpled piece of paper that hid behind it. He smoothed it out on the nightstand and read it,

Salvador and Rosa Gómez have the pleasure of inviting you to a celebration at Rosebud Banquets on Saturday, July 12, 2003, from 7.00 PM to 10:00 PM, in honor of their daughter Lucia's fifteenth birthday.

RSVP by June 12. 708-443-3356

Salvador's heart skipped a beat when he read his name. He had a family: a wife, a daughter, and a son. Everything returned to his memory except how he had reached the motel. A frightening thought assaulted him. He could have wandered over the earth. Some unfortunate people roamed around for years until an incident, or an autopsy unveiled their identities.

Salvador blamed his problem on a psychological shock. He now understood Dr. Whitaker's words forewarning him. His over-whelming efforts to make a reasonable decision turned him into a generic human with no memories or access to the storage of his life experience. The doctor likened the process to the rupture of an abscess under pressure.

Salvador recalled his restless night at the Holiday Inn in Milwaukee. He walked out of the hotel toward his car and heard the noise of something falling from his pocket and hitting the asphalt. He squatted and searched for it, but his recollection ended there. Salvador did not account for the last fourteen hours. His car was parked outside in a spot right in front of his room.

He grabbed the car keys from the nightstand, walked down, and looked for his cell phone in the vehicle. Salvador could not find it and concluded it had dropped from his pocket in the parking lot at the Holiday Inn. An umbrella and two baseball caps rested on the bottom of the trunk. The glove compartment contained the car documents.

Thinking of Elisa brought back his passionate love for her. He recalled her words at the apartment door the last time he saw her. She opened the door, turned to look at him, and bid him goodbye. Her eyes were soft with love. Elisa barely touched his arm. Her nails scratched him like a playful puppy's paws a rubber toy. His skin crawled with gooseflesh, and his body boiled with desire. She stood on her toes and planted a kiss on his right cheek. His lips rooted around to find the lush texture of her mouth. Her hair caressed his shut eyelid as scent wafted from behind her ear and the willowy contour under her chin. Her last words still rang in his mind,

"I'll be waiting for you with open arms. I have passed most of my life waiting for you."

Their love for each other had never blossomed because he did not fight for it. Salvador acknowledged his fault. She left him free to choose. What would have happened if she had gotten married?

Perhaps she would have been happier. But he wondered what would have been his reaction. Would jealousy have haunted him?

Salvador then thought of Rosa's commitment. He reminisced about the day they went to Parque del Valle to enjoy a romantic picnic a few months into their courtship. The young suitor helped her climb a tree and then asked her to jump down, proffering his open arms in jesting. Rosa stared at him, and to his surprise, she plopped into his arms. Laughing, they rolled in the grass as she proclaimed,

"Don't forget, I will always do anything you need."

Salvador knew fate contributed to his decision to marry his wife when it paired him with Rosa at the Bus Cemetery. He did not consider it a blunder because this matrimony best fit his needs then. He fell in love with her. His marriage followed the traditional pattern prevailing in Mexico at the time: the husband was the head of the family, and his wife depended on him. The relationship relied on respect for each other and man's hegemony, reminiscent of a father-daughter interaction.

This union contrasted with the recent development of marriage based on equal partnership and friendship, which was more appropriate for the new era. If he wedded Elisa, theirs would belong to this type, one more propitious for sharing intimate secrets.

Rosa never opened to him, nor did Salvador to her. She never mentioned her venial transgressions or little secrets, and he did not ask. Their physical attraction dazzled them before their marriage as sweet nothings took over their minds and trivialized any relevant conversation. He never told her about his lascivious childhood sin when he contemplated the photograph of Raquel Welch. Nor did he tell her about the sexual abuse he had suffered in the seminary. Salvador wondered whether Rosa would misjudge him.

But, over the years, those untold confidences did not diminish the strength of her love for each other. Salvador recalled the conversation with her before he departed for Milwaukee. The husband sat at the breakfast table across from her over ranch-style fried eggs. She wore near-vision glasses and stared at her left hand as a needle pierced a button of Lucia's shirt. Her gnarled right hand held the garment like a broken dry branch on a tall tree. The pungent aroma of chorizo and an uneasy silence hovered over them.

His wife removed her glasses, lifted her bloodshot eyes on the verge of tears, walked toward him, and hugged him. Rosa kissed him on the forehead. Her lips' warmth lingered as she voiced her thoughts,

"You don't have to leave me. You can have me, and you can have Elisa. Just don't tell me anything about it. I don't want to know."

"What about dignity?"

"Is dignity going to keep you by my side? I don't want to lose you. I'd rather share a piece than have none of you."

"What about Elisa's dignity or my dignity?"

"I can only speak for myself. You'll do what you must do. I know."

Salvador knew Rosa's proposal resulted from a weak moment, and this resolution would not last. Nor would Elisa accept such an arrangement.

The husband appreciated his wife's well-done job. Over the years, Rosa spurred love to grow in her family members and fasten them together like grass to rock cracks. He still loved her. But Salvador fought his love for the other woman for too long, and the uphill battle sickened him. Perhaps if he had listened to his heart, he would have grown into a different man, a better husband, and a father.

Someone slid a paper under the door and broke Salvador's deliberations. It was addressed to Florencio Guzman and informed him of the checkout at 11:00 AM. There was no need to disburse any money since he had already paid. Salvador wondered how he had come up with his brother's first name. Lake Geneva was 57 miles from Milwaukee, so his trip should have lasted about one hour. His mind did not register driving. But he must have been aware of his surroundings. Otherwise, he would not have kept an adequate distance between cars, obeyed traffic lights and highway signs, and changed lanes. There was no ticket or evidence of an accident.

Salvador did not know why he had ended up in Lake Geneva, an unfamiliar town in the middle of nowhere. He walked down to the reception room to determine whether the front desk clerk had noted any alteration in his alertness the previous evening. The guest used the excuse of requesting an iron to smooth out his pants. The receptionist made no remarks. Salvador asked himself how, in his state of oblivion, he had inquired about a room, registered as a guest, and exchanged a few words with the motel personnel.

By now, Salvador thought Rosa might fear he suffered an accident. He dialed his home number and left a message on the recorder to let her know his whereabouts. The machine captured his plan to spend three weeks away to disconnect from everything. The husband also requested that his wife notify his employer he had taken his long-overdue vacation. The message never reached Rosa. Lucia inadvertently erased it along with several others. Her intended target was one from a boy at her school who had a crush on her. Salvador also called Elisa, but her phone was busy. He tried several times and concluded she had inadvertently left the receiver unhung. Since she had no cell phone, he decided to notify her the next day.

Before leaving the motel, he pulled the drawers out and collected his belongings. A Bible rested on the nightstand. He riffled some pages and found an advertisement for the Sacred Heart Retreat Center for Catholic men in Fontana. This resort town was across the water on the southwest side of Lake Geneva.

Salvador stared at the holy book with skepticism. Inside were the passages that loomed before him as the most significant obstacles to making a fair choice between the two women in his life. The texts favored his wife over the other one. But Elisa deserved an equal chance. All these years, he went through the quotidian routine, fulfilling his duties to God like an obedient soldier in combat. But now, he had to question His orders to make a fair decision.

35

GOD'S PRANK

O n his way to the retreat, Salvador watched rolling hills as he drove along a two-lane road that climbed and slid down like a smooth roller coaster. The vegetation teemed with giant pine, oak, and crabapple trees with purple leaves. An iron fence with a closed main gate surrounded the center. A statue of Jesus with His Sacred Heart stood a few feet away next to a narrow path that led to a basilica with slender twin belfries.

A three-story residence was next to the church. For a modest fee, the bucolic grounds were open to those who wanted to reassess their lives away from the chaotic daily routine. Salvador registered, went to his room, and then walked into the cafeteria. Groups of men from various religious organizations in Milwaukee crowded the place. Some sat alone and kept to themselves. The institution discouraged phone calls. Salvador penned a message to Elisa on guest-room stationery and handed the envelope to a busy clerk at the front desk.

Salvador strolled into the forest and read the Bible for the next several days. He asked God for wisdom to find an answer to his predicament. But he felt somewhat at odds with Him. The Almighty wrote the laws, the Bible spoke for Him, and His scriptures condemned his love for Elisa. But those passages were written thousands of years ago and might need to be interpreted in the light of current times. He likened them with the old geographical charts that depicted an abyss beyond Hercules' columns — the Gibraltar Strait — as a warning to ships to sail no farther.

Salvador resorted to his conscience to find God's response to his questions. His search led nowhere. He understood the human mind's limitations because its voice did not speak for the Deity. The moral sense of right and wrong came from parents, religion, school, culture, and society. All our biases, prejudices, and misconceptions formed part of this entity. What was ethical for one person was unethical for another. People committed atrocities with no remorse, justifying their hateful acts with outrageous reasoning that appeased their minds. Our conscience did not bear impartial positions.

These considerations strengthened Salvador's decision to restudy the Bible. He reviewed many paragraphs. A verse harkened Salvador back to the crucial moment he enjoyed the intimate encounter with Elisa and procreated their beloved son:

"Let the marriage bed be undefiled," (*Hebrews 13:4.*)

Back then, amid his passion, Salvador espied the image of Christ on the crucifix that came into view over the bed. Christ's eyes were open. His dangling head rested on His chest as if He were watching their intimacy. Salvador disregarded the image. He loved Elisa, and she loved him. Even in the middle of the fiery passion, she whispered her deep affection for him. How could an act of the highest emotion desecrate a bed? Salvador countered the biblical text with another quote from the Scriptures:

"Whoever does not know love, does not know God because God is love," (*1 John 4:8.*)

Love stemmed from God. This finding uplifted his mood. Salvador was as proud as a well-trained defense lawyer. His optimism ushered him into speculations. His finding implied that, perhaps, a husband who loved someone else would defile his beloved's bed if he engaged in sex with his wife. In his case, he besmirched no bed. He loved both women.

Salvador took a break and went for a walk. The sunset flamed on the horizon, wrapping the branches of the giant oaks in crimson red.

Cardinals and robins whistled and warbled, grateful for the repose the night would bring. He did not view his present irresoluteness as a character defect. He had made tough decisions. A wishy-washy man would not leave his family and homeland for a foreign country. Nor would he forgo the priesthood for an uncertain future.

His digression evoked the day Salvador left the seminary: He regarded the white walls and two large wooden crucifixes above two small beds. A gray blanket covered his mattress, and his black biretta lay on the folded black cassock. A shaft of sunrays seeped through the window and lit his abandoned clerical attire. He felt no misgivings. Salvador examined himself in the small mirror behind his closet door and saw his eyes sparkle. He wore a gray suit and tied a symmetrical knot in his blue tie. The regular clothes aroused a cheerful sensation as if he were going to his hometown's festivities. His roommate had already hugged him and said some kind words before leaving for the daily muster roll in the inner courtyard,

"I'll miss you. The church loses a great priest, better than me for sure."

Salvador then lifted his two bags. Under their weight, he strode toward the school dorm door, kneed it open to slide his luggage through a narrow exit, and never looked back. Salvador wondered whether resolving his current predicament would also uplift his mood. His reaction to its resolution might differ from that of his previous one. He expected no happiness but knew it needed to be done.

After a while, Salvador returned to his room in the retreat center. He sat at his desk and continued his research. In chapter two, God urged the faithful to follow His commandments. Salvador analyzed Exodus, reached the seventh mandate, and His words impacted him:

"Thou shalt not commit adultery."

Salvador studied the sentence. This mandate had resounded in his mind over and over in the seminary. But now it was as if the stone slab with God's laws had just hit him in the head. The might of the verb "Thou shalt not" hammered at him. It was not "Thou will not,"

"Thou must not," or "Thou should not," but an adamant, unmovable, irrevocable "Thou shalt not." Moses received these rules thirty-five hundred years ago. Some had changed. Yet, prohibiting physical relationships outside of marriage remained untouched.

Until the wee hours of the morning, Salvador searched for a paragraph that would mitigate the power of this tenet. As time elapsed, he watched that goal recede further, like the retreat of glaciers millennia ago that forced monarchs northward in pursuit of food. Salvador could not find the text anywhere. He bumped into a verse whose words haunted him,

"Everyone who divorces his wife forces her to commit adultery," (*Matthew 5:31-32.*)

The statement appeared firm and menacing. Why should Salvador condemn Rosa? He might blame himself for the sake of fairness, but not his wife. She did not harm. Helplessness overcame him and exhausted him. He fell asleep, and a restless slumber took over until a dream broke in:

Salvador was on an island with Rosa, Humberto, and Lucia. He admired the intense blue sky, basked in the fresh air, and ran toward a cliff peak with Rosa. Seawater lay far below. Unaware that a rope teetered his wife to him, he jumped down, dragging her over the abyss edge amid her loud cries. Salvador carried a parachute and voiced out the combination numbers to unfurl the device. But their fall accelerated so quickly that they crashed into the ocean before completing his task.

A few minutes later, Salvador opened his eyes. The first morning lights seeped through the middle crack between the window blinds. The green of the walls was barely perceptible. An icy breeze cooled the day as a wet-earth scent oozed from outside. He pulled up a brown blanket and tucked himself under it. The nightmare unsettled him, and its violent meaning lashed at him with alarming force. The words of the Holy Scriptures reverberated in his mind, each echo worsening their ominous significance. Salvador sat up in bed, bent the pillow in half, and propped his body against it. His eyes roved over the semidark room. A black leather-bound Bible was on the nightstand.

Next to the closed door, a portrait of Fray Leopold gazed at him. The friar's baldness contrasted with a huge white beard over his chest. Salvador shut his eyes, but the accusatory stare remained locked as soon as he opened them. The image stirred up a thought in Salvador. Why did God subject me to such a terrible prank and cruel mockery?

God's behavior was no different from the use of civilians as human shields. Salvador's uproar revved up and burst into a crushing panic attack. His breathing rushed, his heart raced, and sweat cropped upon his forehead. He pushed his hands against the mattress and bent his shoulders backward to expand his chest. A sharp wail erupted from his windpipe. He grabbed his throat and stretched it out to let the air in. Palpitations rushed as drops of sweat ran down his face. The picture of Fray Leopold grew blurred, the brown habit overflowed the frame, and the green walls faded into sallow yellows. In the final throes of consciousness, Salvador noticed his hands cramped into painful fists as his lips raged with numbness. Darkness enveloped him and knocked him out.

Salvador woke up, exhausted, lying in bed with sore muscles. Sharp pain ravaged his tongue from a bite, and the sheets bristled with bloodstains. He must have passed out for a while because sunrays flooded the room through the window crack. His spell cleansed his anxious apprehension and replaced it with an inner peace without sadness or concerns. His clean conscience mirrored the one Salvador had enjoyed in his childhood.

This feeling led him to believe the blackout might have exorcised the remnant of his sin from his soul. He conjured up God to rejoice in His nearness. But only profound silence hovered around him.

Salvador did not sense anything, not even a distant presence, nor did he perceive — as in the past — the void left by the Deity. There was nothing. It was as if a black hole had sucked God in. Salvador confronted the truth. All his prior perceptions of Him were figments of his imagination. His sense of the Almighty Father's nearness or distant presence had always been an illusion.

After this epiphany, Salvador realized God did not have to respond to his beckoning calls. One could find Him everywhere. The new convert to common sense Christianism acknowledged this delusion helped him as a young man. But it backfired later and made him feel at the mercy of God's whims. The frustrated attempts to connect with Him suctioned his energy, distorted his view of the world, and corrupted his decisions.

Salvador looked at himself in a mirror and felt like a grown monarch that had just torn through its chrysalis shell, stretched out its wings, and flown for the first time. A smile carved deep folds into his cheeks and revealed a blissful expression. His forehead had no furrows, and dark eyebrows crowned a serene gaze. His eyes sparkled with self-confidence and determination.

Some questions loomed before him: What do I want from life? Does my existence have a purpose? And if so, what is it? I wonder whether, as young adults, we make sounder decisions. One may reach them with the youth's innocence, adaptability, and purity without the corruption that besieges us as we grow older — lust, selfishness, jealousy, distrust, disappointments, lies, and deceitfulness. Or do mature people enjoy better judgment? After all, aging brings wisdom, experience, and perspectives gained over time.

Salvador regarded the sky from the window through the tops of oaks and pines. The cloudscape pirouetted in the immense blue, forming valleys, mountains, cathedrals, and cities that seemed made of cotton. The celestial design soon unraveled into alligators, turtles, birds, donkeys, and even elephants. The scene loomed before him like a reenactment of creation, reassuring him God had not abandoned him.

Salvador went out, lumbered through the forest, and came across Patrick Millen. He saw him before because they had breakfast in the dining room every morning. Yet they never conversed. The fellow pilgrim sat, crying, at the foot of a large oak tree flanking a narrow dirt path. The newcomer approached him and asked if he could assist him. The older man looked at him with teary eyes but uttered no words. Salvador sat beside him, propped his back against the trunk, and stared at the forest.

Patrick Millen kept silent for a while and let his companion adjust his eyes to the lush foliage. Playful lights seeped through the leaves, casting capricious spots on the ground that drifted with the breeze. A mint fragrance wafted from the undergrowth. Two joyful blue jays and a proud grey robin with a brown belly flew from branch to branch as their merry-making warbles and songs hovered over them.

"I'm glad you joined me," Patrick said. "We all came here for a reason. Talking with a stranger may clear the mind and find a solution."

"I wanted to find help in the Bible. But I got nowhere."

"The faithful often do not reach God through holy books. He is one thing, and religion is another."

"I concluded there is a God, but not exactly the one I thought."

"We all see Him differently."

The calmness around his old companion made Salvador relax and open to him. He recounted his story from quitting the seminary to his present problem. The fellow retreatant looked at him and said,

"Let me recount my story. It might aid you."

Patrick owned a beer company in Madison, Wisconsin. The brewer enjoyed his life with his wife, Cynthia, his daughter, Emily, and his two grandchildren, Martha and Johnny. Patrick drove to Wisconsin Dells with his family six years ago when a trucker rammed his semitrailer against his car. Everyone died except him.

"I saw my inert body, unconscious, next to the vehicle and then a tunnel with an enormous light at the end. I wished I had died, but God woke me up a week later."

"I asked Him the reason He had spared me. It took me a while to get my answer on these holy grounds. "

A terrible act of neglect had haunted Patrick for a long time, but he ignored it. The pilgrim was born in Belfast, Ireland, soon after his father's death. As a lad, he left the island for the US, intending to help his mother, his disabled brother, and his little sister. Success provided him with plenty of material possessions. But he never went back, not even to his mother's funeral, and let his brother and sister lead a life of significant poverty. After the accident, Patrick returned to his ancestral home, found his siblings, and fulfilled his promise.

Patrick looked at his companion and said,

"Your predicament entails more than choosing between those wonderful women. You can pick either. If the election does not conform to the Christian commandments, God will pardon you like you would your son."

These words reassured Salvador because he had already reached the same conclusion.

36

AS MUSIC ROLLED

The following day, Salvador's three-week break ended, and he drove on the roads back to Chicago. He passed barns with red and gray silos, grasslands, wood fences, grazing cows and horses, and cornfields. The landscape teemed with small hills, flatlands, forests with tall oak trees, apple orchards, and strawberry patches. There were homes atop hills, lagoons with small boats, bait shops, quilting shops, and little restaurants. The views infused him with wonder. The road ended in an expansive expressway that led to Chicago.

When Salvador arrived home, he found no one. It was unusual to walk into an empty house on a Sunday afternoon. He noticed a sensation of unreality as if he were contemplating his home for the first time or perhaps the last time. A brisk chill ran from head to toe. Rosa and the children must have left in a hurry. A box of cards was open on top of the table at the entrance, and pieces of ribbons lay on the floor.

He regarded the gray wooden plaque with golden letters on the back of the door. The head of the household saw it every time he left home but reread it,

"This is my command—be strong and courageous! Don't be afraid or discouraged, for the Lord your God is with you wherever you go," (Joshua 1:9.)

The words made him resent the former excessive clutches of religion. A sensation of letdown overtook him. So many anxious years went by under this roof — years of religious duties in the will of a misperceived God.

On the right side, a large pot with a peace lily stood in the corner under the small window overlooking the front yard. Sunrays seeped through the narrow cracks between the white horizontal laths. The white blossoms were wilted, heaps of white pollen lay next to the pot, and the overdone flower scent floated through the foyer. The vision evoked a thought. During the long time he had lived here, he felt like a starving monarch butterfly, flittering, and fluttering around to search for nectar on limp flowers.

But Salvador considered this period a necessary phase. Life could toy with us as if we were marionettes. But he would not have wasted all his efforts if he did not opt for Rosa. His two beautiful children and loving wife blessed his life as precious gifts. He walked into the family room, sat on the lazy chair, cooled down from the long trip, and regarded the photographs hanging on the wall:

The black-and-white picture of his wedding caught his attention. Rosa looks gorgeous. She wears a ground-length white dress with a high collar and embroidered flowers around the cuffs and hem. The bodice and skirt stress her curves, and a crown of white flowers sets off her long, dark hair. Her eyes shine with joy. Her left hand grabs a long rosary with a silver cross, and her right hand holds onto Salvador's left elbow. He sports a dark suit and a tie with diagonal stripes. His eyes radiate a stern expression as his mouth opens with a stiff smile. His tension affects his hands, where his bent fingers form in a tight fist. His arms rest down along his body.

At the altar, a commanding image of Christ towers over the newlyweds. Salvador remembered what he had pondered at that moment. No foreboding loomed before him, just trepidation because of his experience at home. He thought of the unhappiness that crept into his parents' relationship. The many months that mother and father spent ignoring one another. Their love ebbed over time, and the spouses ended up in a loveless cohabitation.

Back then, Salvador thought Rosa was beautiful and would be a good wife and a superb mother for their future children. They understood each other well. His girlfriend loved him with all her heart—he could sense it. She craved his protection; he would gladly provide it because he had fallen head over heels for her. His courtship lasted over seven years, and he could not wait to get married and make love to her.

Next to this photo, another one caught Salvador's attention. Rosa stood behind the home window in Toultuca, where its sill held two pots with geraniums in bloom. It was taken shortly after they had built their house. His newlywed wife laughs and covers her cheeks with her hands as a tender sign of shyness. Everything speaks of happiness, and that brought back memories of their suffering and sacrifice when he left for El Norte. His words to Rosa resonated as if he were witnessing his departure in 1981,

"Is my life better than my father's? Was my father's better than my grandfather's? I want a bright future for our child and ourselves."

At first, Rosa didn't support their move to El Norte. Salvador remembered her words,

—"In El Norte, dollars don't grow on trees."

But she risked her life—and that of their son—to save their marriage. From then on, she joined the project of achieving the American dream for the couple and a better life for their descendants. However, she did so with certain reservations due to the living conditions and injustices they endured. Both shared many trials.

The United States was a grateful nation. Its citizens received what they deserved for their hard work. Efforts were rewarded unlike anywhere else on earth. But for them, there was an additional obstacle: their race. Nevertheless, the couple fought and achieved the American dream. Now, they strived for the second and most important goal: their children's success in the promised land. That was the most crucial initial purpose when they moved to El Norte.

But situations change over time. Didn't the American Constitution emphasize the individual pursuit of happiness as the nation's fundamental principle? A new life with Elisa attracted him as something just and desirable. For years, his love for her cried out from the depths of his soul. Salvador resisted the assaults of his mind, social rules, and Christian laws. He could envision a marriage based on intimate friendship without religious restrictions.

The husband wasn't discontent with his wife, but his life with her languished with joy, without passion, as calm as the waters of Lake Michigan on windless days. Not all that glitters is gold in marriages. Happiness should be toiled on, nurtured, and given a preferential place in spouses' lives, like a painting that presided over a living room. That task was difficult to accomplish. *Mea culpa*, he hadn't done it. But Salvador had kept between his wife and himself mutual respect and acceptance of each other's deficiencies. In his case, Rosa's lack of trust in him for many years. He recognized that this resulted from his love for Elisa and his indecision in dealing with that issue. Correcting all that mess would be difficult; it might even be too late.

Those who believe that you only live once would have no doubt. To a certain extent, Salvador envied these people who passed through the world caring only about themselves. They don't worry about the long-term future and exclaim, 'God will provide.' For those of us who look to the future as the result of logical actions taken, life behaves like a formidable opponent in a game of chess. It is always ready to surprise us with the unexpected move of a piece that we must face as best as possible. But for others, life is a roulette.

Salvador observed the other framed pictures documenting the family's journey in the United States. In one, Rosa, Humberto, and Lucía stood looking out at the Chicago skyline on the day of a visit to the Planetarium. In another black and white photograph, Rosa held Humberto in her arms. The proud dad had kept it since they lived in the trailer in California. Others testified to their children's growth: Lucía, at six years old, smiling in her school uniform on the day she sang in the choir at Christmas. Humberto, alongside a group of friends at high school. The teenager stood upright in the back as he looked forward with challenging eyes, imbued with determination to succeed, even stronger than his parents'.

Had they already prepared him for that challenge? Of course, that question also applied to Lucía. If the answer were negative, a divorce could derail the goal. But did their obligation to complete that task extend beyond his happiness?

Salvador walked to the family room, phoned Antonio, and inquired about his family's whereabouts. His friend could not believe his ears. After his initial shock, he informed him that everyone — including Elisa and Carlos — was attending Lucia's graduation at Roseland Junior High. The news struck Salvador dumb with astonishment. His unintended missing status created ties between Rosa and Elisa. The fortunate irony made him feel more at ease.

The sun was in Salvador's eyes when he walked through his front yard. Oak trees flanked the street. One threw its tilted shadow upon his home's façade beyond the railing fence and the grass. A few customers sat at the tables near the windows in the café across the street, the aroma of coffee wafting toward him.

Salvador pulled up his car and purchased three bouquets at a florist shop — one with pink roses, one with white roses, and one with red roses. He wrote three small cards. The first expressed his parental devotion, the second, his affection and respect, and the third, his unconditional love. He tucked one in each of the bouquets.

He placed the flowers on the passenger seat and looked at the bouquet of red roses where he had stuck the love note for Rosa. He prided himself on his decision. Salvado knew he had chosen duty over passional love so their home and hearth could continue the unfinished project. This resolution grew warmer and more intense with every yard that got him closer to the school.

An American flag waved atop a tall post. It announced Salvador's arrival at the building where the graduation ceremony was underway. There was no traffic. Cars filled the parking lots and the sides of the circular road in front of the entrance. Salvador found a spot far from the building under an oak tree, next to where the students chained their bicycles to the racks.

As he walked in, the president of the university, Mr. Edward Larson, was addressing the audience and dedicating a few words to Latino students,

"By 2050, Hispanics are projected to constitute 25% of the United States population, positioning this nation as the second-largest Spanish-speaking country, trailing only behind Mexico. I urge you to enrich this land with your language, culture, and lore."

From afar, Salvador saw Rosa and Elisa with Antonio. The women's awestruck faces revealed happiness at his presence and the reaction reassured him. Carlos raised his hand and waved at him, his joyful and teary eyes expressing his love. Then, Mr. Larson's concluding words resounded in the auditorium,

"Set your sight on college education and claim your rightful place among the elite to lead this proud republic."

Jubilation erupted. Salvador saw Lucia smiling and tossing his blue graduation cap high toward the ceiling. He instantly felt more part than ever of his children's American dream. An uplifting freedom overtook him. If he had wings, he would have flown like a monarch butterfly that sensed nearby milkweed.

And the sun shone outside, and blossoms flourished in the forests and gardens, on the grass and prairies, in the mountains and valleys, in the towns and fields. Monarchs were flitting from flower to flower, displaying beautiful wings, depositing pollen in each of them, infusing them with life, toiling without rest, embellishing the surroundings, and contributing to America's greatness.

ABOUT THE AUTHOR

Louis Villalba was born in Spain in 1945 and has resided in the US since 1970. He completed his neurology training at Chicago Medical School, where he became a clinical professor, taught for over thirty years, and published many scientific articles, and several monographs and books of the same nature. Villalba has authored the following literary works of fiction and nonfiction:

The Silver Teacup: Tales of Cadiz (Createspace, 2012) contains short stories. The accounts take place in his hometown, Cadiz, Spain, shuttling the reader to a world full of historical fiction, human drama, and fantasy.

La Tacita de Plata: Cuentos de Cádiz (Createspace, 2012). Villalba rewrites the stories of his first book in Spanish.

The Stranger's Enigma (Createspace, 2014) features the first book of a two-part series. Kirkus Reviews praises it as "a provocative character study of a man facing a personal and professional crisis."

Afterlife Tracks: Glimpses of the Occult (Createspace, 2015). The author recounts the paranormal events that occurred in his thirty-four-year neurology practice.

Cuban Seeds (Floricanto Press, December 2016) narrates the memoir of a widow who pursues her children's American dream after defying the Cuban tyranny.

The Series of Tales of Cadiz (Gades Books, 2017) re-edits and publishes ten stories about his hometown in Kindle format.

Uprooted Agave (Gades Books, 2018) contains thirteen short stories that deal with the struggle of Latino Immigrants in the US.

The Series of Hispanic Immigrants' Stories (Gades Books, 2020.) Eight short stories in Kindle format.

Born of Dreams (Gades Books, 2021.) This is the second book of the series *The Stranger's Enigma.* A righteous man from a utopian land engages in the conquest of a woman he has fallen in love with.

For further info, please visit www. TheClassicWriter. com, www.LouisVillalba.com, or www.GadesBooks.com

AUTHOR'S NOTE

Dear Reader,

Thank you for taking the time to read "The Monarch's Flight." If you enjoyed it, please post a brief review on www.Amazon.com — a few sentences describing what you liked about the story. Your words will help others discover the book.

Thank you again,
Louis Villalba

OTHER BOOKS
BY
LOUIS VILLALBA

The Silver Teacup
La Tacita de Plata
Afterlife Tracks
Cuban Seeds
The Series of the Tales of Cádiz
Uprooted Agave
The Stranger's Enigma
The Series of Hispanic Immigrants' Stories
Born of Dreams